Praise for *New York⬛*
MARY⬛

"Cleverly plott⬛⬛⬛
and flawlessly written."
—*Library Journal* (starred review)
on *Never Less Than a Lady*

"The enchanting first Lost Lords novel
confirms bestseller Putney as a major force
in historical romance."
—*Publishers Weekly* (starred review)
on *Loving a Lost Lord*

Praise for *New York Times* bestselling author
KRISTIN JAMES

"Ms. James creates a fiery romance
between her two unexpected lovers and
throws the party to end all parties in the process."
—*RT Book Reviews* on *The Last Groom on Earth*

"Ms. James turns the heat way, way up…"
—*RT Book Reviews* on *Once in a Blue Moon*

Praise for
CHARLOTTE FEATHERSTONE

"A wonderful old-fashioned love story…
[with] plenty of sizzle and emotional clout."
—*RT Book Reviews* on *Addicted*

"Featherstone knows how to write sexy
in this unusual tale of the fey."
—*RT Book Reviews* on *Lust*

MARY JO PUTNEY

The WEDDING of the Century

& other stories

KRISTIN JAMES

CHARLOTTE FEATHERSTONE

HQN™

Recycling programs
for this product may
not exist in your area.

ISBN-13: 978-0-373-77550-7

THE WEDDING OF THE CENTURY & OTHER STORIES

Copyright © 2011 by Harlequin Books S.A.

The publisher acknowledges the copyright holders
of the individual works as follows:

THE WEDDING OF THE CENTURY
Copyright © 1994 by Mary Jo Putney

JESSE'S WIFE
Copyright © 1994 by Kristin James

SEDUCED BY STARLIGHT
Copyright © 2011 by Charlotte Featherstone

This edition published by arrangement with Harlequin Books S.A.

For questions and comments about the quality of this book
please contact us at Customer_eCare@Harlequin.ca.

® and TM are trademarks of the publisher. Trademarks indicated with
® are registered in the United States Patent and Trademark Office, the
Canadian Trade Marks Office and in other countries.

www.HQNBooks.com

Printed in U.S.A.

CONTENTS

THE WEDDING OF THE CENTURY   7
Mary Jo Putney

JESSE'S WIFE   139
Kristin James

SEDUCED BY STARLIGHT   245
Charlotte Featherstone

THE WEDDING
OF THE CENTURY

Mary Jo Putney

To Mama Rekus, who always loved a good story.

CHAPTER ONE

Swindon Palace
Spring 1885

AFTER TWO WEEKS OF DIZZYING social activity in London, a visit to the English countryside was an enchanting change of pace. Nature had cooperated by blessing the garden party with flawless weather. Puffs of white cloud drifted through a deep blue sky, the grass and trees were impossibly green, and the famous Swindon gardens were in glorious flower.

Yet the grounds were not half so splendid as the guests, who were the cream of British society. All of the men were aristocratically handsome and all of the women graceful and exquisitely dressed. At least, that was how it seemed to Miss Sarah Katherine Vangelder, of the New York Vangelders. As she surveyed her surroundings, she gave a laugh of pure delight.

The woman beside her said, "Don't look so rapturous, Sunny. It simply isn't done."

Sunny gave her godmother a teasing glance. "Is this the Katie Schmidt of San Francisco who scandalized English society by performing Comanche riding stunts in Hyde Park?"

A smile tugged at the older woman's lips. "It most certainly is *not,*" she said in a voice that no longer held any trace of American accent. "I am now Katherine Schmidt Worthington, Countess of Westron, a very proper chaperon for her exceedingly well-brought-up young American goddaughter."

"I thought that we American girls were admired for our freshness and directness." A hint of dryness entered Sunny's voice. "And our fortunes, of course."

"The very best matches require impeccable manners as well as money, my dear. If you wish to become a duchess, you must be above reproach."

Sunny sighed. "And if I don't wish to become a duchess?"

"Your mother has spent twenty years grooming you to be worthy of the highest station," Lady Westron replied. "It would be a pity to waste that."

"Yes, Aunt Katie," Sunny said meekly. "If I'm very, very impeccable, may I view the rest of the gardens later?"

"Yes, but not until you've met everyone worth meeting. Business before pleasure, my dear." Katie began guiding her charge through the crowd, stopping and making occasional introductions.

Knowing that she was being judged, Sunny smiled and talked with the utmost propriety. She even managed not to look too excited, until she was introduced to the Honorable Paul Curzon.

Tall, blond and stunningly handsome, Curzon was enough to make any woman gape. After bowing over her hand, he said, "A pleasure to meet you, Miss Vangelder. Are you newly arrived in England?" His question was accompanied by a dazzling smile.

If it hadn't been for her rigorous social training, Sunny would have gaped at him like a raw country girl. Instead, she managed to say lightly, "I've been in London for the last fortnight. Before that, we were traveling on the Continent."

"If you'd like to visit the Houses of Parliament, Miss

Vangelder, I'd be delighted to escort you. I'm a member."
Curzon gave a deprecatory shrug. "Only a backbencher,
but I can show you what goes on behind the scenes
and treat you to tea on the terrace. You might find it
amusing."

"Perhaps later in the season Miss Vangelder will have
time," Katie said as she deftly removed her charge.

When they were out of earshot, Sunny said with awe,
"Mr. Curzon is the handsomest man I've ever seen."

"Yes, but he's a younger son with three older brothers,
so he's unlikely ever to inherit the title." Lady Westron
gave a warning look. "Not at all the sort your mother
wants for you."

"But as a Member of Parliament, he actually does
something useful," Sunny pointed out. "My grandfather
would have approved of that."

"Admiral Vangelder would *not* have wanted a penniless
younger son for his favorite granddaughter," Katie said
firmly. "Come, I want you to meet Lord Traymore. An
Irish title, unfortunately, but an earl is an earl, and he's
charming. You could do worse."

Dutifully Sunny followed her godmother to the next
knot of guests, though she promised herself that she would
slip off and view the famous water garden before she left.
Until then, she would enjoy the color and laughter of the
occasion.

She was also guiltily glad to be free of her mother's
rather overpowering presence for a day. Augusta Vangelder was the most devoted and solicitous of parents, but
she had very firm ideas about the way things ought to be.
Very firm. Unfortunately, she was laid up in their suite
at Claridge's with a mild case of the grippe, so Sunny
had the benefit of the more liberal chaperonage of her
godmother. Not only did Lady Westron know everyone,

but she made racy comments about them. Sunny felt very worldly.

While a courtly old judge went to fetch them refreshments, she asked, "Where is the Duke of Thornborough? Since he ordered a special train to bring his guests from London for the day, I should at least know whom to be grateful to."

Katie scanned the crowd, then nodded toward the refreshment marquee. "That tall, fair chap."

After a thorough examination, Sunny observed, "He's almost as handsome as Mr. Curzon, and has a most distinguished air. *Exactly* what one would expect of a duke."

"Yes, and he's delightfully witty, as well," Katie replied. "Very prominent in the Prince of Wales's Marlborough House set. I'll introduce you to him later."

Sunny glanced at the other woman suspiciously. "Am I to be paraded in front of him like a prize heifer?"

"No," Katie said with regret. "Thornborough won't do—his taste runs to ladies who are…rather excessively sophisticated. He's expected to offer for May Russell soon."

"The American Mrs. Russell?" Sunny asked, surprised.

"Mad May herself. She's a good choice—having had children by two husbands already, she shouldn't have any problems giving Thornborough an heir, and her fortune is immense." Katie gave a little sniff. "Heaven knows that Thornborough needs it."

"Who's the man standing by the duke?"

"Oh, that's just the Gargoyle."

"I beg your pardon?" Sunny glanced at her godmother, not sure that she'd heard correctly.

"Lord Justin Aubrey, Thornborough's younger brother, better known as the Gargoyle," Katie explained. "He manages the duke's estate, which means he's scarcely more than a farmer."

A line etched between her brows, Sunny studied the dark young man. While not handsome, his face had a certain rugged distinction. "Why was he given such an unkind nickname? He's no Mr. Curzon, but neither is he ugly."

"The Aubreys are known for being tall, blond and aristocratic, and Lord Justin is none of those things. He's always scowling and has no conversation at all." Katie smiled naughtily. "One would have to question what his dear mother had been up to, except that every now and then the Aubreys produce one like him. The youngest Aubrey daughter, Lady Alexandra, resembles him, poor girl. I imagine she's around here somewhere. She's known as the Gargoylette."

Sunny's frown deepened. "I'm sorry to think that these handsome people have such cruel tongues."

"They are no more and no less cruel than New York society," Lady Westron said dryly. "Human nature is much the same everywhere."

Sunny's gaze lingered on Lord Justin. Though not tall, neither was he short; he appeared to be of average height, perhaps an inch or two taller than she. She guessed that he was in his late twenties, but his stern expression made him seem older. He also looked as if he thoroughly disapproved of the splendid gathering around him.

Her thoughts were interrupted by Katie exclaiming, "Lord Hancock is over there! I had hoped that he would be here today. Come along, dear, you must meet him."

After another wistful glance at the gardens, Sunny obediently followed her godmother.

THE EIGHTH DUKE OF THORNBOROUGH sampled a strawberry from one of the mounds on the refreshment table.

"Splendid flavor." He reached for another. "You've been getting remarkable results from the greenhouses."

Justin Aubrey shrugged. "I only give the orders, Gavin. It's the gardeners who do the real work."

"But someone must still give the right orders, and it isn't going to be me." The duke consumed several more strawberries, then washed them down with champagne. "Relax, Justin. You've worked for weeks to make my fete a success, so you should try to enjoy the results. Everyone is having a cracking good time."

"That's fortunate, considering that this little event is costing over two thousand pounds." Money which could have been much better spent.

Gavin made an airy gesture. "The Duke of Thornborough has an obligation to maintain a certain style. After I marry May, there will be ample money for those boring repairs that you keep talking about."

Justin gave his brother a shrewd glance. "You and Mrs. Russell have reached a firm understanding?"

Gavin nodded. "We'll be making an announcement soon. A late summer wedding, I think. You can plan on fixing the roof directly after, so it will be right and tight by winter." He cast an experienced eye over the crowd. "I see that Katie Westron has a lovely creature in tow. It must be the Gilded Girl. I hear she's cutting quite a swath through London society. The Prince has already invited her to visit Sandringham."

"Then her social reputation is made," Justin agreed with barely perceptible irony. "But who *is* the Gilded Girl?"

"Sarah Vangelder, the fairest flower of the Vangelder railroad fortune." The duke's tone turned speculative. "They say she's the greatest heiress ever to cross the Atlantic."

Justin followed his brother's gaze to where the heiress

stood talking with three besotted males. As soon as he located her, his heart gave an odd lurch. Sarah Vangelder was the quintessential American beauty—tall, slender and crowned with a lustrous mass of honey-colored hair. She also had an engaging air of innocent enthusiasm that made him want to walk over and introduce himself. A beautiful woman, not his. The world was full of them, he reminded himself. Aloud, he said only, "Very fetching."

"Perhaps I should reconsider marrying May," Gavin said pensively. "They say Augusta Vangelder wants to see the girl a duchess. Should I offer her the noble name of Thornborough?"

Justin's mouth tightened. Though he loved his brother, he had no illusions about the duke's character. "You'd find a young innocent a flat bore."

"Very likely you're right," Gavin agreed. His gaze lingered. "Still, she's quite lovely."

Three peeresses and two Cabinet ministers came over to pay their respects to their host. Justin seized the opportunity to escape, for the constant chatter was driving him mad. He would have preferred to be elsewhere, but he could hardly avoid a party taking place in his own backyard.

Avoiding the formal parterre where many of the guests were strolling, he made his way to the rhododendron garden, which had been carefully designed to look like wild woods. There was a risk that he would find some of Gavin's fashionable friends fornicating beneath the silver birches, but with luck, they would all be more interested in champagne and gossip than in dalliance.

Half an hour in the wilder sections of the park relaxed him to the point where he felt ready to return to the festivities. Not that anyone was likely to miss him, but he liked to keep an eye on the arrangements to ensure that everything ran smoothly.

As he walked through a grove of Scottish pines, he heard a feminine voice utter a soft but emphatic, "Drat!"

He turned toward the voice, and a few more steps brought the speaker into his view.

It was the Gilded Girl. But that was too flippant a nickname, for the sunlight that shafted through the pine needles made her honey hair and creamy gown glow as if she were Titania, the fairy queen. He halted unnoticed at the edge of the clearing, experiencing again that strange, unsteady feeling.

A vine had snagged the back hem of Miss Vangelder's elegant bustled walking gown, and she was trying to free herself by poking with the tip of her lace parasol. Any other woman would have seemed ungraceful, but not the heiress. She looked playful, competent and altogether enchanting.

In the wooden voice he used to conceal unseemly feelings, he said, "May I be of assistance?"

The girl looked up with a startled glance, then smiled with relief. "You certainly can! Otherwise, my gown is doomed, and Mr. Worth will be terribly cross with me if he ever finds out."

Justin knelt and began trying to disentangle her hem. "Does it matter what a dressmaker thinks?"

"Mr. Worth is not a dressmaker, but an *artiste*. I'm told that I was singularly fortunate that he condescended to see me personally. After examining me like a prize turkey, he designed every ensemble right down to the last slipper and scarf." She gave a gurgle of laughter. "I was informed in no uncertain terms that any substitutions would be disastrous."

The vine was remarkably tenacious. As Justin tried to loosen it without damaging the heavy ecru silk, he asked, "Do you always do what others wish you to do?"

"Generally," she said with wry self-understanding. "Life is easier when I do."

Her skirt finally came free, and he got to his feet. "I'm Justin Aubrey, by the way."

"I'm Sarah Vangelder, but most people call me Sunny." She offered her hand, and a smile that melted his bones.

She was tall, her eyes almost level with his. He had assumed that they would be blue, but the color was nearer aqua, as deep and changeable as the sea. He drew a shaken breath, then bowed over her hand. Straightening, he said, "You should not be here alone, Miss Vangelder."

"I know," she said blithely, "but I was afraid that if I didn't take the initiative, I'd leave without having a chance to really see the gardens."

"Are you rating them for possible future occupancy?" he said dryly. "I regret to inform you that my brother is no longer in the marriage mart."

"I simply like gardens, Lord Justin," she said crisply, her aqua eyes turning cool. "Are you always so rude?"

So the exquisite Miss Vangelder had thorns. Suppressing a smile, he said, "Always. I took a first in rudeness at Oxford."

Her expression instantly transformed from reproval to delight. "You have a sense of humor!"

"Don't spread such a base rumor around. It would utterly ruin my reputation." He offered his arm. "Let me escort you back to the fete."

As she slipped her hand into the crook of his elbow, she asked, "Could we take an indirect route? I particularly want to see the famous water garden."

He knew that he should return her before her chaperon became concerned. Yet when he looked into her glorious eyes, he found himself saying, "Very well, Miss Vangelder."

As they started down the pine-needle-carpeted path, he was very aware of the light pressure of her hand on his arm and the luxuriant rustle of her petticoats. And her perfume, a delicate fragrance reminiscent of violets…

He took a deep, slow breath. "I assume you are related to Admiral Vangelder?"

"You've heard of my grandfather?"

"It would be surprising if I hadn't." He held a branch aside so that she could pass without endangering her deliciously frivolous hat. "He was one of the great American success stories."

"Yes, and something of a robber baron, as well, though he was always a darling to me. I miss him." She chuckled. "He liked people to think that he was called Admiral because of his magnificent yachts, but actually, he got the nickname because his first job was tending mules on the Erie Canal."

"Really?" Justin said, amused by her artlessness.

"Really. In fact, there are grave suspicions that his papa was not married to his mama." She bit her lip guiltily. "You're dangerously easy to talk to, Lord Justin. I shouldn't have said so much—my mother would be horrified if the Admiral's dubious parentage became common knowledge." She grinned again. "Her own family has been respectable for at least a generation longer."

"Your secret is safe, Miss Vangelder," he assured her.

She gave him another entrancing smile that struck right to the heart. For a mad instant, he felt as if he was the only person who existed in her world. She had charm, this gilded girl, a quality as unmistakable as it was hard to define. He drew a shaken breath and returned his gaze to the winding path.

Though she had said he was easy to talk to, in fact he found himself talking more than usual as they strolled through the park. He told her about the history of the estate, answered questions about the crops and tenants. Together they stood in the gazebo that was designed like a miniature Greek temple, and when they visited the picturesque ruins of an old monastery he described what the community would have been like in its heyday.

She was a wonderful audience, listening with a grave air of concentration that was occasionally punctuated by an incisive question. After she asked about the effects of the agricultural depression on the farm laborers, he remarked, "You have a wide range of interests, Miss Vangelder."

"Education is something of an American passion, so my father insisted that I have a whole regiment of tutors. Shortly before he died, he had me take the entrance exams to Oxford and Cambridge. He was quite pleased when I passed with flying colors." She sighed. "Of course there was never any question of me actually going to a university. That would have been shockingly bluestocking."

At least she had been well taught. Like most English girls, his own sisters had received the sketchiest of educations. Only Alexandra, who loved to read, had a well-informed mind. The man who married Sunny Vangelder would be lucky in more ways than one.

Justin had chosen a path that brought them out of the park's wilderness area right beside the water garden. It was an elaborate series of pools and channels that descended across three levels of terraces before flowing into the ornamental lake.

Sunny stopped in her tracks with a soft exhalation of pleasure. "Exquisite. The proportions—the way the statues are reflected in the pools—the way the eye is led gradually down to the lake. It's masterful. And the grass surrounding it! Like green velvet. How do the English grow such perfect grass?"

"It's quite simple, really. Just get a stone roller and use it on the lawn regularly for two or three hundred years."

She laughed and gave him a glance that made him feel as if he was the wittiest, handsomest man alive.

His heart twisted, and he knew that he must get away from her before he started to act like an utter idiot. "I really must take you back now."

"I suppose so." She took a last look at the water garden. "Thank you for indulging me, Lord Justin."

Their walk had taken them around three sides of the palace, and it was only a short distance to the Versailles garden where the fete was being held. As they approached the festivities, a tall man saw them and walked over swiftly. It was Paul Curzon, who had gone to Eton with Justin, though they had never been more than acquaintances. Curzon had been active in the most social set, while Justin had paid an unfashionable amount of attention to his studies.

After giving Justin a barely civil nod, Curzon said, "Lady Westron has been wondering what happened to you, Miss Vangelder."

Justin glanced at his companion and saw how her face lit up when Curzon spoke to her.

"I was in no danger, Mr. Curzon," she said, her voice proper but her eyes brimming with excitement. "I'm an avid gardener, you see, and Lord Justin very kindly consented to show me some of the lesser-known parts of the park."

In a careless tone that managed to imply that Justin was scarcely better than an under gardener, Curzon said, "You could not have chosen a better guide, for I'm sure that no one knows more about such matters than Lord Justin." He offered Sunny his arm. "Now I shall take you to Lady Westron."

Sunny turned to Justin and said with sweet sincerity, "Thank you for the tour, my lord. I enjoyed it very much."

Yet as soon as she took Curzon's arm, Justin saw that she forgot his existence. He watched them walk away together—two tall, blond, laughing people. They were like members of some superior race, set apart from the normal run of mankind.

For the first time in his life, Justin found himself resenting Gavin for having been born first. The Sunny Vangelders of the world would always go to men like Gavin or Curzon.

His aching regret was followed by deep, corroding anger. Damning himself for a fool, he turned and headed toward the house. Gavin's fete could progress to its conclusion without him.

CHAPTER TWO

Swindon Palace
Summer 1885

JUSTIN STARED OUT THE STUDY window at the dreary landscape, thinking that rain was appropriate for the day he had buried his only brother. After a gray, painful interval, a discreet cough reminded him that he was not alone. He turned to the family solicitor, who had formally read the will earlier in the afternoon. "Why did you ask to speak with me, Mr. Burrell?"

"Though I'm sorry to intrude at such a time, your grace," the solicitor said, "there are several pressing matters that must be addressed without delay."

Justin winced inwardly. Five days of being the ninth Duke of Thornborough was not long enough to accustom him to his new status. "I assume that you are going to tell me that the financial situation is difficult. I'm already aware of that."

Another little cough, this one embarrassed. "While you are extremely well-informed about estate matters, there are, ah, certain other items that you might not know of."

With sudden foreboding, Justin asked, "Had Gavin run up extensive personal debts?"

"I'm afraid so, your grace. To the tune of…almost a hundred thousand pounds."

A hundred thousand pounds! How the devil had Gavin managed to spend so much? Justin wanted to swear out loud.

Seeing his expression, Mr. Burrell said, "It was unfortunate that your brother's death occurred just when it did."

"You mean the fact that he died while on his way to marry May Russell? It certainly would have been more prudent to have waited until after the wedding," Justin said bitterly.

It would have been even more prudent if Gavin had stayed in the private Thornborough railway car. Instead, he had been taken by the charms of a French lady and had gone to her compartment. When the train crashed, the duke and his inamorata had both died, locked in a scandalous embrace. If Gavin had been in his own car, he would have survived the crash with scarcely a bruise.

Oh, damn, Gavin, why did you have to get yourself killed?

Justin swallowed hard. "Obviously drastic measures will be required to save the family from bankruptcy."

"You could sell some land."

"No!" More moderately, Justin said, "The land is held in trust for future generations. It should not be sold to pay frivolous debts."

Burrell nodded, as if he had expected that response. "The only other choice is for you to make an advantageous marriage."

"Become a fortune hunter, you mean?"

"It's a time-honored tradition, your grace," Burrell pointed out with dignity. "You have a great deal to offer a well-dowered bride. One of England's greatest names, and the most magnificent private palace in Great Britain."

"A palace whose roof leaks," Justin said dryly. "Even as we speak, dozens of buckets in the attic are filling with water."

"In that case, the sooner you marry, the better." The solicitor cleared his throat with a new intonation. "In fact, Mrs. Russell hinted to me this morning that if you were interested in contracting an alliance with her, she would look with favor on your suit."

"Marry my brother's fiancée?" Justin said incredulously. He thought of how May had looked earlier at Gavin's funeral, weeping copiously, her beautiful face obscured by her black mourning veil. Perhaps if he had looked more closely, he would have seen a speculative gleam in her eyes. "It's hard to believe that even she would go to such lengths to become a duchess."

"The lady implied that she has a certain fondness for you, as well," Burrell said piously.

"The lady has a deficient memory," Justin retorted. It was May Russell who had first called him the Gargoyle. She had been demonstrating her wittiness. Even Gavin had laughed.

"She has a very large fortune under her own control," the solicitor said with regret. "But I suppose you're right—it would be unseemly for you to marry your brother's betrothed. Do you have another suitable female in mind?"

"No. For the last several years, I've been too busy to look for a wife." Justin returned to his position by the window and stared blindly across the grounds. Burrell was right—marriage was the only plausible answer. Justin wouldn't be the first, and certainly not the last, to marry for money.

Even as a younger son, Justin would have had no trouble finding a wife, for he was an Aubrey, had no appalling vices and he had inherited an adequate private income. Yet though Gavin's entertaining had brought a steady stream of polished, fashionable females through Swindon, there had never been one whom Justin had wanted for a wife.

Except...

He closed his eyes, and instantly the memory he had tried to suppress for months crossed his mind—a perfect spring day, a tall, graceful young woman with a smile of such bright sweetness that she was nicknamed for the sun. The image was more real than the foggy landscape outside.

Though Justin had hated himself for his weakness, he had compulsively tracked Sunny Vangelder's triumphant passage through English society. Scarcely an issue of the *Morning Post* had arrived without mentioning her presentation at court, or her glowing appearance at a ball, or the fact that she had been seen riding in Rotten Row. Rumor said that many men had asked for her hand, and daily Justin had steeled himself for an announcement of a brilliant match. Yet at the end of the season, she had left London still unbetrothed.

He drew a painful breath. It was absurd to think of such an incomparable female marrying someone as ordinary as himself. But Gavin had said that she was the greatest heiress ever to cross the Atlantic, which meant that she was exactly the sort of wife Justin needed. And it was also said that her mother wanted to see her a duchess.

Scarcely daring to hope, he asked, "Do you know if Miss Vangelder has contracted a marriage yet?"

"You want to marry the Gilded Girl?" Burrell said, unable to conceal his shock at such effrontery. "Winning her would be quite a coup, but difficult, very difficult. There's a mining heiress from San Francisco who might be a better choice. Almost as wealthy, and I am acquainted with her father. Or perhaps..."

Interrupting the solicitor, Justin said, "I would prefer Miss Vangelder. I met her once, and found her…very amiable."

After a long pause, Burrell said doubtfully, "Of course, you *are* the Duke of Thornborough now. Perhaps it could be done."

Justin smiled humorlessly at the slate-gray pools of the water garden. "How does one go about selling oneself, Burrell? My experience is sadly deficient."

Ignoring the sardonic tone, the solicitor said, "I shall visit Lady Westron. She's the girl's godmother, you know. If she thinks the idea has merit, she can write Augusta Vangelder."

"Very well—call on her ladyship before the roof collapses."

"There is one thing you should consider before proceeding, your grace," Burrell said with a warning note. "Certainly there are more American heiresses than English ones, and they tend to be much more polished, but the drawback of such an alliance is that the families usually drive hard bargains. You would probably have restrictions placed on your control of the dowry, and you might have to return the balance if the marriage ends."

Justin's mouth tightened. "I wouldn't be marrying the girl with the intention of divorcing her, Burrell."

"Of course not," the solicitor said quickly. After a shuffle of papers, he added, "If I may say so, you're very different from your brother."

"Say what you like," Justin said tersely. Yet though he told himself that a rich wife was strictly a practical matter, the possibility of marrying Sunny Vangelder filled him with raw, aching hunger.

If she came to Swindon, there would always be sunshine.

Newport, Rhode Island

LAUGHING AND BREATHLESS from the bicycle ride, Sunny
waved goodbye to her friends, then skipped up the steps
of The Tides, the Vangelder summer home. Like most
Newport "cottages," it would have been called a mansion
anywhere else. Still, the atmosphere was more informal
than in New York, and she always enjoyed the months
spent in Newport.

And this summer was the best ever, because the Honorable Paul Curzon was visiting the Astors. He had arrived
in Newport three weeks earlier, and the first time they
had waltzed together he had confided that he had come
to America to see Sunny.

She had almost expired from sheer bliss, for she had
been thinking of Paul ever since their first meeting. They
had carried on a delicious flirtation throughout the season,
and she had sensed that there were deeper feelings on both
sides; certainly there had been on her part. It had been
a bitter disappointment that he had not offered for her
then.

As they danced, he explained that he had not spoken
earlier for he had feared that he would not be considered
an acceptable suitor. But after weeks of yearning, he had
finally decided to come to America and declare his love.
Breathlessly she had confessed that she also had tender
feelings for him.

Ever since that night, she had been living in an enchanted dream. Each morning she woke with the knowledge that she would see Paul at least once during the day,
perhaps more than that. The business of Newport was
society, and there was an endless succession of balls and
dinner parties and polo matches.

Though the two of them had behaved impeccably in
public, on two magical occasions they had had a moment's

privacy, and he had kissed her with a passion that made her blood sing through her veins. At night, as she lay in her chaste bed, she remembered those kisses and yearned for more.

His courtship had culminated this morning, in the few minutes when the two of them had cycled ahead of the rest of their party. After declaring his love, he had asked her to marry him. Dizzy with delight, she had accepted instantly.

As Sunny stepped into the cool marble vestibule of The Tides, she tried to calm her expression, for she knew that she was beaming like a fool. It was going to be hard to keep her lovely secret, but she must until the next day, when Paul would ask her mother's permission. It was not to be expected that her mother would be enthralled by the match. However, Sunny was sure that she would come around, for Paul came from a fine family and he had a distinguished career in front of him.

She handed the butler her hat, saying gaily, "It's a beautiful day, Graves."

"Indeed it is, Miss Sarah." Taking the hat, he added, "Your mother has asked that you see her as soon as you return home. I believe that she is in her private salon."

Such summons were not uncommon, so Sunny went upstairs with no premonition of disaster. She knocked on her mother's door and was invited in.

When she entered, Augusta looked up from her desk with triumph in her eyes. "I have splendid news, Sarah. I'll admit I was tempted by some of the offers I received for your hand, but it was right to wait." After a portentous pause, she said, "You, my dear, are going to become the Duchess of Thornborough."

The shock was so stunning that at first Sunny could only say stupidly, "What on earth do you mean?"

"You're going to marry Thornborough, of course," her

mother said briskly. "For the last several days cables have been flying back and forth between Newport and England. The essentials have been settled, and Thornborough is on his way to Newport to make you a formal offer."

"But...but I thought the Duke of Thornborough was going to marry Mrs. Russell."

"That was Gavin, the eighth duke. Unfortunately he was killed in a train wreck several weeks ago, two days before he was to marry May." Augusta smiled maliciously. "I would wager that May tried her luck with his successor, but clearly the ninth duke has better taste than his brother."

Feeling ice-cold, Sunny sank into a chair. "How can I marry a man whom I've never even met?" she said weakly.

"Katie Westron said that you did meet him. In fact, you spent a rather indecent amount of time strolling through the Swindon gardens together," her mother said tartly. "He was Lord Justin Aubrey then, younger brother to the duke who just died."

The fete at Swindon was when Sunny had met Paul. Beside that, other events of the day had paled. Dazedly she tried to remember more. The gardens had been superb, and she vaguely recalled being escorted through them by someone. Had that been Lord Justin? She supposed so, though she could remember nothing about him except that he was dark, and quiet, and...unmemorable.

But it didn't matter what he was like, because she wasn't going to marry him. Steeling herself for battle, Sunny said, "I can't marry Thornborough, because I'm betrothed to Paul Curzon."

There was an instant of ominous silence. Then her mother exploded. "I considered putting a stop to that earlier, but I thought it was a harmless flirtation. I couldn't *believe* that you would be so foolish as to entertain thoughts of marrying such a man." Her eyes narrowed. "I trust that at least you've had the sense not to tell anyone about this so-called engagement?"

Sunny shook her head. "Paul only asked me this morning."

"I shall send him a note saying that he is never to call on you, or speak to you again. That will put an end to this nonsense." Augusta drummed her fingers on the elaborate desk as she thought. "Thornborough will be here in nine days. I shall give a ball in his honor a week later, and we can announce the betrothal then. The wedding should take place in October, I think. It will take that long to make suitable arrangements."

Knowing that she faced the fight of her life, Sunny wiped her damp palms on her skirt, then said evenly, "You must cable the duke and stop him from coming, Mother. Paul Curzon and I love each other, and I am going to marry him."

It was the first time she had ever defied her mother, and Augusta's jaw dropped in shock. Recovering quickly, she said in a low, furious voice, "You are a Vangelder, my girl, and I've devoted my life to training you to be worthy of the highest station. I will never permit you to throw yourself away on a worthless, fortune-hunting younger son."

"Paul is no fortune hunter! He said that if you refused permission, we could live on his income," Sunny said hotly. "And he isn't worthless! He's a British aristocrat, exactly what you wanted for me, and he has a great future in British politics. He was recently made a junior minister, and he says that with me by his side he'll soon be in the Cabinet."

"Your money would certainly help his career," Augusta said grimly, "but he'll have to find himself another heiress, because I will never give my consent."

"I don't need your consent!" Sunny said fiercely. "I'm of legal age and can marry whomever I wish. And I *will!*"

"How dare you speak to your mother this way!" Augusta grabbed Sunny's elbow, then marched her down the hall to her bedroom and shoved her inside. "If you think a humble life is so splendid, you can stay locked in here and live on bread and water until you change your mind."

As the key turned in the lock, Sunny collapsed, shaking, on the bed. She had never dreamed how painful defiance could be. Yet she could not surrender, not when her whole life's happiness was at stake.

She must see Paul; he would know what to do.

The thought steadied her churning emotions, and she began to consider what to do. Her bedroom opened onto the roof of one of the porches, and her older brother Charlie had showed her how to climb to the ground. Her mother had never dreamed that her well-bred daughter would behave in such a hoydenish fashion.

Paul was staying at Windfall, which was only a mile away. Would he be there this evening? Yes, he had mentioned that the Astors were giving a dinner party. She would wait until her mother retired, then escape and walk to Windfall. With a veil over her face, no one would recognize her even if she was seen. She'd go to the servants' entrance and ask for the butler. He knew her, and she thought that for a suitable consideration he would summon Paul and let them have a few minutes of privacy.

Once they were together, everything would be all right.

SUNNY'S PLAN WENT SMOOTHLY, and by ten o'clock that evening she was pacing nervously around the Windfall servants' sitting room. She hoped that Paul would be able to slip away quietly when the butler delivered her message. But what if the butler betrayed her to Mrs. Astor? Or if Mrs. Astor suspected that something was amiss and decided to investigate?

The door opened and she whirled around, ready to jump from her skin. With a wave of relief, she saw that it was Paul, devastatingly attractive in his evening dress. Coming toward her with concern on his face, he said, "Darling, you shouldn't risk your reputation like this—but it's wonderful to see you."

He opened his arms, and she went into them eagerly. She loved his height, which made her feel small and feminine. It was the first time they had real privacy, and his kiss far surpassed what they had shared before. Her resolve strengthened. She would never give up his love for the dubious pleasure of marrying a nondescript duke. *Never.*

Remembering the reason for her visit, she reluctantly ended the kiss. "Oh, Paul, something dreadful has happened!" she said miserably. "Today my mother told me that she has arranged for me to marry someone else. I told her about our betrothal, but she won't hear of it. She locked me in my room and swore I'd stay there on bread and water until I changed my mind."

"How dare she treat you in such a way!" Paul exclaimed. "I won't permit it."

"I refused to agree to her wishes, of course, but it was so difficult. I...I think we should elope. Tonight."

"Right now?" he said, startled. "That's not what I want for you, darling. You deserve the grandest wedding of the century, not a furtive, hole-in-corner affair."

"What does that matter?" she said impatiently. "I'm trying to be strong, but my mother is...is not easy to resist."

"Who does she want you to marry?"

"The new Duke of Thornborough, Justin Aubrey. His brother, Gavin, just died, and Justin needs a rich wife."

Before she could say more, Paul said in a stunned voice, "The Duke of Thornborough! You would be one of the most influential women in England."

"And one of the unhappiest." Tears welled in her eyes, and she blinked them back angrily. "I need to be with you, Paul."

"We must reason this out." He stroked her back soothingly. "Your mother flatly refused to consider me as a suitor?"

"She said that it was unthinkable that I should marry a nobody." Sunny relaxed again, comforted by his touch. "Such nonsense! Titles mean nothing. What matters is being a gentleman, and no one is more gentlemanly than you."

There was a long pause. Then Paul said gravely, "Sunny, I can't marry you against your mother's wishes. Though I knew that she would not be enthusiastic about my suit, I thought I would be able to persuade her. But to be Duchess of Thornborough! With that in prospect, she will never accept me."

A tendril of fear curled through Sunny. "It is not my mother's place to choose my husband," she said sharply. "It's mine, and you are my choice. That's all that matters."

"If only it were that simple!" He sighed. "But it's not, my dear. You are not simply my own sweet love, but a national treasure—one of America's princesses. What kind of cad would I be to take advantage of your innocence to keep you from a glorious future?"

Sunny stared at him, thinking that this scene couldn't be real. Perhaps she had fallen off her bicycle and injured her head, and everything that had happened since was only a bad dream. Very carefully she said, "You're saying that you don't want to marry me?"

"Of course I do, but clearly that is impossible. If you marry me, you will become estranged from your family. I don't want to be the cause of that." He gazed lovingly into her eyes. "This won't be so bad, darling. In fact, one could see it as a piece of good fortune. With your influence to further my career, I'll be in the Cabinet in no time."

"Is that what matters most—your career?" she said brittlely.

"Of course not!" He pulled her close again. "The most important thing is our love, and your mother can't take that away from us. After you've given Thornborough an heir and a spare, we'll be free to love each other as we were meant to."

She went rigid, unable to believe what he was saying.

Feeling her withdrawal, he said tenderly, "I don't want to wait, either. If we're discreet, we can be together as soon as you're back from your honeymoon. Believe me, I would like nothing better! We'll have to be careful, of course—it wouldn't do to foist a bastard on Thornborough." He gave a wicked chuckle. "Though if the Gargoyle is unable to perform his duty, I'll be happy to help him. I look more like an Aubrey than he does."

"In other words, I make you a Cabinet minister, and my reward is adultery in the afternoon," she said numbly. "No, thank you, Mr. Curzon." Knowing that she would break down in tears if she stayed any longer, she headed for the door.

He followed her and caught her shoulders. "Don't look at it that way, darling. I promise you that this will turn out all right. We'll be able to enjoy the very cream of love, with none of the dreariness of daily living that kills romance."

He turned her around so that she was facing him. He was as heart-stoppingly handsome as ever, his golden hair glowing in the gaslight, his blue eyes limpid with sincerity.

She drew a shuddering breath. How could she have been such a fool?

His voice richly confident, he said, "Trust me, darling." Then he started to pull her toward him for another kiss.

She slapped him with all her strength. "You're right that this is a fortunate turn of events, because it's given me a chance to see what a swine you are," she said, her voice trembling. "I hope I never see you again, though I don't suppose I'll be so lucky. Goodbye, Mr. Curzon, and good riddance."

As he gaped with shock, the imprint of her hand reddening on his face, she spun on her heel and raced from the room. When she was outside the cottage, she took refuge in the shadowy lee of a huge hedge. There she fell to her knees, heart hammering and tears pouring down her face.

Ever since her childhood, she had dreamed of finding a man who would love her forever. She had wanted a marriage different from the carefully concealed hostility between her parents, or the bored civility common between many other fashionable couples. In Paul, she thought she had found the man she was seeking.

But she had been wrong, so wrong. Oh, he desired her body, and he lusted after her family's money and influence, but that wasn't love—she doubted that he knew what love was. Obviously she didn't know much about it, either. Perhaps the love she craved had never been more than a romantic girl's futile fantasy.

Blindly she stumbled to her feet and began the slow walk to The Tides. After Paul's betrayal, there was no reason to go anywhere else.

THE NEXT MORNING, WHEN a maid delivered a half loaf of freshly baked bread and a crystal pitcher of water on a tray decorated with a fresh rosebud, Sunny summoned her mother and said that she would accept the Duke of Thornborough's offer.

CHAPTER THREE

JUSTIN FOUND AMERICA a mixture of the sublime and the ridiculous. He liked the bustling energy of New York City and the cheerful directness of the average citizen. Yet in what was supposedly a nation of equals, he found people whose craven fawning over his title would have shamed a spaniel.

Newport society, which considered itself the *crème de la crème* of America, apparently wanted to out-Anglo the English when it came to formality and elaborate rules. Augusta Vangelder was in her element as she escorted him to an endless series of social events. She invariably referred to him as her "dear duke." He bore that stoically, along with all the other absurdities of the situation.

But the habits of the natives were of only minor interest; what mattered was Sunny Vangelder. He had hoped that she would greet him with the same sweet, unaffected good nature that she had shown at Swindon, perhaps even with eagerness.

Instead, she might have been a different person. The laughing girl had been replaced by a polished, brittle young woman who avoided speaking with him and never once met his gaze. Though he tried to revive the easy companionship they had so briefly shared, he had no success. Perhaps her stiffness was caused by her mother's rather repressive presence, but he had the uneasy feeling that there was a deeper cause.

His fifth morning in Newport, he happened to find

Sunny reading in the library during a rare hour when they were at home. She didn't hear him enter, and her head remained bent over her book. The morning light made her hair glow like sun-struck honey, and the elegant purity of her profile caught at his heart.

It was time to make his formal offer of marriage. A flurry of images danced through his mind: him kneeling at her feet and eloquently swearing eternal devotion; Sunny opening her arms and giving him that wonderful smile that had made him feel as if he were the only man in the world; a kiss that would bring them together forever.

Instead, he cleared his throat to get her attention, then said, "Miss Vangelder—Sunny—there is something I would like to ask you. I'm sure you know what it is."

Perhaps she had known that he was there, for there was no surprise on her face when she lowered her book and looked up.

"All of Newport knows," she said without inflection.

She wasn't going to make this easy for him. Wishing that he was skilled at spinning romantic words, he said haltingly, "Sunny, you have had my heart from the first moment I saw you at Swindon. There is no one else…"

She cut him off with an abrupt motion of her hand. "You needn't waste our time with pretty lies, Duke. We are here to strike a bargain. You need a fortune and a wife who knows what to do with a dinner setting that includes six forks. I need a husband who will lend luster to my mother's position in society, and who will confirm our fine American adage that anything can be bought. Please get on with the offer so I can accept and return to my book."

He rocked back on his heels, feeling as if he had been punched in the stomach. Wanting to pierce her contemptuous calm, he said with uncharacteristic bluntness, "We're talking about a marriage, not a business. The first duty of a nobleman's wife is to produce an heir, and knowledge of which fork to use will not help you there."

"I've heard that begetting children is a monstrously undignified business, but didn't the Queen tell her oldest daughter that a female needs only to lie there and think of England?" Sunny's lips twisted. "I should be able to manage that. Most women do."

Damning the consequences to Swindon, he said tightly, "There will be no offer, Miss Vangelder, for I will do neither of us a favor by marrying a woman who despises me."

Sunny caught her breath, and for the first time since he had arrived in Newport looked directly at him. He was shocked by the haunted misery in her aqua eyes.

After a moment she bent her neck and pressed her slim fingers to the center of her forehead. "I'm sorry, your grace. I didn't mean to imply that I despise you," she said quietly. "I recently…suffered a disappointment, and I'm afraid that my temper is badly out of sorts. Still, that does not excuse my insufferable rudeness. Please forgive me."

He guessed that only a broken heart would cause a well-mannered young lady to behave so brusquely. He had heard that Paul Curzon had been in Newport until the week before. Could Sunny have fallen in love with Curzon, who had as many mistresses as the Prince of Wales? Recalling how she had looked at the man when she was at Swindon, Justin knew it was all too likely.

The disappointment was crushing. When he had received Augusta Vangelder's invitation, he had assumed that she had obtained her daughter's agreement to the marriage. He should have known that he would never have been Sunny's choice. It was Augusta, after all, who was enthralled by the idea of a dukedom; Sunny was obviously unimpressed by the prospect.

In a voice of careful neutrality, he said, "You're forgiven, but even if you don't despise me, it's clear that this is not a match that you want." His throat closed, and it took an immense effort to add, "I don't want an unwilling bride, so if there is someone else whom you wish to marry, I shall withdraw."

She stared at her hands, which were locked tightly on her book. "There is no one I would prefer. I suppose that I must marry someone, and you'll make as good a husband as any."

He studied the delicate line of her profile, his resolve to do the right thing undermined by his yearning. Then she raised her head, her gaze searching. He had the feeling that it was the first time she had truly looked at him as an individual.

"Perhaps you would be better than most," she said after a charged silence. "At least you are honest about what you want."

It was a frail foundation for a lifetime commitment, but he could not bear to throw away this chance. "Very well," he said formally. "I would be very honored, and very pleased, if you would consent to become my wife."

"The honor is mine, your grace," she said with equal formality.

If this was a normal engagement, he would kiss his intended bride now, but Sunny's expression was unwelcoming, so he said only, "My name is Justin. It would please me if you used it."

She nodded. "Very well, Justin."

An awkward silence fell. Unhappily he wondered how achieving the fondest hope of his heart could feel so much like ashes. "Shall we go and inform your mother of our news?"

"You don't need me for that. I know that she is interested in an early wedding, perhaps October. You need only tell her what is convenient for you." Rubbing her temples, she set aside her book and got to her feet. "If you'll excuse me, I have a bit of a headache."

"I hope that you feel better soon."

"I'm sure I shall." Remembering that she had just agreed to give her life, her person and her fortune into this stranger's keeping, she attempted a smile.

It must not have been a very good attempt, because the duke's face remained grave. His thoughtful eyes were a clear, light gray, and were perhaps his best feature.

"I don't wish to seem inattentive," he said, "but my brother left his affairs in some disarray, and I must return to London the day after your mother's ball. I probably won't be able to return until a few days before the wedding."

"There is no need for romantic pretenses between us." She smiled, a little wryly, but with the first amusement she had felt since discovering Paul's true character. "It will be best if you aren't here, because there will be a truly vulgar amount of publicity. Our marriage will inevitably be deemed the Wedding of the Century, and there will be endless stories about you and me, your noble ancestors and my undistinguished ones, my trousseau, my flowers, my attendants and every other conceivable detail. And what the reporters can't find out, they will invent."

His dark brows arched. "You're right. It will be better if I am on the other side of the Atlantic."

He opened the door for her. When she walked in front of him, on impulse she laid her hand on his arm for a moment. "I shall do my best to be a duchess you will be proud of."

He inclined his head. "I'm sure you will succeed."

As she went upstairs to her room, she decided that he

was rather attractive, in a subdued way. Granted, he wasn't much taller than she, but she was a tall woman. The quiet excellence of British tailoring showed his trim, muscular figure to advantage, and his craggy features had a certain distinction.

The words echoed in her mind, and as she entered her room and wearily lay on the bed, she realized that she had had similar thoughts when she first saw him at Swindon Palace.

That memory triggered others, and gradually fragments of that day came back to her. Lord Justin had been quiet but very gentlemanly, and knowledgeable about the gardens and estate. He had even showed signs of humor, of a very dry kind. It had been a pleasant interlude.

Yet he was still almost entirely a stranger, for she knew nothing of his mind or emotions. He didn't seem to be a man of deep feelings; it was his duty to marry well, so he was doing so, choosing a wife with his head rather than his heart.

Her eyes drifted shut. Perhaps this marriage would not be such a bad thing; she had heard that arranged marriages were happy about as often as love matches. She and the duke would treat each other with polite respect and not expect romance or deep passion. God willing, they would have children, and in them she might find the love she craved.

Certainly the duke had one great advantage: he could hardly have been more different from charming, articulate, false-hearted Paul Curzon.

THE MAID ANTOINETTE MADE a last adjustment to the train of Sunny's ball gown. "You look exquisite, mademoiselle. *Monsieur le Duc* will be most pleased."

Sunny turned and regarded herself in the mirror. Her cream-colored gown was spectacular, with sumptuous embroidery and a décolletage that set off her bare shoulders and arms perfectly. After her hair had been pinned up to expose the graceful length of her neck, fragile rosebuds had been woven into the soft curls. The only thing her appearance lacked was animation. "Thank you, Antoinette. You have surpassed yourself."

The maid permitted herself a smile of satisfaction before she withdrew. Sunny glanced at the clock and saw that she had a quarter of an hour to wait before making her grand entrance at the ball. The house hummed with excitement, for tonight Augusta's triumph would be announced. All of Newport society was here to fawn over Thornborough and cast envious glances at Sunny. There would also be sharp eyes watching to see how she and the duke—Justin—behaved with each other. Antoinette, who was always well-informed, had passed on several disturbing rumors. It was said that Sunny had at first refused to marry the duke because of his licentious habits, and that Augusta had beaten and starved her daughter into accepting him.

Even though there was a grain of truth in the story about her mother, Sunny found the gossip deeply distasteful. She must make a special effort to appear at ease with her mother and her fiancé. She looked in the mirror again and practiced her smile.

The door opened and a crisp English voice said, "How is my favorite goddaughter?"

"Aunt Katie!" Sunny spun around with genuine pleasure. "I had no idea that you were coming for the ball."

"I told Augusta not to mention the possibility since I wasn't sure I would arrive in time." Laughing, Lady Westron held Sunny at arm's length when her goddaughter came to give her a hug. "Never crush a Worth evening gown, my dear! At least, not until the ball is over."

After a careful survey, she gave a nod of approval. "I'm

madly envious. Even Worth can't make a short woman like me look as magnificent as you do tonight. The Newport cats will gnash their teeth with jealousy, and Thornborough will thank his stars for his good fortune."

Sunny's high spirits faded. "I believe he feels that we have made a fair bargain."

Katie cocked her head. "Are you unhappy about the match?"

Sunny shrugged and began carefully drawing an elbow-length kid glove onto her right hand. "I'm sure that we'll rub along tolerably well."

Ignoring her own advice about crushing a Worth evening gown, Katie dropped into a chair with a flurry of satin petticoats. "I made inquiries about Thornborough when his solicitor first approached me about a possible match. He'll make you a better husband than most, Sunny. He's respected by those who know him, and while he isn't a wit like his brother was, and he's certainly not fashionable, he's no fool, nor is he the sort to humiliate you by flaunting his mistress."

Sunny stiffened. "Thornborough has a mistress?"

"Very likely—most men do." Katie's lips curved ruefully. "There's much you need to learn about English husbands and English houses. Living in Britain is quite unlike being a visitor, you know."

Sunny relaxed when she found that her godmother had been talking in general rather than from particular knowledge. Though she knew that fashionable English society was very different from what she was used to, she disliked the idea of Thornborough with a mistress. Acutely.

She began the slow process of putting on her left glove. "Perhaps you had better educate me about what to expect."

"Be prepared for the fact that English great houses

are *cold*." Katie shuddered. "Forget your delicate lace shawls—to survive winter in an English country house, your trousseau should include several wraps the size and weight of a horse blanket. You must have at least one decent set of furs, as well. The houses may be grand, but they're amazingly primitive—no central heating or gaslights, and no hot running water. And the bathrooms! A tin tub in front of the fire is the best you'll do in most houses."

Surprised and a little amused, Sunny said, "Surely Swindon Palace can't be that bad. It's said to be the grandest private home in Great Britain."

Katie sniffed. "A palace built almost two hundred years ago, and scarcely a pound wasted on modernization since then. But don't complain to Thornborough— English husbands, as a rule, are not solicitous in the way that American husbands are. Since the duke will not want to hear about your little grievances, you must learn to resolve matters on your own. I recommend that you take your own maid with you. That way you can count on at least one person in the household being on your side."

Sunny put a hand up. "If you say one sentence more, I will go downstairs and cancel my betrothal," she said, not knowing whether to laugh or cry. "I'm beginning to wonder why any woman would want to marry an English lord, particularly if she isn't madly in love with him."

"I didn't mean to terrify you," Katie assured her. "I just want to make sure that you won't be disillusioned. Once a woman gets past the discomforts, she may have more freedom and influence than she would in America. Here, a woman rules her home, but nothing outside. An English lady can be part of her husband's life, or develop a life of her own, in a way most unusual in America."

Since frankness was the order of the day, Sunny asked, "Are you sorry you married Lord Westron?"

Katie hesitated a moment. "There are times when I would have said yes, but we've come to understand each other very well. He says that I've been invaluable to his political career, and through him, I've been able to bring a little American democracy to some hoary bits of British law." She smiled fondly. "And between us, he and I have produced three rather splendid children, even if I shouldn't say so myself."

Sunny sighed; it was all very confusing. She was glad when a knock sounded on her door. "Your mother says that it is time to come down, Miss Sarah," the butler intoned.

"Don't forget your fan. It's going to be very warm on the dance floor," Katie said briskly. "I'll be down after I've freshened up."

Sunny accepted the fan, then lifted her train and went into the corridor. At the top of the sweeping staircase, she carefully spread the train, then slowly began descending the stairs, accompanied by the soft swish of heavy silk. She had been told that she walked with the proud grace of the Winged Victory. She ought to; as a child, she had been strapped into an iron back brace whenever she did her lessons. Perfect posture didn't come easily.

The hall below opened into the ballroom, and music and guests wafted through both. As she came into view, a hush fell and all eyes turned toward her. The cream of American society was evaluating the next Duchess of Thornborough.

When she was three-quarters of the way down, she saw that her fiancé was crossing the hall to the staircase. The stark black of formal evening wear suited him.

When she reached the bottom, he took her hand. Under his breath, he said, "You look even more beautiful than usual." Then he brushed a courtly, formal kiss on her kid-covered fingers.

She glanced at him uncertainly, not sure if he truly admired her or the compliment was mere formality. It was impossible to tell; he was the most inscrutable man she had ever met.

Then he smiled at her and looked not merely presentable, but downright handsome. It was the first time she had seen him smile. He should do so more often.

Her mother joined them, beaming with possessive pride. "You look splendid, Sarah."

A moment later they were surrounded by chattering, laughing people, particularly those who had not yet met the duke and who longed to rectify the omission. Sunny half expected her fiancé to retreat to a corner filled with men, but he bore up under the onslaught very well. Though he spoke little, his grave courtesy soon won over even the most critical society matrons. She realized that she had underestimated him. Thornborough's avoidance of the fashionable life was obviously from choice rather than social ineptitude.

When she finally had a chance to look at her dance card, she saw that her fiancé had put himself down for two waltzes as well as the supper dance. That in itself was a declaration of their engagement, for no young lady would have more than two dances with one man unless intentions were serious.

When the orchestra struck up their first waltz, Thornborough excused himself from his admirers and came to collect her.

She caught her train up so that she could dance, then took his hand and followed him onto the floor. "It will be a pleasure to waltz," she said. "I feel as if I've been talking nonstop for the last hour."

"I believe that you have been," he said as he drew her into position, a light hand on her waist. "It must be fatiguing to be so popular. In the interests of allowing you to recover, I shan't require you to talk at all."

"But you are just as popular," she said teasingly. "Everyone in Newport wants to know you."

"It isn't me they're interested in, but the Duke of Thornborough. If I were a hairy ape from the Congo, I'd be equally in demand, as long as I was also a duke." He considered, then said with good-natured cynicism, "More so, I think. Apes are said to be quite entertaining."

Though Sunny chuckled, his remark made her understand better why he wanted her to call him Justin. Being transformed overnight from the Gargoyle to the much-courted Duke of Thornborough must have been enough to make anyone cynical.

It came as no surprise to learn that he danced well. She relaxed and let the voluptuous strains of music work their usual magic. The waltz was a very intimate dance, the closest a young woman was allowed to come to a man. Usually it was also an opportunity to talk with some privacy. The fact that she and Justin were both silent had the curious effect of making her disturbingly aware of his physical closeness, even though he kept a perfectly proper twelve inches between them.

Katie had been right about the heat of the ballroom; as they whirled across the floor, Sunny realized that a remarkable amount of warmth was being generated between their gloved hands. It didn't help that their eyes were almost level, for it increased the uncomfortable sense of closeness. She wished that she knew what was going on behind those enigmatic gray eyes.

A month before, she had waltzed like this with Paul Curzon and he had told her that his heart had driven him to follow her to America. The memory was jarring and she stumbled on a turn. If Justin hadn't quickly steadied her, she would have fallen.

His dark brows drew together. "Are you feeling faint? It's very warm—perhaps we should go onto the porch for some air."

She managed a smile. "I'm fine, only a little dizzy. It's absurd that we can turn only one direction during a waltz. If we could spin the other way now and then, it would be much easier."

"Society thrives on absurdity," he observed. "Obscure rules are necessary so that outsiders can be identified and kept safely outside."

While she pondered his unexpected insight, the waltz ended and another partner came to claim her. The evening passed quickly. After the lavish supper was served, the engagement was formally announced. Augusta was in her element as even her most powerful social rivals acknowledged her triumph.

Sunny felt a pang as she accepted the good wishes of people she had known all her life. This was her last summer in Newport. Though she would visit in the future, it would not be the same; already her engagement to an Englishman was setting her apart.

The first phase of her life was ending—and she had no clear idea what the next phase would be like.

IT WAS VERY LATE WHEN the last of the guests left. As her official fiancé, Thornborough was allowed to escort Sunny to her room. When they reached her door, he said, "My train leaves rather early tomorrow, so I'll say good-bye now."

"I'm sorry that you'll have to travel without a proper night's sleep." Almost too tired to stand, she masked a yawn with her hand. "Have a safe and pleasant journey, Justin."

His gaze caught hers, and she couldn't look away. The

air between them seemed to thicken. Gently he curved his hand around her head and drew her to him for a kiss.

Because she didn't love him she had been dreading this moment, yet again he surprised her. His lips were warm and firm. Pleasant. Undemanding.

He caressed her hair, disturbing the rosebuds, and scented petals drifted over her bare shoulder in a delicate sensual caress. She gave a little sigh, and his arms went around her.

The feel of his broad chest and his hand on the small of her back triggered a vivid memory of her last kiss, in Paul Curzon's embrace. All the anger and shame of that episode flooded back. She stiffened and took an involuntary step backward.

He released her instantly. Though his eyes had darkened, his voice was mild when he said, "Sleep well. I shall see you in October."

She opened her door, but instead of entering her room she paused and watched his compact, powerful figure stride down the hall to his own chamber. In spite of the warmth of the night, a shiver went down her spine. Her feelings about Justin were confused, but one thing was certain: it would be disastrous to continue to let the shadow of Paul Curzon come between her and her future husband.

Yet she didn't know how to get rid of it.

CHAPTER FOUR

New York City
October 1885

THE WEDDING OF THE CENTURY.

Justin stared at the blaring headline in one of the newspapers that had just been delivered to his hotel room. It was a rude shock for a man who had disembarked in New York City only two hours earlier.

Below the headline were drawings of Sunny and himself. The likeness of him was not flattering. Were his brows really so heavy and threatening? Perhaps.

He smiled wryly as he skimmed the story; it was every bit as bad as Sunny had predicted. Apparently Americans had a maniacal interest in other people's private business. There was even a breathless description of the bride's garters, which were allegedly of gold lace with diamond-studded clasps. The item must have been invented, since he could not imagine Sunny discussing her garters with a reporter.

The thought of Sunny in her garters was so distracting that he swiftly flipped to the next newspaper. This one featured a cartoon of a couple getting married by a blindfolded minister. The tall, slim bride wore a martyred expression as she knelt beside a dissolute-looking groom who was half a head shorter.

The accompanying story implied rather strongly that

the Duke of Thornborough was a corrupt specimen of European cadhood who had come to the New World to coldly steal away the finest, freshest flower of American femininity. At the same time, there was an unmistakable undercurrent of pride that one of New York's own was to become a duchess. Apparently the natives couldn't decide whether they loathed or loved the trappings of the decadent Old World.

Disgusted, he tossed the papers aside and finished dressing for the dinner that Augusta Vangelder was giving in his honor. Afterward, the marriage settlements would be signed. Yet though that would make him a far wealthier man, what made his heart quicken was the fact that after three long months, he would see Sunny again. And not only see, but touch…

After his Newport visit they had written each other regularly, and he had enjoyed her whimsical anecdotes about the rigors of preparing for a wedding. If she had ever expressed any affection for him, he might have had the courage to tell her his own feelings, for it would be easier to write about love than to say the words out loud.

But her letters had been so impersonal that anyone could have read them. He had replied with equal detachment, writing about Swindon and acquainting her with what she would find there. He had debated telling her about some of the improvements he had ordered, but decided to keep them as a surprise.

He checked his watch and saw that the carriage the Vangelders were sending should be waiting outside the hotel. Brimming with suppressed excitement, he went downstairs.

As he crossed the lobby, a voice barked, "There he is!"

Half a dozen slovenly persons, obviously reporters, bolted across the marble floor and surrounded him. Refusing to be deterred, he kept walking through the babble of questions that came from all sides.

The loudest speaker, a fellow with a red checked vest, yelled, "What do you think of New York, Duke?"

Deciding it was better to say something innocuous rather than to ignore them entirely, Justin said, "A splendid city."

Another reporter asked, "Any of your family coming to the wedding, Duke?"

"Unfortunately that isn't possible."

"Is it true that Sunny has the largest dowry of any American girl to marry a British lord?"

The sound of her name on the man's lips made Justin glad that he wasn't carrying a cane, for he might have broken it across the oaf's head. "You'll have to excuse me," he said, tight-lipped, "for I have an engagement."

"Are you going to visit Sunny now?" several chorused.

When Justin didn't answer, one of the men grabbed his arm. Clamping onto his temper, Justin looked the reporter in the eye and said in the freezing accents honed by ten generations of nobility, "I beg your pardon?"

The man hastily stepped back. "Sorry, sir. No offense meant."

Justin had almost reached the door when a skinny fellow jumped in front of him. "Are you in love with our Sunny, your dukeship, or are you only marrying her for the money?"

It had been a mistake to answer any questions at all, Justin realized; it only encouraged the creatures. "I realize that none of you are qualified to understand gentlemanly behavior," he said icily, "so you will have to take my word for it that a gentleman never discusses a lady, and particularly not in the public press. Kindly get out of my way."

The man said with a leer, "Just asking what the American public wants to know, Thorny."

"The American public can go hang," Justin snapped.

Before the reporters could commit any further impertinence, several members of the hotel staff belatedly came to Justin's rescue. They swept the journalists aside and escorted him outside with profuse apologies and promises that such persons would never be allowed in the hotel again.

In a voice clipped by fury, Justin told the manager, "I hope that is true, because if there is another episode like this I shall move to quieter quarters."

Temper simmering, he settled into the luxurious Vangelder carriage. The sooner this damned wedding was over and he could take his wife home, the better.

SUNNY WAS WAITING IN THE Vangelder drawing room. She came forward with her hands outstretched, and if her smile wasn't quite as radiant as he would have liked, at least it was genuine.

"It's good to see you, Sunny." He caught her hands and studied her face hungrily. "You were right about the publicity surrounding the wedding. I'm afraid that I was just rather abrupt with some members of the press. Has it been hard on you?"

She made a face. "Though it's been dreadful, I'm well protected here. But everyone in the household has been offered bribes to describe my trousseau."

"Gold-lace garters with diamond-studded clasps?"

"You saw that?" she said ruefully. "It's all so *vulgar!*"

She looked utterly charming. He was on the verge of kissing her when the door swung open. Justin looked up to see a tall, blond young man who had to be one of Sunny's older brothers.

"I'm Charlie Vangelder," the young man said cheerfully as he offered his hand. "Sorry not to meet you in Newport, Thornborough, but I was working on the railroad all summer. Have to learn how to run it when my uncle retires, you know."

So much for being alone with his intended bride. Suppressing a sigh, Justin shook hands with his future brother-in-law. A moment later, Augusta Vangelder swooped in, followed by a dozen more people, and it became clear that the "quiet family dinner" was an occasion for numberless Vangelders to meet their new relation by marriage.

The only break was the half hour when Justin met with the Vangelder attorneys to sign the settlement papers. His solicitor had bargained well; the minute that Justin married Sunny, he would come into possession of five million dollars worth of railway stock with a guaranteed minimum income of two hundred thousand dollars a year.

There would also be a capital sum of another million dollars that Justin would receive outright, plus a separate income for Sunny's personal use so that she would never have to be dependent on her husband's goodwill for pin money. As an incentive for Justin to try to keep his wife happy, the stock would revert to the Vangelder family trust if the marriage ended in divorce.

Gavin would have been amused to know that the value of the Thornborough title had risen so quickly. May Russell would have brought only half as much to her marriage.

Impassively Justin scrawled his name over and over,

hating every minute of it. He wished that he could marry Sunny without taking a penny of her family money, but that was impossible; without her wealth and his title, there would be no marriage.

As he signed the last paper, he wondered if Sunny would ever believe that he would have wanted her for his wife even if she had been a flower seller in Covent Garden.

WHEN HER DAUGHTER ENTERED the breakfast parlor, Augusta said, "Good morning, Sarah." She took a dainty bite of buttered eggs. "There's a letter here for you from England."

Sunny tried unsuccessfully to suppress a yawn as she selected two muffins from the sideboard. The dinner party for Thornborough had gone on very late, and she had smiled at so many cousins that her jaw ached this morning.

She wished that she had had a few minutes alone with her future husband; she would have liked to tell him how much she had enjoyed his letters. She didn't know if it had been a deliberate effort on his part, but his descriptions of life at Swindon Palace had made her future seem less alien. His dry wit had even managed to make her smile.

She slit open the envelope that lay by her plate and scanned the contents. "It's from Lady Alexandra Aubrey, Thornborough's youngest sister. A charming note welcoming me to the family."

Uncomfortably Sunny remembered that Katie had said the girl had been nicknamed the Gargoylette. Her lips compressed as she returned the note to the envelope. The girl might be small, shy and seventeen, but she was the only Aubrey to write her brother's bride, and Sunny looked forward to meeting her.

"Are you only going to have muffins for breakfast?" Augusta said with disapproval.

"After the dinner last night, it's all I have room for." Sunny broke and buttered one of the muffins, wondering why her mother had requested this private breakfast.

Expression determined, Augusta opened her mouth, then paused, as if changing her mind about what she meant to say. "Look at the morning paper. Thornborough was intemperate."

Obediently Sunny lifted the newspaper, then blinked at the screaming headline. *Duke Tells American Public to Go Hang!*

"Oh, my," she said weakly. The story beneath claimed that Thornborough had bodily threatened several journalists, then bullied the hotel manager in a blatant attempt to infringe on the American public's constitutional right to a free press. "He mentioned yesterday that he'd been abrupt with some reporters, but surely this story is exaggerated."

"No doubt, but someone should explain to Thornborough that it's a mistake to pick fights with men who buy ink by the barrel." Augusta neatly finished the last of her meal. "A good thing that he was in England until now. Heaven knows what trouble he would have gotten into if he had been here longer."

Feeling oddly protective, Sunny said, "He's a very private man. He must find this vulgar publicity deeply offensive."

"Unfortunately, wealth and power always attract the interest of the masses."

Sunny poured herself coffee without comment. Her

mother might say that public attention was unfortunate, but she would not have liked to be ignored.

Augusta began pleating her linen napkin into narrow folds. "You must be wondering why I wanted to talk to you this morning," she said with uncharacteristic constraint. "This will be difficult for both of us, but it's a mother's duty to explain to her daughter what her...her conjugal duties will be."

The muffin turned to sawdust in Sunny's mouth. Though she didn't want to discuss such a horribly embarrassing subject, there was no denying that information would be useful. Like all well-bred young ladies, her ignorance about marital intimacy was almost total.

Briskly Augusta explained the basics of male and female anatomy. Then, rather more slowly, she went on to describe exactly what a husband did to his wife.

Sunny choked on her coffee. "That's disgusting!" she said after she stopped coughing. She had heard whispered hints and giggles about the mysterious *something* that happened between men and women in the marriage bed, but surely it couldn't be what her mother was describing.

"It *is* disgusting," Augusta agreed, "as low and animal as the mating of hogs. It's also uncomfortable and sometimes painful. Perhaps someday scientific progress will find a better, more dignified way to make babies, but until then, women must suffer for the sins of Eve."

She took a piece of toast and began crumbling it between nervous fingers. "Naturally women of refinement are repulsed by the marital act. Unfortunately, men enjoy it. If they didn't, I suppose there would be no such thing as marriage. All a woman can do is lie there very quietly, without moving, so that the man will please himself quickly and leave her alone."

Lie there and think of England, in other words. Sunny's

stomach turned. Had her tall, athletic father actually done such things to her delicate mother? Was this what Paul Curzon had wanted when he was kissing her? And dear God, must she really allow Thornborough such liberties? Her thighs squeezed together as her body rejected the thought of such an appalling violation.

Seeing her expression, Augusta said reassuringly, "A gentleman will not visit your bed more than once or twice a week. You also have the right to refuse your husband once you are with child, and for at least three months after you deliver." She glanced down at the pile of crumbs she had created. "Last night, after the settlements were signed, I took the duke aside and reminded him that you are gently bred, and that I would not permit him to misuse you."

"You spoke to Thornborough about this?" Sunny gasped, so humiliated that she wanted to crawl under the table and never come out. "How did he reply?"

"He gave me the oddest look, but said that he understood my concern for your welfare, and assured me that he would be mindful of your innocence." Augusta gave a wintry smile. "It was very properly said. He is, after all, a gentleman."

Sunny's mind was a jumble of chaotic thoughts. The marriage bed sounded revolting—yet she had enjoyed Paul Curzon's kisses, and kissing was supposed to be a prelude to doing *it*. Surely the women who carried on flagrant affairs wouldn't do so if they found the whole business distasteful. Timidly she asked, "Do all women dislike the marital act?"

"I wish that I could say that was so, but there is no denying that there are some women of our order who are a disgrace to their sex—low-bred creatures who revel in their animal nature like barmaids. I know that you

are not like that, but you will meet women who are."
Leaning forward, Augusta said earnestly, "I cannot em-
phasize enough that it is fatal to seem to take pleasure in
a gentleman's embrace. If you do, he will instantly lose
all respect for you. A woman who acts like a prostitute
will be treated like one. Always strive to maintain your
dignity, Sarah—ultimately it is all that a lady has."

With horror, Sunny remembered that when Paul had
taken liberties, she had responded eagerly. Was that why
he had made his degrading suggestion that she marry
Thornborough, then have an affair with him? She still
thought his behavior despicable—but perhaps she had
brought it on by her wantonness. Paul had seen her acting
like a slut, so he had treated her like one. It was exactly
what her mother was warning her about.

Apparently a woman who gave in to her animal nature
also risked unleashing a man's worst traits. That had been
bad enough in the case of Paul Curzon, but Thornborough
was going to be her husband; if he didn't respect her, the
marriage would be hellish.

Feeling ill, Sunny said, "I shall remember all you have
said and I will strive to behave in a manner that you would
approve."

"I'm sure you will not disgrace your upbringing."
Augusta bit her lip, her usual confidence gone. "Oh,
Sarah, I'm going to miss you dreadfully. You'll be so far
away."

Sunny resisted the temptation to point out that her
mother should have thought of that before accepting the
proposal of a foreigner. "I'll miss you, too. You must visit
us at Swindon soon."

Augusta shook her head. "Eventually, but not right
away. I know that I'm a strong-minded woman, and I don't
want to cause trouble between you and your husband.

Marriage is a difficult business, and you and he must have time together with as little interference as possible."

At moments like this, Sunny loved her mother with painful intensity. It was true that Augusta was often domineering—yet her love for her children was very real. She was a woman of formidable energy; if she had a railroad or a bank to run, she might have been less absorbed in her daughter's life.

"I'll be fine," Sunny said with determined optimism. "Thornborough is a gentleman, and I am a lady. I'm sure that we can contrive a civilized marriage between us."

She wished that she was certain that was true.

CHAPTER FIVE

TEARS FLOWING DOWN HER face, Sunny stood patiently while her maid laced up her white brocade bridal corset. Then Antoinette dropped the wedding gown over her head. It was magnificent, with foaming layers of Brussels lace and billows of white satin spangled with seed pearls and silver thread. Augusta had been so confident of her daughter's future triumph that she had ordered the gown from Worth when they visited Paris in March, before Sunny had ever set foot in London.

When the gown was fastened, Antoinette lifted the tulle veil and carefully draped it over the intricate coils of Sunny's hair. As the gauzy fabric floated down to her knees, the bride bleakly wondered if it was dense enough to conceal her tears.

Antoinette secured the veil with a coronet of orange blossoms, saying soothingly, "Don't fret, mademoiselle. Every girl is nervous on her wedding day. *Monsieur le Duc* is a fine gentleman, and he will make you very happy."

Sunny's shoulders began shaking with the force of her sobs. Antoinette frowned and gave her a handkerchief, muttering, "Madame Vangelder should not have gone ahead to the church. A girl needs her mother at a time like this."

As Sunny wept into the crumpled muslin square, a knock sounded at the door. Antoinette answered and returned with a large white flower box. "For you, mademoiselle."

"You can open it if you like," Sunny said drearily.

Less jaded than her mistress, Antoinette opened the package, disclosing an exquisite orchid bouquet nestled in layers of tissue paper. "There is a card for you, mademoiselle."

Sunny's puffy eyes widened when she read, *These flowers are from the Swindon greenhouse. If they are suitable, perhaps you might wish to carry them. Fondly, Justin.*

Oblivious to the fate of her five-yard-long train, Sunny dropped into a chair and wept even harder.

"Oh, mam'zelle," Antoinette said helplessly. "What about the orchids makes you weep? They are very lovely."

"Yes, they are." Sunny made a desperate effort to collect herself. "I was…touched by Thornborough's thoughtfulness in having them sent all the way from England."

Though it was not something she could say to her maid, she was even more moved by the fact that he was actually letting her choose whether or not to carry them. Every other detail of the wedding—the trousseau, the decorations, the extravagant reception—had been determined by her mother. Even the eight bridesmaids—including two Vangelder cousins, a Whitney, a Jay and an Astor—had been selected by Augusta for reasons of her own. Sunny had been swept along like a leaf in a torrent.

But Justin had given her a choice. Surely with such a considerate man, she could be happy. Unsteadily she said, "I must look like a fright. Please bring me some cold water and a facecloth." She glanced at the enormous bouquet Augusta had ordered. "You can set that aside. I will carry the orchids."

"But…" After the beginning of a protest, the maid nodded. "Yes, mademoiselle. An excellent choice."

As Antoinette went for the cold water, Sunny found herself wondering if the maid had ever endured the grotesquely undignified process of mating that Augusta had described. The thought almost sent her off in tears again.

For the last two days, at the most awkward moments, she had wondered the same thing about others: her brother Charlie, who was very fond of female company; the wife of the Anglican bishop who was going to perform the ceremony; Thornborough himself. Her morbid imaginings were turning her into a nervous wreck.

Antoinette returned with a basin of water and a cloth, then flipped the veil back over Sunny's head so that her face was bare. "You must hurry, mademoiselle, or you will be late."

As she sponged her stinging eyes with the cool, moist cloth, Sunny snapped, "They can all *wait*."

THE DAY BECAME INCREASINGLY unreal. Fifth Avenue was lined on both sides with policemen assigned to prevent the thousands of spectators from breaking through. The wedding was to be at St. Thomas's Anglican church. Though the Vangelders didn't usually worship there, it was the only fashionable church with enough space for the seventy-voice choir Augusta had chosen.

Inside the church, huge arches of orange blossoms spanned the aisle, and banks of palms and chrysanthemums seemed to cover every vertical surface. Twenty-five excruciating minutes behind schedule, Sunny waited for her entrance, one icy hand clenched around her orchid bouquet and the other locked on her brother Charlie's arm. Though she could not see the guests clearly in the dim light, every pew seemed to be filled.

As the bridesmaids marched smartly down the aisle to the music of the sixty-piece orchestra, Charlie whispered, "Buck up, Sunny. Show them that an American girl is every bit the equal of any European princess."

The wedding march began, and Sunny started the long walk to the altar. If it hadn't been for her brother's firm support, the "American princess" might have fallen flat on her face.

With hysterical precision, she calculated that in the months since she had met Thornborough, they had seen each other for ten days, and been alone together for less than an hour. *Why was she marrying a stranger?* If it hadn't been for the five-yard train, she might have turned and bolted.

The dark figure of her fiancé waited impassively at the altar. Next to him was his best man, a pleasant fellow called Lord Ambridge, an old school friend of Justin's who was currently serving in the British Embassy in Washington.

As Sunny drew closer to her future husband, she saw that his expression was grim. Then she looked into his eyes and realized that he was as nervous as she. Her lateness must have made him wonder if she had changed her mind.

Dear God, how humiliating those long minutes of waiting must have been for him. As Charlie handed her over, she gave Thornborough an unsteady smile of apology.

His expression eased. He took her hand, and the warmth of his clasp was the most real thing she had experienced all day.

They turned to face the bishop, and the ancient, familiar words transformed the stranger beside her into her husband.

THE WEDDING NIGHT WAS a disaster. Later Justin realized that it had been foolish of him to think it could have been otherwise, yet he had had the naive hope that once he and his bride were alone together, they would be able to relax. To become friends.

Instead, the "wedding breakfast" had proved to be a huge reception that seemed as if it would never end. By the time they reached their hotel suite, Sunny's face was gray with fatigue.

He wanted to hold her but restrained himself, for she looked as if she would shatter at a touch. They had a lifetime ahead of them; it would be foolish to rush matters now.

She mutely followed his suggestion that she relax with a long bath. Much later, after Sunny's maid had finished her ministrations and left for the night, he joined his wife in the spacious bedchamber. He expected to find her in the canopied bed, perhaps already asleep. Instead, she stood by the window, gazing out on the lights of New York.

He found her a far more interesting sight than the city. The glossy, honey-gold hair that flowed over her shoulders was even lovelier than he had imagined, and he longed to bury his face among the silken strands. Her white negligee frothed with lace and delicate embroidery, and was so translucent that he could see the lithe shape of her body beneath. It must be another Worth creation; only a master could make a woman look simultaneously pure and provocative.

His wife. He was still awed by the miracle of it.

Justin had been introduced to the dark mysteries of passion when he was sixteen. Deciding it was time his young brother became a man, Gavin had taken Justin to a courtesan. With his usual careless kindness, Gavin had chosen the woman well. Lily was a warmhearted, earthily sensual Frenchwoman who had known exactly how to initiate a shy youth half her age.

Justin's shamed embarrassment had been gone by the end of his first afternoon with Lily. With her he had discovered not only passion, but kindness and mutual affection. He had visited her many times over the ensuing years. When her looks faded and she could no longer support herself as a courtesan, he had quietly bought her a cottage in the south of France so that she could retire in comfort. They still corresponded occasionally.

Because of Lily, he was now able to give his wife the gift of passion. Praying that desire would not make him clumsy, he went to join her by the window. Her delicate violet scent bewitched him, and his hands clenched with the effort of not touching her. Needing a safe, neutral topic, he said, "New York is lovely in a way quite distinct from London or Paris."

"I shall miss it," she whispered.

He glanced over and saw tears trembling in her eyes. "It must be hard to leave one's home," he said quietly, "but you can come back whenever you wish."

"Yes." She drew an unsteady breath. "Still, it hurts knowing that I am no longer an American. Though I understood that marrying a foreigner meant that I would lose my citizenship, I didn't expect to feel it so much."

"The law might say that you are now an Englishwoman, but it can't change what you are in your heart. America made you, and nothing can take that away."

After a long pause, she said in a low voice, "Thank you. I needed to be reminded of that."

Thinking the time was finally right, he put an arm around her waist. For the barest instant, she was pliantly yielding. Then she went rigid, like a small woodland creature holding still in the desperate hope that it would escape a predator's notice.

He turned her toward him and pulled her close, stroking her back in the hope that she would relax, but he was unsuccessful. Though she submitted without protest, her body remained as stiff as a marble statue.

Shyness or nerves were to be expected, but her reaction seemed extreme. He put his hands on her shoulders and held her away from him. "Sunny, are you afraid of me?"

"Not...not of you, really," she said, her eyes cast down.

It wasn't a heartening answer for an eager bridegroom. Patiently he said, "Then are you afraid of...marital intimacy?"

"It's more than that, Justin. I don't know quite how to explain." She pressed her hands to her temples for a moment, then looked into his eyes for the first time in days. "I was raised to be a wife. In the whole of my life, there was never any thought that I would ever be anything else." She swallowed hard. "Only now, when it's too late, does it occur to me that I don't really want to be married to anyone."

Though she claimed that he was not the problem, it was hard not to take her comments personally. Feeling a chill deep inside, he lowered his hands and said carefully, "What do you want me to do—set you up in a separate establishment so that you never have to see me? File for an annulment on the grounds that your mother coerced you into marriage against your will?"

She looked shocked. "Oh, no, of course not. I pledged my word today, and that can't be undone. I will do my best to be a good wife to you—but I don't know if I will succeed."

Some of the pain in his chest eased. As long as they were together, there was hope for building a loving marriage.

Though he had been counting the hours until they could be together, he said, "We needn't share a bed tonight, when you're so tired. It might be better to wait a few days until you're more at ease with me."

She hesitated, clearly tempted, before she shook her head. "I think it will be best to get it over with. Waiting will only give me more time to worry."

He wanted to make love to his wife, and she wanted to "get it over with," like a tooth extraction. Dear God, this was not what he had dreamed of. Yet perhaps she was right. Once she learned that intercourse was not as bad as she feared, she could relax and find pleasure in physical intimacy.

Yet he could not quite suppress the fear that his wife might never come to welcome his touch. He had been concerned ever since Augusta had ordered him to try to control his beastly animal nature. Obviously Augusta had loathed her own marital duties, and there was a strong possibility that she had passed her distaste on to her daughter.

His mouth tightened. Brooding would solve nothing. If his wife wanted the marriage consummated tonight, he would oblige—partly because it might be the wisest course, but more because he wanted her with an intensity that was painful.

"Come then, my dear." He untied the ribbons of her negligee and pushed it from her shoulders so that she was clad only in a sheer silk nightgown that revealed more of her tantalizing curves than it concealed. He drew a shaky breath. It was how he had dreamed of her—and at the same time, it was utterly wrong, for she looked at him with the despairing eyes of a wounded doe.

She colored under his hungry gaze and glanced away. "Could you…would you turn the lamps out?"

Though he yearned to see her unclothed, he said, "As you wish."

As he put out the lights, she drew the curtains so that the windows were covered and the room became suffocatingly dark. Then she climbed into the bed with a faint creak of springs.

After removing his robe, he located the bed by touch and slid in beside her. He would have liked to take his nightshirt off, as well, but a man's naked body might upset her more, even in the dark and under blankets.

He drew her into his arms and kissed her with all the tenderness he had been yearning to lavish on her. Though she did not reject him, her mouth was locked shut and her whole frame was tense and unyielding. No amount of patient skill on his part could soften her; in fact, his feather kisses and gentle stroking seemed to make her more rigid. He felt as if he was trying to ravish a vestal virgin. Despairing, he pushed himself up with one arm and said hoarsely, "This isn't right."

"Please, just *do* it," she said, an edge of hysteria in her voice.

His better nature surrendered, for despite his doubts, his body was hotly ready, burning for completion. He reached for the lotion he had provided to ease this first union.

She gasped when he raised the hem of her gown, separated her legs and touched her intimately. He hoped that she might respond positively to his sensual application of the lotion, but there was no change. She simply endured, her limbs like iron, her breath coming in short, frightened gulps.

Though his blood pounded in his temples, he forced himself to go slowly when he moved to possess her. Her body resisted and he heard the scratch of her nails digging into the sheets, but she made no protest.

When the frail membrane sundered and he thrust deeply into her, she gave a sharp, pain-filled cry. He held still, waves of exquisite sensation sweeping through him, until her breathing was less ragged.

Then he began to move, and his control shattered instantly. He loved her and she was his, and he groaned with delirious pleasure as he thrust into her again and again.

His mindless abandon had the advantage of swiftness, for he could not have prolonged their coupling even if he tried. After the fiery culmination, he disengaged and lay down beside her, trembling with reaction. He yearned to hold her close and soothe her distress, but hesitated to touch her. "I'm sorry I hurt you," he panted. "It won't be this painful again."

"I'm all right, Justin," she said, voice shaking. "It... wasn't as bad as I expected."

It was a lie, but a gallant one. No longer able to restrain his impulse to cradle her in his arms, he reached out. If she would let him comfort her, something good would come of this night. But she rolled away into a tight little ball, and his searching fingers found only her taut spine.

The silence that descended was broken by the anguished sound of her muffled sobs. He lay still, drenched with self-loathing at the knowledge that he had found intoxicating pleasure in an act that had distressed her so profoundly.

After a long, long time, her tears faded and her breathing took on the slow rhythm of sleep. Quietly he slid from the bed and felt his way to the door that led to the sitting room, cracking his shin on a stool as he went.

A gas lamp burned in the sitting room, and he saw his haunted reflection in a mirror on the far wall. He turned away, unable to bear the sight of his own misery.

The suite was the most luxurious in the hotel, though

not as richly furnished as the Vangelder houses. A porcelain bowl filled with potpourri sat on a side table. He sifted it through his fingers, and the air filled with a tangy fragrance.

He had reached for heaven and landed in hell. Their disastrous wedding night had not been the result of anything simple, like shyness on her part or ineptness on his; it had been total rejection. The woman of his dreams couldn't bear his touch, and there seemed little chance that she would change in the future.

Vases of flowers were set all over the room. Some he had ordered, others were courtesy of the hotel, which was embarrassingly grateful to have the Duke and Duchess of Thornborough as guests. He pulled a white rose from an elegant cut-glass vase. It was just starting to open, at the perfect moment when promise met fulfillment.

Inevitably, he thought of Sunny when he had first seen her at Swindon. Exquisite, laughing, without flaw.

And now she lay weeping in the next room, her bright gaiety gone. He supposed that part of the blame for that could be laid to a false lover, and part to Augusta, who loved her daughter with utter ruthlessness. But most of the fault was his. By the simple act of wanting to marry her, he might have destroyed her blithe sweetness forever.

He began plucking out the satiny white petals, letting them drop one by one. She loved him, she loved him not, over and over, like a litany, as the scent of rose wafted around him.

The last petal drifted to the floor. She loved him not.

He lifted the vase and studied the artistry of the cut glass. Then, in one smooth, raging gesture, he hurled it across the room, where it shattered into a thousand pieces.

She loved him not.

CHAPTER SIX

JUSTIN GLANCED OUT THE TRAIN window at the rolling English landscape. "We'll reach Swindon station in about five minutes."

Sunny lifted her hat from the opposite seat and secured it to her coiled hair with a pearl-headed hat pin. Since they were traveling in the luxurious solitude of the Thornborough private car, she had had ample space for her possessions.

As she prepared for their arrival, she surreptitiously studied her husband. His expression was as impassive as always, even though he was bringing his bride home for the first time. Didn't he ever feel anything? In three weeks of marriage, he had never been anything but unfailingly polite. Civil. Kind. As remote as if he were on the opposite side of the earth.

Not that she should complain, for his calm detachment had made it possible to reach a modus vivendi very quickly. In public, she took his arm and smiled so that they presented a companionable picture to the world.

Naturally neither of them ever referred to what happened in the silence of the night. Justin always ordered suites with two bedrooms so they could sleep separately. Every three or four days, with his gaze on the middle distance, he would ask if it was convenient for him to visit her.

She always gave her embarrassed assent, except for once when she had stammered that she was "indisposed."

She would have died of mortification if he had asked what was wrong, but he had obviously understood. Five days passed before he asked again, and by then she was able to give him permission to come.

As he had promised, there had been no pain after the first occasion, and soon her fear had gone away. Dutifully she obeyed her mother's dictum and lay perfectly still while her husband did what husbands did. The marital act took only a few minutes, and he always left directly after.

Once or twice, she had felt his fingers brush through her hair before he climbed from the bed. She liked to think that it was a gesture of affection, though perhaps it was mere accident, a result of fumbling in the dark.

But her mother had been right; passive acceptance of her wifely role had won Justin's respect. Besides treating her with the utmost consideration, he also encouraged her to speak her opinions. That was certainly an unusual sign of respect, as well as a pleasure few wives had.

They discussed a wide variety of topics—British and American politics, art and music, architecture and history. Though Justin was never talkative, his observations were perceptive and he seemed to genuinely enjoy listening to her chatter. Best of all, the conversations were slowly building a rapport between them. It wasn't love—but perhaps someday it might be.

She prayed that that would happen, for living without love was a sad business.

Getting to her feet, she pulled on her sable-lined coat. Though it would warm her on the raw November day, that practical use was secondary. Before they left New York, her mother had emphasized that it was essential to wear her furs as a sign of wealth when she was first introduced to her new home and family. A good thing it wasn't August. Unable to see all of herself in the mirror, she asked, "Do I look all right?"

Her husband studied her gravely. "You look very lovely. Exactly as a duchess should, but seldom does."

The train squealed to a halt, and she glanced out to see a bunting-draped platform. "Good heavens," she said blankly. "There are hundreds of people out there."

"I did warn you." He stood and walked to the carriage door. "It's probably the entire population of Swindon Minor and everyone for five miles around. The schools will have given a holiday so that the pupils can come and wave flags at you."

"It's different actually seeing them." Observing her husband's closed expression, she said, "You don't look very enthusiastic."

"Gavin was much better at this sort of thing."

Perhaps that was true, but when Justin opened the door and stepped onto the platform, a roar of welcome went up. He gave a nod of acknowledgment, then turned to help Sunny step down. Another cheer went up, so she gave a friendly wave.

She met a blur of local dignities, all of whom gave speeches of welcome. Luckily she was good at smiling graciously, and the sables kept her from freezing in the damp air.

The only part that stood out in her mind was the little girl who was pushed forward, clutching a bouquet in her tiny hands. "Give the posies to the duchess, Ellie," her mother hissed.

Unclear on the theory, Ellie swept the bouquet around in circles. With a grin, Sunny intercepted it, then dropped a kiss on the child's soft brown curls. "Thank you, Ellie."

Another cheer arose. Sunny blushed; her gesture had

not been calculated, but apparently kissing babies was good policy everywhere.

The mayor of the borough assisted her into the waiting carriage and Justin settled beside her. However, instead of starting for the palace, there was a delay while the horses were unhitched. A dozen men seized the shafts and began pulling the carriage up the village high street as the church bell began to ring clamorously. Sunny gave her husband a doubtful glance. "This seems dreadfully feudal."

He lifted his hand in response to a group of exuberant uniformed schoolchildren. "This isn't really for you, or for me, either. It's a celebration of continuity—of a life lived on this land for centuries. Swindon Palace belongs as much to the tenants as it does to the Aubreys."

She supposed he was right, and certainly the crowd seemed to be having a very jolly time. Nonetheless, her democratic American soul twitched a bit. Trying to look like a duchess, she smiled and waved for the slow two miles to Swindon Palace.

Another crowd waited in the courtyard. After the newlyweds had climbed the front steps, Justin turned and gave a short thank-you speech in a voice that carried easily to everyone present. Gavin might have had a talent for grand gestures, but the tenants had had more daily contact with Justin, and they seemed to heartily approve of him.

After one last wave, she went inside with her husband. The greetings weren't over yet, for a phalanx of Aubrey relations waited with a sea of servants behind them.

As she steeled herself for more introductions and smiles, two huge wolfhounds galloped toward the door, nails scrabbling on the marble floor. The sight of the enormous dogs charging full speed at her made Sunny give a small squeak of alarm.

Before the beasts could overrun them, Justin made a quick hand gesture and commanded, "Sit!"

Instantly the wolfhounds dropped to their haunches, though they wriggled frantically for attention. Justin stroked the sleek aristocratic heads, careful not to neglect either. "These were Gavin's dogs. They miss him dreadfully."

To Sunny, it looked as if the wolfhounds were perfectly satisfied with the new duke. It took a moment to realize that Justin's comment was an oblique admission of his own grief. She was ashamed of the fact that she had not really considered how profoundly he must feel his brother's death. Though the two men had been very different, the first time she had seen them they had been standing side by side. They must have been close, or Justin would not have chosen to manage the family property when he could have done many other things.

While she was wondering if she should say something to him, the relatives descended. First in consequence was the dowager duchess, Justin's mother, who wore mourning black for Gavin. Her forceful expression reminded Sunny of her own mother, though Augusta was far more elegant.

After a fierce scrutiny of the colonial upstart, the dowager said, "You look healthy, girl. Are you pregnant yet?"

As Sunny flushed scarlet, Justin put a protective arm around her waist. "It's a little early to think about that since we've been married less than a month, Mother," he said calmly. "Sunny, I believe you already know my older sisters, Blanche and Charlotte, and their husbands, Lord Alton and Lord Urford."

Sunny had met all four in London during the season. The sisters were in the same mold as Gavin: tall, blond, handsome Aubreys whose self-absorption was tempered by underlying good nature. They examined Sunny's furs with frank envy, but their greetings were friendly. After all, it was her money that would keep up the family home.

Next in line was Lady Alexandra, the Gargoylette. She hung back until Justin pulled her into a hug. It was the most affectionate Sunny had ever seen him. "I don't believe you've met my little sister, Alexandra."

He accompanied his introduction with a speaking look at his wife. Sunny guessed that if she was dismissive or abrupt, he would not easily forgive her.

Alexandra stammered a greeting, too bashful to meet her new sister-in-law's eyes. Dark and inches shorter than the older girls, she looked very like Justin. There was nothing wrong with her appearance except that her mother dressed her very badly.

Following her instinct, Sunny also hugged her smallest sister-in-law. "Thank you so much for your letter," she said warmly. "It was good to know that I would have a friend here."

Alexandra looked up shyly. Her gray eyes were also like Justin's, but where he was reserved, she was vulnerable. "I'm glad you're here," she said simply. "I saw you when you came to the garden fete last spring, and thought you were the loveliest creature in the world."

A little embarrassed at such frank adoration, Sunny said lightly, "It's amazing what a good dressmaker can do."

Then it was onward to sundry Aubrey cousins and shirttail relations. After that, the butler and housekeeper—two *very* superior persons—welcomed her as their new mistress and presented her with a silver bowl as a wedding gift from the household. While Sunny wondered how much the poor servants had been forced to contribute, she was paraded past ranks of maids and footmen as if she were a general reviewing troops.

Finally it was time to go upstairs to prepare for dinner. Justin escorted her to her new rooms.

The duchess's private suite was rather appallingly magnificent. Eyeing the massive, velvet-hung four-poster bed, Sunny asked, "Did Queen Elizabeth sleep there?"

"No, but Queen Anne did." The corner of Justin's mouth quirked up. "I know it's overpowering, but I didn't order any changes because I thought you'd prefer to make them yourself."

Sunny thoughtfully regarded a tapestry of a stag being torn apart by a pack of dogs. "I don't care if it is priceless—that tapestry will have to go. But I can bear it for now. How long do I have until dinner?"

"Only half an hour, I'm afraid. There's more to be seen, but it can wait." He gestured to a door in the middle of one wall. "That goes directly to my bedchamber. Don't hesitate to ask if there's anything you need."

"I'm too confused to know what I need, but thank you." Sunny took off her hat and massaged her throbbing temples. "Should you and I go down together for dinner?"

"Definitely," he replied. "Without a guide to the dining room, you'd probably get lost for a week."

After Justin left, Antoinette emerged from the dressing room. "While everyone was welcoming you, madame, I had time to unpack your clothing. What do you wish to wear tonight? Surely something grand to impress the relations."

"The butter-cream duchesse satin, I think." Sunny considered. "I suppose I should also wear the pearl and diamond dog collar, even though it chafes my neck."

The maid nodded with approval. "No one will be your equal."

After Antoinette disappeared to prepare the gown, Sunny sank into a brocade-covered chair. It was hideously uncomfortable, which was fortunate, because otherwise she might fall asleep.

It was pleasant to have a few minutes alone. In spite of the wretched chair, she was dozing when Antoinette bustled back. "Madame, I have found something wonderful! You must come see."

Sunny doubted that anything was worth such enthusiasm, but she obediently rose and followed her maid into the dressing room. Two doors were set into the opposite wall. Antoinette dramatically threw open the right-hand one. "Voilà!"

Sunny's eyes widened. It was a bathroom that would have impressed even Augusta Vangelder. The mahogany-encased tub was enormous, and the floor and walls had been covered in bright, exquisitely glazed Spanish tiles. "You're right—it's the most gorgeous bathroom I've ever seen."

"And the next room over—" the maid pointed "—is a most splendid water closet. The chambermaid who brought in the towels said that *Monsieur le Duc* had all this done for you after the betrothal was announced."

Amused and touched, Sunny stroked a gleaming tile. It appeared that she would not have to suffer the country house horrors that Katie Westron had warned her about. "Perhaps later tonight I will take advantage of this."

Wanting to give credit where credit was due, she went to her bedchamber and opened the connecting door to the duke's suite. "Justin, I have found the bathing room and—"

In the middle of the sentence, her gaze found her husband and she stopped dead. She had caught him in the middle of changing his clothing. He had just taken off his shirt, and she blushed scarlet at the sight of his bare chest.

Though his brows rose, he did not seem at all discomposed. "Having seen the wonders of modern American plumbing, I knew that you would find Swindon rather primitive," he said. "Making some improvements seemed like a more useful wedding gift than giving you jewels."

Though she tried to look only into his eyes, her gaze drifted lower. He was broad-shouldered and powerfully muscled, which was why he didn't have a fashionable look of weedy elegance. She wondered how the dark hair on his chest would feel to her touch. Blushing again, she said hastily, "Your idea was inspired. I've always loved long baths, and I'd resigned myself to having to make do with a tin tub in front of the fire."

"Speaking of fires, I decided that it was also time to install central heating." Justin casually pulled on a fresh shirt, though he didn't bother to button it. "It will be a long time until the whole building is completed, but I had the workers take care of this wing first, so you would be comfortable. I know that Americans like their houses warm."

Only then did she notice that the rooms were much warmer than she should have expected. "Thank you, Justin. I think you must be the most considerate husband on earth." She crossed the room to her husband's side and gave him a swift kiss.

It was the first time she had ever done such a thing, and she wondered belatedly if he would think her too forward. But he didn't seem to mind. His lips moved slowly under hers, and he raised his hand and massaged the back of her neck. He had a tangy masculine scent that was distinctly his own. Succumbing to temptation, she let her fingers brush his bare chest as if by accident. The hair was softer than she had expected, but she felt unnerved when his warm flesh tensed at her touch. Hastily she lowered her hand.

But the kiss continued, and she found that she was in no hurry to end it. Very gently, his tongue stroked her lips. It was a new sensation, but pleasant. Very pleasant…

The clamor of a bell reverberated brassily through the corridors. Both of them jumped as if they had been caught stealing from the church poor box.

After he had caught his breath, Justin said, "The predinner bell. We must be downstairs in ten minutes."

"I barely have time to dress." Embarrassed at how she had lost track of time, Sunny bolted to her own room. As soon as the connecting door was closed, Antoinette started unfastening her traveling dress so that the duchesse satin could be donned.

Yet as her maid swiftly transformed her, Sunny's mind kept returning to the kiss, and her fingertips tingled with the memory of the feel of her husband's bare body.

DINNER WAS ANOTHER STRAIN. Sunny sat at the opposite end of the table from her husband, so far away that she could barely see him. Before the first course had been removed, it was obvious that the dowager duchess was a tyrant, with all the tact of a charging bull. She made a string of remarks extolling Gavin's noble spirit and aristocratic style, interspersed with edged comments about the deficiencies of "poor, dear Justin."

Charlotte tried to divert the conversation with a cheerful promise to send Sunny a copy of the table of precedence so that she would never commit the cardinal crime of seating people in the wrong order. That inspired the dowager to say, "There are about two hundred families whose history and relationships you must understand,

Sarah. Has Justin properly explained all the branches of the Aubreys and of my own family, the Sturfords?"

"Not yet, Duchess," Sunny said politely.

"Very remiss of him. Since he wasn't raised to be a duke, he hasn't a proper sense of what is due his station." The dowager sniffed. "So sad to see poor, dear Justin in his brother's place—such a comedown for the family. You must be quick about having a child, Sarah, and make sure it's a boy."

Sunny was tempted to sling the nearest platter of veal collops at her mother-in-law, but it seemed too soon to get into a pitched battle. A quick glance at her husband showed that he had either not heard his mother, or he chose to ignore her. Clearly Alexandra had heard, for she was staring at her plate.

Carefully Sunny said, "The eighth duke's death was a great tragedy. You all have my sympathies on your loss."

The dowager sighed. "Gavin should have betrothed himself to you, not that Russell woman. If he had, he might be alive now, in his proper place."

Sunny had heard enough gossip to know that the fatal problem had not been Gavin's fiancée, but his inability to keep his hands off other women, even when on the way to his own wedding. Hoping to end this line of discussion, she said piously, "It is not for us to question the ways of heaven."

"A very proper sentiment," the dowager said. "You have pretty manners. One would scarcely know you for an American."

Did the woman suppose that she was giving a compliment? Once more Sunny bit her tongue.

Yet in spite of her good intentions, she was not to get through the evening peacefully. The gauntlet was thrown down at the end of the lengthy meal, when it was time for the ladies to withdraw and leave the gentlemen to their port. Sunny was about to give the signal when the dowager grandly rose to her feet and beat Sunny to it.

As three women followed the dowager's lead, Sunny's blood went cold. This was a direct challenge to her authority as the new mistress of the household. If she didn't assert herself immediately, her mother-in-law would walk all over her.

The other guests hesitated, glancing between the new duchess and the old. Sunny wanted to whimper that she was too *tired* for this, but she supposed that crises never happened at convenient times. Though her hands clenched below the table, her voice was even when she asked, "Are you feeling unwell, Duchess?"

"I am in splendid health," her mother-in-law said haughtily. "Where did you get the foolish idea that I might be ailing?"

"I can think of no other reason for you leaving prematurely," Sunny said with the note of gentle implacability that she had often heard in her mother's voice.

For a moment the issue wavered in the balance. Then, one by one, the female guests who had gotten to their feet sank back into their seats with apologetic glances at Sunny. Knowing that she had lost, the dowager returned to the table, her expression stiff with mortification.

As she waited for a decent interval to pass before leading the ladies from the table, Sunny drew in a shaky breath. She had won the first battle—but there would be others.

THE EVENING ENDED WHEN the first clock struck eleven. Accompanied by the bonging of numerous other clocks, Justin escorted his wife upstairs. When they reached the door of her room, he said, "I'm sorry that it's been such a long day, but everyone was anxious to meet you."

She smiled wearily. "I'll be fine after a night's sleep."

"You were a great success with everyone." After a moment of hesitation, he added, "I'm sorry my mother was so…abrupt. Gavin was her favorite, and she took his death very badly."

"You miss him, too, but it hasn't made you rude." She bit her lip. "I'm sorry, I didn't mean to sound impertinent."

"My mother is a forceful woman, and I don't expect that you'll always agree. Blanche and Charlotte used to have terrible battles with her. Just remember that you are my wife, and the mistress of Swindon."

"I shall attempt to be tactful while establishing myself." She made a rueful face. "But I warn you, I have trouble countenancing unkind remarks about other people."

That sensitivity to others was one of the things he liked best about her. A volatile mix of tenderness and desire moved through him, and he struggled against his yearning to draw her into his arms and soothe her fatigue away.

He might have done so if he hadn't been aware that the desire to comfort would be followed by an even more overwhelming desire to remove her clothing, garment by garment, and make slow, passionate love to her. With the lamps lit, not in the dark.

Innocently she turned her back to him and said, "Could you unfasten my dog collar? It's miserably uncomfortable."

The heavy collar had at least fifteen rows of pearls. As he undid the catch and lifted the necklace away, he saw that the diamond clasp had rubbed her tender skin raw. He frowned. "I don't like seeing you wearing something that hurts you."

She sighed. "Virtually every item a fashionable woman wears is designed to hurt."

He leaned forward and very gently kissed the raw spot on her nape. "Perhaps you should be less stylish."

She tensed, as she did whenever he touched her in a sensual way. "A duchess is supposed to be fashionable. I would be much criticized if I didn't do you credit." Eyes downcast, she turned and took the jeweled collar, then slipped into her room.

He felt the familiar ache as he watched her disappear. Who was it who said that if a man wanted to be truly lonely, he should take a wife? It was true, for he didn't recall feeling lonely before he married.

But now that he had a wife, his life echoed with loneliness. The simple fact was that he wanted more of her. He wanted to hold her in his arms all night while they slept. He wanted her to sigh with pleasure when he made love to her. He wanted to be with her day and night.

He drew a deep breath, then entered his room and began undressing. He had hoped that with time she might come to enjoy intimacy more, but every time he came to her bed, she became rigid. Though she never complained, or spoke at all, for that matter—it was clear that she could scarcely endure his embraces.

Yet she didn't seem to dislike him in other ways. She talked easily and was willing to share her opinions. And she had given him that shy kiss earlier. In her innocence, she had not understood that she set the blood burning through his veins. But even going to her bed would not have quenched the fire, for he had found that quick, furtive coupling was more frustrating than if he had never touched her.

As he slid into his bed, he realized how foolish it was of him to object to a necklace that chafed her neck when his conjugal demands disturbed her far more. He despised himself for taking that which was not willingly given—yet he was not strong enough to prevent himself from going to her again and again. His twice weekly visits were his compromise between guilt and lust.

He stared blindly into the darkness, wondering if he would be able to sleep.

If you would be lonely, take a wife.

CHAPTER SEVEN

Swindon
February 1886

SUNNY ABANDONED HER LETTER writing and went to stand at her sitting-room window, staring out at the gray landscape. In the distance was a pond where long ago a footman had drowned himself in a fit of melancholy. As the dreary winter months dragged by, she had come to feel a great deal of sympathy for the poor fellow.

The loudest sound was the ticking of the mantel clock. Swindon was full of clocks, all of them counting out the endless hours. She glanced at the dog curled in one of the velvet-covered chairs. "Daisy, how many of the women who envied my glamorous marriage would believe how tedious it is to winter on an English country estate?"

Daisy's floppy-eared head popped up and she gave a sympathetic whimper. Unlike the beautiful but brainless wolfhounds, Daisy, a small black-and-tan dog of indeterminate parentage, was smart as a whip. Sunny liked to think that the dog understood human speech. Certainly she was a good listener.

Sunny's gaze went back to the dismal afternoon. Custom decreed that a bride should live quietly for a time after her wedding, and at Swindon, that was very quietly indeed. Apart from the newlyweds, Alexandra and the dowager were the only inhabitants of the vast palace.

There were servants, of course, but the line between upstairs and downstairs was never crossed.

The best part of the daily routine was a morning ride
with Justin. Sunny never missed a day, no matter how
vile the weather, for she enjoyed spending time with her
husband, though she couldn't define the reason. He was
simply…comfortable. She only wished that she understood him better. He was like an iceberg, with most of
his personality hidden from view.

After their ride, she usually didn't see him again until
dinner, for estate work kept him busy. Occasionally he
went to London for several days to attend to business. He
was gone now, which made the hours seem even longer.

The high point of country social life was making brief
calls on neighbors, then receiving calls in turn. Though
most of the people Sunny met were pleasant, they lived
lives as narrow and caste-ridden as Hindus. Luckily even
the most conventional families usually harbored one or
two splendid eccentrics in the great British tradition.
There was the Trask uncle who wore only purple clothing, for example, and the Howard maiden aunt who had
taught her parrot all the basic social responses so that the
bird could speak for her. Such characters figured promi-
nently in Sunny's letters home, since little else in her life
was amusing.

A knock sounded at the door. After Sunny called permission to enter, her sister-in-law came into the sitting
room. "A telegram arrived for you, Sunny, so I said I'd
bring it up." Alexandra handed it over, then bent to scratch
Daisy's ears.

Sunny opened the envelope and scanned the message.
"Justin finished his business early and will be home for
dinner tonight."

"That's nice. It's so quiet when he's away."

"Two months from now, after you've been presented to

society and are attending ten parties a day, you'll yearn for the quiet of the country."

Alexandra made a face. "I can't say that I'm looking forward to being a wallflower at ten different places a day."

"You're going to be a great success," Sunny said firmly. "It's remarkable what good clothing can do for one's confidence. After Worth has outfitted you, you won't recognize yourself."

Unconvinced, Alexandra returned to petting Daisy. Though young in many ways, the girl was surprisingly mature in others. She was also well-read and eager to learn about the world. The two young women had become good friends.

Deciding that she needed some fresh air, Sunny said, "I think I'll take a walk before I bathe and change. Would you like to join me?"

"Not today, thank you. I have a book I want to finish." Alexandra grinned, for at the word *walk,* Daisy jumped to the floor and began skipping hopefully around her mistress. "But someone else wants to go. I'll see you at dinner."

After Alexandra left, Sunny donned a coat—not the sables, but a practical mackintosh—and a pair of boots, then went down and out into the damp afternoon, Daisy frisking beside her. Once they were away from the house, Sunny asked, "Would you like to play fetch?" Foolish question; Daisy was already racing forward looking for a stick.

Sunny had found Daisy on a morning ride not long after her arrival at Swindon. The half-grown mongrel had been desperately trying to stay afloat in the overflowing stream where someone had probably pitched her to drown. Driven frantic by the agonized yelps, Sunny had been on the verge of plunging into the water when Justin had snapped an order for her to stay on the bank. Before she could argue, he dismounted and went in himself.

When Sunny saw her husband fighting the force of the current, she realized that he was risking his life for her whim. There had been one ghastly moment when it seemed that the water would sweep him away. As her heart stood still, Justin managed to gain his footing, then catch hold of the struggling dog. After sloshing out of the stream, he had handed her the shivering scrap of canine with the straight-faced remark that it was quite an appealing creature as long as one didn't have any snobbish preconceptions about lineage.

The sodden pup had won Sunny's heart with one lap of a rough tongue. Sunny had almost wept with gratitude, for here was a creature who loved her and whom she could love in return.

Naturally the dowager duchess had disliked having such an ill-bred beast at Swindon, but she couldn't order the dog out of the house when Justin approved. The dowager had resorted to mumbled comments that it was natural for Sunny to want a mongrel, since Americans were a mongrel race. Sunny ignored such remarks; she had gotten very good at that.

As always, Daisy's desire to play fetch exceeded Sunny's stamina. Abandoning the game, they strolled to the little Greek temple, then wandered toward the house while Sunny thought of changes she would make in the grounds. A pity that nothing could be done at this time of year, for gardening would cheer her up.

In an attempt to stave off self-pity, she said, "I'm really very fortunate, Daisy. Most of Katie Westron's dire warnings haven't come true. Justin is the most considerate of husbands, and he is making the house very comfortable." She glanced toward the palace, where men were laboring on the vast roof, in spite of the weather. "My ceiling hasn't leaked since before Christmas."

She made a wry face. "Of course, it might be considered a bit strange that I talk more to a dog than to my husband."

One of Katie's warnings haunted her—the possibility that Justin might have a mistress. Could that be the real reason for his business trips? She loathed the thought that her husband might be doing those intimate, dark-of-the-night things to another woman. She tried not to think of it.

The dull afternoon had darkened to twilight, so she summoned Daisy and headed toward the house. If the best part of the day was riding with Justin, the worst was dining with the dowager duchess. Familiarity had not improved her opinion of her mother-in-law. Most of the dowager's cutting remarks were directed at Justin, but she also made edged comments about Alexandra's lack of looks and dim marital prospects. She usually spared Sunny, rightly suspecting that her daughter-in-law might strike back.

Sunny wondered how long it would be before she disgraced herself by losing her temper. Every meal brought the breaking point closer. She wished that Justin would tell his mother to hold her tongue, but he was too courteous—or too detached—to take action.

When she got to the house, she found that her husband was in the entry hall taking off his wet coat. She thought his expression lightened when he saw her, but she wasn't sure; it was always hard to tell with Justin.

"Hello." She smiled as she took off her mackintosh. "Did you have a good trip to London?"

As the butler took away the coats, Justin gave Sunny a light kiss on the cheek, then rumpled Daisy's ears. He was rather more affectionate with the dog. "Yes, but I'm glad to be home."

He fell into step beside her and they started up the main stairs. The thought of a possible mistress passed through Sunny's mind again. Though she knew that it was better not to probe, she found herself saying, "What are all these trips about, or wouldn't I be able to understand the answer?"

"The Thornborough income has traditionally come from the land, but agriculture is a chancy business," he explained as they reached the top of the stairs. "I'm making more diverse investments so that future dukes won't have to marry for money."

She stopped in midstride, feeling as if he had slapped her. When she caught her breath, she said icily, "God forbid that another Aubrey should have to stoop to marrying a mongrel American heiress."

He spun around, his expression startled and distressed. "I'm sorry, Sunny—I didn't mean that the way it sounded."

Her brows arched. "Oh? I can't imagine any meaning other than the obvious one."

When she turned and headed toward the door of her suite, he caught her arm and said intensely, "You would have been my choice even if you weren't an heiress."

Her mouth twisted. "Prettily said, but you needn't perjure yourself, Justin. We both know this marriage wouldn't have been made without my money and your title. If you invest my money wisely, perhaps our son, if we have one, will be able to marry where he chooses. I certainly hope so."

Justin's hand fell away and Sunny escaped into her sitting room, Daisy at her heels. When she was alone, she sank wretchedly into a chair. She had been better off not knowing what Justin really felt. Before she had wondered if he had a mistress; now, sickeningly, she wondered if he had a woman who was not only his mistress, but his beloved. There had been a raw emotion in his voice that made her think, for the first time, that he was capable of loving deeply. Had he been forced to forsake the woman he loved so that he could maintain Swindon?

Sensing distress, Daisy whimpered and pushed her cool nose into Sunny's hand. Mechanically she stroked the dog's silky ears. What a wretched world they lived in. Yet even if Justin loved another woman, he was her husband and she must make the best of this marriage. Someday, if she was a very good wife, perhaps he would love her, at least a little.

She desperately hoped so, for there was a hole in the center of her life that the frivolity of the season would never fill.

SUNNY'S DEPRESSION WAS not improved by the discovery that the dowager duchess was in an unusually caustic mood. Throughout an interminable dinner, she made acid remarks about the neighbors, the government and most of all her son. As fruit and cheese were served, she said, "A pity that Justin hasn't the Aubrey height and coloring. Gavin was a much more handsome man, just as Blanche and Charlotte are far prettier than Alexandra."

Sunny retorted, "I've studied the portraits, and the first duke, John Aubrey, was dark and of medium build. Justin and Alexandra resemble him much more than your other children do."

The dowager sniffed. "The first duke was a notable general, but though it pains me to admit it, he was a very low sort of man in other ways. A pity that the peasant strain hasn't yet been bred out of the family." She gave an elaborate sigh. "Such a tragedy that Justin did not die instead of Gavin."

Sunny gasped. How *dare* that woman say she wished Justin had died in his brother's place! Justin was worth a dozen charming, worthless wastrels like Gavin. She glanced at her husband and saw that he was carefully peeling an apple, as if his mother hadn't spoken, but there was a painful bleakness in his eyes.

If he wouldn't speak, she would. Laying her fork beside her plate, she said, "You must not speak so about Justin, Duchess."

"You forget who I am, madame." The dowager's eyes gleamed with pleasure at the prospect of a battle. "As the mother who suffered agonies to bear him, I can say what I wish."

"And you forget who *I* am," Sunny said with deadly precision. "The mistress of Swindon Palace. And I will no longer tolerate such vile, ill-natured remarks."

The dowager gasped, her jaw dropping open. "How dare you!"

Not backing down an inch, Sunny retorted, "I dare because it is a hostess's duty to maintain decorum at her table, and there has been a sad lack of that at Swindon."

The dowager swept furiously to her feet. "I will not stay here to be insulted by an impertinent American."

Deliberately misinterpreting her mother-in-law's words, Sunny said, "As you wish, Duchess. I can certainly understand why you prefer to have your own establishment. If I were to be widowed, I would feel the same way. And the Dower House is a very charming residence, isn't it?"

The dowager's jaw went slack as she realized that a simple flounce from the table had been transformed into total eviction. Closing her mouth with a snap, she turned to glare at Justin. "Are you going to allow an insolent American hussy to drive me from my own home?"

Justin looked from his mother to his wife, acute discomfort on his face. Silently Sunny pleaded with him to support her. He had said that she was the mistress of Swindon. If he didn't back her now, her position would become intolerable.

"You've been complaining that the new central heating gives you headaches, Mother," Justin said expressionlessly. "I think it an excellent idea for you to move to the Dower House so that you will be more comfortable. We shall miss you, of course, but fortunately you won't be far away."

Sunny shut her eyes for an instant, almost undone by relief. When she opened them again, the dowager's venomous gaze had gone to her daughter. "The Dower House isn't large enough for me to have Alexandra underfoot," she said waspishly. "She shall have to stay in the palace."

Before her mother-in-law could reconsider, Sunny said, "Very true—until she marries, Alexandra belongs at Swindon."

"*If* she ever marries," the dowager said viciously. Knowing that she was defeated and that the only way to salvage her dignity was to pretend that moving was her own idea, she added, "You shall have to learn to run the household yourself, Sarah, for I have been longing to travel. I believe I shall spend the rest of the winter in southern France. England is so dismal at this season." Ramrod straight, she marched from the room.

Sunny, Justin and Alexandra were left sitting in brittle silence. Not daring to meet her husband's eyes, Sunny said, "I'm sorry if I was disrespectful to your mother, but...but I'm not sorry for what I said."

"That's a contradiction in terms," he said, sounding more weary than angry. After a long silence, he said, "By the way, I saw Lord Hopstead in London, and he invited us for a weekend visit and ball at Cottenham. I thought

the three of us could go, then you could take Alexandra
on to Paris for her fittings."

Relieved that he didn't refer to her confrontation
with the dowager, Sunny said, "That sounds delightful.
Are you ready for your first ball, Alexandra? I have a
gown that will look marvelous on you with only minor
alterations."

"That's very kind of you," a subdued Alexandra
said.

For several minutes, they stiffly discussed the proposed
trip, none of them making any allusion to the dowager's
rout. It was like ignoring the fact that an elephant was in
the room.

Finally Sunny got to her feet. "I'm very tired tonight.
If you two will excuse me, I'll go to bed now."

Her temples throbbed as she went to her room, but
under her shakiness, she was triumphant. Without the
dowager's poisonous presence, life at Swindon would
improve remarkably.

She changed to her nightgown and climbed into bed,
wondering if Justin would visit her. Ordinarily he did
after returning from a journey, but perhaps he would stay
away if he was displeased with the way she had treated
his mother.

Though it shamed her to admit it, she had come to
look forward to his conjugal visits. One particular night
stood out in her mind. She had been drifting in the misty
zone between sleep and waking when her husband came.
Though aware of his presence, she had been too drowsy
to move her languid limbs.

Instead of waking her, he had given a small sigh, then
stretched out beside her, his warm body against hers,
his quiet breath caressing her temple. After several minutes he began stroking her, his hand gliding gently over
her torso. She had lain utterly still, embarrassed by the

yearning sensations that tingled in her breasts and other unmentionable places. Pleasure thickened inside her until she had had to bite her lip to keep from moaning and moving against his hand.

Fortunately, before she disgraced herself, he dozed off, his hand cupping her breast. Slowly her tension had dissipated until she also slept. Her rest was remarkably deep, considering that she had never in her life shared a bed with another person.

But when she awoke the next morning, he was gone. She might have thought she had dreamed the episode if not for the imprint of her husband's head on the pillow and a faint, lingering masculine scent. It had occurred to her that people who could not afford to have separate bedrooms might be luckier than they knew.

She had been mortified by the knowledge that she had the nature of a wanton. The next time she saw Katie Westron, she must find the boldness to ask how a woman could control her carnality, for surely Katie would know. Until then, Sunny would simply have to exercise will-power. She could almost hear her mother saying, "You are a lady. Behave like one."

Yet still she longed for her husband's company. She had almost given up hope that he would join her when the connecting door quietly opened and he padded across the deep carpet. As he slipped into the bed, she touched his arm to show that she was awake and willing. He slid his hand beneath the covers and drew up the hem of her nightgown.

Perhaps the evening's drama was affecting her, for she found it particularly difficult to keep silent while he prepared her for intercourse. Those strange feelings that were part pleasure, part pain, fluttered through her as he smoothed lotion over her sensitive female parts.

When he entered her, heat pulsed through those same

parts, then expanded to other parts of her body. She caught her breath, unable to entirely suppress her reaction.

Immediately he stopped moving. "Did I hurt you?"

"N-no." She knotted her hands and pressed her limbs rigidly into the mattress. "No, you didn't hurt me."

Gently he began rocking back and forth again. The slowness of his movements caused deeply disquieting sensations. Yet curiously, instead of wanting them to stop, she wanted more. It was hard, so hard, to be still....

His breathing quickened in the way that told her that the end was near. He gave a muffled groan and made a final deep thrust. Then the tension went out of him.

She felt a corresponding easing in herself, as if her feelings were intertwined with his. She was tempted to slide her arms around him, for she had a most unladylike desire to keep his warm, hard body pressed tightly against her. Perhaps he might fall asleep with her again.

But that was not what men and women of good breeding did. Her parents had not shared a room. After Sunny's birth, they had probably not even had conjugal relations, for she was the youngest in the family. Once her father had two sons to work in the business and her mother had a daughter for companionship, there had been no need for more babies.

Justin lifted his weight from her. After pulling her gown down again, he lightly touched her hair. She wanted to catch his hand and beg him to stay, but of course she didn't.

Then he left her.

When the connecting door between their chambers closed, Sunny released her breath in a shuddering sigh, then rolled over and hugged a pillow to her chest. She felt restless impatience and a kind of itchy discomfort in her female parts. Her hand slid down her torso. Perhaps if she rubbed herself there...

Horrified, she flopped onto her back and clenched her hands into fists. Her nurse and her mother had made it clear that a woman never touched herself "down there" unless she had to.

She closed her eyes against the sting of tears. She was trying her very best to be a good wife. But from what she could see, a good wife was a lonely woman.

IN A FLURRY OF TRUNKS AND contradictory orders, the Dowager Duchess of Thornborough moved herself and a substantial number of Swindon's finest antiques to the elegant Dower House on the far side of the estate. Then she promptly decamped to the French Riviera, there to flaunt her rank and make slanderous hints about her son's inadequacies and her daughter-in-law's insolence. The one thing Justin was sure she would not say was the truth— that a slip of a girl had maneuvered the dowager out of Swindon Palace.

Life was much easier with his mother gone. He and Sunny and Alexandra dined *en famille,* with much less formality and far more enjoyment. His sister was blossoming under Sunny's kind guidance, and no longer dreaded her social debut.

What wasn't prospering was his marriage. Ever since his incredibly clumsy remark about sparing future dukes the necessity of marrying for money, there had been strain between him and Sunny. What he had meant was that he wanted financial considerations to be irrelevant.

Unfortunately, she had believed the unintended insult rather than his heartfelt declaration that he would have wanted to marry her anyhow. Because he had accidentally hurt her, she had struck back, hurting him in return when she had underlined the fact that their marriage had nothing to do with love.

Fearing that more explanations would only make

matters worse, he hadn't raised the subject again. Eventually memory of the incident would fade, but in the meantime Sunny had pulled further away from him. She was courteous, compliant—and as distant as if an ocean still divided them. Sometimes she trembled during their wordless conjugal couplings, and he feared that she was recoiling from his touch. If she had verbally objected, perhaps he could have controlled his desires and stopped inflicting himself on her. But she said nothing, and he did not have the strength to stay away.

As they prepared to go to the ball at Cottenham Manor, he hoped that Sunny's return to society would cheer her. She deserved laughter and frivolity and admiration.

Yet though he wanted her to be happy, the knowledge that she would be surrounded by adoring, predatory men terrified him. If she was miserable in her marriage, how long would it be before she looked elsewhere?

If you would be troubled, take a wife.

CHAPTER EIGHT

Cottenham Manor
March

COTTENHAM MANOR, SEAT of the Earl of Hopstead, was almost as grand and large as Swindon Palace. Lord and Lady Hopstead were famous for their entertainments, and Sunny had spent a long and happy weekend at Cottenham the previous summer. It was a pleasure to return, and as her maid fastened a sapphire and diamond necklace around her neck, she hummed softly to herself.

"Madame is happy tonight," Antoinette observed as she handed Sunny the matching eardrops.

Sunny put on the eardrops, then turned her head so she could see the play of light in the sapphire pendants. "I've been looking forward to this ball for weeks. What a silly custom it is for a bride to rusticate for months after the wedding."

"But think how much more you will appreciate society after wintering in the depths of the English countryside."

"That's true." Sunny rose with a rich whisper of taffeta petticoats. She was wearing a sumptuous blue brocade gown, one of Worth's finest, and she was ready to be admired.

"You must sit until I have put on your tiara," Antoinette said reprovingly.

Obediently Sunny sat again and braced herself for the

weight of the Thornborough tiara. The massive, diamond-studded coronet would give her a headache, but it wouldn't be proper for a duchess to attend a ball without one, particularly since the Prince of Wales would be present.

Just as the maid was finishing, a hesitant knock sounded at the door. Antoinette crossed the room and admitted Alexandra. Dressed in a white silk gown that shimmered with every movement, the younger girl had a fairylike grace. Her dark hair had been swept up to show the delicate line of her throat, and her complexion glowed with youth and good health.

"You look marvelous," Sunny said warmly. "Turn around so I can see all of you."

Her sister-in-law colored prettily as she obeyed. "You were right about the gown. Even though this one wasn't made for me, it's so lovely that one can't help but feel beautiful."

"It looks better on you than it ever did on me. You'll be the belle of the ball."

"No, you will." Alexandra chuckled. "But at least I don't think that I'll be a wallflower."

Another knock sounded on the door. This time it was Justin, come to take his wife and sister down to the dinner that would precede the ball. Sunny had hoped that there would be so many people at Cottenham that they would be put in the same room, but such intimacy was unthinkable in the fashionable set. The previous night, she had slept alone. Perhaps tonight…

Hastily she suppressed the improper thought.

After he examined them both, Justin said gravely, "You will be the two most beautiful women at the ball. Alex, I shall have a dozen men clamoring for your hand before the evening is over."

As Alexandra beamed, he offered one arm to his wife and one to his sister, then led them into the hall. As they descended the broad stairs, Sunny asked, "Will you dance with me tonight?"

He gave her a quizzical glance. "You would dance with a mere husband?"

"Please." Afraid that she might sound pathetic, she added lightly, "I know that it's not fashionable to dance with one's spouse, but it isn't actually scandalous."

He gave her one of the rare smiles that took her breath away. "Then it will be my very great pleasure."

As they entered the salon where the other guests had gathered, Sunny's heart was already dancing.

THE HOPSTEADS' BALL WAS an excellent place to rejoin society, and Sunny enjoyed greeting people she had met the year before. During a break after the fourth dance, she came across her godmother, who was resplendent in coral-and-silver silk. "Aunt Katie!" Sunny gave her a hug. "I hoped you would be here. You're not staying at Cottenham, are you?"

"No, I'm at the Howards'. Every great house in the district is full of guests who have come for this ball." Katie affectionately tucked a tendril of Sunny's flyaway hair in place. "You're in fine looks. By any chance are you…?"

"Please, don't ask me if I'm expecting a blessed event! I swear, every female at the ball has inquired. I'm beginning to feel like a dreadful failure."

"Nonsense—you've only been married a few months." Katie chuckled. "It's just that we're all such gossips, and like it or not, you're a subject of great interest."

Sunny made a face. "Luckily there will soon be other heiresses to capture society's attention." The two women chatted for a few minutes and made an engagement for the next morning.

Then Sunny glanced beyond Katie, and her heart froze

in her breast. On the far side of the room was Paul Curzon, tall and distinguished and heart-stoppingly handsome.

As if feeling her gaze, he looked up, and for a paralyzing instant their eyes met. Shocked by the way her knees weakened, Sunny turned to Katie and stammered, "I must go now. I'll see you tomorrow."

Then she caught her train up with one hand and headed for the nearest door, scarcely noticing when she bumped into other guests. Sometimes escape was more important than manners.

ONE OF THE DRAWBACKS OF socializing was the number of people who hoped to enlist ducal support for some cause or other. This time, it was a junior government minister talking about an upcoming bill. Justin listened patiently, half of his attention on the minister, the other half anticipating the next dance, which would be with Sunny. Then, from the corner of his eye, he saw his wife leave the ballroom, her face pale. He frowned, wondering if she was feeling ill.

He was about to excuse himself when he saw Paul Curzon go out the same side door that Sunny had used. Justin's face stiffened as a horrible suspicion seized him.

Seeing his expression, the minister said earnestly, "I swear, your grace, the scheme is perfectly sound. If you wish, I'll show you the figures."

Justin realized that he couldn't even remember what the damned bill was about. Brusquely he said, "Send me the information and I'll give you my decision in a week."

Hoping desperately that he was wrong, he brushed

aside the minister's thanks and made his way after his wife and the man whom she might still love.

WITHOUT CONSCIOUS THOUGHT, Sunny chose the conservatory for her refuge. It was at the opposite end of the house from the ball, and as she had hoped, she had it to herself.

Cottenham was noted for its magnificent indoor garden, and scattered gaslights illuminated banks of flowers and lush tropical shrubbery. Though rain drummed on the glass panels far above her head, inside the air was balmy and richly scented.

She took a deep breath, then set out along one of the winding brick paths. It had been foolish to become upset at the sight of Paul Curzon, for she had known that inevitably they would meet. But she had not expected it to be tonight. If she had been mentally prepared, she would have been able to accept his presence with equanimity.

Yet honesty compelled her to admit that in the first instant, she had felt some of the excitement she had known in the days when she had loved him. In the days when she *thought* she loved him, before she had discovered his baseness.

As always, nature helped her regain her composure. If she hadn't been dressed in a ball gown, she would have looked for some plants to repot. Instead, she picked a gardenia blossom and inhaled the delicate perfume.

As she did, a familiar voice said huskily, "The conservatory was a perfect choice, darling. No one will see us here."

"Paul!" The shock was as great as when she had first seen him, and spasmodically she crushed the gardenia blossom in her palm. After a fierce struggle for control, she turned and said evenly, "I didn't come here to meet you, Paul, but to get away from you. We have nothing to say to each other."

Unfortunately the way out lay past him. As she tried to slip by without her broad skirts touching him, he caught her hand. "Sunny, don't go yet," he begged. "I'm sorry if I misunderstood why you came here, but I wanted so much to see you that hope warped my judgment. I made the worst mistake of my life with you. At least give me a chance to apologize."

Reluctantly she stopped, as much because of the narrow aisle as because of his words. "I'm not interested in your apologies." As she spoke, she looked into his face, which was a mistake. He didn't look base; he looked sincere, and sinfully handsome.

"If you won't let me apologize, then let me say how much I love you." A tremor sounded in his voice. "I truly didn't know how much until I lost you."

Reminding herself that he had looked equally honest before he had broken her heart, she tried to free her hand, saying tartly, "Perhaps you think that you love me *because* you lost me. Isn't that how people like you play at love?"

His grip tightened. "This is different! The fact that you were willing to marry me is the greatest honor I've ever known. But I let myself be blinded by worldly considerations, and now I'm paying for my folly. Both of us are."

"There's no point in talking like this! The past can't be changed, and I'm a married woman now."

"Perhaps the past can't be changed, but the future can be." He put his hand under her chin and turned her face to his. "Love is too precious to throw away."

His gaze holding hers, he pressed his heated lips to her gloved fingers. "You are so beautiful, Sunny. I have never loved a woman as much as I love you."

She knew that she should break away, for she didn't love him, didn't really trust his protestations of devotion.

Yet her parched heart yearned for warmth, for words of love, even ones that might be false.

Her inner struggle held her paralyzed as he put his arms around her and bent his head for a kiss. In a moment, she would push him away and leave. Yet even though it was wrong, for just an instant she would let him hold her....

THE CONSERVATORY SEEMED like the most likely spot for dalliance, but Justin had only been there once, and he lost precious time with a wrong turn. His heart was pounding with fear when he finally reached his destination and threw open the door. He paused on the threshold and scanned the shadowy garden, praying that he was wrong.

But through the dense vegetation, he saw a shimmering patch of blue the shade of Sunny's gown. Down a brick path, around a bend...and he found his wife in Paul Curzon's arms.

The pain was worse than anything Justin had ever known. For a moment he stood stock-still as nausea pulsed through him.

Then came rage. Stalking forward, he snarled, "If you expect me to be a complaisant husband, you're both fools."

The two broke apart instantly, and Sunny whirled to him, her face white. Justin grabbed her wrist and pulled her away from Curzon. Then he looked his rival in the eye and said with lethal precision, "If you ever come near my wife again, I will destroy you."

"No need to carry on so, old man," Curzon said hastily. "It was merely a friendly kiss between acquaintances."

Justin's free hand knotted into a fist. *"I will destroy you."*

As Curzon paled, Justin turned and swept his wife

away, heedless of the difficulty that she had keeping up in her high-heeled kid slippers. When she stumbled, his grip tightened to keep her from falling, but he did not slow down.

Wanting to ease the rage in his face, she said desperately, "Justin, that wasn't what you think."

He gave her a piercing glance. "It looked very much like a kiss to me. Am I wrong?"

"Yes, but…but it didn't really mean anything."

"If kisses mean nothing to you, does that mean you'll give them to any man?" he asked bitterly. "Or only those with whom you have assignations?"

"You're deliberately misunderstanding me! I went to the conservatory to avoid Paul, not to meet him. I know that I shouldn't have let him kiss me, but it was just a…a temporary aberration that happened only because there were once…warmer feelings between us."

"And if I hadn't come, they would have become warmer yet. If I had been ten minutes later…" His voice broke.

Guilt rose in a choking wave. Though she had not sought the encounter with Paul, she had not left when she should, and she had allowed him to kiss her. Might the warmth of Paul's embrace have dissolved her knowledge of right and wrong? She wanted to believe that morality would have triumphed—but treacherous doubt gnawed at her. Since she had discovered her wanton nature, she could no longer trust herself.

They reached the hallway below the main staircase. Several couples were enjoying the cooler air there, and they all turned to stare at the duke and duchess. Dropping her voice, Sunny whispered, "Let go of me! What will people think?"

"I don't give a tinker's dam what anyone thinks." He began climbing the staircase, still holding tightly to her wrist to keep her at his side. "Your behavior is what concerns me."

He followed the upstairs corridor to her bedchamber, pulled her inside, then slammed the door behind them and turned the key in the lock. The room was empty, lit only by the soft glow of a gas lamp. She edged uneasily away, for this furious man was a stranger, and he was starting to frighten her.

They stared at each other across the width of the room. With the same lethal intensity he had directed at Paul, Justin growled, "In the Middle Ages, I could have locked you in a tower or a chastity belt. A century ago, I could have challenged any man who came near you to a duel. But what can a man do about a faithless wife in these modern times?"

His words triggered her secret fear. "What about faithless husbands?" she retorted. "I've been told that men like you always have mistresses. Is the real reason for your trips to London another woman—one that you couldn't have because you had to marry for money?"

Renewed fury blazed in his gray eyes, and a dark hunger. "I have not looked at—or touched—anyone else since I met you. I wish to God that you could say the same. But since you choose to act like a whore, I will treat you as one."

Then he swept across the room and shattered her with a kiss.

Sunny had thought that her months of marriage had educated her about what happened between husband and wife, but nothing had prepared her for Justin's embrace. The quiet consideration to which she was accustomed had been replaced by blazing rage.

Trapped in the prison of his arms, she was acutely aware of his strength. Even if she wanted to resist, any effort on her part would be futile. Yet as they stood locked together, his mouth devouring hers, she sensed that his fury was changing into something that was similar, but was not anger at all. And it called to her.

Her head tilted and the heavy tiara pulled loose and fell to the carpet, jerking sharply at her hair. When she winced, his crushing grip eased and he began stroking her head with one hand. His deft fingers found and soothed the hurt. She didn't realize that he was also removing the pins until coils of hair cascaded over her shoulders.

He buried his face in the silken mass, and she felt the beating of his heart and the soft exhalation of his breath against her cheek. "Oh, God, Sunny," he said with anguish. "You are so beautiful—so painfully beautiful."

Yet his expression was harsh when he straightened and turned her so that her back was to him. First he unhooked her sapphire necklace, throwing it aside as if it was a piece of cut-glass trumpery. Then he started to unfasten her gown.

She opened her mouth to object, but before she could, he pressed his mouth to the side of her throat. With lips and tongue, he found sensitivities she hadn't known she possessed. As he trailed tiny, nibbling kisses down her neck and along her shoulder, she released her breath in a shuddering sigh, all thoughts of protest chased from her mind. Potent awareness curled through her, pooling hotly in unmentionable places.

When the gown was undone, he pushed it off her shoulders and down her arms. The rough warmth of his fingers made an erotic contrast to the cool silk that skimmed her flesh in a feather-light caress, then slithered in a rush to the floor, leaving her in her underthings. Instinctively she raised her hands to cover her breasts, stammering, "Th-this is highly improper."

"You have forfeited the right to talk about propriety." He untied her layered crinolette petticoat and dragged it down around her ankles. Then he began unlacing her blue satin corset. Stays were a lady's armor against impropriety, and she stood rigidly still, horribly aware that every inch of her newly liberated flesh burned with life and longing.

Then, shockingly, he slid his hands under the loose corset and cupped her breasts, using his thumbs to tease her nipples through the thin fabric of her chemise. It was like the time he had caressed her when he thought she slept, but a thousand times more intense. Unable to suppress her reaction, she shuddered and rolled her hips against him.

"You like that, my lady trollop?" he murmured in her ear.

She wanted to deny it, but couldn't. Her limbs weakened and she wilted against him, mindlessly reveling in the waves of sensation that flooded through her. The firm support of his broad chest, the silken tease of his tongue on the edge of her ear, the exquisite pleasure that expanded from her breasts to encompass her entire being, coiling tighter and tighter deep inside her...

She did not come to her senses until he tossed aside her corset and turned her to face him. Horrified by her lewd response and her near-nakedness, she stumbled away from the pile of crumpled clothing and retreated until her back was to the wall. "I have never shirked my wifely duty," she said feebly, "but this...this isn't right."

"Tonight, right is what I say it is." His implacable gaze holding hers, he stripped off his own clothing with brusque, impatient movements. "And this time, I will have you naked and in the light."

She could not take her eyes away as he removed his formal garments to reveal the hard, masculine body beneath. The well-defined muscles that rippled beneath his skin...the dark hair that patterned his chest and arrowed down his belly…and the arrogant male organ, which she had felt but never seen.

She stared for an instant, both mortified and fascinated, then blushed violently and closed her eyes. No wonder decent couples had marital relations in the dark, for the sight of a man's body was profoundly disturbing.

A Vienna waltz was playing in the distance. She had trouble believing that under this same roof hundreds of people were laughing and flirting and playing society's games. Compared to the devastating reality of Justin, the outside world had no more substance than shadows.

Even with her eyes closed, she was acutely aware of his nakedness when he drew her into his arms again, surrounding her with heat and maleness. Her breath came rapid and irregular as he peeled away the last frail protection of chemise, drawers and stockings. His fingers left trails of fire as they brushed her limbs and torso.

She inhaled sharply when he swept her into his arms and laid her across the bed, his taut frame pinning her to the mattress. Though she tried to control her shameful reactions, she moaned with pleasure when his mouth claimed her breast with arrant carnality.

No matter how hard she tried, she could not lie still as he caressed and kissed and tasted her, the velvet stroke of his tongue driving her to madness. His masterful touch abraded away every layer of decorum until she no longer remembered, or cared, how a lady should act. In the shameless turmoil of intimacy, she was tinder to his flame.

She was lovely beyond his dreams, and everything about her intoxicated him—the haunting lure of wild violets, her tangled sun-struck hair, the lush eroticism of removing layer after layer of clothing until finally her flawless body was revealed. Her lithe, feminine grace wrenched his heart.

Yet side by side with tenderness, he found savage satisfaction in her choked whimpers of pleasure. His wife might be a duchess and a lady, but for tonight, at least, she was a woman, and she was *his*.

This time there would be no need of lotion to ease their joining. She was hotly ready, and she writhed against his hand as he caressed the moist, delicate folds of female flesh. Her moan gave him a deep sense of masculine pride, dissolving the aching emptiness he had known in their inhibited marriage bed.

When he could no longer bear his separateness, he entered her. The voluptuous welcome of her body was exquisite, both torment and homecoming. Trembling with strain, he forced himself to move with slow deliberation. This time he would not let their union end too quickly.

Vivid emotions rippled across her sweat-sheened face. But he wanted more; he wanted communion of the mind as well as the body. He wanted acknowledgment of the power he had over her. Hoarsely he asked, "Do you desire me?"

"You...you are my husband." She turned her head to the side, as if trying to evade his question. "It is my duty to comply with your wishes."

Mere obedience was not what he wanted from his wife. He repeated, *"Do you desire me?"* Slowly, by infinitesimal degrees, he began to withdraw. "If not, perhaps I should stop now."

"No!" she gasped, her eyes flying open for an instant and her body arching sharply upward. "Don't leave me, please. I couldn't bear it...."

It was what he had longed to hear. He responded to her admission by surrendering to the fiery need that bound them. No longer passive, she was his partner in passion, her nails slashing his back as they thrust against each other. She cried out with ecstasy as long, shuddering convulsions rocked them both, and in the culmination of desire he felt their soaring spirits blend.

In the tremulous aftermath, he gathered her pliant body into his arms and tucked the covers around them. As they dozed off together, he knew they had truly become husband and wife.

JUSTIN WAS NOT SURE HOW long he had slept. The ball must have ended, for he could no longer hear music and laughter, but the sky outside was still dark. He lay on his side with Sunny nestled along him, her face against his shoulder.

Not wanting to wake her, he touched the luscious tangle of her hair with a gossamer caress. He had never known such happiness, or such peace. Not only was she the loveliest and sweetest of women, but she was blessed with an ardent nature. If he hadn't been so blasted deferential, he would have discovered that much sooner. But now that they had found each other, their lives would be different.

Her eyes opened and gazed into his. For a long moment, they simply stared at each other. He stroked the elegant curve of her back and prepared to make the declaration of love that he had never made to any other woman.

But she spoke first, saying in a thin, exhausted voice, "Who are you?"

A chill touched his heart as he wondered if she was out of her senses, but she seemed lucid. Carefully he replied, "Your husband, of course."

She gave a tiny shake of her head. "You are more a stranger to me now than on the day we married."

He looked away, unable to face the dazed bleakness in her aqua eyes. He had known that she had not yet been unfaithful; not only was she not the sort of woman to engage lightly in an affair, but buried at Swindon she hadn't even had an opportunity. Yet seeing her in Curzon's arms had devastated Justin because it was a horrific preview of the possibility that he would lose her.

Despair had made him furiously determined to show her what fulfillment was. He had wanted to possess her, body and soul, to make her his own so profoundly that she would never look at another man. He realized that he had also hoped to win her love by demonstrating the depth of his passion.

But the fact that he had been able to arouse her latent ardor did not mean that she suddenly, miraculously loved him. With sickening clarity, he saw that in his anger he had ruthlessly stripped away her dignity and modesty. Instead of liberating her passion, he had ravished her spirit, turning her into a broken shadow of the happy girl who had first captured his heart.

His unspoken words of love withered and died. Instead he said painfully, "I am no different now from what I was then."

He wanted to say more, to apologize and beg her forgiveness, but she turned away and buried her face in the pillows.

Feeling that he would shatter if he moved too suddenly, he slid from the bed and numbly dragged on enough clothing to make his way the short distance to his room.

As he left, he wondered despairingly if he would ever be able to face his wife again.

CHAPTER NINE

SUNNY AWOKE THE NEXT morning churning with tangled emotions. The only thing she knew for certain was that she could not bear to face a house full of avid-eyed, curious people. With a groan, she rolled over, buried her head under a pillow and did her best not to think.

But her mind refused to cooperate. She could not stop herself from wondering where Justin was and what he thought of the events of the previous night. She was mortified by memories of her wantonness, and angry with her husband for making her behave so badly. But though she tried to cling to anger over his disrespect, other things kept seeping into her mind—memories of heartwarming closeness, and shattering excitement....

At that point in her thoughts, her throat always tightened. Justin had said he would treat her as a whore, and her response had confirmed his furious accusation.

For the first time in her life, Sunny understood why a woman might choose to go into a nunnery. A world with no men would be infinitely simpler.

Eventually Antoinette tiptoed into the dim, heavily curtained room. "Madame is not feeling well this morning?"

"Madame has a ghastly headache. I wish to be left alone." Remembering her obligations, Sunny added, "Tell Lady Alexandra not to be concerned about me. I'm sure I'll be fine by dinner."

There was a long silence. Even with her eyes closed,

Sunny knew that her maid was surveying the disordered bedchamber and probably drawing accurate conclusions. But tactful Antoinette said only, "After I straighten the room, I shall leave. Perhaps later you would like tea and toast?"

"Perhaps."

As the maid quietly tidied up the evidence of debauchery, someone knocked on the door and handed in a message. After the footman left, Antoinette said, "*Monsieur le Duc* has sent a note."

Sunny came tensely awake. "Leave it on the table."

After the maid left, Sunny sat up in bed and stared at the letter as if it were a poisonous serpent. Then she swung her feet to the floor. Only then did she realize that she was stark naked. Worse, her body showed unaccustomed marks where sensitive skin had been nipped, or rasped by a whiskered masculine face. And her body would not be the only one marked this morning....

Face flushed, she darted to the armoire and grabbed the first nightgown and wrapper she saw. After she was decently covered, she brushed her wild hair into submission and pulled it into a severe knot. When she could delay no longer, she opened the waiting envelope.

She was not sure what she expected, but the scrawled words, *I'm sorry. Thornborough* were a painful letdown. What was her husband sorry about—their marriage? His wife's appallingly wanton nature? His own disproportionate rage, which had led him to humiliate her? The use of his title rather than his Christian name was blunt proof that the moments of intimacy she had imagined the night before were an illusion.

Crumpling the note in one hand, she buried her face in her hands and struggled against tears. The wretched circle of her thoughts was interrupted by another knock.

Though she called out, "I do not wish for company," the door swung open anyhow.

In walked Katie Westron, immaculately dressed in a morning gown and with a tray in her hands. "It's past noon, and you and I were engaged to take a drive an hour ago." She set the tray down, then surveyed her goddaughter. "You look quite dreadful, my dear, and they say that Thornborough left Cottenham this morning at dawn, looking like death."

So he was gone. Apparently he couldn't bear being under the same roof with her any longer. Trying to mask the pain of that thought, Sunny asked, "Are people talking?"

"Some, though not as much as they were before I said that Thornborough had always intended to leave today because he had business at Swindon." Briskly Katie opened the draperies so that light flooded the room. "And as I pointed out, who wouldn't look exhausted after a late night at such a delightful ball?"

"He *was* planning to leave early, but not until tomorrow." Sunny managed a wry half smile. "You lie beautifully."

"It's a prime social skill." Katie prepared two cups of coffee and handed one to Sunny, then took the other and perched on the window seat. "There's nothing like coffee to put one's troubles in perspective. Have a ginger cake, too, they're very good." After daintily biting one, Katie continued, "Would you like to tell me why you and Thornborough both look so miserable?"

The scalding coffee did clear Sunny's mind. She was in dire need of the advice of an older and wiser woman, and she would find no kinder or more tolerant listener than her godmother.

Haltingly she described her marriage—the distance between her and her husband, her loneliness, her encounter with Paul Curzon and the shocking result. Of the last she said very little, and that with her face burning, but she suspected that her godmother could make a shrewd guess about what went unsaid.

At the end, she asked, "What do you think?"

"Exactly why are you so upset?"

After long thought, Sunny said slowly, "I don't understand my marriage, my husband or myself. In particular, I find Justin incomprehensible. Before, I thought he was polite but basically indifferent to me. Now I think he must despise me, or he would never have treated me with such disrespect."

Katie took another cake. "Do you wish to end the marriage?"

"Of course I don't want a divorce!"

"Why 'of course'? There would be a ghastly scandal, and some social circles exclude all divorced women, but as a Vangelder, you would be able to weather that."

"It…it would be humiliating for Thornborough. If I left him, people would think that he mistreated me horribly."

Katie's brows arched. "Aren't you saying that he did exactly that?"

"In most ways, he's been very considerate." She thought of the bathroom that he had had installed for her, and almost smiled. Not the most romantic gift, perhaps, but one that gave her daily pleasure.

"You'd be a fool to live in misery simply to save Thornborough embarrassment," Katie said tartly. "A little singed pride will be good for him, and as a duke he will certainly not be ruined socially. He can find another wife with a snap of his fingers. The next one might not be able to match your dowry, but that's all right—the Swindon roof has already been replaced, and you can hardly take it back. What matters is that you'll be free to find a more congenial husband."

The thought of Justin with another wife made Sunny's hackles rise. "I don't want another husband." She bit her lip. "In fact, I can't imagine being married to anyone else. It would seem wrong. Immoral."

"Oh?" Katie said with interest. "What is so special about Thornborough? From what you say, he's a dull sort of fellow, and he's not particularly good-looking."

"He's *not* dull! He's kind, intelligent and very witty, even though he's quiet. He has a sense of responsibility, which many men in his position don't. And he's really quite attractive. Not in a sleek, fashionable way, but very... manly."

Her godmother smiled gently. "You sound like a woman who is in love with her husband."

"I do?" Sunny tried the idea on, and was shocked to realize that it was true. She was happy in Justin's presence; on some deep level that had nothing to do with their current problems, she trusted him. "But he doesn't love me—he doesn't even respect me. Last night he said that since I had behaved like a...a woman of no virtue, he would treat me like one." A vivid memory of his mouth on her breast caused her to blush again.

"Did he hurt you?"

"No, but he...offended my modesty." Sunny stared at her hands, unable to meet her godmother's gaze. "In fairness, I must admit that I did not behave as properly as I should. In fact...I was shocked to discover how wantonly I could behave."

"In other words, your husband made passionate love to you, you found it entrancing as well as alarming, and are now ashamed of yourself."

The color drained from Sunny's face, leaving her white. "How did you know?"

Setting aside her coffee cup, Katie said, "The time has come to speak frankly. I suppose that your mother told you that no decent woman ever enjoyed her marriage bed, and that discreet suffering was the mark of a lady."

After seeing her goddaughter nod, she continued, "There are many who agree with her, but another school of opinion says that there is nothing wrong with taking pleasure in the bodies that the good Lord gave us. What is the Song of Solomon but a hymn to the joy of physical and spiritual love?"

Weakly Sunny said, "Mother would say you're talking blasphemy."

"Augusta is one of my oldest and dearest friends, but she and your father were ill-suited, and naturally that has affected her views on marital relations." Katie leaned forward earnestly. "Satisfaction in the marriage bed binds a couple together, and the better a woman pleases her husband, the less likely he is to stray. And vice versa, I might add." She cocked her head. "If you hadn't been raised to believe that conjugal pleasure was immodest, would you have enjoyed the passion and intimacy that you experienced last night?"

The idea of reveling in carnality was so shocking that it took Sunny's breath away—yet it was also powerfully compelling. She had come to look forward to Justin's visits and to long for more of his company. The idea that her response was natural, not wanton, was heady indeed.

More memories of the previous night's explosive passion burned across her brain. Though the episode had been upsetting, there had also been moments of stunning emotional intimacy, when she and her husband had seemed to be one flesh and one spirit. If such intensity could be woven into the fabric of a marriage, it would bind a man and woman together for as long as they lived. And if passion made a marriage stronger, surely fulfillment could not be truly wicked.

There was only one problem. "I'd like to think that you're right, but what does it matter if I love my husband and he holds me in contempt? Justin has never said a single word of love."

Katie smiled wryly. "Englishmen are taught to conceal their emotions in the nursery, and the more deeply they care, the harder it is for them to speak. In my experience, the men who talk most easily of love are those who have had entirely too much practice. The more sparingly a man gives his heart, the more precious the gift, and the less adept he is at declarations of love. But deeds matter more than words, and an ounce of genuine caring is worth a pound of smooth, insincere compliments."

Abruptly Sunny remembered that Justin had said that he hadn't looked at another woman since meeting her. She had thought that was merely a riposte in their argument, but if true, it might be an oblique declaration of love. Hesitantly she said, "Do you think it's possible that Justin loves me?"

"You would know that better than I. But he seems the sort who would be more of a doer than a talker." Katie's brows drew together. "Men are simple creatures, and for them, love and passion often get knotted up together. If he does love you in a passionate way, the kind of restrained marriage you have described must be difficult for him."

And if he was finding the marriage difficult, he would withdraw; that much Sunny knew about her husband. She had regretted the fact that he had never reached out to her with affection—yet neither had she ever reached out to him. Perhaps she was as much responsible for the distance between them as he was. Attempting lightness, she said, "I suppose that the way to find out how he feels is to hand him my heart on a platter, then see whether he accepts it or chops it into little pieces."

"I'm afraid so." Katie shook her head ruefully. "All marriages have ups and downs, particularly in the early years. I was once in a situation a bit like yours, where I had to risk what could have been a humiliating rejection. It wasn't easy to humble myself, but the results were worth it." She smiled. "A witty vicar once said that a good marriage is like a pair of scissors with the couple inseparably joined, often moving in opposite directions, yet always destroying anyone who comes between them. The trick is for the blades to learn to work smoothly together, so as not to cut each other."

That's what she and Justin had been doing: cutting each other. Feeling a century older than she had the day before, Sunny gave a shaky smile. "Apparently I must learn to speak with American bluntness."

"That's the spirit. But first, you might want to ask yourself what you want out of your marriage."

"Love, companionship, children. I certainly don't want to withdraw entirely from society, but the fashionable world will never be the center of my life, the way it is for my mother." Her brow wrinkled. "Perhaps if my parents had been happier together, my father would not have worked so hard, and my mother would not have cared as much about society."

"I've often suspected that many of the world's most dazzling achievements are a result of a miserable domestic situation." Katie considered. "You might want to wait until both you and Thornborough have had time to recover from what was obviously a distressing episode. You were about to take Alexandra to Paris, weren't you? In your place, I would carry on with my original plans. That will give you time to think and decide exactly how to proceed."

"I'm going to need it." Sunny rose and hugged her godmother. "Thank you, Aunt Katie. What can I do to repay you?"

"When you're old and wise like me, you can give worldly advice to other confused young ladies." Katie smiled reminiscently. "Which is exactly what I was told by an eccentric, sharp-tongued Westron aunt who sent me back to my husband when I was a bewildered bride."

Sunny nodded gravely. "I promise to pass on whatever womanly wisdom I acquire."

But before she was in a position to give good advice, she must fix her own frayed marriage. And that, she knew, would be easier said than done.

CHAPTER TEN

ALEXANDRA LOOKED EAGERLY from the carriage window. "Almost home! It's hard to believe that it's been only a month since we left Swindon. I feel *years* older."

Sunny smiled, trying to conceal her frayed nerves. "Paris has that effect on people. You really have changed, too. You left as a girl and are returning as a young woman."

"I hope so." Alexandra grinned. "But I'm going to go right up to my room and take off my wonderful Worth travel ensemble. Then I'll curl up in my window seat and read that new Rider Haggard novel I bought in London. Though Paris was wonderful, there's nothing quite like a good book."

"You've earned the right to a little self-indulgence." Sunny gave her sister-in-law a fond smile. Petite and pretty, Alexandra would never be called the Gargoylette again, and the difference was more than mere clothing. Now that Alexandra was free of her mother's crushing influence, she was developing poise, confidence and a quiet charm that would surely win her whatever man she eventually honored with her heart.

The carriage pulled up in front of the palace and a footman stepped forward to open the door and let down the steps. Even though Sunny had lived at Swindon for only a few months, and that interval had been far from happy, she felt a surprising sense of homecoming. It helped that the full glory of an English spring had arrived. All nature

was in bloom, and the sun was almost as warm as high
summer.

As they entered the main hall, Sunny asked the butler,
"Is my husband in the house or out on the estate?"

She assumed the latter, for Justin was not expecting
them to return until the next day. But the butler replied,
"I believe that the duke is taking advantage of the fine
weather by working in the Greek gazebo. Shall I inform
him of your arrival?"

Sunny's heart lurched. She had thought she would
have several hours more before confronting her husband
about the state of their marriage, but perhaps it would be
better this way. "No, I shall freshen up and then surprise
him."

As she walked toward the stairs, a black-and-tan whirlwind darted across the hall and leapt against her, barking
joyfully. "Daisy! Oh, darling, I missed you, too." Sunny
knelt and hugged the slender little dog, feeling that such
a warm welcome was a good omen.

A moment later, the wolfhounds thundered up and
greeted Alexandra eagerly, then escorted her upstairs.
Canine snobs of the highest order, they could tell aristocratic British blood from that of an upstart American, and
they reserved their raptures for Justin and his sisters.

Sunny didn't mind. Her charming mongrel at her heels,
she went to her room and changed from her traveling suit
to her most flattering tea gown, a loose, flowing confec-
tion of figured green silk that brought out the green in
her eyes.

She chose the costume with care, and not just because
it was comfortable. The free and easy design of a tea gown
was considered rather daring because it hinted at free and
easy morals. She hoped that Justin would see her garb as
the subtle advance that it was.

Because he always seemed to like her hair, she let it

down and tied it back with a scarf. She needed all the help she could get, for she was terrified by the prospect of baring her heart to the man who could so easily break it. Apart from a brief note that she had written to inform Justin of their safe arrival in Paris, there had been no communication between them. For all she knew, he was still furious over Paul Curzon's kiss.

Fortunately, she had news that should mollify any lingering anger. God willing, it would also bring them together.

Chin high, she sailed out of the house and down the path toward the gardens.

A BREEZE WAFTED THROUGH the miniature Greek temple, carrying exuberant scents of trees and spring flowers. Justin scarcely noticed. He was hardly more aware of the pile of correspondence that lay on the cushioned bench beside him, for thoughts of his wife dominated his mind. All of his grief, guilt and anguished love had been intensified by that night of heartbreaking passion, when he had briefly thought that their spirits and bodies were in total harmony.

Sunny had sent him a single impersonal note from Paris. Though it gave no hint of her feelings, its civility implied that she was willing to go on as if nothing had happened.

Yet he feared her return almost as much as he longed to see her. Having once found passion in her arms, it was going to be almost impossible for him not to try to invoke it again, whether she was willing or not.

Absently he slit an envelope with the Italian dagger that he used as a letter opener. Before he could pull out the folded sheet inside, a soft voice said, "Good day, Justin."

He looked up to see Sunny poised on the edge of the

folly, her right hand resting on one of the Ionic columns
that framed the entrance. She wore a flowing green tea
gown that made her look like an exquisite tree nymph.
The garment was distractingly similar to a nightgown,
and the breeze molded the fluttering, translucent layers
of fabric to her slim figure.

For an instant all his tormented desire must have
showed in his face. He wanted to cross the marble floor
and draw her into his arms and never let her go. But he
didn't. She looked ready to run if he made a move toward
her, and it was unbearable to think that she might fear
him.

He set the pile of letters on the bench beside him and
courteously got to his feet. "I hope you had a good journey. I wasn't expecting you and Alex until tomorrow."

"Rather than spend another night in London, we decided to come home early."

"I'm glad. The house has seemed empty without the
two of you." Afraid to look at her because of what his
expression would reveal, he turned the dagger over and
over in his hands. The impact of her presence had driven
away all of the eloquent, romantic speeches he had been
rehearsing in his mind.

After a strained silence, she said, "I have good news.
I'm almost certain that…that I am with child."

His first reaction was delight, but that was instantly
shadowed by the implications. Augusta Vangelder had
told him that once her daughter conceived, she was not
to be troubled by husbandly lust. The fact that Sunny was
brandishing the possibility of her pregnancy like a shield
was clear proof that she welcomed the excuse to ban him
from her bed.

His fingers whitened around the handle of the dagger.
If she bore a son, her obligation to the Aubrey name would
be fulfilled, and their marriage would effectively be over.

Driving the dagger into his belly would have hurt less than that thought.

During the last lonely month, he had resolved to take advantage of the quiet intimacy of the marital bed to speak more openly to his wife. If she was willing, perhaps they could build a closer, warmer relationship. Now that hope was gone; any discussions between them must endure the harsh light of day.

Knowing that the silence had been too long, he said, "Excellent. I hope you are feeling well?"

She nodded.

After another awkward pause, he said, "Good. We shall have to get a London physician here to make sure that your health is all it should be." He laid the dagger precisely on top of his correspondence so that the letters would not blow away in the wind. "You need not worry that I will continue to…force my attentions on you."

"Very well." She bent her head, and a slight shiver passed through her. Relief, perhaps. "I'm a bit tired. I think that I'll skip dinner and have a tray in my room."

Thinking that she looked pale, he said, "Of course. You must take good care of yourself."

Back straight and head high, she turned and started down the grassy path. Every inch a lady, and as unapproachable as Queen Victoria herself.

He watched her leave, very aware of what an effort it was to breathe. Inhale, exhale. Inhale, exhale. He had been breathing all his life, yet never noticed before how difficult it was.

There was a tearing sensation deep inside, as if his heart was literally breaking, and he knew that he could not let the deadly silence continue. He called out, "Sunny!"

She halted, then turned slowly to face him. In the shadows cast by the tall boxwoods that lined the path, he could not see her face clearly.

He stepped from the folly and moved toward her, then stopped when she tensed. "Sunny, I want to apologize for what I did at Cottenham. I am profoundly sorry for distressing you."

"You were within your rights, and your anger was justified," she said expressionlessly.

"Perhaps, but that doesn't make it right to mistreat you. It won't happen again."

"Should I be grateful for that?" she said with sudden, chilling bitterness. "That night was upsetting, but it was also the one time in our marriage that you have shown any feelings about me. I have begun to think that even anger is better than indifference."

The gay ribbons on her gown shivered as she bowed her head and pressed her fingertips to her brow. When she looked up, her eyes were bleak. "We can't continue to live together as strangers, Justin. I can't endure it any longer."

Her words struck with the force of a blow, nearly destroying his fragile control. It seemed impossible that their marriage could be ending like this, on a day full of sunlight and promise. Yet he could not hold her against her will; somehow he must find the strength to let her go. "If you wish to be free of me," he said tightly, "I will set no barriers in your way."

Her mouth twisted. "Is that what you want—to end our marriage now that you have your damned roof?"

"I want you to be happy, Sunny." Hearing the anguish in his voice, he stopped until he could continue more steadily. "And I will do anything in my power that might make you so."

The air between them seemed to thicken, charged with indefinable emotions. Then she said passionately, "What I want is to be a real wife! To be part of your life, not just another expensive bauble in Swindon Palace." Her hands clenched at her sides. "Or perhaps I should wish to be your mistress, since English lords seem to save their hearts for women who are not their wives."

Stunned, he stammered, "I don't understand."

"It's a simple matter, Justin. I want you to love me," she said softly. "Do you think that you ever could? Because I'm horribly afraid that I love you."

He felt as if his heart had stopped. Her declaration was so unexpected that it seemed she must be mocking him. Yet it was impossible to doubt the transparent honesty in her eyes.

Before he could find the words to answer, her face crumpled and she spun away from him. "Dear God, I'm making a fool of myself, aren't I? Like the brash, vulgar American that I am. Please—forget that I ever spoke."

Justin's paralysis dissolved and he caught her arm and swung her around before she could dart down the path. To his horror, tears were coursing down her face. The sight delivered a final, shattering blow to his reserve. Crushing her in his arms, he said urgently, "Don't cry, Sunny. If you want my love, you already have it. You always have."

Though her tears intensified, she did not pull away. Instead, she wrapped her arms around him and hid her face in the angle between his throat and shoulder. She was all pliant warmth, honeyed hair and the promise of wild violets.

He groped for the best way to tell her how much he loved her until he realized that words had always failed and divided them. Action would better demonstrate the depth of his caring. He raised her head and brushed back her silky hair, then kissed her with all of the hunger of his yearning spirit.

Salty with tears, her lips clung to his, open and seeking.

Subtle currents flowed between them—despair and

comfort, wonder and promise, trust and surrender. In the stark honesty of desperation, there was no place for shame or doubt or misunderstanding. One by one, the barriers that had divided them crumbled away to reveal the shy grandeur of love.

At first the sweetness of discovery was enough, but as the kiss deepened and lengthened, sweetness slowly blossomed into fire. Murmuring her name like a prayer, he kneaded the soft curves that lay unconstrained beneath her flowing gown. She pressed against him, breathless and eager, and he drew her down to the sun-warmed grass.

They had had dutiful conjugal relations, and once they had come together with chaotic, disquieting passion. This time, they made love. She yielded herself utterly, for the awesome needs of her body no longer frightened her now that she knew she was loved.

Rippling layers of green silk were easily brushed aside, buttons undone, ribbons untied. Then, too impatient to wait until they were fully disrobed, they joined in the dance of desire. Swift and fierce, their union was a potent act of mutual possession that bound them into one spirit and one flesh.

Only afterward, as she lay languidly in the haven of his arms, did she realize the scandalousness of her behavior. The Duchess of Thornborough was lying half-naked in the garden, as bold as any dairymaid in a haystack. How strange. How shocking. How right.

His head lay pillowed on her shoulder, and she slid her fingers into his tousled dark hair. "How is it possible for us to say so much to each other in ten minutes when we didn't speak a single word?" she asked dreamily.

"Words are limiting. They can only hint at an emotion as powerful as love. Passion comes closer because it is itself all feeling." Justin rolled to his side and propped himself up on one elbow, his other arm draped over her waist to hold her close. Smiling into her eyes, he said, "For someone who seemed to hate being touched, you have developed a remarkable talent for physical intimacy."

She blushed. "At first I was afraid of the unknown. It wasn't long until I began to look forward to your visits, but I was ashamed of my desire. And…and my mother said that a man would never respect an immodest woman who reveled in her lower nature."

"In this area, your mother's understanding is sadly limited. There may be men like that, but for me, the knowledge that we can share our bodies with mutual pleasure is the greatest of all gifts." He leaned over and dropped a light kiss on the end of her nose. "Let us make a pact, my love—to pay no attention to what the world might say, and care only about what the two of us feel."

With one hand, she unbuttoned the top of his shirt and slipped her fingers inside so she could caress his warm, bare skin. "I think that is a wonderful idea. I only wish that we had started sooner. I was so sure that you married me only because you needed my fortune."

Expression serious, he said, "Don't ever doubt that I love you, Sunny. I have since the first time we met, when you were the Gilded Girl and I was an insignificant younger son who could never dare aspire to your hand."

Her eyes widened. "We hardly even spoke that day."

"On the contrary—we walked through the gardens for the better part of an hour. I could take you along the exact route, and repeat everything you said. It was the most enchanting experience of my life." His mouth quirked up wryly. "And you don't remember it at all, do you?"

"I do remember that I enjoyed your company, but I was meeting so many people then. You were simply a quiet, attractive man who didn't seem interested in me."

She looked searchingly into his eyes. "If you loved me, why didn't you say so sooner?"

"I tried, but you never wanted to hear." He began lazily stroking her bare arm. "Since it never occurred to me that you could love me, there was no reason to burden you with my foolish emotions, even if I had known how to do it."

A vivid memory of his proposal flashed through her mind. He had said then that she had had his heart from the moment they met. There had been other occasions when he had haltingly tried to declare himself, plus a thousand small signs of caring, from his wedding orchids to the way he had risked his life to rescue a puppy for her. Yet because of her pain over Paul's betrayal and her conviction that Justin had married her only for money, she had spurned his hesitant words and gestures, convinced that they were polite lies. Dear heaven, no wonder he had preferred to conceal his feelings.

"I'm the one who must apologize. Because I was hurting, I ended up hurting you, as well." She laid her hand along his firm jaw, thinking how handsome he looked with that tender light in his eyes. "Yet you were always kind to me."

He turned his head and pressed a kiss into her palm. "We gargoyles are known for kindness."

"I *hate* that nickname," she said vehemently. "How can people be so cruel? You are intelligent, amusing, considerate, and a gentleman in the best sense of the word."

"I'm very glad you think so, but society loves cleverness, and a good quip counts for more than a good heart," he said with dry amusement. "The fact that you love me is clear proof that much of love comes from simple proximity."

"Nonsense," she said tartly. "Proximity can just as easily breed dislike. But it's true that I would never have learned to love you if we hadn't married. You are not an easy man to know."

"I'm sorry, my dear." He sighed. "As you know, my mother can be...difficult. I learned early that to show emotions was to risk having them used against me, so I became first-rate at concealing what I felt. Unfortunately, that made me at a flat loss at saying what matters most. I promise that from now on, I will say that I love you at least once a day."

"I'd rather have that than the Thornborough tiara." Shyly she touched her abdomen, which as yet showed no sign of the new life within. "Are you happy about the baby? You didn't seem very interested."

"I'm awed and delighted." A shadow crossed his face. "If my reaction seemed unenthusiastic, it was because I feared that if it was a boy, you would go off to Paris or New York and never want to see me again."

"What a dreadful thought." She shivered. "May I ask a favor?"

"Anything, Sunny. Always." He laced his fingers through hers, then drew their joined hands to his heart.

"I would very much like it if we slept together every night, like people who can't afford two bedrooms do." Her mouth curved playfully. "Even with central heating, it's often chilly here."

He laughed. "I would like nothing better. I've always hated leaving you to go back to my own cold and lonely bed."

"We can start a new fashion for togetherness." She lifted their clasped hands and lovingly kissed his fingertips.

He leaned over and claimed her mouth, and the embers of passion began glowing with renewed life. As he slid his hand into the loose neckline of her gown, he murmured,

"We're both wearing entirely too many clothes, especially for such a fine day."

Remembering their surroundings, she said breathlessly, "Justin, don't you dare! We have already behaved disgracefully enough for one day."

"Mmm?" He pulled her gown from her shoulder so that he could kiss her breasts, a process that rendered her quite unable to talk. She had not known that there was such pleasure in the whole world.

She made one last plea for sanity as he began stripping off his coat. "If someone comes along this path and sees us, what will they say?"

"They'll say that the Duke of Thornborough loves his wife very much." He smiled into her eyes with delicious wickedness. "And they'll be right."

* * * * *

JESSE'S WIFE

Kristin James

CHAPTER ONE

AMY MCALISTER HAD NEVER done anything so daring.

She glanced up at her companion as she tucked her hand in his arm and strolled out through the hall and kitchen onto the back porch. The color was high in Amy's cheeks, partially from the exercise of dancing in which they had been engaged, but just as much from her heightened excitement. It would not be terribly improper to walk with Mr. Whitaker out onto the front porch, for there was such a crush of people inside the house that more than one gentleman and lady had stepped outside on this balmy October evening for a breath of air.

However, it was quite another matter for them to have slipped out onto the small back porch, where there was no one but them. Still worse, Mr. Whitaker was taking her hand and leading her down the steps onto the packed earth of the backyard and across toward the corral. To be alone with a man in the darkened night was not at all proper, especially when he had asked her to slip away with him for a moonlight stroll. In any other woman, such behavior would have been termed loose. In herself, Amy knew, such carelessness would be classified as mere naiveté, for the quiet, plain Amy was "such a *good* girl," and, moreover, not the sort to drive a man to an act of unbridled passion.

The idea rankled. It wasn't that Amy wished to be thought of as a "bad" girl, or to have some harridan like old Mrs. Gooden call her an "incorrigible flirt"—as she had Amy's sister, Corinne. She simply found it singularly depressing to know that everyone thought her so indifferent in looks and boring in personality that she would never even be afforded the opportunity to break society's rules.

Amy had unhappily admitted the truth—that she was, indeed, just plain and uninteresting. All the looks in their family had fallen to her younger sister, Corinne, whose blond curls, sparkling blue eyes and creamy complexion had entranced most of the men of the area ever since she grew old enough to put her skirts down and her hair up.

Amy, on the other hand, had rather mousy light brown hair, which she usually wore carelessly screwed up into a knot, a style that did nothing for her features. Her eyes, though large and expressive, were an ordinary brown. Her skin was nice enough, her figure was neat and becomingly curved, and her features were not unpleasing. But Amy had none of her sister's vivacity. Rather than sparkling and flirting, she was apt to be tongue-tied in a man's presence. She tended to look down when she talked, and she avoided talking to people if she possibly could. Moreover, she was well-known around the county as a scholar, and few people were interested in the sort of things she liked to talk about.

As a result, Amy was something of a wallflower. It was a good thing, her mother maintained, that Amy was a calm, sensible girl, obviously happy being immersed in her books, and with no interest in a husband or family.

In that, Mrs. McAlister was wrong. Although Amy was generally calm and sensible, inside her beat the heart of a romantic. She read everything she could get her hands on, from dull histories to the thoughts of philosophers, but what she loved most of all were novels, especially romantic ones, and those she read over and over. Therefore, when Charles Whitaker had leaned down and whispered in her ear at the end of the dance, suggesting that they slip away from this tiresome crowd and go for a stroll in the moonlight, she had readily agreed.

Her pulse was skittering madly now as she walked with him across the yard. One of his hands covered hers as it lay in the crook of her elbow, warm and full of meaning. He glanced down at her and smiled, his eyes caressing her face. Amy drew in a little breath and gazed up into his face, which was washed romantically by moonlight. Looking at him made her knees a trifle weak.

Charles Whitaker was a handsome man, one who could, indeed, have stepped from the pages of one of her novels. His hair was jet black and thick, springing back from a high, fair brow, and his eyes were dark and intense. From the moment he had ridden into Portersville a few weeks before, he had been the center of intense female interest.

There was a faint air of melancholy about him, and though he was mysteriously silent regarding his past, one or two things he had let drop indicated that his family, once the proud possessors of a plantation in Virginia, had lost it all in the war some twenty-four years before. Amy didn't hold his loss against him. After all, Amy's own father had come to Texas after the war from his native Louisiana with his friend Cal Boudreaux. He had worked hard and built up one of the biggest ranches in the state.

To Amy's surprise, however, her father seemed to have little sympathy for Charles Whitaker. He had accepted Whitaker in the friendly way people had here, without questions as to his past, but after a few weeks he had taken a dislike to Charles. He had said Charles was lazy and frivolous, and wondered why he hadn't taken a job, as any other man would have. He had told his daughters grimly that he suspected the man was a fortune hunter, and warned them to stay away from him.

Corinne, of course, had merely laughed and continued to do as she pleased, flirting with Mr. Whitaker as she did with her other many beaux. Even Amy, usually obedient to her father's wishes, thought he was being unkind and unfair, and when Charles had begun paying decided attention to her, she had disregarded her father's warnings. She was thrilled that a man like Charles Whitaker had stopped hanging about her beautiful sister and had chosen her company instead.

They reached the corral, and Whitaker drew Amy into the shadow of the barn. In the distance, Amy heard a trill of laughter from the porch, but it merely blended into the soothing night noises—the shuffle of horses' hooves within the corral, the croak of frogs down by the stock tank, the call of a night bird. She felt wrapped in the darkness, and giddy to be standing so close to Charles and in such a situation.

He smiled down at her, taking her hands in his. "You must think me very presumptuous."

Amy mutely shook her head. She was more afraid that he would think her overly bold than the other way around.

"I had to speak with you…to be alone with you."

"Why?" she asked honestly.

Whitaker looked a trifle taken aback by her bluntness. "But surely you have guessed…"

Amy continued to look at him uncertainly. She had noticed that the past few times she had seen Mr. Whitaker, he had paid particular attention to her, no longer dangling after Corinne. But she had refused to let herself believe it, certain that she simply had been reading too much into a look or into the number of times he asked her to dance.

"Mr. Whitaker, I'm not sure—"

She broke off, whirling as the barn door scraped across the earth with a loud noise. A man stepped out of the barn and into the moonlight. He stopped abruptly when he saw them, and his eyes narrowed.

"Oh! Jesse!" Amy breathed a sigh of relief. "You startled me."

The man walked toward them, his eyes flickering over Charles Whitaker, then coming to rest on Amy. His gaze was expressionless, but still Whitaker shifted a little beneath it. Jesse Tyler was young, no more than twenty, and he was not a big man, but he was leanly muscled and strong. There was about him an air of toughness. Whitaker wasn't sure what it was—perhaps the hard expression in his cool green eyes, or the carefully blank, hard set of his face or even the rough clothes he wore and his slightly shaggy, too-long hair—but it was clear that Jesse Tyler was not a man to tangle with.

"What are you doing out here, ma'am, so far from the party?" Tyler asked Amy mildly, but the suspicious look he shot at Whitaker was anything but mild.

"Just taking a stroll," Amy answered. "It was awfully hot in there, dancing. You know."

Jesse nodded, biting off the end of his cheroot, then putting it in his mouth and lighting it. Amy eyed him uncertainly. She liked Jesse; he was one of her dearest friends. Though others often said he was tough, even mean, Amy had never seen anything like that in him. She reached out and placed a hand affectionately on Jesse's arm. He paused in the act of lighting his cheroot and looked up at her. His gaze was long and considering.

"You won't say anything about my being out here, will you, Jesse?"

"I don't think your pa would like it," he responded.

"Perhaps not, but there's nothing wrong with it. You

know I wouldn't do anything wicked or reckless, don't you?"

"*You* wouldn't," he said with careful emphasis, and his eyes flickered to Whitaker.

"I'm in good hands with Mr. Whitaker," Amy replied blithely, and smiled. "You mustn't worry about that."

Tyler continued to stare at Whitaker, his gaze hard. "Yes. I'm sure Mr. Whitaker will be very careful to take good care of you."

Charles raised his brows in lazy disdain at the hint of a threat in the other man's words, but he sketched a little bow, inclining his head to show that he understood Tyler's implication.

"Good night, Miss Amy."

"Good night, Jesse."

Tyler strolled away in the direction of the house. Charles and Amy did not watch him go, so neither of them saw him stop when he reached the shadows of the house and turn back to look at them. He ground out his cheroot in order to rid himself of its red glow, and he crossed his arms over his chest and leaned back against the side of the house, studying the couple by the corral.

Charles took Amy's hands in his. "Please, Miss Mc-Alister, come for a stroll with me—away from the yard. If we stay here, we'll only be interrupted again."

Amy paused uncertainly. She was dazzled by the attention Mr. Whitaker was paying her; no man had ever flirted with her so assiduously, or paid her such pretty, extravagant compliments. It made her feel almost beautiful, as if she were a belle of the county like her sister, instead of a washed-out nonentity, relegated to line the wall with the matrons and the other spinsters while the sought-after girls danced.

She knew that it would be improper to walk out of the yard alone with a man late at night. Why, it wasn't really proper to have come this far away from the others with him! Yet she could not bear to give up this chance to be with him and hear the wonderful things he had to say. He seemed to actually be smitten with her, and it would have taken a stronger woman than she—or one far more sure of herself—to give up this opportunity.

"All right," she murmured, her pulse racing as he took her hand and led her away from the corral and barn. "But only for a little while."

"Of course."

They took the path that led toward Rock Creek. The moonlight made it easy for them to pick their way along. Some distance behind them, Jesse Tyler left the shadow of the house and followed.

Amy was grateful that Charles kept up a constant flow of conversation as they walked along, for she usually found herself without anything to say around gentlemen.

They reached the creek, whose banks were lined with trees, and Amy started to turn back, assuming that this was as far as they would go. But to her surprise, Charles led her along the bank of the creek. The moonlight filtered down through the branches, and now and then, in an open place, it sparkled on the water, a beautiful and romantic sight. They reached a grove, and Amy came to an abrupt stop. There, at the edge of the grove, was a horse and buggy, unattended. Amy stared at it in surprise.

"What in the world? Who—" Her heart began to thump, and she glanced around nervously. There must be someone else here.

"Charles, let's go," she whispered urgently.

"No. Wait. Don't be scared. This is my buggy. There's no one here."

"Yours?" Amy looked at him in blank surprise. "But what is it doing here?"

"It's a surprise." Again that beautiful white smile

flashed on his face, asking her to share in his pleasure. "I put it here because I wanted to surprise you."

"Surprise me? But I don't understand." Amy was puzzled, yet she let him pull her along to the buggy.

"You'll see." He put his hand at her elbow to help her into the buggy. When she hesitated, he murmured, "Please, don't spoil the moment, darling."

Darling! Heat rose in her face at his use of the endearment, and her stomach knotted. She knew that her mother would not approve of her doing this, but... Was it really so improper? After all, it was merely a ride in the moonlight with a gentleman. No doubt Corinne and other girls like her had done it many a time; it was just an indication of her own inexperience that she had never been asked to do it. She felt silly, yet at the same time thrilled by the loving word that had slipped from his lips, and both sensations served to drown her unease at being alone in a buggy at night with a man.

She climbed into the buggy, and they started off across the land, coming out at last on a narrow, rutted road that marked the end of her father's land on the south side. The land was lovely, bathed in moonlight, and it was breathlessly exciting to be alone with Charles, but gradually her uneasiness won out. She was sure she should not be doing this.

"Perhaps we'd better start back now," she murmured.

"In just a moment," Charles replied. "There's a place I want to show you."

The buggy rattled across the old wooden bridge spanning the creek and stopped on the small rise just beyond. It was a pretty view. Even the old sheepherder's hut below them, abandoned years before, took on a romantically ruined aspect in the pale wash of the moonlight.

Charles got down and came around to help Amy out of

the buggy, taking her arm and drawing her over to look at the view.

He turned and looked down at her seriously. "Miss McAlister, I don't know whether you are aware of the high esteem in which I hold you."

Pleased, Amy smiled, but could think of no way to answer his remark.

"I have tried to contain my feelings. I know I am unworthy of you."

Amy's heart began to beat faster. She had never received a proposal, but she had heard about several of them secondhand from Corinne and some of her friends, and this sounded suspiciously like one. However, she could hardly believe that Charles Whitaker would actually be making an offer of marriage to *her!*

"Amy—my love makes me bold to call you that—"

"It's all right," Amy reassured him softly.

Annoyance flickered in his eyes for an instant at her interruption, but was quickly gone, replaced by a look of melting love.

"Amy, my dearest, I cannot hold back my feelings any longer. I have fallen deeply, desperately, in love with you. I want you for my wife. Say you'll marry me, and you'll make me a happy man." He smiled down into her face.

Amy gazed at him in amazement and uncertainty. *She had finally had a proposal of marriage!* No one could ever again say that she had been utterly unwanted. Her heart swelled with feeling. Charles Whitaker was everything a woman could want in a man—handsome, courteous, sophisticated. It would be very easy to fall in love with him; in fact, already she thought she was halfway to that point—aflutter with nerves whenever he was around, dreamily imagining him as the hero of her stories. The only problem was...

"But I don't know you!" she blurted out.

His expectant face fell, and Amy realized how grace-less her response had been.

"I'm sorry. It's not that I don't have a—a great deal of regard for you, Mr. Whitaker. But, well, I haven't known you long. And marriage is such a major step. A lifetime, in fact." It occurred to her that she sounded deadly dull and sensible. Corinne, she knew, would have groaned at such a practical response.

Charles took her hands in his, squeezing them and saying passionately, "Love can happen in an instant! I cannot stop thinking about you, dreaming about you."

He raised her hands to his mouth and began to press his lips feverishly against them. Amy stared at him, feeling ri-diculous and embarrassed. She had imagined many times a man saying words such as this to her, and now, when it was actually happening, it sounded rather absurd.

"Mr. Whitaker, please…" Amy tugged her hands out of his grasp. "I think it's time we returned to the house."

Charles grabbed her shoulders. "Please!" he exclaimed passionately. "Tell me that you return my feelings! I burn for you!"

He jerked her to him and kissed her hard. Amy, shocked, froze for a moment, unable to move or even think. Then his tongue thrust against her lips, wet and disgusting, and she began to struggle, twisting her face away.

"No! Stop!" She wriggled and squirmed, trying to break the bond of his arms around her, but he was stronger than she. Strangely, he seemed to enjoy her struggles.

"Ah!" he said, the loverlike tone gone from his voice, replaced by a coarse quality. "Maybe this won't be such a chore after all. You might be a little interesting."

"What!" Amy went still, all the color leaving her face. "What do you mean?"

He grinned, one hand coming up to crudely encircle

her breast. "Just that there's some fire in you, after all. I think I may enjoy 'compromising' you."

Hurt and rage surged through her, and Amy brought her foot down with all her might on his instep, wishing that her dancing slippers had higher heels.

What they did have proved quite enough. Whitaker let out a howl of pain, and his arms slackened around her.

Amy tore out of his grasp and darted off.

CHAPTER TWO

WHITAKER STOOD BETWEEN Amy and the buggy, so when she ran away from him, she ran away from it, too. Instinctively she headed toward the only shelter within reach: the decaying sheepherder's hut. She knew that even though she had gotten a head start on Whitaker, he would soon catch up with her, hampered as she was by her dress and petticoats, her flimsy dancing slippers and the stays that fashionably bound her waist. Her only hope was to reach the hut before he did and somehow bar it against him.

But before she could reach the shack, Whitaker caught her. He grasped the back of her dress, pulling her to a stop. Her dress ripped, tearing down to her waist in back. Amy twisted, trying to pull loose, but she succeeded only in tearing her bodice further, so that it slid down her arms, exposing her chest, which was clad in only her chemise and stays.

Whitaker threw her to the ground, knocking the breath out of her. He dropped down to his knees, straddling her prone body, and began to rip at the laces of her stays. Amy struggled, but her arms were hampered by her fallen bodice. He grabbed the bodice, twisting it around her wrists and jerking them up above her head, immobilizing her arms.

Amy bucked and struggled impotently, sobbing, but Whitaker only leered down at her, his grin widening. She realized with horror that her movements were arousing him. She let out a scream of rage, and he slapped her, almost casually, then chuckled.

"Who do you think's going to hear you out here?"

"My father will kill you!" she spat.

"I doubt it," he retorted cheerfully. "More likely he'll insist that I marry you."

Fury surged through Amy. She hated him, and she hated herself for letting him trick her so. She redoubled her efforts to escape, twisting and kicking. Her pulse hammered in her ears, so hard that for a moment she thought the drumming she heard was merely that. Then it registered that it was hoofbeats, bearing down on them fast.

She turned her head, hope dawning on her face. A horse was thundering toward them, and a man leaned low over its neck. Amy recognized both horse and man in the bright moonlight.

"Jesse!"

A look of such dismay crossed Whitaker's face that Amy would have laughed in any other circumstances. He scrambled to his feet and started to run, but the horse was upon them now, and Jesse leaped off the horse onto him. The men tumbled onto the ground and rolled. Quickly Jesse was on top, his fists pummeling Whitaker. Amy scrambled to her feet, impatiently disentangling her torn bodice from her wrists. She stumbled toward the men.

"Jesse! No! Please! Stop! You'll kill him!" The rage drained from her at the sickening sounds of his fists thudding into flesh. She ran to Jesse and tugged at his arm.

He turned and looked up at her. His pale eyes were bright, close to madness, and Amy drew in a quick breath, almost afraid of him. Then reason returned to his face, and he was once again the Jesse she knew well. He rose to his feet, brushing back his hair with his hand. His eyes ran down her body, and then he averted his head.

Amy realized then that she was embarrassingly close to nakedness. Her bodice was completely gone, and her stays, with their laces halfway undone, sagged open, exposing her chest almost to her waist in only the thin covering of her chemise. She looked down at herself. The dark circles of her nipples showed through the thin cloth, plainly visible to Jesse, and as the breeze brushed over her naked shoulders and arms, she shivered and her nipples tightened, turning into hard little buds.

Thoroughly humiliated, Amy crossed her arms over her chest, huddling into herself, as a burning blush spread over her throat and face. Tears sprang into her eyes, and she struggled not to cry in front of Jesse, feeling that somehow that would be the final humiliation. *Whatever must he think of her?* Somehow it seemed the worst of the whole mess that she should be humiliated in front of a man who had for many years been her friend.

"I'm sorry," she mumbled miserably, tears leaking out of her eyes.

"Sorry!" Jesse exclaimed, impulsively going to her and curling his arm protectively around her shoulders. "What in the blue blazes do you have to be sorry for? That scoundrel over there's the one who ought to feel sorry, and, by God, he will by the time I get through with him."

"No!" Amy leaned against Jesse, grateful for his strength and reassurance, her hand clenching in the front of his shirt. "Please, don't do anything else. It'll only make it worse! I've created such a scandal. Oh, what will Mama and Papa say?"

She burst into sobs at the thought, and Jesse held her, murmuring soft words of sympathy and stroking her hair awkwardly. He couldn't help but be aware of Amy's nearly naked chest against his. Her breasts pressed into him, the nipples pointing, and he could feel the warmth of her skin beneath his arms. Her hair, tumbling down from its elegant roll, was sweet-smelling, and soft as satin. He could feel his own body hardening. He was a scoundrel himself to respond to her that way, he thought, when she was in such distress from the lustful pawings of another man.

But he could not help it. Holding Amy in his arms was something he had wanted to do for years, though under normal circumstances he would never have allowed himself to. He knew it was hopeless, but he had loved Amy for years—from the first moment he'd seen her, when he was fifteen and she was thirteen, and she'd come charging in like a wildcat to save him.

Jesse had been an orphan, and had made his way in the world since he was ten years old, when he went to work for a brutal man named Olen Sprague. Amy and her father had come to Sprague to purchase a horse from him, and they had arrived just as Sprague was whipping Jesse for yet another infraction. Amy, horrified, had run in between Sprague's belt and Jesse, and had commanded him to stop, her usual shyness and reserve melted by her anger. Mr. McAlister had wound up offering Jesse a job at his ranch, and they had left, without the horse for Amy, but with Jesse.

He had remained with them ever since, and had become one of Mr. McAlister's most trusted employees, breaking and training cow ponies. He held McAlister responsible for changing his life, and there was nothing he would not do for the man—or for Amy. Amy, he thought, was pure gold, clever and sweet, worth ten of her prettier sister. She was far out of the reach of most men, though, including himself. She was an innocent, a child, and it made him burn with rage to think what Charles Whitaker had tried to do to her—and made him feel ashamed of himself that he could have such a basic masculine response to the feel of her in his arms.

"Come, I'll take you back to the house," he said quickly to cover his discomfort. He looked down at her state of undress. He couldn't take her back this way. Quickly he stripped off his jacket and handed it to her. "Here, put this on."

Gratefully Amy slipped into his jacket. It looked ludicrous, of course, and its buttons started so far down that one could easily see that she had no dress on beneath it, but at least she was decently covered. She clung to Jesse, still sniffling, as he led her to his horse and helped her up onto it. Then he swung up behind her and, cradling Amy in his arms, turned the animal toward home.

Amy snuggled into Jesse's chest, grateful for his strength—and his silence. She was unbearably humiliated, and knew she could not answer any questions or face a lecture right now. Jesse, however, was comforting and uncensorious. He had long been one of the few people to whom she could talk easily; he was quiet and undemanding, the only man she knew besides her father who seemed to pay any attention to her. She often sat out on the corral fence and watched him break a horse, and it was easy to smile at him and chat with him when he took a break for a drink of water. He had even sat, his fingers busy cleaning and polishing the tack and saddles, and listened to her talk about the exciting things she discovered in books, something that even her father usually didn't have time for.

Thank God it was Jesse who had found her in that awful situation, and not someone else.

Tears started to leak from her eyes again as she thought about what had happened, but after a while they subsided. It was so comfortable leaning against Jesse. She began to feel calmer. She had been a fool, she thought wearily. She should have known that no man would truly be interested in her, as Charles Whitaker had pretended to be. She had doubtlessly mired her family in an awful scandal. Just thinking of that man's hands and mouth on her made her shudder. Jesse had rescued her from the horror of what Charles had tried to do, and she was enormously grateful to him, but that would not prevent a scandal. All she could do was pray that somehow she could keep all the people at the party from finding out what had happened.

Jesse was thinking the same thing. He hoped that if he rode quietly into the yard and left his horse by the corral, perhaps he could get Amy in the back door without anyone seeing her. Then he could find Mr. McAlister and explain to him what had happened and trust in him to hush the matter up.

Unfortunately, there was no possibility of entering the ranch house secretly. When they were still some distance from the house, Jesse caught sight of the bobbing lights of lanterns and torches all around the yard and outbuildings and even beyond.

He slowed down, wondering how he could manage to evade the well-meaning searchers, but just then a man's voice cried, "There! Miss Amy! Is that you?"

A rider moved out of the shadow of the trees and trotted toward them. It was Hank Westruther, a neighboring rancher, and the husband of one of the biggest gossips in the county. Grimly Jesse pulled up.

"Mr. Westruther, please, could you—"

He interrupted gleefully. "Miss Amy! It is you!" The man turned, waving his lantern wildly, and shouted in the direction of the house, "I've found her! Here! McAlister!"

He turned his attention back to Jesse and Amy. "You're one of Lawrence's men, aren't you? What happened?"

"Yes, sir, I'm Jesse Tyler."

"Of course. The wizard with horses." Westruther peered at Amy, who kept her face turned into Jesse's chest. "Is she all right? What happened to the girl? Don't seem like that little Amy to go wandering off like this."

"She's fine," Jesse replied, ignoring Westruther's other questions. He touched his heels to his horse's sides, urging him into a trot. The best thing he could do now was get Amy into McAlister's hands as quickly as possible.

But as they rode into the yard, people on foot and horseback seemed to converge on them from all directions. The yard was soon full of lights and people, babbling questions. McAlister and his wife came out onto the porch, their faces white and worried, followed by their daughter Corinne, who looked sulky. They stopped when they saw Jesse and Amy and stared at them. Corinne's mouth fell open.

Amy, in an agony of embarrassment, hid her face against Jesse's chest. He had to dismount and help her down, however, and when he did so, she was fully exposed to everyone in her state of deshabille—hair tumbling down to her shoulders and a man's coat over her almost bare chest.

Amy wrapped Jesse's jacket tightly around her and ducked her head. The crowd pressed in on her from all sides, and she whirled back to Jesse. "Jesse…"

"Stand back," he ordered the people around them, then swept Amy up into his arms to carry her up the steps to her parents.

"Oh, Amy!" Mrs. McAlister reached out her hand to her daughter's head. "Are you all right, honey?"

"Take her into the back parlor, Jesse," her father ordered gruffly. Mrs. McAlister followed Jesse, leaving her husband to reassure all the guests, and Corinne trotted behind her, her face alight with curiosity.

"What happened?" Corinne asked breathlessly. "Amy, what did you do?"

"Is she hurt?" Mrs. McAlister's forehead was knotted with worry. "Corinne, honey, stop asking questions and go get a wet cloth for your sister."

Corinne grimaced, but turned and went off to the kitchen. Mrs. McAlister gripped Jesse's arm, pulling him to a stop. "What happened, Jesse? Where's that Whitaker fellow? Pat Spielman said they left the house together. Did he—"

"*Nothing* happened," Jesse stated firmly. "I found them and I took care of the son—of Whitaker. I don't think he really hurt her, only scared her."

"Oh, thank God."

"I'm all right," Amy said, turning her head and looking at her mother for the first time. "I'm so sorry, Mama."

Unlike Jesse, Mrs. McAlister was not at all surprised at her daughter's apology, and she understood very well why she offered it. Tears began to pour afresh from Mrs. McAlister's eyes. "Oh, Amy! What are we going to do?"

Jesse carried Amy into the parlor and carefully set her on the sofa. Amy took his hand, reluctant to let him go. His quiet strength had been so reassuring.

"Thank you," she whispered.

"No need to thank me." He squeezed her hand.

Corinne hurried into the room, carrying a wet cloth, and handed it to her mother, who began to bathe Amy's face. She stepped back, looking down at her sister. "Everybody's been running around like chickens with their heads cut off," she announced, looking rather put out.

"I'm sorry," Amy murmured again.

Mr. McAlister came into the room and shut the door firmly behind him, turning the key in the lock. "Damned busybodies," he growled. "I wouldn't put it past that Mrs.

Bowen to come bustling in here on some excuse or other."
He strode over to the sofa and shook Jesse's hand firmly.
"Thank you, Jesse. I could never repay you for what
you've done."

Jesse looked embarrassed and shook his head. "There's
no need to thank me, sir. Anyone would have done the
same. When I saw Whitaker take her off like that, I figured he was up to no good. I'm just sorry I didn't get
after them any quicker. I had to go back and saddle my
horse. I hadn't figured on him having a horse and buggy
hidden."

"You were wonderful, Jesse," Amy told him, her eyes
glowing. She turned to her father. "Papa, you should have
seen him! He knocked that—that *man* right to the ground,
and—"

"Yes, dear," Lawrence McAlister said, interrupting her.
"I'm sure Jesse did what was necessary and proper. But
now I want you to tell me what happened. *Exactly* what
happened."

Amy blushed and swallowed, seeming to search for the
right words to say. Finally she began to talk in a hurried,
trembling voice. Jesse edged toward the door. He didn't
want to be a party to such an intimate family scene. But
he couldn't escape unnoticed; Mr. McAlister had locked
the door and pocketed the key. He retreated to a corner of
the room and leaned against the wall, crossing his arms
and doing his best to appear invisible.

Amy's voice faltered as she told of agreeing to go for a
ride with Charles Whitaker, and then dropped almost to a
whisper as she described how he had proposed to her, then
attacked her. Corinne gasped, and her eyes grew huge
as she stared at her sister. Mrs. McAlister moaned and
leaned back in her chair, as if the last ounce of strength
had been drained from her.

"What are we to do now?" Sylvia McAlister wailed. "Amy's reputation is ruined! Utterly ruined!"

"But, truly, he didn't do anything to me," Amy protested weakly. "Except for a few bruises. He didn't…well, violate me."

"Hush!" Mrs. McAlister cried. "Don't even say such a thing!" She began to cry, her hands going up to her face. "You're ruined anyway. It's almost two o'clock in the morning! To have been out at that hour with a man—and to come home looking like that, with Jesse carrying you on his horse! Well, anyone could guess what happened. Except that they'll all presume it was even worse. I don't know what we're going to do."

"Amy, how could you!" Corinne added. "What if people stop inviting us to parties? What if—"

"Well, there's nothing for it. Amy has to marry the fellow," Mr. McAlister announced heavily. "Whitaker's seen her in an indecent state of dress, he's ruined her name, he's…he's touched her in a lewd way."

Jesse stirred uneasily. *His sweet little Amy couldn't be made to marry that villain!* The whole idea was repulsive. His fists clenched as he remembered seeing the man holding Amy down on the ground, his hands moving over her.

Amy colored to the roots of her hair at the disgust on her father's face, but her agitation was greater than her embarrassment, and she leaped to her feet, her fists clenching. "No! I could not marry that man! I won't!"

"You have to," her father said wearily. "I don't like it, either. He's a blackguard. But the only thing that can save your reputation is for you to marry, and at once. Why, half the county was in the yard and saw you ride in. Hell's bells, Amy, it's you I'm thinking of. You'll be snubbed. People will gossip about you. You won't have a chance of marrying."

"I didn't, anyway," Amy replied, fighting back her panic.

"*None* of us will be able to hold up our heads," her mother went on tearfully. "What happened was bad enough, but if you don't get married, then everyone will say you're outright brazen."

"But I don't want to marry him!"

"You should have thought of that before you went out riding with Charles Whitaker at eleven o'clock at night!" Mrs. McAlister retorted. Now that she knew her daughter was safe, her former worry was rapidly turning into anger.

"I can't! I can't marry him!" Amy wailed. "Papa, you don't understand. He did it so this very thing would happen. He as good as told me so. He was trying to…to force you to make me marry him."

"Well, he was right," Mr. McAlister said grimly. "He knew that the only thing that could bring you out of this disgrace would be an immediate marriage. I know he's a cad. That's obvious. But if I pay him something, no doubt he'll be willing to give you his name and then disappear. Hopefully you won't have to be bothered by his presence."

Amy stared at her father. "But then I'll be married and have no husband!" It seemed a worse fate than being a spinster or a widow or even an outcast: to be tied legally to a man she despised, with no hope of ever finding love. It would be a kind of living death. "I can't. Please, Papa, don't ask me to do that! I'll do anything else. I'll go away somewhere, so that you all won't have to bear the stigma of what I've done. Or…or…"

Her voice trailed off miserably. She could think of nothing else she could do. No other man would want to marry her, now or ever. She would be regarded as Charles Whitaker's leavings. Her family would bear the burden of the awful scandal that had been caused by her own thoughtlessness. It was only right that she should be punished, not they. But Amy quailed at the thought of the price she would have to pay to make up for her folly. Whatever infatuation she had felt for Charles Whitaker had fled as soon as he began to kiss her. She hated and feared him, and the thought of marrying him made her feel ill.

But how else could she get out of this mess she had created? She glanced up at her father's stern countenance. He was a good man, but he abhorred the idea of any sort of blot on his family's name. He was a man who lived by a strict code of honor, and he expected everyone else to follow that code, no matter what sacrifices were involved. For once, Amy knew that she could expect no leniency from him.

She let out a long, shuddering sigh. She would have to marry Whitaker. She drew a breath to speak.

Suddenly Jesse shoved away from the wall, blurting out, "Then marry me."

CHAPTER THREE

THERE WAS A MOMENT OF stunned silence in the room. Everyone turned to stare at Jesse. Amy went white, then pink, and dropped her face into her hands.

"Are you serious?" Lawrence McAlister studied Jesse, frowning.

"Yes, sir." Jesse came toward him. "You know I wouldn't normally have asked. I'm not nearly good enough for Amy."

"Don't say that!" Amy stuck in fiercely, raising her face from her hands, eyes blazing. "You're the best man in the world!"

Jesse cast her a faint smile. "I'm glad you think so, ma'am. But your father knows as well as I do that I'm not the sort of man you should be marrying." He turned and fixed Mr. McAlister with a serious gaze. "But you can't deny that I'm a hell of a lot better than that blackguard Whitaker. Sir, you can't be easy at the thought of giving Amy to him."

"No, of course I'm not. But, Jesse, there's no reason why you should sacrifice—"

Jesse's face tightened, and he said shortly, "It's no sacrifice!"

"Well, of course, I didn't mean that marrying Amy would—" McAlister bumbled to a stop, reddening. "What I meant was, you're young, and you have your whole life in front of you. You'd be giving up the chance to find and marry a woman you love someday. There's no reason for you to do that. Why, you saved Amy!"

"I know. But the same applies to me as to Whitaker. I saw her with her dress torn off. I—I touched her." His color heightened a little as he remembered the wayward reaction of his body to touching her, and he hoped her father wouldn't guess how lascivious his own response had been. "I held her in my arms all the way back to the house. The only difference is that I didn't try to harm her."

"No. Of course not." McAlister was still somewhat stunned by Jesse's offer, but he couldn't help but feel relief. He loved his daughter, and he hated to think of her marrying a man like Whitaker. She would be safe with Jesse. He would respect her and care for her, even if he did not love her. Jesse knew Amy well, and would not be impatient with her or scornful of her odd, dreamy, bookish ways.

He glanced toward his wife, who was still staring at Jesse, openmouthed, then toward his daughter. Amy was gazing at Jesse, her face troubled. "Well, Amy, what do you say?"

She turned to him, frowning. "But, Papa…it wouldn't be fair. Jesse, it wouldn't be right!"

Jesse flushed at her words. "I know it's not. I told you that. But I don't see what else to do."

"I don't mean that nonsense about you not being good enough to marry me," Amy retorted scornfully. "I mean, it wouldn't be fair to you. *You* haven't done anything wrong. I was the one who…who was so stupid and wicked. And there's no reason why you should be punished because of what I did!"

Jesse gazed back at Amy levelly. "Sometimes you *are* foolish. Why do you insist on saying that marrying you would be punishment? Any man would be honored to be your husband."

She averted her face. "No. That's not true. I'm in disgrace. And that's not all—I'm difficult to live with. Ask anyone in my family." She gestured vaguely toward the others. "They can tell you. Half the time I don't pay attention, I've always got my nose stuck in a book, I'm not much of a housekeeper, and I don't care about cooking or clothes or…oh, all kinds of things."

Jesse grinned. "Well, now, that is too bad, 'cause I don't care much for those things, either. We just might starve."

Amy couldn't keep from smiling at his words, and she cast him a glance of amusement. "You think you're joking." She stood up and faced him, setting her face into stern lines. "The truth is, I'm not…I'm not like other people."

"Now, Amy…" protested her father with a groan.

"No, it's true, Papa, and you know it, however much you love me." She looked Jesse straight in the eye. "I'm a bookworm. I read all the time. I read poetry and novels and…and everything I can. And that's not all. I write things, too…poems and stories…" she said with the melancholy of one confessing to murder. "I can put my hair up in only one style, and my favorite dress is three years old, and I wear it because it's comfortable, not because it's pretty."

Jesse's lips twitched. "You may not believe me this, ma'am, but I count that an advantage. I don't know what I'd do with a wife who wanted new clothes all the time."

"Jesse! Stop being obtuse. You know that's not the worst of it. That's just what makes daily life with me so uncomfortable. After tonight, my reputation is in shreds.

You can't want a wife whom everyone in the county has branded a slut!"

Jesse's face hardened. "No one would call you such a thing," he retorted. "I'd like to see anyone try!"

"Well, they might not in your presence," Amy admitted candidly. "But they'd say so behind your back. People would—would ridicule you. They'd say that you had to marry me, that Papa made you. That he bought me a husband because I was such a disgrace. I would ruin your name just as surely as I've ruined mine."

"That's not true, dear," Mrs. McAlister answered, feeling on firm ground when it came to social problems. "Not if you married Mr. Tyler. Now, if you remained unmarried, it's true that it would cast a shadow over you all your life, but if you marry, why, it'll all blow over in a few months. Before you know it, everyone will have completely forgotten about it. Or at least they'll stop talking about it."

"Mama, you don't understand." Amy shot her mother a dark glance. "I can't bear for Jesse to be forced into marrying me to save my name. And for Jesse's name to be tarred with the same brush because he married me!"

"I'm not being forced," Jesse put in quietly. He looked over at Amy's father. "Sir, could I talk to Amy alone just for a moment?"

McAlister hesitated. It wouldn't be proper, of course, but, after what had happened already tonight, it seemed a minor breach of society's rules. "Well, all right, I suppose so, but only for a few minutes."

He took his wife's arm and led her out of the room, Corinne trailing reluctantly after them, and pulled the door almost completely shut. Jesse walked over to Amy and took her hand.

"Let's sit down."

Amy nodded, and they sat down side by side on the

sofa. Jesse was still holding her hand. It felt odd, she thought, to have a man's hand around hers. Jesse's hand was strong and roughened by calluses, and it completely covered hers. She thought about Jesse and the way he handled the horses, his hands patient and gentle yet strong. It made her feel warm and safe to have his hand on hers, and she remembered how pleasant it had been to lean her head against his chest.

"It could never be a burden to marry you," Jesse told her. "It would be a privilege. An honor. You must believe that. You and your father have done so much for me. You took me away from Sprague and showed me how good and kind people can be. Before that I had given up hoping, given up believing that things could be any better. Before I knew you I was nothing.... I had nothing."

"That's not true. You're very talented. Papa has said so often. Why, remember how that man from San Antonio tried to hire you away from Papa?"

Jesse shrugged. "I'm good with horses. But that's not what I'm talking about. Nobody ever considered me as a person before. But you and your pa took me in and...and were good to me. Ah, hell, ma'am, I'm no good at saying things!"

"I understand what you're saying," Amy said reflectively. "You want to marry me so you can repay your debt to Papa and me."

Jesse's mouth tightened. "You persist in looking at everything the worst possible way. I want to marry you," he said obstinately. "Why can't you just accept that?"

Amy cast a sideways glance at him, a smile touching the corners of her mouth. "Don't you agree that this desire came upon you rather suddenly?"

He couldn't tell Amy that he wanted to marry her because he loved her, that he had loved her for years. It would only make her feel bad and guilty. To Amy he was merely one of the workers, someone to whom she was kind, as she was to everyone. It was impossible that she would have any interest in him. She was too smart and educated for an ignorant cowpoke like himself. She had spent her life among fine things and people of good manners. And he was a man who had grown up hardscrabble, fighting for everything he got.

Besides, she was in love with another man. She was so infatuated with Charles Whitaker, in fact, that she had thrown caution to the winds and gone out driving with him late at night. Jesse was sure that it had hurt Amy terribly to discover that Whitaker was using her for his own ends, that he had not loved her as she had loved him and was not the sterling man she thought he was, but a fortune hunter who was willing to do anything to gain a rich wife. For that reason, she had been repelled by the idea of having to marry Whitaker, but Jesse didn't fool himself that her refusal meant she didn't still love Whitaker.

Jesse was an astute young man, however, and he'd been around Amy long enough to have some idea how to get around her. So he sighed now and stood up, moving away from her.

"All right. I won't press you. I know I'm not a proper husband for you. I was presumptuous to even ask you. It'd be absurd for a lady like you to be married to me."

"Jesse! That's not the reason at all!" Amy protested, as he had known she would, her face filled with dismay. "It's not because I'm a 'lady,' or whatever strange notion you've gotten into your head."

"It's the truth. Everyone would say we wouldn't suit. They'd talk about how you had 'married beneath you,' and you shouldn't have to put up with that. I wouldn't even have suggested it if it hadn't been for the circumstances. I thought maybe marriage to me would be preferable to the scandal and all. But likely you'll live that down after a while. No one could seriously believe you've done anything wicked. Whereas if you married me, you'd have to put up with that inequity all your life."

"How can you talk such nonsense?" Amy said fuming, her cheeks pink with indignation. "Do you really believe I'm that shallow, that snobbish?"

"You know I don't think anything bad of you. I just told you I don't blame you for not wanting to marry me."

"Jesse!" Amy frowned in frustration. "You're turning my words all around. It's not that I don't want to marry you. I don't want to marry anyone!"

"I know that, ma'am. The only thing is, you really sort of have to, don't you, or else you and your family are going to be dragged through the dirt? I know you don't want that."

Amy looked anguished. "No, I don't. It would be so awful for Corinne and Mama. Papa, too, though he'd try hard to bear up under it. But, Jesse, I can't ask you to make that sacrifice for my family!"

"I keep telling you, it's not a sacrifice. It's what I want to do. It's the only chance I've ever been given to help you and your father. Besides, it'd be my chance to have a family. I've never had that."

Amy hesitated, looking at him uncertainly. Everything Jesse said made sense. The thought of marriage was rather frightening, but it would be less so with Jesse than with anyone else she could think of. But she could not help feeling guilty at the thought of Jesse marrying her in order to save her reputation. It seemed so unfair to him!

Seeing her hesitation, Jesse went on, "I wouldn't push you, if that's what you're worrying about. I mean, I wouldn't presume to, well, exercise my—my marital rights."

He looked highly uncomfortable, and Amy blushed

scarlet at his words. She wasn't sure exactly what marital rights were, but it was something women talked about in hushed tones, which meant it was secret and rather scandalous.

"I know I shouldn't say anything like this to a lady, but, well, I don't know how else to reassure you, if that's what you're worried about. I would never try to force you like Whitaker did, just because we're married. I'd, well...I mean, I know you don't love me, and you'd feel awkward." He stumbled to a halt, unnerved by Amy's beet-red face and the anguish of embarrassment in her eyes.

"Thank you," Amy said softly. She might not know exactly what he was talking about, but she would certainly be grateful not to be subjected to the kind of pawing and kissing that Charles Whitaker had done to her—not that she could really imagine Jesse acting that way, anyway. "I— Well, all right, I will marry you. I mean, if you're still sure that that's what you want."

"Yes, ma'am." He smiled at her, suddenly looking shy. "I'm positive."

"Well. Then, I—I guess we better tell Mama and Papa."

She went to the door and looked out into the hall. Her parents and sister were huddled together at the foot of the stairs, and they turned at the sound of the parlor door opening and hurried back into the parlor. Mr. and Mrs. McAlister were obviously relieved to hear that Amy had accepted Jesse's offer, and they fell immediately to making plans.

"It will have to be soon, I'm afraid," Sylvia McAlister mused. "I'd like to wait, just to prove to everyone that she doesn't have to...but that would keep the gossip alive that much longer. Better to get it over with, and then everyone will begin to forget."

"You're right," her husband agreed. "Can you manage it in a week or two?"

"Yes. We'll keep it small. Just the family."

Amy retreated from the group, feeling lonely and cold—not at all the way a bride should feel. And her wedding wouldn't resemble the romantic occasion she had dreamed of. She could feel tears welling up inside her, and she had to struggle to hold them back. Amy turned away. She wished she could run away, wished she did not have to face all this.

But she could not do that, of course. She had already brought too much disgrace upon the family. She would simply have to endure it.

Amy glanced back over her shoulder at Jesse. He was standing, listening to her father talk. As she looked at him, he suddenly seemed a stranger to her. She did not really know him, and yet before long she would be living with him, married to him for life! It was a disturbing thought, and she turned quickly and left the room.

She started toward the stairs and the peace and safety of her own room, but before she reached the bottom stair, Corinne came after her and grabbed her by the arm and pulled her back around.

"What did you think you were doing?" she asked furiously. "Now you've ruined everything!"

"I know." Tears welled up in Amy's eyes. "I'm sorry." She and Corinne were not the good friends that some sisters were, but she hated to have her angry at her.

"People will talk about me," Corinne went on, fueled by her favorite topic—herself. "They'll wonder if I'm loose like my sister."

"Corinne!" Amy cried, stung. "I'm not! You know I'm not!"

Corinne made a dismissive gesture. "Of course not," she said disgustedly. "You would never do anything wrong. But that's what people will say. How could you have been so stupid? Did you actually believe that Charles was interested in you?"

"I—I couldn't quite believe it," Amy admitted. "But he *seemed* to be."

"Oh, for heaven's sake! I knew right away what he was. That's why I turned him down. It was me he wanted, you know. He was always hanging around. He asked me twice to marry him, but I turned him down. That's the only reason he started dangling after you."

Amy looked down at the floor, struggling not to burst into tears. Corinne was right, of course; she should have known that a man could not possibly be interested in her, especially not with a beauty like her sister around. She had been foolish to let Charles turn her head, and now her whole family would pay for her misdeed. Even though she could contain the scandal by marrying Jesse, there would still be whispers.

And Jesse would pay most of all. It seemed awful that he, innocent of any wrongdoing, should have to suffer for her foolishness. But how else could she save her family? She told herself that she would not have agreed to his proposal just to save herself the shame and scandal. She would have endured it, knowing that she deserved it. She was marrying Jesse for Mama's and Papa's sake. And Corinne's, too. Corinne had been blameless and, for once, far wiser than Amy had.

"I know," Amy admitted, her voice barely a whisper. "I was so silly and wrong. I'm sorry. Oh, I wish I could go back and do it all over. Poor Jesse!"

"Poor Jesse?" Corinne repeated scornfully. "I wouldn't waste my time feeling sorry for him. He gets to marry the rancher's daughter! He's gaining wealth and position. Why, I bet Papa even gives him some land for you all to live on. He'll make quite a profit off the deal."

Amy's head snapped up, and she glared at Corinne. "Jesse would never do it for that!" she protested fiercely.

Corinne's eyes widened with surprise at her meek sister's transformation, and she took a step backward.

"He did it to be kind, not for any thought of profit," Amy went on. "He is giving up his whole life, his chance at ever loving someone, just to save me! Just to help our family! Now, you take back what you said about him!"

"All right, all right." Corinne turned her hands out, palm up, in an exculpatory gesture, though her voice was still laced with sarcasm. "I'm sure Jesse has done no wrong."

"Well, he hasn't!" Amy thrust her chin out defiantly, and she gave her sister a look of warning. "And I don't want to hear anyone around here saying another bad word about him."

With that, Amy turned and stalked up the stairs, leaving Corinne staring after her in amazement.

CHAPTER FOUR

THE NEXT TWO WEEKS WENT by in a whirlwind of activity. Amy did not realize it, but much of the work was orchestrated by her mother with the primary purpose of keeping Amy's mind off the scandal and the approaching nuptials. Mrs. McAlister took her youngest sister's wedding dress, only seven years old, down from the attic and tailored it to fit Amy's smaller frame. She also bought two lovely bolts of material from the mercantile store in town and made Amy new dresses, declaring that she could not send her off to her husband looking like a ragamuffin.

She set the girls to washing the linens in Amy's hope chest, making sure that all of them were as fresh and neat as the day they had sewn them. When they weren't busy sewing, they were cooking or cleaning the house, for even though it was to be a small wedding, attended only by family, there would be plenty of guests, since Sylvia McAlister had been born here and had dozens of aunts, uncles and cousins. Also, a few very close friends, like the Boudreaux family, would be invited, and, of course, all the ranch hands. It added up to quite a few people, and there would be a celebration afterward. Sylvia McAlister was not about to send her elder daughter off without any ceremony, no matter what the haste. Therefore, the house must be spotless and the larder well stocked.

As Corinne had predicted, Amy's father had decided to give the young couple a piece of land as a wedding present. It was not large, but it was plenty for Jesse to break and train wild horses and sell them, which was what he wanted to do. The land had an old line shack on it at present, and Jesse and a couple of the other hands were staying there until the wedding, getting the house in suitable shape. So Amy did not see her future husband until the wedding.

She thought many times about what her marriage would be like, and was nervous, scared and excited by turns. She wondered about the wedding night, and what it was exactly that Jesse had promised not to demand of her. *Was it the same thing that happened when animals mated?* Amy couldn't quite imagine how it would work, and it made her blush to think of it.

Sylvia tried to talk to her about her marital obligations once, but she stumbled and blushed and tiptoed around the subject so much that Amy could make little sense out of it—although she assured her quickly that she understood, just to put her mother out of her misery.

Amy knew that Jesse would keep his promise, and that she did not need to be nervous or shy, but she thought that surely he would *someday* expect her to be a real wife to him. He was probably giving her time to get adjusted to the idea, to him…unless, of course, he found her so unattractive that the thought of coupling with her repelled him. Perhaps that was why he had been so quick to promise not to push her sexually. Saddened by that thought, Amy found herself hoping that he didn't really intend to keep his promise forever.

Amy might not know anything about her "marital duties," but she knew well enough that she did not want to spend the rest of her life being a sham of a bride—a wife in name only—with a husband who tolerated her just because he had to pay back a debt to her father.

Such thoughts kept her worried and on edge until the day of the wedding. She had seen Jesse only once since their wedding was announced, and that had been the day before the wedding, when he had returned from the line shack he was rebuilding for them. He had come up to see her that evening, but both of them had been awkward and had little to say to one another. Jesse had seemed like a stranger to Amy, and her stomach had knotted more tightly than ever.

The wedding ceremony was late morning the next day. Amy's mother and sister helped her into her aunt's wedding dress, and Sylvia arranged her hair into a thick roll, with little tendrils of hair escaping and curling around her face. Then she stepped back and smiled into the mirror at her daughter's image.

"You look beautiful," Sylvia assured her. "Just as a bride should. Doesn't she, Corinne?"

"Yes," Corinne responded grudgingly.

Amy looked at herself in the mirror. She thought that she did, in fact, look rather good today. So often the fussy frills and bows of fashionable dresses overwhelmed her petite figure, but the elegant simplicity of this dress, a few years out of fashion, suited her, and its creamy yellow color warmed her pale skin. Her mother's pearls, lent for the occasion, glimmered at her ears and throat, as smoothly beautiful as the satin of the dress. Her cheeks were faintly flushed, and her big brown eyes were bright with excitement. She smiled back at her image. *Would Jesse look at her and find her beautiful?* Suddenly she wanted that more than anything in the world.

Corinne and Mrs. McAlister left Amy's bedroom and swept down the staircase. Amy followed them, alone, a moment later. As she neared the bottom, Amy drew in her breath sharply. The parlor was filled with people, and at the sound of her footsteps they all turned to look at her. Amy was not used to being the center of attention, and her stomach turned to ice. She faltered on the stairs and reached out to grasp the banister to steady herself. She went down the last few steps, feeling more and more nervous with each movement.

How could there be this many people here? Her nerves multiplied the number until the waiting crowd seemed like a vast blur of unfamiliar faces. Then her eyes fell on Jesse, standing at the front of the parlor with the minister from their church. He was smiling at her, and her nerves settled a trifle. She started walking toward him. As long as she concentrated on Jesse and ignored the staring faces around her, she was all right. She didn't even look over to where her mother and father sat, suddenly afraid that looking at them would make her start to shake or, worse, to cry.

She reached the front, and Jesse took her hand. Her hands were freezing, and she knew he must feel that through her lace mitts. He squeezed her hand reassuringly, and she was grateful for the warmth and strength that seemed to course through his hand into hers. She looked up at him, and he smiled down at her, giving her a wink that somehow relaxed her.

The minister began the ceremony. Jesse's replies were strong and sure. Amy had been afraid that she would stumble over her words or forget what she was saying, but she managed to get everything out, even if it was in a rather soft voice.

Then, suddenly, it was over. The minister was smiling at her, and Jesse turned and bent to give her a brief kiss. His lips barely brushed hers, but she could feel his breath against her skin, the warmth of his flesh, and it was a strange sensation—but not unpleasant. It reminded her of the way it felt when she ran her horse—a little scary, but exciting, too.

They turned away, and Amy's parents came up to them immediately, shaking Jesse's hand and hugging her. Tears

sparkled in Mrs. McAlister's eyes, and she squeezed Amy
to her tightly before she stepped back to let her husband
and Corinne have their turns. After that, there were all the
relatives to greet, as well as the ranch hands, but for once
Amy felt too relieved to dislike the crush of people.

Afterward, they ate at trestle tables set up in the side
yard, for the day was sunny and mild, despite the fact
that it was almost November. Of course, the men got
into games of skill, as they usually did, while the women
cleaned up after the meal. The men laughingly excluded
Jesse from the riding competitions, such as racing or leaning down out of the saddle to swoop up an object from the
ground, saying that as groom he wasn't allowed to enter.
Jesse protested, saying that they were cutting him out only
because they knew he would win. But his protests were
faint, and he seemed quite happy to sit beside Amy on
the porch with the older relatives and watch the sport.

Later in the afternoon, when the games finally wound
down and the children had been put down for naps upstairs, Uncle Tyrah got out his fiddle and struck up a tune,
accompanied by another man, who pulled a harmonica
from his back pocket.

"First the bridal couple has to dance!" Amy's great-
aunt Hope called out as people began to gather around.

"Well, I reckon we'd better oblige," Jesse said, holding
out his hand to Amy and leading her into the center of
the yard, where a circle had formed to watch the bridal
couple.

Amy followed him, picking up the train of her skirt
and looping it over her arm. Her stomach was dancing
with nerves, and she hoped she wouldn't stumble or do
anything to disgrace herself. "I—I don't dance very well,"
she said in a stifled voice, keeping her eyes down.

Jesse reached out and put his hand on her waist, taking
her other hand in his. "You'll do fine."

Amy looked up into Jesse's face, warmed by his reassuring words. *How handsome he was!* She wondered why she had never noticed before. But, no, she realized, he wasn't handsome, exactly. His hair was a little too long and shaggy, and his features were a trifle too rough. He looked like a man who had seen more of life than anyone should have had to at his age, and yet…there was a certain sensitivity to his wide mouth, a kind of wary vulnerability in his eyes that refuted the wildness. He looked, not handsome, but…intriguing. Desirable.

At that thought, Amy glanced quickly away. The music started, and they began to dance. Jesse danced competently, and he kept a firm grasp on Amy's waist, guiding her without hesitation. Amy found that it was easy to follow his lead, and she looked up at him again and smiled.

He grinned back at her triumphantly, and his face lit up, his eyes taking on a twinkle and suddenly looking very green. He looked different—younger and even a little mischievous, a lurking charm overwhelming his usual tight, tough control.

A funny fluttering started inside Amy. She was very aware of her hand in his, his callused palm rough against her skin. His other hand felt very large upon her side, the fingers curling around onto her back. She could feel their heat even through the cloth of her dress. It was curiously exciting.

This man seemed like a different Jesse from the one she had known for five years. He was no longer just one of her father's employees whom she liked, but one of those vaguely frightening creatures known as eligible males, the sort of person with whom she was expected to talk and dance and around whom she was tongue-tied and stumbling. She could feel the smooth power of his muscles as he guided her around the outdoor dance floor, the leashed force of the male being, and the thought made her shiver. She wondered if Jesse had any idea of the effect he was having on her. Amy hoped not; she imagined that he would be disappointed in her if he learned that only two weeks after he'd found her in a compromising situation with one man, she was feeling these strange stirrings about another man.

Amy wondered if she was abnormal. She had heard other girls talk of love, of feeling faint or dazzled or breathless when this man or that talked to them or took their hand for a dance, but she had never heard any of them mention the odd, faintly sizzling sensations that she was experiencing right now. No one spoke of being supremely aware of a man's body close to her own, of the sinew and muscle that lay beneath the firm flesh, or of the heat of the skin. She had never heard anyone describe the hot, melting feeling growing in the pit of her stomach. And it seemed to her decidedly unladylike to be imagining Jesse's hand gliding down her back, where it now rested, and over her hips and legs.

Amy blushed at her own thoughts. *Did the things she was thinking about have anything to do with the "marital duties" Jesse had spoken of?* She suspected that they did, and she suspected, further, that Jesse would be shocked to know what she was thinking. He believed her to be pure and innocent, the sort of woman who would recoil from bedding a man she did not love. Yet here she was thinking about doing that very thing, and feeling not repulsed but excited. She knew that she must not let him know what she was thinking. When the dance ended, Jesse's arms relaxed and fell away from her slowly. Amy murmured, "Thank you," and looked up into Jesse's face. He was not smiling, and there was an odd glint in his eyes. Amy wasn't sure what it meant, but her heart began to beat a little faster.

"Thank *you*." Jesse's voice came out a trifle hoarse, and he had to clear his throat. His eyes moved over her face, and Amy wondered what he was thinking.

As the next song started, other couples broke from the circle around them and began to dance. Jesse raised his eyebrows questioningly, and Amy nodded. He took her in his arms again, and they began to waltz. Amy felt as if her feet were floating across the ground.

They danced several more dances, but then her mother pulled her away, reminding her that they'd better be on their way before it grew dark. Her father's buggy was brought up from the barn. Amy's trunk and a carpetbag were strapped to the back. The rest of their things, including furniture, had been taken over to their new home in a wagon the day before, as had their riding horses.

There was no getting away without a shivaree, a wedding custom in which the bridal couple were sent off with a maximum of noise. A couple of boys set off firecrackers, and everyone shouted out good wishes and jests, many of them bordering on the bawdy. Amy suspected that they got off lightly because she was the daughter of most of the men's boss, although sometimes the jests were enough to make women cover their ears. Cal Boudreaux's son, Joe, and two of her cousins mounted their horses and rode madly around the buggy and across the yard, firing their guns in the air and letting out rebel yells. Jesse grinned and slapped the reins across the horses' backs, letting them have their heads. Amy twisted around in her seat and looked back. Her parents and Corinne stood on the steps in front of the porch, waving.

Tears filled Amy's eyes, and an ache bloomed in her chest. She was leaving her family forever; after this, she would return only as a visitor. She waved and blew them a kiss, continuing to wave until the figures had receded into the distance and she could no longer make out anything but the shape of the house. At that point their last two pursuers pulled up and swept their hats from their heads, waving goodbye. Amy and Jesse tossed them a last salute, and Amy turned back around to face the fast-approaching sunset. Her throat felt tight with unshed tears, and a confusion of emotions tumbled inside her. She glanced over at Jesse, and he smiled at her.

Amy smiled back tremulously. *She was a married woman now, and this man was her husband.*

CHAPTER FIVE

IT WAS ALMOST TWILIGHT when Jesse and Amy reached their new home. The sun was slipping below the horizon, and the area was bathed in a golden glow. As they approached the house, Amy, who had seen the place several times in the past, looked at it with new interest. She leaned forward, and as they drew closer, she sucked in her breath sharply.

"Why, Jesse! It looks so...so different!"

He smiled, casting her an uncertain glance. "Do you like it?"

"Oh, yes! It's wonderful." Jesse had obviously replaced the bad boards and painted the whole thing a crisp, clean white. He had even added dark green shutters to the windows.

"I wanted to put on a porch in front, too," he told her, "but I didn't have time. I'll get it done before next spring, though. That way we can sit out and look at the wildflowers over there. There's a pastureful of them every spring."

"And watch the fireflies in the evening," Amy added, her lips curving upward into a smile.

"Sure."

"I can plant flowers in front of the porch. Mama'll give me cuttings from her rosebushes."

They smiled at each other in perfect agreement, the sweet pride of ownership swelling in their breasts. Though Amy had grown up in comfort, she had never really had anything of her own except for her books, and Jesse had had less than that, not even a true home. This small house with the new corral beside it was a treasure to them.

They pulled up in front of the house, and Jesse leaped down to help Amy out of the buggy. She looked at the house, then back at him. Jesse smiled at her, relieved that she liked the place. He'd worked like a demon on it the past two weeks, and he'd driven the other two men with him until they regretted agreeing to help him. He was proud of the results and already filled with love for his first home, but he had been afraid that Amy, used to the large main house of the ranch, would not like it. He had known that she would be too kind to say anything bad, yet had worried that her face would fall in disappointment. But even a sweet disposition such as Amy's would not account for the clear joy that he had read in her unguarded face as she looked at their home.

"Come on, I want to see what it's like inside," Amy said, starting forward.

"No, wait. It's bad luck." Jesse stopped her and bent to sweep her up in his arms. "I have to carry you across, or we'll have bad luck."

Amy giggled. It was strange to be held like this by a man, to have his arms around her at the knees and chest, to feel his hand there, just below her breast, and his own chest so firm and warm against her other side. She could see straight into Jesse's face. His eyes looked so green this close, and she was fascinated by the texture of his tanned skin, and the blending of blond and brown strands in his hair.

He felt her gaze and turned his head to look into her eyes. He went still, and for a moment they remained motionless, gazing at each other, aware of nothing except how close they were and every place that their bodies touched. Amy felt suddenly hot and breathless, and she wanted to move her hand from its place on Jesse's shoulder and weave her fingers into his hair. Her eyes went to his mouth, and she wondered what it would feel like if he kissed her—really kissed her, not like the respectable peck that he had placed on her lips at the end of the wedding ceremony.

Then Jesse moved, breaking their trance, and carried her through the front door. He set her down, and Amy looked around delightedly. No one would have recognized this for the line shack it had once been. It was still only one big room, of course, kitchen, bedroom and parlor all in one, but it had been transformed with loving care. The walls had been sanded and painted, and the floor, which had been merely packed earth, was now laid with pine planks, carefully varnished. There were only a few pieces of furniture, and though they was not new, they had been handpicked by Amy from the things in the McAlister attic. The big brass bed and the lyre-backed oaken washstand had been her grandmother's. The hutch and table in the kitchen area were the ones they had used when she was a child, replaced years ago by more expensive ones her mother had ordered from San Antonio. The braided rug in front of the couch came from Amy's own bedroom at home; her grandmother had given it to her when she turned sixteen. She loved everything in the room, and it made the house seem immediately her home.

"Oh, Jesse!" she breathed, her eyes shining as she turned slowly, taking it all in. "It's beautiful. It's perfect."

Jesse grinned. "You really think so?"

"Oh, yes!"

"I didn't have time to get everything done, of course, but I can get to the rest of it this winter. I thought that I could build shelves for your books along that wall behind the couch."

"Really?" Amy turned big eyes brimming with gratitude and happiness toward him. "Jesse, you are so sweet. How could I ever thank you?"

"You don't need to thank me, ma'am." He looked embarrassed. "You're my wife now. Why wouldn't I try to make you comfortable here?"

"Since I'm your wife now," Amy told him teasingly, "you might stop calling me ma'am."

"I know. I'm sorry. It slipped out. It seems so odd.... It'll take me a little while to get used to it."

"Me, too," Amy admitted. She turned back to survey the room once more, and was filled with housewifely pride and a sudden nesting instinct. "I'll need to make curtains for the windows. That's all it's lacking. And maybe braid a rug for beside the bed."

She colored faintly and turned away. Abruptly the free-and-easy camaraderie between them, the shared happiness, was gone. Amy could have kicked herself for mentioning the word *bed*.

"I, uh...I better unharness the horses and turn them out in the pasture," Jesse said stiffly, and left the house.

While he was gone, Amy spent the time exploring the house more thoroughly, opening the doors and drawers in the kitchen and bedroom areas. When Jesse returned, carrying her trunk, Amy turned, her brow knit in puzzlement.

"Jesse, where's the stove?"

He checked for an instant, then continued to carry the trunk over to the wardrobe. "Well, there isn't one, for the moment."

"There isn't one," Amy repeated blankly.

Jesse nodded. "I'm sorry. I know it's not convenient, but the line shack didn't have one, and Hansom's Store didn't, either. He had to put one on order for me. It should be in in a week or two."

"But, Jesse, what are we going to do until then? How will I cook?"

He jerked a thumb toward the fireplace at the kitchen end of the room. Amy turned and looked at it, and her eyes widened.

"The fireplace!" She turned back to Jesse, panic on her face. "But, Jesse, I don't know how to cook over an open fire!"

"Well," Jesse said reasonably, "it can't be all that hard. People did it for years before they had stoves. Mrs. Sprague still cooked that way."

"But you don't understand." Amy's voice rose in a wail.

Jesse's face tightened. "I'm sorry, Amy. I know it's not what you're used to."

Heedless of what he was saying, Amy plunged on. "You don't know what an awful cook I am! Even Ines said so, and you know how sweet she is. I was already afraid that you'd hate what I cooked for you, so I was going to start out with the two or three things that I know I can do all right, like scrambled eggs and stew and bean soup. But I don't even know how to cook *them* in a fireplace." Tears started in her eyes. "It'll be awful, and you'll be sorry you ever married me, and— Oh!" She broke off, the tears rolling out of her eyes and down her cheeks, and she looked at Jesse with such exaggerated distress that it was almost comical.

Jesse couldn't help but chuckle, relieved to find that Amy wasn't upset because cooking in the fireplace was "beneath her." "Ah, Amy…" he said, starting toward her.

"Don't you laugh at me!" She took a step backward. "It's not funny."

"Well, maybe not, but it's not a tragedy, either." He took her arms in his and gave them a gentle shake. "I don't care whether you can cook. I'm sure I've eaten worse than anything you could dish out. There've been times when I've had nothing but hardtack or jerky for days."

Amy looked at him doubtfully. "But at least it wasn't burned—or, worse, half burned and half raw."

He laughed at her expression. "Then we'll eat jerky and hardtack instead. We have a supply, you know. Or I can manage a pot of beans over the fire, I think. Besides, it's only for a little while. The stove'll come in soon enough."

"I guess you're right." Amy heaved a sigh. "But I'd hoped I could conceal my ineptitude from you for a time, at least. Now you know."

"So you aren't a good cook. It's not the end of the world. There are lots of people who can't do things that you're good at. It all evens out."

"No." Amy shook her head. "I'm not good at anything practical." She moved away and plopped down in one of the chairs by the table. "All I'm good at is reading and daydreaming."

"It's hard to get by if you can't read," Jesse said tersely. "Believe me."

Amy looked at him oddly. "Why do you say it that way?"

Jesse shrugged and turned away. "No reason. I'm just saying that you don't think enough of yourself. You're always trying to make less of yourself than you are. Imagination's a grand thing, and there are plenty of people who could use a little of it. Why, how else would all those people who write those books you like to read do it? You know a lot about all sorts of things—history and such. You've got what somebody like me will never have. I've heard you. You know dates and places, and the why and wherefore of things. That's more important than knowing how to cook, isn't it?"

"Not if you're hungry," Amy replied drily.

Jesse chuckled, shaking his head. "I forgot to mention, you know how to argue, too. I never met such a one for always having to have the last word."

"That's not true!"

Jesse cast her a speaking look, and Amy burst out laughing. "All right, point taken." She paused, looking at him, and said finally, "You really don't mind?"

"Well, I doubt I'll enjoy it. But it won't last forever. Anyway, I know you, and you're too clever to let something buffalo you. Pretty soon, you'll be cooking up a storm."

"I've never done it before."

"Ah, but this is the first time there won't be somebody there to cook something good when you ruin it." He cocked an eyebrow at her.

"Jesse Tyler! Are you saying I ruined my dishes on purpose just to get out of doing it?"

"Nope. Just saying that you never had much reason to learn before. I wouldn't think there's anything you can't learn if you put your mind to it."

Amy smiled. "Thank you. I hope you'll say the same after you've eaten a few of my meals."

"Well, at least that won't start tonight," Jesse said jovially, crossing to the front door and picking up a box there. "Before we left, Ines gave me this. Said she reckoned we wouldn't have any interest in trying to fix a meal tonight."

Amy grinned. "She was trying to save me embarrassment on my first night in our new home."

"Well, whatever, she sent us quite a spread." He set the box down on the table and began taking things out of it. "What do you think of this, Mrs. Tyler?"

Amy glanced up, startled, then smiled shyly at Jesse. It sent a funny fizzy sensation through her to hear herself called by her new married name. There was something even more tingling about hearing Jesse say the words.

"I think it looks scrumptious," she retorted. "And," she continued, leaning across the table and putting her hand on his, "I think you are the best and dearest of men, and I'm terribly, terribly lucky to have you for a husband."

He was still for a moment, his eyes gazing deeply into hers, almost as if he were searching for something there. Then he grinned in his usual way and said lightly, "Now, there is one of the few times when you aren't right. *I'm* the one who's lucky. Let's sit down and sample Ines's present."

They sat down to eat the delicious meal. Amy found it easy to be with Jesse. He made some light conversation, but he seemed just as content to be silent. Normally, when Amy sat in silence with someone, she was very aware of her inability to make conversation and felt guilty for the awkwardness, and then she became even more tongue-tied. But Jesse's easy acceptance of the quiet, perversely enough, freed Amy to talk, and she soon was chatting away about her plans for their home.

After the meal, when Jesse went out to check on the animals and Amy cleared the table and washed up, she began to think about the night ahead of her and wonder what was going to happen. Jesse had told her that he wouldn't expect anything like that from her, so tonight would not be a real "wedding night."

She cast a glance at the large brass bed in one corner of the house. Did Jesse expect them to sleep together in the same bed? There really was nowhere else *to* sleep, but, on the other hand, Amy could not imagine climbing into bed with a man and going to sleep, cocooned with him there under the blankets, with nothing between them except a few inches of air and the cotton of her nightgown. Amy drew in a shaky breath just thinking about it.

The dishes were few, and she finished them quickly.
Then Amy turned to unpacking the things from her trunk.
Keeping busy helped hold off the thought of what this
evening would bring.

After a while Jesse came in, carrying a hammer and
nails, and went over to the bedroom area, where Amy
was working. Amy glanced over her shoulder at him. She
felt awkward, being with him here, so she turned away
quickly and resumed her task, keeping an eye on him as
she worked. Jesse pounded a stout nail into the wall at
a level with the top of his head, and left it protruding an
inch or so, then tied a piece of thick twine to it. Stretching
the twine out, he curved it around the back of the large
wardrobe, making a ninety-degree angle, and up to the
side wall, where he pounded another nail into the wall
and tied the other end of the twine to it.

Amy glanced at the twine, puzzled. It formed a sort of
imaginary wall, enclosing the bedroom on the two open
sides. "What's that?" she asked. "Are you going to build
walls there?"

"Nah. I thought about it, but I figured it'd make the
bedroom too small and dark." He finished tying the twine
and stepped back to look at it. "I'm probably going to have
to tack it into the back of the wardrobe, if you don't mind.
I'll use a little nail so it won't leave much of a hole."

"That's all right. But what's it for?"

"Cloth walls," Jesse replied with a flash of a grin. "We
can hang some of those sheets and things in that trunk
your ma sent out here." He nodded his head toward the
cedar hope chest.

"Oh! I see. We can pin them up like on a clothes-
line."

"Right. Then you can have some privacy. I'll bunk
down out there." He gestured toward the living area.

"But where? On the sofa? It's too short, surely."

"You're right about that. Then I'll just spread out my bedroll on the floor."

"Oh, no! Jesse, you can't mean to sleep on the floor!"

He shrugged. "Why not? I've slept on the floor before, believe me."

"That may be, but not here—not in your own house."

"But where else am I going to sleep?" he asked reasonably. "There isn't another bed, and I prefer the floor to that couch—I hate running up against the back of it every time I turn over." He paused and looked at her. "What did you think, Amy? That I was going to break my promise to you?"

"No! No, of course not." Amy hastened to reassure him, worried that she had hurt him, that he would think she didn't trust or believe him.

"Because I won't," he went on flatly. "Ever."

"I know you wouldn't. I just didn't think about…the practicalities of the situation before. It seems so awful that you should have to sleep on the floor in your own house."

He smiled at her, and Amy thought what a warm green his eyes turned when he smiled like that, like leaves struck by the sun. "You're too softhearted. I don't mind, really. Later, when I have the time, I'll build me a truckle bed."

"All right. If you're sure." Amy went to the trunk and pulled out several sheets.

Together they hung them on the twine with clothespins. They met in the middle, and their hands happened to reach up to the line at the same time, and they brushed against each other. A little thrill ran through Amy at the contact, and she pulled her hand back self-consciously, unable to look at Jesse. She felt more than saw him turn away.

He gathered up his hammer and nails, saying stiffly, "Well, I'll take these back out to the toolshed."

Amy nodded. She suspected that he was giving her this time to undress and put on her nightgown. She was grateful to him for that. Even with the sheets up, she thought, she would have felt embarrassed at undressing in the same room with him. As soon as he closed the front door behind him, she skinned out of her clothes as fast as she could.

Jesse was gone long enough that she was able to not only undress, but wash up and go through her other nightly routines, as well. She blew out the oil lamp beside the bed and crept in under the covers. She curled up and closed her eyes. The bed was deliciously soft, and the sheets smelled faintly of lavender, but these things made little impression upon Amy. She was more aware of the tight, cold little ball of loneliness that was centered in her chest.

Sometime later she heard the door open and Jesse come in. She did not open her eyes, just lay still, listening to the soft noises he made as he laid out his blankets on the floor and rolled up in them. Somehow the sound of his presence only made Amy lonelier. She thought how pleasant and comforting it would be to have Jesse's arms around her, as he had held her that night when he rescued her from Charles. Amy could not recall ever having felt quite that safe and warm.

Did Jesse mean to keep his promise not to touch her forever? If that was his intention, then she knew that he would stick to it. Jesse was a strong person. *Or perhaps,* she thought, *it wouldn't require any strength of will on his part. Perhaps it was just that he found her too unappealing to even desire to sleep with her.*

With that thought, tears seeped out from between her lids, and she turned her face into the pillow and cried, softly, so that Jesse would not hear her.

CHAPTER SIX

JESSE PAUSED, WIPING the sweat from his brow, and looked over his shoulder at the western horizon. The sun was sinking fast, and soon the light would fade too much for him to see. It was time to quit.

Amy would have supper ready soon, anyway, and he couldn't deny his eagerness to get back inside and see her. His stomach rumbled, and he grinned to himself. It wasn't desire for food that was calling him home. If he was lucky, enough of the meal would be salvageable to fill his stomach, but with Amy's cooking, even that wasn't always a possibility.

They had been married for a little over a week now, and in that time decent meals had been few and far between. The first meal Amy had cooked, breakfast the day after their wedding, had been an unmitigated disaster, with blackened bacon, fried eggs that were raw on top and scorched on the bottom, and toast that was the color and consistency of charcoal. Even Jesse, despite a valiant effort, had been unable to eat it. They had wound up eating the leftovers from their packed supper of the night before.

Amy had finally gotten the knack of cooking eggs and bacon over the fire, and her toast now was only a little burned around the edges, making breakfast the best meal of the day. A rump roast the other evening had been charred on the outside and still raw in the center, and her vegetables usually wound up a big, gluey blob that was almost unrecognizable. Jesse still wasn't sure what the thick green mass the other night had been, though he suspected beans or peas. Her corn bread was passable, as long as he left the bottom crust stuck to the pan and ate only the top portion.

Jesse drove in a final nail, hung the hammer through his belt and climbed lithely down from his perch on the crosstimber of the barn. He strode toward the house, stretching out his tired muscles. He was working harder than he ever had, but he didn't mind it. Everything he did was for him and Amy, and that made it a joy. Once he finished getting this barn built for the protection of their horses and the hay, he would be able to start doing the work he really loved: hunting, capturing and training the wild mustangs that still roamed the range. His life, he thought, was almost perfect. He was married to the woman he loved, they had their own cozy little home, and he was doing the work he loved, the work he excelled at. It couldn't have been better—except for the fact that he couldn't sleep with his wife.

The frustration was eating him alive. He had sworn not to make love to his wife, thinking that he could live like that. After all, he had loved Amy for years, had seen her often at the ranch, and he had managed to keep his desire and love for her in check, hiding it from everyone.

But he was finding out how different a situation it was, actually living in the house with Amy, sitting across from her at every meal, seeing her when he awoke and at night before he went to sleep, talking and laughing with her, sharing thoughts with her. His love for her seemed to grow with each passing day, and his promise became harder and harder to keep.

He was coming to know all her different expressions—

the bemused, vague look she turned on him when his voice pulled her away from the book she was reading, the flashing anger that made her eyes huge and glowing when she talked about some wrong, the way her eyes brimmed with merriment and her mouth twitched upward when she was amused. He was learning her thoughts and dreams, discovering the fascinating breadth of her imagination. He had heard that familiarity bred contempt, but in him it was drawing forth a deeper, stronger love—and an equally strong desire. The more he knew Amy, the more he wanted her.

Yet he could not have her. He was sworn to keep his hands off her, and if he broke that promise, if he tried to seduce her, to kiss and caress her into giving in to him, then she would lose faith in him. Once her trust in him was gone, he would have no chance of winning her love. The only hope he had with Amy was to give her time to get over her love for Charles Whitaker, and then maybe, just maybe, she would come to return *his* love. He knew how to be patient; he used that skill every time he broke and trained a horse. He knew how to coax and wait, how to take his gains in small increments.

He also knew how badly a mistake could ruin the whole careful plan and make a horse skittish again, setting him back. That was why he had to move so carefully with Amy, why he had to stick to his promise until *she* urged him to break it. Unfortunately, maintaining that promise was the hardest thing he'd ever had to do. Sometimes he thought that he would rather put up with ten Olen Spragues than have to live like a eunuch with the woman he loved.

Jesse reached the house and went inside. It was warm and scented with the smell of a wood fire. There was also a charred odor, one with which he had grown quite familiar the past few days. Jesse stopped, and his eyes went warily to the fireplace. Well, at least there was no food actually in flames, as the sausages had been last Thursday.

He strode over to the fireplace, picked up the hot pad lying there and pulled out the spider skillet. Lifting the lid, he found several pork chops. They were barely brown on the top, but Jesse had learned not to be fooled by that. He grabbed a fork from the table and lifted one of them from the skillet. It came up slowly, sticking to the hot metal, and when he got it turned over he saw that the bottom was almost black. Shaking his head, he turned the other two, covered the pan again and set it back at the edge of the fireplace. The other pot was causing the smell. In it were four small, blackened, roundish objects; he wasn't sure what they were, but they had obviously gone long past the point of being cooked.

Jesse set the pan down on the counter and turned, looking for Amy. As he had expected, she was curled up in the comfortable chair in the corner of the room beside the window. In one hand she held a meat fork, in the other, a book, tilted to catch the last dying rays of the sun. Her lower lip was caught between her teeth, and her eyes were darting back and forth, devouring the lines. She whipped the page over and started avidly down the next one.

Jesse had to grin. It was impossible for him to get angry with Amy. She looked so sweet and intent, so amusingly lost to the world. Sometimes he felt as if he had married a sprite or a fairy, blissfully disconnected from the concerns of other human beings because she was attached to another world, one in which mere men like him could never enter.

"Amy…" he began. Then, he cleared his throat and said, in a much louder voice, "Amy!"

She jumped, her eyes flying up from the book to where he stood. "Jesse!"

A delighted smile broke across her face, and whatever fragments of irritation he felt with her quickly flew away. "Good afternoon, Mrs. Tyler." The term of address was the closest he allowed himself to come to an endearment. It carried for him the warm, even titillating knowledge that she belonged to him now.

Amy uncurled her legs and stood up. "I didn't hear you come in. I was reading my favorite book, and I was at the very best part." She paused and sniffed the air. "What's that smell?"

He said nothing, only raised his brows, and Amy wailed, "Have I burned dinner again?"

She dropped her book and raced toward the fireplace, but Jesse caught her by the shoulders. "It's all right. I already turned the pork chops, and I took the, uh, the other things off the fire."

"The other things?" Amy looked at him blankly, and then her eyes widened in horror. "You mean the potatoes?"

"Is that what they were?" An amused grin tilted up the corners of Jesse's mouth.

"Yes! Where are they?" He gestured toward the counter, and she went over to them. When she saw them, her hands flew to her cheeks, and she cried, "Jesse! They're ruined!"

She turned to him, her eyes filling with tears. "I've done it again! I am so sorry."

"It could happen to anyone," he replied soothingly.

Amy's lips twitched with disgust. "No, it couldn't, and you know it. Honestly, Jesse, I'm such a mess! I'm the most awful wife, and you are always so sweet and kind about it. I feel terrible!"

"Would you rather I growled at you or banged on the table?" he inquired politely, his eyes lighting with amusement. "I suppose I could manage to work up a tantrum or two."

Amy managed a small, watery smile. "Sometimes I almost wish that you would. I feel so guilty—you're so good to me, and I'm managing wretchedly. Oh, Jesse! You must regret marrying me!" Tears began to spill over out of her eyes.

"Never!" Jesse retorted fiercely, reaching out to grasp her shoulders. At his touch, she gave way to her tears and threw herself against his chest, crying.

"You don't even know the worst," she told him, sobbing. "I—I finished the curtains this afternoon, and they're horrid! I ruined them!"

"Sweetheart…" Jesse uttered the endearment without thinking as he curled his arms around her. She felt so good in his arms that he almost let out a sigh of pure pleasure. Amy was warm and pliant against him. He could feel the soft pressure of her body all the way up and down his, and it sent an enticing, sensual thrill through him. Jesse ached to help her, to comfort and reassure her. Yet he ached just as much to squeeze her closer to him and let his hands run free over her body.

But he knew that she trusted him, and so he could not do what he wanted. It would be taking advantage of her weakness and her unhappiness, it would be going back on his word to her. And no matter how painful it might be at times to keep his promise, he was determined to do so.

So Jesse contented himself with laying his cheek against her soft hair and breathing in the delicious scent of it as he cuddled her body against his. He hoped that Amy was too naive to notice or that the clothing between

them was thick enough to hide the instinctive reaction of
his body from holding her this close.

Amy's tears stopped, and she let out a little sigh, snug-
gling closer. That little movement almost undid Jesse's
resolve, expressing as it did Amy's enjoyment of being
held by him. Jesse wondered if she might feel some bit
of desire for him, too. Could she sometimes feel lonely in
that bed by herself at night and wish that their marriage
was of a different kind?

He could not let himself believe it. It was just his wish-
ful thinking, his own willful longings, that made him
impute his desires to Amy. Amy was too sweet and naive,
too innocent, to think of such things. He remembered how
disgusted and angry she had been when Charles Whitaker started mauling her that night—and she had been in
love with him. How much less would she welcome the
advances of a man she didn't even love!

Jesse forced himself to loosen his arms around her and
move back a little. Amy, too, stepped back and raised her
face to look up at him. Tears glistened on her pale cheeks
and swam in her eyes, making them huge and luminous.
Her mouth was soft and almost trembling, deliciously
pink and moist; it seemed to call out to be kissed. Instinctively he began to lower his face toward hers, but then he
caught himself. Drawing in a harsh breath, he released
her completely and moved away.

"Uh...well, why don't you show the curtains to me?
They couldn't be that bad."

Amy hesitated, then said in a muted voice, "All
right."

She went listlessly to her bedroom, which was still
roped off by sheets, and returned a moment later, two
pieces of material in her hands. Mutely she held them
out to Jesse, and he took them.

"Why, they look fine to me," he told her heartily, and carried them over to the window. The material was attractive, and the two sides looked to be the same length; his fear had been that one was longer than the other. "Look," he said cheerfully as he held them up on either side of the window. "Oh."

Now he could see the problem. Both sides might be the same, but they were too short. The curtains ended, ludicrously, a good two inches higher than the windowsill. He looked back at Amy, who was standing watching him, her arms folded across her chest. He hoped she wouldn't start crying again. He could think of nothing to say to make her feel any better about the curtains.

To his surprise, a smile twitched across Amy's face, and she had to bring up her hands to cover a laugh. Her eyes twinkled merrily above her hands, and suddenly she couldn't hold it in anymore. She began to laugh. "Oh, Jesse! I—I'm sorry." She tried to swallow her laughter and regain a sober expression, but it was a losing battle from the start, and she once again burst into giggles. "But that look on your face!"

She gave way to her laughter, and Jesse couldn't keep from joining in. The curtains were, after all, absurd. So, for that matter, were the potatoes she'd cooked. He laughed harder, thinking of all the silly mistakes she'd made over the past week and how hard-pressed he'd been not to laugh at most of them. Now he released the amusement he had so valiantly held in—and, with it, much of the tension that had strung his nerves taut. The more he laughed, the more Amy laughed, too, until finally their sides were aching from their merriment.

His laughter slowed, then stopped as Jesse released a sigh and leaned against the wall, recovering his breath.

Amy flopped down onto a chair, holding her sides. She wiped her eyes and looked at him.

"I didn't know being married would be this much fun," Amy confessed naively.

Suddenly, as hard and fast as a fist to the gut, desire slammed through Jesse. He wanted to charge across the room and pull Amy to her feet and kiss her again and again, so deep and hard that they melted into one another. He clenched his teeth together hard to keep back the words that threatened to tumble from his mouth, words of love and yearning and hot, youthful passion.

"Do you really not mind the things I do?" Amy went on.

Jesse levered himself away from the wall. "No, I don't mind." His voice came out hoarsely. He jammed his hands in his pockets and turned aside, clearing his throat. "Amy, I didn't marry you to get a cook or a seamstress. I've told you before."

"But why? What do you get out of it? I mean, I got my reputation saved. I can sit around and read and let the dinner burn, and you don't mind. But what do you get?"

"I get you," he answered honestly.

Amy blinked. "But that's not much."

"It's all I want."

Realizing how much he had revealed, Jesse swung around. "Come on," he said brusquely. "Enough of this. Let's see if there's anything we can save out of those potatoes."

Amy watched him, frowning, as he crossed the room to the ruined potatoes. She looked as if she would like to question him further, but in the end she said nothing, just followed him to the table.

They scooped out the centers of the burned potatoes

and ate the half-burned pork chops. Jesse said little. He was aware of Amy studying him curiously from time to time, but he couldn't bring himself to meet her eyes. He wondered what she was thinking, and whether she had guessed his feelings from what he had said. He cursed his wayward tongue.

Later, after they had eaten, Amy cleared off the table and washed the dishes. Jesse watched her, thinking it must be a sign of how badly he was smitten that he enjoyed so much watching Amy do even a simple thing like washing dishes. It was knowing that she did it for him, that she was his wife, in his home, that made his loins turn hot. He thought about going up to Amy and slipping his arms around her waist, bending down to nuzzle the bare back of her neck. He thought about sliding his hands up her torso to her breasts and cupping them possessively. He could imagine their soft, warm weight through the cotton of her dress, the hard prickling of her nipples as he touched them.

Jesse knew he was insane to do this to himself. He should leave and let his senses calm down. He should force his mind onto something else. But he could not. Instead, his imagination rolled onward, picturing how he would take her in his arms and kiss her, how he would lift her up and carry her to this very table and lay her down upon it, shoving up her skirts and letting his hands roam her legs…

"Jesse? Are you all right?"

"What?" He came back to reality with a crash. Amy was standing at the counter, staring. "I—I'm sorry. I didn't hear you. I was daydreaming."

"It must have been an odd daydream," Amy commented. "You looked as if you were in pain."

"No, I— Really, it was nothing. Just foolishness. Now, what were you saying?"

"I was asking you if you'd mind reading to me while I worked. Corinne and I used to do that sometimes. It made the work go faster."

Jesse went cold inside; her words were as effective in cooling him down as a bucket of ice water in his face. "Read?" he repeated blankly. "Read what?"

"I don't know. Whatever you want to. Why don't you pick out a book from one of the boxes?"

"Uh..." Jesse stood up, glancing from Amy to the boxes of books stacked in the corner. "If you don't mind, I have some chores I need to finish outside. I really should do them first."

"In the dark?"

"I'll take a lantern."

"Oh. All right, if that's what you want." Amy looked disappointed, but she went back to her work without any complaint.

Jesse hurriedly left the room. He went to the corral and looked at the horses, resting his arms on the upper rail. He tried to think of some chore to do out here. At least it would make his words a little less of a lie. He hated lying to Amy, who was so trusting and sweet.

But he hadn't known what else to say. And he couldn't tell her the truth. It would be too humiliating. Not that Amy would say anything unkind. But he could imagine the dismay that would leap into her eyes, quickly followed by pity. And he could not bear to see her look at him like that.

THE FOLLOWING SATURDAY, Amy and Jesse rode into town to get their stove, stopping at the McAlisters' ranch house to borrow their wagon. The McAlisters greeted

Amy with hugs and cries of glee. It was less than two weeks since they had seen her, but somehow the fact of her marriage made it seem as if it had been longer.

They picked up their supplies in town, and Jesse and the store clerk loaded the small but heavy stove into the back of the wagon while Amy watched them, fairly bubbling with excitement over their new purchase.

Afterward, as Jesse started to help her into the wagon, Amy said, "No, wait. We have to go to the post office and pick up Papa's mail. I promised him that we would."

"All right." They walked across the street, and Jesse got Mr. McAlister's mail.

As he returned, Amy asked eagerly, "Is the *Hancock's Quarterly* there? It has a continuing story I've been reading."

"I don't know. Here, you look for it." Jesse handed her the stack of mail.

"Why, silly," Amy said with a smile, "it's right here on top. See?" She pointed to the cover of the magazine on the top of the stack.

"Oh," Jesse said shortly, glancing at the periodical. "I—I guess I didn't look at the name."

Amy gave him an odd look, but she said nothing, just walked with him out to the wagon and climbed in. But inside, her brain was busily whirring. It was hard to see how Jesse could have missed seeing the name on that magazine. It was written in huge letters across the top of the cover. She thought back to the way he had left the house so abruptly the other night after she asked him to read aloud while she finished the dishes. It had seemed odd that he had such urgent chores to do, when up until then he had been sitting around, obviously enjoying the opportunity to relax after a hard day's work. She remembered, too, the time when he had been reminding her of her abilities and accomplishments, and reading had been the first thing he mentioned. Could it possibly be that Jesse could not read?

But he had signed his name on their wedding certificate. She had seen him do it. How could he write if he couldn't read? That didn't make any sense. Amy told herself that she must be wrong, and yet she could not quite get rid of her suspicions. She thought about it on the way home, and she soon concocted a plan.

That night after supper, she asked casually, "Jesse, would you help me take some of these books out of the boxes? I'm looking for something."

"Sure." He rose with alacrity and walked over to the boxes. Squatting down beside one, he opened it and began to pull out books.

"Why don't you look in that box?" Amy suggested, kneeling in front of another box. "I'll look in this one. I'm looking for *Gulliver's Travels.*"

Jesse's hands stilled. He pulled another two handfuls of books out and said slowly, "Why don't I take them out, and you look for the book? That'll be quicker."

He set the books down beside Amy and delved into the box again, avoiding her eyes. Thoughtful, Amy shuffled through the books he had given her. Then she suddenly held one out in front of Jesse, saying, "Why, look what I found!"

He gazed at the book blankly. "Yes. I see. The book you wanted."

"No," Amy said, watching him carefully. "It's not *Gulliver's Travels.* It's a book of poetry."

"Oh." A dull flush mounted in Jesse's cheeks. He turned away. "Do you want me to keep on looking, then?"

"No, I don't. I never wanted the book."

He glanced at her in surprise. "Then why the hell—"

"I just wanted to see something. You can't read, can you?"

Jesse's eyes flashed, and he rose quickly to his feet. "That's why you asked me to help you? It was a trick?"

"Yes, I guess it was," Amy admitted, rising. "I suspected you couldn't, but you didn't tell me, so I thought I could find out if I—"

"Congratulations!" Jesse snapped. He looked so furious that Amy stepped back involuntarily. "You proved it. I can't read. I can't write. Now you know. You married a fool who doesn't know anything but horses!"

Jesse whirled around and strode out of the house, slamming the door behind him.

CHAPTER SEVEN

"JESSE! JESSE, WAIT!" Amy cried, running after him. She caught up to him near the corral and grabbed his arm. "Jesse, I'm sorry. Please, wait, listen to me."

He stopped and swung around. His face was dark with anger, and he snapped, "What?"

"I'm sorry," Amy went on breathlessly. "Please believe me, I didn't mean to upset you. I—I shouldn't have done that. Mama always said I was far too inquisitive for a lady. I'm sorry."

"Stop apologizing. It's not your fault," he responded tightly. "You didn't do anything wrong. Anyone would be shocked to find that a grown man can't read or write."

"I wasn't shocked," Amy protested. "There are lots of grown men who can't read or write. Why, old Herman, for one, and Sam Dougherty, and I bet lots of other hands that I never even knew about."

"Yeah, but you didn't make the mistake of marrying one of them."

"Mistake? Why do you say that? Just because you can't read?"

"Just?" he repeated sarcastically. "Maybe not, if you were some poor nester's daughter, or a washerwoman. But you— My God, Amy! You're the smartest person I've ever met, man or woman. Why, your dad swears that you've read all the books in his library twice over, and some of them a lot more than that. How are you going to feel sometime when we're around other people,

people like your family, and somebody realizes that I can't read?"

Amy shrugged. "I don't know. I haven't thought about it."

"Well, I'll tell you. You'll be humiliated. It's not right. I—I used to watch you sometimes, sitting out on your front porch, reading.…"

"You did?" Amy looked at him, surprised.

"Yes. I saw how you devoured those books. I've seen you writing in your pad, too."

Amy colored. "Well, yes, sometimes I do. I— Mama says it's foolish."

"It's not foolish. It's wonderful. But don't you see? How can you bear to have a dumb lump of a husband like me? I don't even know what you're talking about half the time."

"Well, how could you, if you've never read the books?"

"That's what I mean! I don't know anything."

"Don't talk that way!" Amy retorted fiercely, reaching out to grab his hand and squeeze it tightly between her own. "You know lots and lots! There's nobody around here who knows horses like you do."

Jesse snorted derisively, but Amy pressed on. "Well, that's a lot more useful knowledge than some of the things I know, like…like when the Battle of Hastings was, or Marco Polo's trade route to the Orient. There are lots and lots of things that I can't do, but you don't hold me in contempt for them. You saw how my curtains turned out, and you know how terrible my cooking is. I could never build a barn, the way you're doing. Why, I hardly know how to hammer a nail. I wish I could do it, but nobody ever thought it was a fit thing to teach a girl. But that doesn't make me a dummy or a fool, any more than it makes you one for not being able to read. I would never, *never* feel humiliated because you are my husband."

Jesse gazed at her, his brows drawn together in puzzlement. He lifted his forefinger and trailed it softly down her cheek. "You're something special. It truly doesn't bother you that I can't read?"

"No. Why should it?" Amy smiled up at him. "Am I forgiven now? Will you come back inside with me?"

"Of course. I wasn't angry with you. It was with me. With life."

Amy linked her arm through Jesse's, and they started back to the house. "Tell me something—why can't you read?"

Jesse shrugged. "'Cause I never learned. I didn't go to school. My ma couldn't read, either, and she didn't see the sense in it. Besides, she always needed me at home to help her, so she didn't send me. And after she died, I had to make my way in the world. I didn't have time to go to school, and anyway, I was getting too old."

"How were you able to sign your name on our marriage certificate? That made me think I must be wrong about you not being able to read."

Jesse grinned shamefacedly. "Oh, that. I knew I was going to have to sign it, and I didn't want you to see that I couldn't write. So I had one of the other hands teach me how to write my name. He wrote it down for me, and I practiced it over and over until I could do it. That's all."

Amy remembered the slow, careful way Jesse had made his signature. She had thought he was taking his time because it was an important thing. "Oh. I see."

They reached the house and went inside. Amy went over to the boxes and piled the books back in. Jesse began to help her. Amy turned to him impulsively and laid her hand on his arm.

"I truly am sorry about what I did. I didn't mean to

hurt you. I didn't realize why you wouldn't tell me, or how much it meant to you. So many people think reading and history and things like that are pretty useless knowledge."

"It's all right." He smiled at her. "You didn't do anything wrong."

"Jesse…would you like to learn to read? I was thinking that I could teach you."

He glanced at her sharply. "No, that's too much trouble for you."

"How can that be trouble? I love books—you just told me that yourself. It would be fun for me."

"Teaching me my ABCs?" He looked skeptical.

"Yes. That's something that I *am* good at, something I can help you with. And it would make me happy. You've been so good and patient with me, it's the least I could do for you. And with you, I don't think it'd be boring at all."

Something flashed in Jesse's eyes, and a thrill ran through Amy. She thought about sitting beside Jesse every night and working with him. It didn't sound dull to her.

"But I'm too old to learn it now."

"Why? You're not senile yet, are you?"

He shrugged. "I don't know. It just seems foolish. It would take so long, and there are so many things I need to do. It'd waste a lot of time."

"Reading is *not* a waste of time," Amy told him severely. "Besides, I was thinking I could help you more with the outside chores. I mean, all I do now is feed the chickens and cook and keep the house clean. Keeping this place clean is hardly anything, it's so small. Now, with the stove, cooking's going to be a lot easier, too. Anyway, it doesn't take up all my time, either. The fact is, I don't have enough to do. I'm being lazy."

"That's all right."

"Not while you're working yourself into the ground, it's not. I bet there are lots of things I could do to help you, and that way you'd have time to spare for learning. I could even help you build the barn. You could show me how to do some things—I'd really like to learn!—and I could help you. Hold things in place while you nail them down, maybe, or fetch and carry for you, at least. Please?"

Amy folded her hands in an exaggeratedly prayerful attitude, and Jesse had to chuckle. "Sure, you can help me if you want."

"And you'll let me help you with reading?"

Confusion flitted across his face. Finally he said, "Amy, what if I can't? What if I really am stupid, like Sprague said?"

"Jesse Tyler." Amy put her hands on her hips and gave him an exasperated look. "You are *not* stupid. Tell me something—who do you think knows more, me or Olen Sprague?"

Jesse chuckled. "What a question! You, of course."

"Then why do you persist in believing him over me? I'll tell you why." She shook her forefinger sternly at him. "Because you're flat scared of something you don't know. You know the way to get over something you're scared of is to just do it. So you *have* to let me teach you."

"I never knew what a bossy woman I was marrying," Jesse marveled, grinning.

"Well, you did marry me, and now you're stuck with me."

His grin broadened. "I don't mind."

Amy felt suddenly breathless. Jesse's eyes were so warm when he looked at her, and the way his mouth curved upward did strange things to her stomach. She wished he would lean over and kiss her. She wanted to feel his mouth against hers, to taste his lips.

She looked away, confused and embarrassed, and

Jesse stood up. The moment was over. "All right," he said, reaching down a hand to pull her to her feet. "We might as well get started...teacher."

OVER THE COURSE OF THE next few weeks, Amy and Jesse were always together. During the day she helped him build the barn, and in the evenings they worked on Jesse's reading. Amy felt that neither of those occupations could really be called work. Though the carpentry was sometimes tiring, she found it fun and intriguing, as well. She caught on quickly for she did not find it boring, unlike most of her house chores. Jesse's praise of her ability made her smile and flush with pleasure.

To her amazement, she found that her other skills even began to improve. The new stove was a vast help with her cooking, and now that she had chores outside to help with, she had less time to spend on the cooking, and consequently she cooked the meal all at once, remaining at the stove the whole time, instead of getting distracted by a book and forgetting what she was doing. She began to realize that Jesse was right; she wasn't incompetent in all practical matters.

Another thing Amy discovered she could do well was teach. Jesse was learning how to read by leaps and bounds. She taught him the alphabet quickly, and after that she rode over to her parents' house one day to retrieve a small trunk full of her old schoolbooks. They started on the primer, chuckling a little over the childishness of the book. Amy found herself looking forward all day to teaching Jesse his lessons in the evening. She enjoyed helping him. She enjoyed watching his earnest concentration. Quite frankly, she liked simply sitting beside him or watching his hand move across the paper.

She loved his hands. They were strong and slender, callused yet capable of gentleness. She found herself looking at his hands often as they worked together, and she could not keep from thinking wild, crazy things about his touching her. It was embarrassing, even though, of course, Jesse had no idea what she was thinking.

At first Jesse was embarrassed to be seen struggling over the simple words, but after a time, when Amy was neither impatient nor scornful of his efforts, he shed most of his embarrassment and concentrated on his studies. He worked his way steadily through the primer, and as he conquered each new word or sentence, Amy was as proud of his success as he was.

When Jesse read the last sentence of the last page of the primer, he closed the book with a snap and turned to smile triumphantly at Amy, who was seated beside him at the kitchen table.

Amy let out a squeal. "You did it! I knew you could!"

Without thinking, she leaned across the few inches that separated them and hugged him enthusiastically. Jesse froze for an instant, and then his arms clamped around her like steel bands and his mouth came down, seeking hers.

His kiss startled Amy, and she let out a little squeak of surprise. But then the feel of Jesse's mouth against hers drove out all other thoughts and feelings. His lips were pliant, but insistent and determined, pressing deeper and deeper into hers. Their velvet pressure threw Amy's insides into turmoil, opening her up to wild, chaotic yet delightful sensations.

Jesse's tongue slid delicately along the joining line of her lips, and Amy drew in a startled breath. He seized the opportunity, thrusting his tongue between her lips and into her mouth, his own lips pressing hers open for him. Amy remembered that Charles Whitaker had tried to do the same thing, but it felt incredibly different when

Jesse did it. It wasn't scary, it was exciting. Amy shivered and leaned into him, giving herself up to the delightful exploration of his tongue.

With a groan, Jesse pulled Amy out of her chair and into his lap, cradling her tightly against his chest. One of his arms was around her shoulders, pressing her to him, and the other drifted lower, his hand sliding down her back and over the curve of her buttock. Heat blossomed between Amy's legs, growing as Jesse kissed her again and again. His skin was feverishly warm and his breath came out in a hot shudder against her cheek. The evidence of his response to her excited her almost as much as his mouth on hers. Amy had never experienced this sort of heat within herself before, this odd feeling of ripeness, as though she were loosening and opening to him. Her breasts seemed swollen and heavy, aching, and she wanted Jesse to touch them. It was a scandalous thought, she supposed, but at the moment she didn't care. She wanted to stretch and purr on his lap like a cat and have him stroke her all over.

She shifted on his lap, bracing her hands on his shoulders, and Jesse went still. He lifted his head, and his hands fell away from her. Amy looked up at him, her eyes wide with surprise and confusion. *Why was he stopping?*

"Jesse?" she began uneasily.

"Oh, God." He looked appalled. "No. No. I'm sorry. Oh, Amy, I didn't mean to—"

He jumped to his feet, setting her away from him hastily. "Please, Amy, I—I don't know what happened. But I swear, I'll be more careful next time. I won't let it happen again."

She gazed at him blankly, seeing disgust, even horror, in his eyes. *What had she done wrong?* Panic-stricken, she couldn't think what to say or do.

"I'm sorry," he said again, stiffly. "I—I'll leave you alone now."

He turned on his heel and strode quickly out the door. Amy stood for a long moment, gazing at the blank door. Everything had happened so fast that it left her stunned. She turned and walked blindly into the bedroom area, seeking the illusive protection of the cloth walls. She sat down on the bed and thought about what had happened. *Why had Jesse stopped kissing her so abruptly? Why had he left?*

Obviously he didn't want any passion between them. When he had made her that promise, she had thought that he was doing it for her sake, so that she would feel at ease until she got to know him better. Now she began to wonder if he had not meant it for his sake, as well. Perhaps Jesse had no interest in making love to her, now or ever. Maybe he found her uninteresting. Unattractive.

But if that was true, Amy couldn't understand why he had kissed her. She had leaned over to hug him in her enthusiasm, but Jesse had kissed her. He had pulled her right out of her chair and onto his lap. She remembered the sound of his labored breathing, the searing touch of his skin. *Surely those things betokened desire, not indifference.* He had wanted her. She didn't think she could be that wrong about what had transpired.

She tried to remember exactly when he had broken off their kiss. It had been when she squirmed in his lap, restlessly seeking satisfaction for the fiery ache within her, and her hands clamped onto his shoulders.

Amy frowned, thinking. Jesse had stopped when she responded to him, not just letting him take her lips, but actively urging him on with her body. She remembered her mother talking once about Mabel Holloway and how she was always chasing the boys. "Men don't like an aggressive female," Mrs. McAlister had declared, casting an admonishing eye toward Corinne. "You mark my words. She'll have trouble ever getting a husband. I heard she went out in the garden alone with Henry Smithson at the Patterson dance last month—and was gone for ten minutes. Well, she'll get a reputation acting that way, I can tell you."

And even Corinne, who had grimaced at her mother's remark, had once said something similar to her. "Men like a chase," Corinne had told her, explaining why she had turned down Geoffrey Ames for a dance, even though she had one open on her dance card. "You can't let a fellow know that you like him, or he loses interest."

It had sounded rather strange to Amy at the time, for it seemed to her that a man ought to be pleased and reassured to know that a woman he was interested in was interested in him, too. But now, thinking about the way Jesse had just acted, she wondered if Corinne and her mother were right. Maybe men didn't want a woman to be too eager.

It was obviously terribly important to a man that a woman be pure; that was why her driving out with Charles that night had ruined her. Perhaps a man even wanted his wife to be so pure-minded that she did not want to touch him or to rub herself against him as Amy had just done.

Jesse must have been appalled at her wantonness. That was why there had been disgust in his eyes. He had thought her too bold, too forward. Maybe he even thought she would respond like that to any man. After all, only a few weeks ago, she had driven out with Charles Whitaker at night, which no lady should have done. Jesse might think that she had acted the same way with Charles as she had with him. He wouldn't know that she had never felt for Charles Whitaker the kind of passion she felt for him. Jesse couldn't know how much she loved him.

Amy sat bolt upright. *Where had that thought come from? She loved Jesse Tyler?*

But of course, she realized, a tiny smile playing at her lips. It was obvious: she loved him. She had probably loved him for a long time and not realized it. Love was not the silly infatuation she had had for Charles Whitaker for a time. That had simply been her overactive imagination. Love was the emotion inside her now, this sweet, aching yearning. Love was wanting to be around Jesse all the time. It was enjoying talking to him and laughing with him. It was the quiet, certain knowledge of Jesse and what he would do, the faith and trust she had in him.

She wasn't sure when it had happened, if love for Jesse had grown from being married to him or if it had been inside her earlier, hidden and waiting to reveal itself. The important thing was that she did love him.

Amy slid off the bed, about to run out and find Jesse and tell him. She would explain that she loved him, that she wanted to be a real wife to him, that she had never really loved Charles Whitaker.

But she stopped herself before she reached the front door. There was that boldness again, that impulsiveness that always got her into trouble. She seemed to have difficulty acting in a proper, maidenly way. However, this time she had to make herself do what she should. Jesse and her marriage were too important for her to make a mistake.

Amy turned and walked back into the bedroom and sat down once again on her bed to think. She realized that she should not boldly announce her love and her intention to have a real marriage. For one thing, Jesse would no doubt be appalled at this further demonstration of her forwardness. Secondly, he did not return her love. He had married her merely to pay back the debt of gratitude that he owed her and her father. Therefore, Amy realized, she must conceal her own feelings, while at the same time getting Jesse to fall in love with her. For him to feel right about it, he must pursue her.

She almost started crying at that thought. It seemed hopeless. She had never been the kind of girl men fell in love with. Jesse probably thought of her as a sort of sister.

Well, perhaps not exactly as a sister. A wicked grin touched her lips. He hadn't kissed her as if she were his sister tonight. He did feel desire for her. She could not be mistaken about that. What she needed to do was to entice and attract him, to encourage that passion, so that he would start to kiss her again and want to share her bed. Then, surely, when they were truly husband and wife, he would grow to love her.

The trick, she knew, would be in enticing him without appearing bold or sluttish. Her actions must appear entirely innocent. It seemed impossible. But Amy was a smart girl with a fertile imagination, and as she got undressed and crawled into bed to go to sleep, her brain was buzzing with schemes.

She embarked on her plan first thing the next morning. First, she knew, she must follow her sister's advice and look as alluring as she could. She spent much more time than usual over her hair, finally getting it pinned into a full, soft style that flattered her face. Next she pulled out one of the new dresses that Corinne had insisted enhanced her coloring. The final touch was a spot of rose water behind her ears and on her wrists. Then she walked out of the little bedroom to face Jesse, her color high with excitement.

Jesse was putting wood in the new stove, and he swiveled around at the sound of her approach. His expression was uncertain, and he wiped his hands down his trouser legs nervously. "Amy."

Amy smiled brilliantly at him. "Hello, Jesse."

Jesse blinked in surprise, but he smiled back and returned to laying the fire. Amy walked over to the stove and bent down beside him to peer into the firebox. He glanced at her, his eyes traveling over her body, then hastily turned back to finish his job.

Over the next few days, Amy did her best to subtly entice her husband. Every evening as they worked together on Jesse's reading, she leaned close to him on the pretext of looking at his book. When she refilled his glass at dinner, she made sure her hand or arm brushed his. Once, in the evening, she came out of the bedroom pretending to remember that she had to tell Jesse something. She was careful to forget her dressing gown, so that she was clad only in her lace-trimmed white nightgown. Of course, it was hardly revealing, being high-necked and long-sleeved and made of cotton, but at least it flowed down along the lines of her body, without all the petticoats and undergarments that a lady wore under her dresses.

Seeing the way Jesse's eyes flickered down her body and the way he rose from his bed on the floor, almost as if drawn up by force, Amy was certain that her attire had had the effect she desired. She deliberately walked up to him, gazing into his face. He reached out to touch her hair, which was flowing loosely over her shoulders, then snatched his hand back and clasped his hands behind his back. Amy could almost feel the heat from his body, and she could see the tension in his face, the involuntary slackening of his lips, and a triumphant satisfaction rose up in her. Her doubts were resolved. She had been right; he *did* want her, no matter how much he tried to hide or deny it.

After that night, she had the courage to take her sensual teasing to a new level. In the past she had waited modestly each evening for Jesse to make his nightly trip around the yard before she went into her bedroom area and undressed. But the next night, instead of waiting for him to leave, she bid him a pleasant good-night, picked up her kerosene lamp and sailed into the bedroom, leaving Jesse gazing after her.

She set the lamp down on the night table and began to unpin her hair. Though the sheets hung around the room ostensibly gave her privacy, Amy was aware that with the light of her lamp behind them, the sheets were almost transparent. Though the image would not be clear, Jesse would be able to see her every move. She brushed out her hair and began to undress, her ears cocked for the sound of the front door opening and closing. It didn't come, and Amy smiled to herself, knowing that Jesse must be watching her.

It was embarrassing to know that he could see her pull off her skirt and blouse, then her undergarments, until finally she was completely nude, and she blushed as she did it. But it was exciting at the same time, and she felt a delicious thrill at the thought of Jesse watching her.

However, much to her disappointment, it seemed as though all her efforts were doomed to failure. Jesse did not try to kiss her, did not even make a move toward her. If anything, he began to avoid her company. Amy suspected that if not for their lessons, she would hardly have seen him at all. Sadly she began to wonder if, instead of luring him into loving her, she was actually driving him away!

She would give it a few more days, she thought, and then, if Jesse still had made no move toward her, she would give up and let things return to the way they had been.

CHAPTER EIGHT

JESSE DUNKED HIS HEAD and chest under the pump spout outside. The water was bitterly cold, and he shivered, but he grimly continued to wash off. It helped to cool him down, which, heaven knew, he needed before he went into the house and saw Amy. The pain seemed an apt punishment for the sins he usually contemplated when he was with her.

Jesse wasn't sure how much longer he could last. It seemed as if nowadays all he could think about was making love to Amy. He knew it would be disastrous if he did, that he would be breaking every vow he had made to her, that he would be letting his lust destroy their marriage. But it was reaching the point where the need was so strong in him that he almost didn't care about the consequences, as long as he could finally satisfy the craving that was rampant in him.

Ever since that night when he had kissed her, his life had been a living hell of desire. He had managed to pull himself together then and get out, to quell the hunger that was raging in him, and he had sworn that after that he would keep a firmer hold over his passions. But no matter how hard he tried, the yearning in him only grew worse. Amy seemed prettier and more desirable every day. He knew it must be only his hunger that made it appear so, but everything Amy did now seemed full of sexual allure. Now it seemed as if she accidentally brushed against him frequently, as if she leaned in closer to look at his schoolwork, tantalizingly warm and smelling of roses, as if when she smiled at him her eyes were warm with sensual promise.

Worst of all had been the one night she had gone into her bedroom to undress before he left the house. He had been surprised, but he supposed he must have been late in going, and she had gotten tired of waiting. He knew that she did not realize how her lamp turned the barrier of the white sheets translucent, making all her movements visible to him. She had undressed and put on her nightgown, and he had stood and watched. He had known guiltily that he should go, that he was invading her privacy, that he was only making his own situation more untenable. But he had been unable to tear himself away. Every night now he waited for her to go into the bedroom and innocently undress before his gaze. He hated himself for doing it, yet he could not make himself leave. Every night he vowed that this night would be different, but it never was. No matter how much he reviled himself for it inwardly, he could not walk out the door.

Shivering, Jesse blotted his chest and arms dry with a towel and pulled his shirt back on. He buttoned it quickly and grabbed his jacket from the hitching post, where he had hung it while he washed up. He cast a last look toward the barn. They had finished it days ago, and now the horses were safe inside its shelter. Every time Jesse looked at it, he was filled with pride.

He strode across the yard and into the house, bracing himself mentally against the desire that always flooded him when he saw his wife. Amy turned and smiled at him as he stepped inside. She was prettily flushed from the heat of the stove, and little tendrils of hair had escaped her bun and were curling softly around her face. Even knowing how he always reacted to her, Jesse was amazed by the desire that slammed into his gut.

They ate supper. Though Amy's meals were much improved since the arrival of the stove, Jesse hardly tasted
his food. He was too aware of Amy's presence, desire
already tightening his loins just from looking at her and
listening to her voice.

Afterward they got out the books and worked at the
table. Jesse tried to lose himself in the work, but he
found it almost impossible to concentrate with the scent
of Amy's perfume tickling his nostrils. She laid her hand
on his arm while she explained a word to him, and his
skin burned where she had touched it.

Finally they finished their lesson and Jesse put away
the books. Amy picked up the kerosene lamp and turned
to go into the bedroom area. Jesse watched her, knowing
that he should leave. He stood up, but he did not move
toward the door. His breathing accelerated, and his flesh
tingled in anticipation. He gripped the back of his chair,
his eyes remaining on Amy's form, visible through the
sheets.

She set the lamp down on the nightstand and began to
unpin her hair. Jesse's loins tightened. He knew what was
coming, and that made it somehow even more exciting.
Her hair tumbled down slowly. Then she picked up her
brush and began to brush through it in long, even strokes.
Watching her dark form, he could almost feel her hair
sliding through the brush, could almost hear the crackle
of electricity.

When she finally set down the brush, her fingers went
to the buttons of her bodice, and she undid them slowly,
then peeled the bodice off. She folded it neatly, put it
away, and began on her skirt. Soon it drifted down over
her hips and along her petticoats, pooling at last at her
feet. Jesse watched as she bent to pick it up. He wished
he could see her in detail, not just this dark figure against

the sheets. He wanted to see the tones of her skin, each individual feature of her face and body.

Slowly, one by one, she took off her petticoats. With each movement, Jesse's skin flamed hotter, until he felt as if he were on fire. His hands clenched tightly around the posts of the chair, his knuckles white with tension. Amy reached down and removed her shoes, then rolled down each stocking, her hands gliding along her legs. Jesse swallowed hard as her fingers went next to the ribbons of her chemise. She untied them and pulled the chemise off, and he could see the globes of her breasts swing free, high and firm, swaying with her movements. Heat flooded his loins, and his manhood swelled, pressing against his trousers.

Jesse wanted her so much he thought it might kill him. He could think of nothing but her, the beauty of her body and the sweet wonder of taking her. She untied her pantaloons and pulled them down, revealing her soft feminine shape entirely. Jesse was on fire, hard and throbbing. She reached for her nightgown. He began to walk to the bedroom.

He knew he should stop, should go back, but tonight he could not bring himself to listen to reason. He was drawn to her in a way that surpassed all reason, all thought. There was nothing in him right now but need. Jesse reached out his hand and took the edge of one sheet, pulling it aside.

Amy jumped, gasping, and instinctively jerked the nightgown in her hand up to her torso, partially concealing her nakedness. "Jesse!"

She stared at him, her eyes wide and startled, yet luminous. His eyes went down to her mouth, soft and pink, then farther down, to her bare shoulders and arms, above the nightgown crumpled to her chest. Her skin was just as satiny as he had known it would be, a lovely creamy white. His eyes moved down the line of her hips and legs. She was perfectly formed.

Hunger pulsed in him. He wanted to snatch away the gown and reveal all her body to him. He wanted to lay her down on the bed and crawl on top of her, to sink into her delicious softness.

"Oh, God, Amy…" He closed his eyes. He thought he might explode. "Please…I want you."

Amy stared at Jesse's tortured face. Her heart twisted within her. As much as she wanted him, as much as she had tried to get him to desire her, she had never intended that he feel the kind of pain that was in his eyes now.

"Jesse." Tears clogged her voice. She didn't know what to say. It occurred to her that she had done nothing but bring misery to this man whom she loved so much.

"I'm sorry," he went on hoarsely. "I know I promised you, and I meant it. I— But, Lord, when I see you, I—I don't think I can keep from making love to you."

Amy forgot about concealing her boldness, about pretending that she did not feel the wanton desire that blossomed inside her. She could not think about the consequences, or about how Jesse's feelings for her might change if he knew how she really felt. All she could see was Jesse and his anguish. All she could think of was easing it.

"Then don't try to," she said, dropping her nightgown to the floor.

Jesse blinked, unable to believe his ears or eyes. He stared at Amy's naked body—slender and feminine, inviting. Blood roared in his head and coursed through his body. *Amy was giving herself to him.*

He started toward her. He half expected her to back away from him or blurt out that she didn't mean it or even suddenly run away. But she did not. She simply stood, watching him with wide eyes.

There was something a little frightening about Jesse, Amy thought. Power and heat radiated from him intimidatingly, and there was something more—a wildness barely held in check. But that very wildness was exciting, too. It was a heady feeling to know that she had the ability to arouse him to such overwhelming desire.

Jesse stopped only inches from her. Carefully he put his hands on her shoulders. His fingers seared her skin. He gazed down into her eyes, his face taut, his eyes blazing bright green. Slowly he bent and sealed her mouth with his. Heat flamed up instantly in Amy, and she moved into him, her arms going around his waist. It was strange and rather titillating to feel his clothes against her naked flesh. Amy moved against him, provoking a deep groan from Jesse, and her nipples hardened as they rubbed against the cloth of his shirt.

His kiss was hungry and deep, and his hands slid over Amy's body, as though he wanted to touch her everywhere at once. His tongue plunged deep into her mouth, and his fingers dug into her buttocks, lifting her up into him. The denim cloth of his trousers was rough upon her skin, and under it she could feel the hard insistence of his desire. She shivered, trembling with need for him.

"I'm sorry," he murmured, releasing her. "You're cold." He pulled down the bedspread and picked her up and settled her in the deep feather mattress. He reached down and jerked off his boots, then began to unbutton his shirt.

Amy was a trifle chilled, but she didn't pull the cover up over her. She liked the way Jesse gazed at her all the time he was undressing, as if he could not get his fill of looking at her body. He peeled his shirt back off his shoulders and down his arms; when it stuck at the still-buttoned cuffs, he swore and yanked at it. Amy heard the buttons pop off and bounce across the floor. He unfastened his belt buckle and started on the metal buttons of his trousers, but then he broke off, as if he could not hold back a moment longer, and bent to kiss her thoroughly, his hands plunging into her hair. He pulled away and continued to undress, his eyes eating her up all the while.

Finally he finished and stood naked in front of her. Amy gazed at him in love and wonder. He was lean and ridged with muscle, his skin smooth and tanned. Amy longed to reach out and run her hand along the washboardlike expanse of ribs and muscles. It was like satin laid over rock. Her eyes drifted lower, to his flat abdomen and the naked, thrusting maleness riding between his legs. She drew in a shuddering breath.

"Oh, Jesse, how can—? Do you think it'll work?"

Her naive remark drew a chuckle from him, despite the passion now tearing at his vitals. He climbed into the bed and lay down beside her, saying, "I'm not sure, sweetheart. I've never actually tried it. But I presume it must, given all the children that are produced."

"Do you mean—?" Amy sat up, amazement stamped on her face, and she gazed down intently into his face. "Are you saying that you've never—?"

He shook his head, smiling faintly. "No. Disappointed?"

"No! I—" She began to smile. "It's rather nice, actually, to know that you haven't—that no other woman has…well, you know."

"Yes, I know." He stroked his knuckles down her cheek. "I feel the same about you."

"It's just, well, I suppose it would be better if one of us knew what they were doing."

His grin grew broader, and he curved his hand around her neck, pulling her down toward him. "I think we'll muddle through well enough."

Amy melted into him, delighting in the feel of his

naked chest against hers. Their mouths met and clung, and the heat that had abated slightly while Jesse undressed flared up with renewed force. Jesse rolled over, taking Amy under him. They kissed deeply, tongues entwining.

Jesse pulled his mouth free and rained kisses over her face and down her neck, murmuring, "Sweet, so sweet. I'm glad I have never lain with another woman. I want to learn every pleasure with you. I want every flicker of your desire to be for me."

"It is," she assured him, her hands sweeping down his back and buttocks onto his hair-roughened thighs.

His mouth moved lower, onto the soft curve of her breast, and Amy drew in her breath sharply.

His head came up, and he frowned in concern. "Did I hurt you?"

"No! Oh, no. Please...keep on."

She moved a little beneath him, urging him on, and he quickly returned to what he had been doing. His mouth trailed across her breast, and his hand came up to cup it. Her nipple hardened at the soft, moist touch of his mouth, and Jesse stroked his thumb across the little bud, watching in fascination as it tightened even more. He teased the nipple with his thumb and forefinger, gently squeezing and caressing it until Amy's breath was ragged and she was rolling her head restlessly from side to side, eyes closed against the sweet, almost painful pleasure. Jesse looked at her face, drinking in the passion there, and then, at last, he lowered his head and took her nipple into his mouth. Amy let out a shuddering moan as he began to suck, enveloping her sensitive nipple with moist heat as his mouth pulled gently at it.

Amy had never experienced anything like the hot tremors of sensation that ran through her now. Passion blossomed in her abdomen, turning it waxen and heavy.

Heat throbbed between her legs, where she suddenly, embarrassingly, flooded with moisture. She clamped her legs together to ease the sensation, but it wasn't enough; it wasn't what she wanted.

But Jesse seemed to know exactly what she wanted. His hand slid down her smooth stomach and abdomen and into the tangle of curls there. His movement startled her, but she reacted instinctively, opening her legs. His finger slipped down between her legs, delving into the slick, satiny folds of flesh. Amy groaned and moved her legs restlessly.

Jesse lifted his head and looked down into her face as his fingers explored her; the desire on her face excited him almost past bearing. He leaned down and teased her other nipple into hot, pulsing life with his tongue, while his fingers searched her soft secret flesh, delving into her heat, until she was panting and writhing with passion.

"Please, Jesse, please," Amy murmured.

Jesse moved quickly between her legs, lifting her buttocks and probing gently, his shaft instinctively seeking its home. He pushed into her, feeling her tighten at the pain. He wanted to stop, to not hurt her, but he was past that point now. He thrust into her, quick and hard, and she gasped, but now he was deep inside her, gloved by her sweet, tight femininity. Jesse groaned and took a long, slow breath, fighting the desire that threatened to swamp him. He had never felt anything so pleasurable, so good. It was as if he had found his home. His life.

He pulled back and plunged more deeply, sending waves of pleasure through them both. He tried to move slowly, but the pleasure was too intense, the passion too strong. It swept him along, making him move faster and faster. Amy was moving beneath him, panting, her fingers digging into his back. Her desire multiplied his, driving him higher and higher, until finally Amy convulsed around him, letting out a noise of surprised pleasure. Feeling her passionate release ignited his own, and Jesse cried out, releasing his seed into her and sweeping them both into a dark, mindless whirl of pleasure.

Finally Jesse rolled off her, curling his arm around her and cradling her head on his shoulder. They lay together silently, dazed by the storm of pleasure they had just experienced. Jesse turned his head to look into Amy's eyes. She smiled shyly at him, suddenly a little embarrassed by what she had just done. *Would he think her loose now? Overly bold?* But he had enjoyed it; innocent as she was, Amy could not believe that she was mistaken about his response. Jesse had been in the grip of passion, and surely he would not blame her for feeling the same way. She remembered the words of desire he had spoken, the endearments he had murmured as he kissed and caressed her. Why, he had called her "sweetheart" and "love"! Hope fluttered in her chest.

Jesse smoothed a finger down Amy's cheek. "You are so beautiful," he murmured. "Even more beautiful than I imagined."

Amy blushed and had to look away, thrilled by his words. "Thank you." Her voice was barely audible.

"Thank *you*." He kissed the top of her head. "You gave me a glimpse into heaven tonight."

"Jesse! That's blasphemous!" But she had to giggle, warmed by his words. She hesitated, then went on, "Did you really...enjoy it? Was it what you wanted?"

"Couldn't you tell? Of course it was what I wanted. It was everything I have ever dreamed of."

"I'm glad." She looked at him with glowing eyes. "I was afraid you might be disappointed with me."

"Don't be absurd." He brought her hand up and placed a kiss on the back and then on the palm. "You're everything any man could want." He spoke slowly, punctuating every word with a kiss on one of her fingertips.

He was quiet for a moment, and then he went on in a constrained voice. "What about you? Were you...content? I hope I didn't hurt you."

She shook her head, her hair brushing across his skin. "No. Only a little. And after the hurt, it was so wonderful." Amy blushed furiously. "I didn't know what to expect, what I would feel, but I never dreamed it would be like that."

Jesse smiled and twisted down to kiss her lips. Then he lay back with a sigh of contentment. He gazed up at the ceiling, idly twisting a strand of Amy's hair around his finger. Finally he asked softly, "Why did you—do that this evening? Why did you drop your nightgown and invite me in?"

"Oh. Were you upset with me?"

"For that? Good God, no, why would I be upset with you for giving me what I wanted?"

"I mean, because I so bold. I didn't act much like a lady. But you looked so unhappy—I never meant to make you unhappy."

"You made love with me because I looked unhappy? Because you felt sorry for me?"

"No. I didn't say I made love with you because you were unhappy. I already wanted to do that. I said I *dropped the gown* tonight because I couldn't bear to go on hurting you. Before then, I really hadn't thought about whether I was causing you pain—you know, with the things I was doing."

"Things you were doing?" he repeated, realization dawning in his voice. "You mean you did that on purpose?" Jesse sat straight up and gazed down at her in shock. "Undressing in here with the lamp on? You meant for me to see that every night?"

Amy glanced at him uncertainly. "Yes. And the other things, like sitting too close to you while you studied and wearing rose water all the time."

"My God." Jesse rubbed his hands over his face. "I can't believe this. All that time you were *trying* to get me to break down? You *wanted* to seduce me?"

"I'm sorry." Amy's voice trembled, and she bit her underlip. "Oh, please, Jesse, don't be mad. I didn't realize that it would upset you so. I just wanted you to love me, and I didn't want you to think I was too bold. Mama and Corinne told me how men like to pursue a woman. I saw how you looked that time after we kissed, and you were so disgusted with me. When you said that it would never happen again, I didn't want you to think I was loose and terrible. So I figured if I made all those things seem innocent, then maybe you wouldn't be repulsed."

"Repulsed!" He shoved his hands back into his hair. "I must be going mad. I was not repulsed by you. I never have been—I don't think I could be. I didn't sleep with you because I had promised you I wouldn't! I couldn't break my vow! And how could I try to seduce you, knowing that you loved another man?"

Amy frowned, looking puzzled. "Ano— Oh! You mean Charles Whitaker?"

"Yes. Charles Whitaker," he agreed grimly. "Unless there's someone else that you love lurking around."

"Only you," Amy replied simply. "I never loved Charles. I was infatuated with him for a time, but I never really loved him."

But Jesse seemed to have heard only the first part of her statement. "Only me?" he repeated in a dazed voice. "Are you saying that you love me?"

"Of course! That's what I've been talking about. That's why I was trying to trick you into desiring me. The night we kissed, I realized that I loved you. I thought if I could make you want me, then maybe that desire would grow into love. I wanted you to love me. I wanted to be truly your wife. I wanted to have you kiss me again and touch me and—make love to me."

Jesse groaned comically and flopped back onto the bed. He began to laugh, and Amy stared at him. "Oh, Amy, Amy...what a pair of fools we are! You didn't have to seduce me into loving you. I already loved you! Why do you think I offered to marry you? Why do you think I never slept with any of the whores in town? I went there with the other hands, but when I got into a room with the girl, I looked at her and knew I couldn't—because she wasn't you. You were the only one I wanted. I've loved you for years, almost from the first moment I saw you."

"Me?" Amy asked in disbelief. "You love me?"

"Yes!" He rolled onto his side, bracing his head on his bent arm. "Yes, I love you." He leaned over and began to kiss her lightly all over her face and neck, saying, "I love you, I love you, I love you."

Amy laughed out loud and threw her arms around his neck. "Oh, Jesse, how can we have been so foolish?" She smiled brilliantly up at him.

Jesse bent to kiss her again, but he stopped abruptly. Amy frowned up at him, puzzled. "What is it? What's the matter?"

"I don't know. I thought—I thought I heard something." He turned his head, listening. Suddenly his body went taut. "The horses! I did hear something."

He got up and went over to the window, pulling aside the curtain and peering out into the night. "I don't see anything...."

With an uneasy expression he turned back to her. "I better check."

"What is it?" Amy sat up, clutching the sheet to her naked bosom, his sudden odd mood infecting her, too.

"I'm not sure." Jesse quickly pulled on his trousers and shoved his feet into his boots. He grabbed his shirt from the floor, where he had dropped it earlier, and headed for the door.

Alarmed, Amy got out of bed and began to put on her clothes, too. She heard Jesse open the door, and then she heard a loud, abrupt oath from him, and he exclaimed, "The barn's on fire."

"On fire!" Amy ran to the window, and now she could see what Jesse had not been able to earlier: flames were licking up from the back of the barn, eerie and orange against the night sky.

She saw Jesse run across the yard toward the barn. She knew he would first run to save his horses. But then he would return to fight the fire, she knew, and her mind busily spun ahead to what she should do to help him.

Quickly she thrust her feet into her shoes, not bothering to tie them, and ran from the room. She finished buttoning her dress as best she could as she hurried into the kitchen and began pulling out her largest tubs and pots, as well as the pails in which she carried water and feed for the chickens. She carried them out to the pump outside.

The horses thundered out of the barn past her, terrified by the fire. She knew Jesse had released the horses from their stalls and he would be here in a moment to grab the pots of water. She pumped as hard as she could, filling up the two pails and then starting on the largest tub.

She realized that Jesse should have gotten one of the pails by now, and fear clutched at her heart. She straightened and looked toward the barn. There was no sign of Jesse. Her fear deepened. She picked up the pails and began to walk to the barn, expecting at any moment to see him come running toward her to take the pails.

He did not.

Amy's heart began to thunder in her chest, and she set
down the pails and ran to the barn. Just as she reached
the barn door, a figure came out of the darkened corral,
stretching out an arm toward her. Amy shrieked and
jumped, startled.

"Shh... Don't be afraid. It's me."

Amy stared through the darkness at the man, only a
few feet away from her. "Charles?" she asked in aston-
ishment. "What in the world are you doing here?" Then
she shook her head; there was no time for explanations.
"Come on and help me. Jesse's still in the barn."

She started forward again, and he grabbed her arm,
pulling her to a halt and turning her around. "No,
don't!"

"What? Let go of me." She twisted, but he clung to her
tightly.

"Don't go in there! You'll ruin everything. Besides,
you can't save him. He's out cold."

"Out cold! Why? What do you mean?" Amy went icy
inside, too scared to move.

"I hit him. I had to. He discovered me."

Amy glanced toward the barn, now blazing brightly.
She could feel the heat from its flames. "You mean you
set this? And then you hit Jesse and left him to die in
there?"

He nodded. "I had to. I told him I'd get back at him.
No one can get away with treating Charles Whitaker like
that."

"Let go of me!" Amy began to struggle wildly, released
from her momentary paralysis.

"No, wait!" He grabbed her with both hands, holding
on tightly even though she kicked and swung and twisted,
fighting to get away from him. "Don't! Think— Once he's
gone, you won't have a cowhand for a husband. You and
I can be married. You wouldn't have turned me down if

you'd known that you'd have to marry your father's horse trainer instead. You deserve better than that. Leave him alone, and we—"

"Are you insane!" Amy brought her heel down hard on his instep and twisted away with all the strength she possessed, driven by fear. At last she was able to tear free from him. She ran straight into the burning barn, screaming, "Jesse! Jesse!"

"Amy, no!" Whitaker came after her, trying to pull her back.

Amy grabbed the closest thing she could find, a shovel that was leaning against the barn wall, and she whirled around, slamming it into Whitaker. She connected solidly with his head and shoulders, and he crumpled to the floor. Amy dropped the shovel and ran deeper into the barn, calling Jesse's name.

Smoke roiled through the barn, blinding her and making her cough. The heat was intense. High above her head, flames licked at the rafters of the barn. But Amy thought of none of it, only of Jesse and the fact that she could not let him die. She screamed his name over and over as she made her way toward the back of the barn, peering through the smoke.

Her foot hit something soft, and there was a groan. "Jesse!"

She sank down on her knees beside him, coughing from the smoke, and shook his arm. "Jesse! Jesse, wake up! We have to get out of here."

He stirred and mumbled, coughing, but he didn't open his eyes. Grimly Amy shoved her arms under his shoulders and locked them across his chest. She pulled and tugged frantically, but she could budge him only inches. Tears streamed down her face, and she repeated his name over and over, begging him to wake up, to help her. She pulled, straining every muscle, digging in her heels, and slowly she moved his body. Inch by precious inch they moved across the floor, and all the while the flames licked over the rafters, sending down sparks and waves of heat.

Finally Jesse groaned, and his eyes fluttered open.

"Jesse!" Amy exclaimed in relief and collapsed beside him. "Get up! Help me! Come on."

His eyes rolled, and for an awful instant she thought he had lost consciousness again, but then he groaned and rolled over, coughing, and began to try to rise. Jesse made it up to his hands and knees, and Amy put her shoulder under his arm, lifting with all her strength.

He staggered to his feet and, with him leaning woozily against her, they stumbled and weaved toward the barn door. It was an agonizingly slow journey, and Amy's heart was in her mouth with each step as the rafters groaned above them. Then, at last, they were free of the barn and sucking in the fresh air of the outdoors. They collapsed against the corral fence, coughing.

"What—what happened?" Jesse gasped.

"Charles Whitaker tried to kill you." Quickly Amy related what had happened.

"You mean—" Jesse looked back at the barn. Flames licked across the roof and up the walls. A rafter crashed, engulfing the rear of the barn in flames. "You mean Whitaker's in there?"

"Yes." Amy, too, looked at the barn, frowning with worry. Charles was a low human being, but she hated to think of him burning to death in the inferno he had created.

Jesse sighed and started back to the barn.

"No! Jesse! You might get killed, too! He's not worth it."

He smiled at her, but shook off her restraining hand. "I can't just let a man burn to death."

Jesse loped into the barn, and Amy waited in breathless suspense. Moments later, Jesse reemerged, dragging Charles Whitaker. A great groan sounded from the barn, and the central beam broke and crashed in flames to the ground. The barn roof collapsed, sending flames leaping and sparks shooting out.

Jesse stood looking at the barn for a long moment, then sighed and turned away. "We better tie this fellow up. I'll take him in to the sheriff tomorrow. This time I'm not letting him get away."

As soon as they had tied Whitaker up, Jesse and Amy raced to water down the area around the barn. Although the barn itself was beyond help, they had to keep the fire from spreading to the corral and the grass beyond. They soaked the corral fences nearest the barn, as well as the ground around it for several feet.

By the time they finished, they were tired and sore, but they saw with satisfaction that the fire was not spreading. Amy turned from the grim sight of the barn burning to the ground and looked down at Jesse. He reached up and wiped a smudge of soot from her cheek, and then he smiled tenderly into her eyes.

"You saved my life." His voice was soft, almost wondering.

"Of course. I love you. I couldn't let you die."

Any lingering doubts he had had about her love melted away. She had risked her own life to save his.

Amy looked back at the barn, and her eyes flooded with tears. "Oh, Jesse. I'm so sorry. All your hard work…"

Jesse glanced at the rubble of the barn, then turned back to Amy. "I can rebuild a barn. What's important is that I have you. You're my wife, in every way, and that's all that matters to me. We can do anything together."

Amy threw her arms around his neck and went up on

tiptoe to brush her lips against his. "Oh, Jesse, I love you so."

"And I love you, Mrs. Tyler." His arms tightened around her, and he kissed her deeply. "I love you."

* * * * *

SEDUCED
BY STARLIGHT

Charlotte Featherstone

Acknowledgments

Special thanks for this incredible opportunity
to be part of this anthology goes to Tara Parsons
and Margo Lipschultz of the HQN Books team
and also to Tracy Martin for editing this novella.
And to Susan Swinwood, because she's the
best editor a neurotic writer could ever have!
I can't tell you how thrilled I am to make
my debut with HQN Books with this anthology,
and with these characters. Thank you.

Dedication

To all the readers who wrote asking for more of the
Addicted world, I hope this satisfies, and gives you a
glimpse of how passionate and happy Lindsay and
Anais, and Jane and Wallingford's lives are.
It truly was so much fun to revisit their world
and watch their children fall in love.

To the most excellent kitties
at the Pussycat Parlor—Beth, Cyn, Amy, Stephanie,
Holly, Kelly, Alycia, Cheryl, Cherra, Dhes, Rach,
Maureen, Tracy and Heidi! Your friendship is
everything, and your exuberance for life, passion and
love most inspiring. I treasure the stories, the laughs
and the support and all those naughty pictures in
the Wet Man Thread—you really know how to
get the muse moving! I dedicate this book to you!

PROLOGUE

March 1874
Bewdley, Worcestershire, England

THE LATE WINTER SNOWSTORM had come and gone, leaving the garden resembling an enchanted fairyland, glittering with crystal displays of frosted tree limbs and dagger-sharp icicles that shone like prisms, radiant and iridescent, almost blinding as they sparkled in the brilliant afternoon sun.

The grass, which in the summer resembled green velvet, was dusted with snow, reminding Blossom of icing sugar delicately sprinkled on sponge cake. There was beauty to the garden like this. Beneath snow and the crackling iced tree limbs there was simplicity. Crispness. She longed to end her walk and run to her studio to capture the brilliance of the day on canvas. It would be a challenge to turn this vista from cold, bleak slumber to a magical land of ice and snow, but she was up for it, if only this impromptu promenade would come to an end.

They had been walking for some time now, her gloved fingers lying delicately upon the arm of his wool greatcoat. In silence they strolled, both lost in thoughts—and perhaps dreams of the future. Their future.

Beneath her fur-lined hood, Blossom stole a look at the man who walked silently beside her. Samuel Markham, the Marquis of Weatherby's second son. And her fiancé. In three very short months he would be her husband.

Samuel was a handsome man, tall and dark-haired like his father, but he lacked the marquis's curling hair and green eyes. His elder brother had inherited those—not that she cared, she quickly reminded herself. Jase, the eldest son and heir, was a renowned rake and shameless heartbreaker. She'd gotten the better of the two as far as she was concerned.

Betrothed since she was a child, they liked to joke between themselves. Blossom had even stole the opening line of Jane Austen's famous work *Pride and Prejudice* and tailored it to her own. "It was a truth universally acknowledged that the beloved daughter of the Duke and Duchess of Torrington was going to marry the handsome second son of the Marquis and Marchioness of Weatherby—no other suitors need apply." Samuel had laughed himself silly. So had she.

However, it was not so very far from the truth. From early childhood their mothers had plotted and planned, and here they were, three months from their wedding date, strolling among her parents' beautiful gardens—*unchaperoned*.

There was no need for concern for her reputation. There really was little to cause anxiety. Everything was set. The wedding invitations had already been printed, the church reserved and the breakfast menu decided upon. If indeed something scandalous happened out here in the gardens, her name, and good reputation, were safe, for the wedding was nearly upon them. But Blossom was not worried, Samuel was nothing but a consummate gentleman. Only chaste kisses and handholding had ever passed between them.

Yes. She had gotten the better of the Markham boys. Samuel was safe, Jase was anything but. Samuel would make a very fine husband, and Jase... He would bring a wife nothing but grief and heartache. She'd known that for years, despite the fact she had once fancied herself enamored of Jase, and perhaps just a touch in love with him. But all that had changed during her first Season.

After discovering Jase's true personality, Blossom had given a very hearty prayer of gratitude that her mother had chosen the right Markham son to marry her off to. Never let it be said that the spare was any less worthy than the heir.

"Are you cold?" Samuel asked after clearing his throat. "I felt you shiver."

Strange, she hadn't noticed. Had thoughts of Jase made her tremble? *Impossible.*

"We could go to the temple, if you like. The wind shouldn't be too bad there."

He was different somehow today. She hadn't seen him in weeks. He'd been in the south, in Devon, painting a seascape which Lord Heversham had commissioned for his library. He'd only just returned, and immediately set out to see her. A young woman couldn't ask for a more diligent and thoughtful suitor. *Fiancé,* she reminded herself as she stole a look at him once more. He was going to be her husband. They would share a future. A life. A bed.

"Blossom."

Her name was whispered so softly, so painfully, that she stopped, reached for his gloved hand, halting him on the snow-dusted path. "What is it?"

He cast his gaze away, and she felt something dark and frightening curl deep in her belly. Something was wrong. This was not the Samuel she had known since childhood. The easy banter, the good humor that always flowed between them, had been replaced with an intensity and underlying current of...of... She could not name it. Only knew it wasn't right.

"Oh, God, how do I tell you this?" he said to the ground

as he raked his gloved hands through his hair. When he at last looked upon her, his expression was solemn, his eyes rimmed with dark circles that showed how tired he truly was.

"You're frightening me," she whispered. "Please, tell me. Whatever it is, I'm certain it is not as grievous as the expression you're presently wearing."

"Blossom." He swallowed hard, and she felt her fingers curl tightly in her gloves, waiting for something terrible to be said. "I…I…" He blew out a breath, which turned to gray vapor in the chilly air. "I've fallen in love with someone else."

Shocked. Stunned. Blossom could only blink. She was certain her mouth opened, then promptly shut, emitting no words, only a quiet little "Oh."

"I didn't mean for it to happen," he rushed on, the words spilling from his mouth as he cupped her cheeks in his hands. "It…it just did. And I'm sorry. Oh, God, I'm so, so sorry."

She wasn't exactly certain what she felt. Surprise was an understatement. Alarm, perhaps. Astounded…most likely. Curiously, she did not feel pain. Perhaps she was in a state of shock, after all.

"You're in love—with someone else?" she repeated as though she were a simpleton. He glanced away sheepishly, then turned to look at her. No, not merely gaze, but stare forthrightly into her eyes.

"Yes. Most ardently and passionately."

Ardent. Passionate. He had not been that with her. Nor had she felt that way with him. She loved him, of course. But it was not that blind, all-consuming love and passion that books by the Brontë sisters wrote of. It was a quiet love. One of companionship, and familiarity. Rather the sort of love she held for her brother, Edward, without the desire to share a kiss, of course.

Oh, Lord, she was rambling.

"Say something," Samuel entreated. "I cannot bear the look in your eyes."

How did she appear to him? she wondered. Crushed? Heartbroken? Or was her expression blank? Masked by good breeding and ladylike decorum.

"Damn it," he cursed. It was so strange to hear it from his lips—he was never anything but proper and controlled. "Please say something."

Suddenly, "something" came to mind. Where the question sprung from, she had no idea; the words were out and spoken before she could think, or take them back.

"Do you love her so much that you would do anything to have her? Are your thoughts fixated by her? Are you even now thinking of her, and when you might see her again?"

"Blossom," he chastised, "how could you—"

"We've always been honest with each other, Samuel. Now is not the time for half-truths. Our future is at stake here, and I believe that I am owed at least the truth. Tell me."

Holding her gaze, he reluctantly nodded. "Yes. I'm consumed by her, and yes, God help me, I have thought of her while with you. Forgive me, Blossom."

Something inside her broke and swelled, then flew free. "Then you must marry her, and love her long and well, Samuel Markham."

He stared at her as if she were mad. As if he didn't dare allow himself to believe what he'd just heard.

"We are both artists, both so passionate in our work, but we've never been passionate toward each other, have we? We are friends. As close as any friends could be. But we are not lovers. It would be a travesty to deny each other of that—passion and pleasure. Do we not owe it to ourselves to experience such bliss? To discover what it means to be someone's lover?"

As if to test her words, Samuel, still cupping her cheeks in his palms, lowered his mouth to hers. Softly, he brushed his lips to her mouth, then again, then once more, widening her lips, pressing his tongue inside. He had never kissed her like this, this intimately, and the experience was pleasant. Nice.

When he pulled away, they both knew the truth. While they enjoyed each other's company and shared many interests, the passion was only lukewarm. It was not the unbridled passion of their kind—poets, writers and artists.

"What does your heart tell you?" she whispered.

Closing his eyes, he held his breath, then released it in a long rush. "That you deserve much more than I can give you."

"I wish you only the best, Samuel."

Resting his forehead against hers, he murmured, "I never, ever wanted to hurt you. I was quite content to marry you and be your husband, but then—"

"You discovered what it was to truly, passionately love someone. I understand. And I'm not hurt. I'm glad that we shall remain friends. Marriage might have ruined that. I can tolerate the idea of not marrying you, but I cannot abide the thought of never having your friendship."

"You will *always* have that." Tipping her face up to look at him, he smiled, and brushed his thumb across her kiss-swollen mouth. "You're so lovely, and some man is going to come by and sweep you off your feet and love you with such a passion it will take your breath away."

She smiled then. Truly, honestly smiled, and threw her arms around him. "Will you promise me that, Samuel?"

"I will more than promise. I will vow it, on my honor

as a gentleman, that there is a man out there who will love you as well and as thoroughly as any woman could ever desire."

"And as passionately?"

"Yes, Blossom. Passion will be yours."

Separating, their hands lingered, entwined, as they stared at each other.

"You would have married me, wouldn't you? Despite loving another."

Glancing away, he shrugged. "You mean so much to me, and I would have gone through with it, if you hadn't released me. But I felt I needed to tell you the truth. That you would only have part of me."

"Thank you for that. For not robbing both of us of a life of love and desire."

"I will see you happy, Blossom. I swear it."

Already she could see the change in him. He was different. Love had made him this way. Passion had changed him. And she wanted that, too. To experience what he had. To learn the difference between a congenial love and a fierce, consuming love.

"Shall I go with you to tell your parents?"

Nodding, she placed her hand on his coat sleeve and glanced around the garden, which suddenly looked so very different to her. She saw possibilities where none had been before. Life, where only snow and ice had resided.

The spring was not far off, and her future called, beckoning her excitement. Tears welled in her eyes, but it was not from what had transpired between her and Samuel, but what was happening now. Her future was unfolding. And somewhere, out there, was a man waiting to fall hopelessly, ardently and most passionately in love with her.

CHAPTER ONE

June 1874
North Yorkshire Moors

"Damn it, he's won again!"

Jase Markham slammed his cards down on the make-shift table and smiled in triumph. "That's a hundred quid from you, Trevere."

The duke frowned and lifted his tankard of ale as he cast his gaze out the grime-covered window. "It's early yet, let's have another hand."

"We've been at this all night," Maxime Carrington grumbled. "Why are you avoiding your bed, and its lovely occupant?"

Trevere scowled and motioned to the deck. "Will someone deal?"

The cards were picked up, shuffled, and Merrick Carrington, the Marquis of Winterborne, began to toss out cards as he shared a smile with his twin, who sat opposite him. "Are you certain Her Grace won't mind?" he teased, sending the proper Trevere frowning once again. "You have been gone all night. No doubt Her Grace will want an explanation for this behavior. Wives are like that, or so I've been told."

"What do you know of wives, Winterborne?"

"That they generally become rather miffed when their husband spends the night away, consumed by ale and deep play."

"Don't remind me," Trevere said with a forlorn glance at the tally of winnings. "I'm nearly five hundred pounds lighter than when I arrived."

"I told you when you decided to flee your house that nothing good would come of it."

"Sod off," the duke snapped at Winterborne, sending the table laughing.

Evan Westlake, the head of the notorious Westlake clan, was hiding out in a stable instead of facing his wife after a row. Jase found that fact rather ridiculous. The imposing duke cowed to no one, but one little, dark-haired woman with large brown eyes sent him running. Strange how the man who was once known as the wicked and wanton Westlake had changed so much.

"Five years," Maxime murmured as he glanced at his cards and shared a looked with his brother, Merrick, "and you've never had a row before now? Remarkable."

"I prefer not to talk about wives at the present," the duke grumbled. "I want more ale, and to win back some of my money."

Maxime snorted and leaned toward Jase. "What do you think of this business of wives and holy matrimony, Raeburn?"

Swallowing a long draft of warm ale, Jase contemplated his answer. He wasn't opposed to marriage per se. His parents enjoyed a long and glorious union. They were as passionately in love to this day as they were on their wedding day. One could not be surrounded by such bliss and not ache but for a measure of the same happiness. But marriage for him was out of the question. So was discussing it.

"Ha!" Winterborne said with glee. "His expression says it all. You look like you've swallowed sour milk, Raeburn."

Jase placed his pewter tankard down on the wooden

pallet that acted as their card table. Behind them, the soft whinnies of horses could be heard. Before him were three of his closest friends—all school chums from Eton and Cambridge.

He didn't want to dwell on Edward, because thoughts of him lead to other, more dangerous thoughts. Mainly a raven-haired temptress with large, dark blue eyes and curves that made a man mad with desire.

"Come, let's play," he muttered as he reached for his hand. "We've been at this all night, and if we don't get His Grace home, he'll have a devil of a time explaining things to his wife. And I, for one, have no wish to be cornered by her and interrogated. I fear she could make the Spanish Inquisition look like child's play."

Everyone laughed, except the duke, of course, who had been irritable and distracted all night. After five years of marriage, and repulsive displays of matrimonial bliss, all was not as it once was. Despite not wanting to marry himself, Jase didn't want to see his friend suffer. Jase knew how much his friend adored his duchess, just as Trevere knew his sordid secret.

"Your brother is for the noose later this month, is he not?" Winterborne asked. "The Duke of Torrington's delightful daughter. Gorgeous girl."

Trevere shot him a look over the tops of his cards. Jase cleared his throat.

"Yes, as a matter of fact he is."

And that was all he intended to say on the subject. But Winterborne was in his cups, and he wanted to talk, not play cards.

"I danced with her once, at Lady Steepes's musicale— delightful armful. I was dashed disappointed to discover that she was intended for someone else."

He was, as well, but there it was. Blossom was engaged to marry his brother. It was a love match. And he would be forced to bear witness to the happy union in three weeks, one day and—he glanced down at his pocket watch—five hours.

"I've never seen her. Is she pretty?" Maxime asked. "I adore pretty girls. Especially intended ones," he teased.

Jase ground his teeth together and reminded himself that these were his friends. He liked his friends. He didn't want to murder them, but if they kept on about marriage and Blossom, he was going to have to bash them both.

"Oh, aye, gorgeous," Winterborne said as he finished off his ale. "Striking, to say the least. Dark exotic features with a rather—" he cast a glance to Jase "—desirable form."

That description of her was bland and uninspiring. Jase much preferred his own—that of an angelic succubus, created to tempt men like him. Her hair was black and thick, her eyes blue and innocent. Her lips red and succulent, the kind you could kiss and suck at for hours. Her skin was pale, unblemished, and her body was full and voluptuous and made for the dreams—and desires—of men. Innocence and sensuality. He wanted to ravish her, just as much as he wanted to protect her. *That* was the fitting description of Blossom.

"What do you think of her, Raeburn?" Maxime questioned.

Jase didn't dare glance at Trevere when he replied, "Tolerable."

"Tolerable?" Maxime laughed. "Does that mean you will be able to abide her company during the Christmas holidays? Or does it mean she's an inch away from your scathing regard?"

Hell, no! He could hardly stand to be in the same county as she. How would he ever be able to bear seeing the woman he desired with his brother? Witnessing their conjugal bliss was going to be soul-shattering, just as it had been to watch their love grow.

"What of you? Will you be next?" Winterborne taunted. "You can hardly stand to be outdone by your younger brother."

Jase frowned and tossed a card out. Hearts were trump and he lead with a measly ten of hearts. His mind was not on the hand, but rather on the image of a very delicious raven-haired nymph. Which really was rather disturbing seeing that she was going to be his sister-in-law.

"Come now, Raeburn, you've got a title to be conscious of. What of the proverbial heir and a spare?"

He glared at Winterborne. "What of you, old boy? You've got a title, as well, and as far as I know, the only women you get close to have long snouts and tails."

Maxime laughed and tipped his head back. "True enough. But my brother does put in all sorts of effort in breeding—it's just the wrong sort of species."

As if on cue, a pretty brown filly snorted and stomped in her stall.

"Come now, this is putting a depressing shade on our game," Winterborne snapped. "I've got a winning hand here, and I intend to make good use of it."

"Agreed. I'm not risking the wrath of my wife for talk of horses or marriage and women," Trevere grumbled. Tossing the ace of hearts on the pile, he signaled Jase to pick up the trick. "Cease this prattle and let's play."

Grumbling, the Carrington brothers focused their attentions on the cards. But damn them, after all this talk of marriage Jase could not think of anything other than Blossom and how he would have to return home to Bewdley in a few weeks and watch the one woman he yearned for above all others marry his brother.

Damn the Fates! He wanted to curse and rail, and yes...

abduct her from her home and ravish her so thoroughly she would be ruined for any other man but him.

Oh, he'd thought of it—thousands of times—what it would be like to have those lovely blue eyes on him, or those luscious red lips beneath his, and on other parts, as well. He'd debauched her in his mind, and craved her from afar, for so long that he almost felt wedded to her. He'd never met with another woman who made his body feel like Blossom's did. One glance from her was like watching fireworks.

Melodramatic fool. It was unhealthy, this obsession with her. Nothing could come out of it. Passion was all well and good, and he was certain he could tempt her with seduction if he truly desired to. All young women could be persuaded to succumb to a kiss and a caress. But there was the undeniable and infuriating fact that Blossom loved his brother. And Samuel loved her. Passion was never a replacement for love. He of all people knew that. So, he had stepped back and allowed his brother to love Blossom, while he had tried—most unsuccessfully—to bury his feelings.

"Pray, excuse me, milord, but a telegraph has just arrived for Lord Raeburn."

Four sets of eyes peered up from the cards. Winterborne's footman was standing in the stable opening, the early-morning sun outlining his tall figure.

"A telegraph," he found himself saying. "When did you decide to avail yourself of modern convenience?"

Winterborne waved the footman in. "Since I found it necessary to expand my breeding business after I inherited this deuced indebted estate up in the north, where there is nothing but sheep and cattle and little of anything that is convenient."

Ignoring Winterborn's rant, Jase reached for the missive and glanced around. His friends, the nosy blighters,

watched as he opened the paper. Who could it be from? he
wondered. He'd been nomadic these past months, restless
as the impending wedding came closer. He'd felt out of
sorts, and he'd left Bewdley for the north where he and his
father bred Arabian horses. After a few months there, he'd
been lonely and isolated. He'd come to North Yorkshire to
search out his friends. He'd been here ever since, but he
hadn't written home to tell his family. His mother, who
knew of his affliction, would only wish him back. No
doubt, she would have a gaggle of young ladies for him
to meet. To his mother, there was nothing better than to
ease a broken heart with the promise of new love.

His darling mother. He did adore her, but sometimes
he wished he had not unburdened himself when she had
come across him after Samuel had announced his engagement. He still cringed at the memory, and at the way he
had allowed himself to be comforted in her arms.

Met a lovely girl—a ballet dancer. Stop. Ran off
to Gretna Green and am now blissfully married.
Stop. Come home. Stop. Mum is worried sick about
you. Stop.

Barely breathing, Jase stared at the telegraph and the
name of the sender. Samuel. He'd met a ballet dancer
and eloped to Gretna Green? Was this some sort of jest?
Or had his brother finally lost his mind in prewedding
nerves?

The ramifications of such an act ran through his
thoughts—so, too, did the possibilities. Blossom was free.
Brokenhearted, no doubt, and shamed by his brother's
rash actions, but free nonetheless.

"What is it?" Trevere asked.

The paper flitted from his trembling fingers down to
the table, and Trevere reached for it. Their gazes collided

and then his friend, who had been so taciturn and utterly miserable all night long, smiled.

"I have a cottage in the Lakes. Lovely old place. Secluded. Romantic. A most excellent location. And it can be had on short notice. Just let me know when you want it, and it's yours."

Jase looked between his friends—Trevere, who was still smiling, and the Carrington twins, whose mouths were hung open in question. And then, despite the lack of sleep, and too many cups of ale, Jase jumped up from his chair and snatched the missive out of Trevere's hand. "I'll be taking you up on that offer, Your Grace! Just you wait and see."

CHAPTER TWO

TWO LARGE HANDS PLANTED themselves palms down on either side of her. "Another masterpiece, sweetheart."

Brushing the black paint in fine strokes, Blossom smoothed the lines with the tip of her brush, blending it until it looked soft and feathery.

"The shadowing is perfect. You have a gift in that regard. Masterpiece," he said again.

Smiling, she couldn't help but let out a little laugh. "Papa, you think everything I paint is a masterpiece. Why, you still have the portrait of our family framed on your desk—the one where we're all stick people with big heads and frighteningly large smiles."

Laughing, he dropped a kiss to the top of her head. "My love, that was your first masterpiece. Everything else only gets better."

Muttering to herself, she continued to paint, aware of the large presence of her father looming over her, studying her technique. He had taught her to draw and paint. She had been his apprentice, and now she was her own master.

"This is a plate from the commission you took?"

"Yes. A retelling of Lord Tennyson's *The Lady of Shallot*."

"I like it—it's a balance of colors and shading. The jeweled tones give it a feel and atmosphere—one of substance, and a certain sensuality, I might say. Most striking.

But who is this?" he asked, pointing to the dark-haired character on horseback.

"Lancelot."

"I thought Lancelot was supposed to be a fair and golden knight?"

Lifting her brush from the plate, Blossom studied what she had sketched. Frowning, she suddenly recognized who she had drawn, and prayed her father wouldn't notice—or, heavens above, comment on the resemblance. How unfortunate it was that Jase seemed to be creeping into her thoughts. Subliminal or not, she was most perturbed. Where these thoughts had sprung from she had no idea. She hadn't thought of him in *that* way for years.

"Well?"

"Fair and golden is tired, Papa. Dark and mysterious is far more enticing, don't you think? Art is, after all, open to interpretation."

He laughed, a deep chuckling sound that made her smile. Her father was her greatest champion. He loved her. Wanted only her happiness. When she and Samuel had broken the news of their canceled wedding, her father had been the first to hug her. To tell her that it was all right to follow her heart.

Her parents had a love match, a most passionate one, even to this day. It was what she had wanted, too. What she had hoped one day might flower between her and Samuel. But it had not, and these past months after her ended engagement had been the most freeing of her life.

"Dark and mysterious, eh?" he asked, once more perusing the portrait. "It is indeed most becoming in art, but not in life."

She turned and looked at him over her shoulder. "Papa, are you warning me off of a certain type of gentleman?"

"Never! If I did, it would only draw you to that sort of man, wouldn't it? You have too much of me in you, I'm afraid. Headstrong, willful child."

"I'm no longer a child."

He sighed and moved away. "Don't I know it. These past few days have disabused me of the thought. Now, about these men who have asked for an audience with me. What do you want me to do?"

Blossom thought of the barrage of male guests who had been invited to her parents' party, and the handful of them that seemed to be her most ardent pursuers. "You may do precisely what you've done with the past four offers for my hand. Politely decline. I have no wish to marry a man who sees me as way to forge a connection with a powerful duke, or worse, a bank note."

Laughing, her father moved away to gaze out the window. Blossom knew that below, on the grass, was a group of gentlemen playing lawn bowling. They were the same gentlemen who would not leave her be. The ones who spoke of her beauty, ad nauseam. They didn't even know her, and not one of them had ever truly tried to. They thought her a frivolous, featherbrained female who wished her vanity to be stroked. Little did they comprehend that she despised vanity and empty compliments. What she wanted was a man who was truthful, honorable—and passionate. The men her father was currently watching were only ardent about advancing their reputations and estates—with her dowry.

"Very well, I shall send them all away, desolate and brokenhearted."

Snorting, she dabbed the tip of her brush once more into the ink. "I have a feeling that if you offered them a couple hundred pounds their desolation would evaporate and their broken hearts would miraculously mend."

"Such a cynic," her father teased. "I wonder from whom you inherited that flaw?"

Laughing, she looked up. "I think we both know the answer to that. Now, if we are done here, talking about bloodthirsty suitors, would you close the curtains, Papa? The sun is causing a glare on the canvas."

"Enough for now, Blossom. Mama wishes you to come to the salon."

"So you've turned traitor, have you?"

"No, I have not. But your mother has gone to a lot of work planning this party, and you will partake of it—at least some of it. Besides, I of all people know that one cannot shut one's self up forever. It's good for you to get out and meet new people. I'm certain that there is at least one gentleman present who can come up to scratch."

"I'm not—"

"You're avoiding the male guests, my dear. Understandable, of course, but you're doing yourself a disservice. You know your mother and I would never force you to wed where your heart didn't lie. But we never promised to not encourage it along. Come, your mother wishes to see you."

Mama... Sighing, Blossom dropped her paintbrush in the jar of turpentine and wiped her hands on the white cloth that lay beside her. Mama had not accepted the news of her aborted wedding quite as well as Papa had. Oh, she had supported her decision not to marry where she did not love. But her mother, being a woman madly in love these past twenty-odd years, could not stand idly back and allow love to find her daughter. No, Mama sought out love with a vengeance. Hence, the enormous house party that was under way, and the dozens of single gentlemen milling about the estate.

"Lord Halston has spoken with me. He asked for the

honor of taking tea with us this afternoon. Naturally I agreed."

Blossom quirked a perturbed brow in her father's direction. "Naturally. He's Mama's choice."

Halston. He was a kind fellow, and handsome, too. He was a sporting man, and one of good spirits and jovial conversation and one of her more attentive and genuine admirers. Many of the single ladies grew tongue-tied in his presence, and more than once, Blossom had heard girls gossiping behind their fluttering fans about Halston, and the fact he was this Season's catch.

Glancing at her gown, and the stained apron she wore, Blossom sighed and held up a white flag of surrender. "I will just change."

Her father uncrossed his arms and reached for her hand. "You'll do no such thing. Besides, we've seen you in stained aprons for years."

Oh, good Lord, her mother was going to be perturbed. But her father was right. She had no plans to give up her painting after marriage. Best to set out the ground rules now.

With the duke's boots ringing a commanding tattoo on the marble floor, Blossom walked beside her father, down the private wing of the family's residence, to the yellow salon that belonged to her mother. It smelled of her—soap and orange blossoms—and she smiled, thinking of how many days she had spent there, listening to her mother's stories.

"My dear, I have dragged our daughter out of her studio for a spot of tea."

In the process of pouring, her mother glanced up, then took in her state of dress. With a knowing smile, she nodded, and indicated the chair beside her.

"Come, Blossom. You can pour."

Bounding up from his chair, the Earl of Halston turned

to greet her. His smile was bright and charming, until his gaze, which lingered a trifle too long on her face and bosom, descended—to the white apron splotched with oil paint.

"Forgive me," she said in a hurry as she untied the strings to the apron. Tossing it aside, she placed it on a small table and headed for Halston, where she dropped into an elegant curtsy before him.

"Good day, my lord."

He cleared his throat as he reached for her. Taking her bare hand in his, he helped her up. Blossom could not help but noticed how her fingertips—stained black—stood out against Halston's perfectly manicured ones.

"You look lovely today, Lady Blossom," he murmured, and she thought she heard her father's deep chuckle.

"I've been painting," she admitted as he released her hand and took the seat next to her mother.

"Do you do that often?" the earl asked as he sat down beside her.

"Oh, yes, every day."

"Nearly all day," her mother teased as she slid the china teapot to her. "Always in her studio."

Holding out his cup and saucer, Halston smiled at her as she poured. "I think it charming when ladies paint."

A chuckle from her father. Their eyes met as Blossom poured her father's tea. There was mischief in his eyes, and a shared look between her parents.

Turing back to Halston, Blossom attempted to clarify the earl's misdirected belief.

"I'm afraid I'm not a dabbler, my lord. Painting for me is not just another female accomplishment. It is as necessary as breathing. It fulfills me, and gives me purpose."

Halston blinked, and tried to prevent choking on his tea.

"You have heard that I'm a professional artist, my lord? I take commissions."

He did choke then. And her father most definitely did nothing to conceal yet another outburst of mirth—a sardonic one at that.

"You're a...a..." Halston looked to her father, then to her, floundering for the correct word.

"A career woman?" She brightened and straightened in her chair. "Indeed, I guess I am. I make a very comfortable living working for commission."

"Surely you don't have to." He glanced at her father, whose expression turned glacial. "That is to say, you would not need to continue in that vein if you were to say...marry advantageously."

"I'd like to meet the man who tries to dissuade her from her painting," her father muttered. "And no, she need not paint to keep us afloat, Halston. She does it because it is in her soul. Do you know nothing of the arts? An artist, whether they be painter, sculptor, poet or writer, cannot just stop doing what calls to them. It's in their blood, man. Who they are. Surely you would not wish to change what is in one's soul?"

Lord Halston flushed, and notched his chin, as though his necktie were choking him. "Of course not," he said, smiling weakly. "And if one were truly worthy, they would not force you to abandon your...vocation," he said in a strangled voice.

"Do you fish, Lord Halston?" her mother asked as she lowered her cup to the saucer. "The lake is well stocked with trout."

"I do," he said, brightening. "It's been an age since I've done so, however."

"Oh, do you fly-fish?" Blossom asked, excited at last.

"Yes. Perhaps you might come and watch me, if that would be permissible. Your Grace?"

"Watch?" Blossom snapped at the same moment her father inclined his head, giving the earl permission to take her to the lake. "Whatever would I wish to watch for? No, I fly-fish, too."

This time, Halston's eyes bulged out of his head, and his face turned red. "I...beg your pardon, Lady Blossom... I..."

"She's better than her brother," her father drawled, a faint smile curling his lips. Her father was actually enjoying himself!

"I suppose you thought I might sit on a blanket, surrounded by a picnic lunch, while you entertain me with your skill."

Halston squirmed in his chair. She was being far too forward, and rude, but she could not help it. She had no intention of lingering on the ground watching, idle, while Lord Halston strutted about, showing off his skills. She would never be that sort of wife, one content to sit back and admire. She wanted to participate—as her mother had always done. She wanted a partnership, a truly mutual companion.

Recovering with aplomb, Halston set his saucer atop the table. "I would be delighted to join you, Lady Blossom. Perhaps tomorrow morning, then?"

Blossom didn't know what to make of him. Did he legitimately wish to spend time with her, or was he merely placating her? His shock had been so evident, his disdain so transparent. What had made him change his mind? Was it her dowry, which was one of the largest on the Marriage Mart, or was it something else? Genuine affection?

Blossom could not summon the belief it was the latter. Halston, while handsome and personable, had proved himself a bit too traditional, too...male in his thinking. He could never truly desire to have her as his wife.

While she desired passion and love in her marriage,

she also wanted freedom. Freedom to paint and continue with her commissions. Freedom to be the sort of woman she had always been.

Her mother had reared her to be free thinking, liberal and self-sufficient. She found herself wondering what the old-fashioned Earl of Halston would think if he were to discover she could cook herself a hot pot and scones? Another of her mother's doings.

Her mother was a duchess, had been for twenty-five years, but before her marriage to the duke, Jane had been a common woman. A woman forced to work. An independent woman. And despite her title, and the fact that her daughter was born into the nobility, her mother had made it her mantra to raise her daughter in an independent fashion. Blossom had no need, or desire, to be dependent upon a man.

Would Halston accept her as she was? No, never mind acceptance. Would he *love* her as she was?

"Well, this has been a beautiful afternoon," Halston commented. "And lovely tea. But you will forgive me. I promised Lady Billings that I would take a walk with her and her daughter in your beautiful gardens and I see it is the time that was set for us to meet. Till later, Lady Blossom."

Blossom watched Halston retreat as though a pack of hellhounds were hard upon his boots. When the door closed firmly behind him, her mother and father sat back in their chairs, relaxed and reposed, and smiling at each other.

"Darling Jane, you are the most cunning of women," her father drawled as he reached for a biscuit. "How I admire you, dearest."

"I had a wonderfully gifted tutor," her mother said with a knowing smile.

"I thought he'd choke on his tongue." Her father laughed. "Poor fellow, he was ambushed."

"Nonsense," her mother scoffed. "It was only a little test of his character. And he did surprisingly well, under the circumstances. Perhaps he was a little…off center, but I have not given up all hope yet that he might come up to scratch."

"Mama," Blossom asked, suspicion in her voice, "did you and Papa plan for me to come into this room wearing my apron?"

"Of course, child," her mother replied. Her fair complexion was positively beaming, and her green eyes sparkling with mischief behind her spectacles. "You have to be absolutely certain what sort of man you're getting involved with. While I will agree, Lord Halston is very handsome and his manners impeccable, it is not those two virtues you are marrying. It is the man himself."

"And you knew what sort of man Papa was, then?"

Her mother's gaze softened; mischief was replaced with a deep and abiding love. "Yes," she whispered, and Blossom saw her flush as the afternoon sun shone upon her mother's red hair, which was streaked at the sides with gray. "I knew exactly what sort of man your father was. The very sort worth fighting for. And that, my dear, is the kind of man you want. The sort who will walk through fire to have you. Who will give you everything you want—not baubles and material things," she clarified, "but the things that mean something. Objects that money cannot buy. That is the sort of man that makes a husband, Blossom. One who loves you for you. Not for what you come from."

"Your mother is right. No man who was less than that would ever be worthy of you. And let me tell you, no man is truly content with a wife who is a copy of every other man's wife. A man wants his own—teeth, claws and all."

"Thank you, both. Not many women my age could boast of having such understanding parents."

"I should say not. You've been positively ruined by your indulgent father and spoiling mother."

"Papa." She laughed as he teased her. She kissed him on the cheek, and then her mother. "Now, then, may I be excused?"

"Naturally," her father said. "But do have a care with poor old Halston. His unfortunate showing at tea aside, I quite like the fellow."

"I shall keep that in mind, Papa." Quickly she left the salon. She needed to think, and the best thinking spots were outside by the lake. Before closing the door, she heard her mother's quiet whisper.

"Do you think we've destroyed all hope for her?"

"No, my love. He is truly smitten by her, I think. If he wants her bad enough, he'll find her paint-stained fingers charming, and the fact she fly-fishes better than her brother an intriguing notion."

"I want her happiness, Matthew, that is all."

"As do I. But what you forget, my love, is that she is very much like us. She has your teeth, and my claws. Blossom will stay true to herself. She will not allow a man to railroad her into marriage. On that, I can promise you."

CHAPTER THREE

"LADY BLOSSOM, A LETTER for you."

Blossom reached for the missive the butler was holding out to her. "Thank you, I think I shall read it during my walk. I'll be going to the Temple and back, Thompson, if my parents should happen to ask after me."

"Very good. Ah, I see you have your bonnet. The sun is very hot today, miss."

"Thank you, Thompson. I shall take every care."

Stepping outside, Blossom heard the door close behind her. Ensuring that no one was around, she raised the hem of her skirt and petticoats and ran down the gravel drive, to the side path that led to the garden. She would walk to the lake, and linger on the bridge for a few moments. There she would find a measure of peace and tranquility, away from her eager suitors and zealous penniless men searching for an heiress.

In these past few months, she had learned what it was like to be hunted and desired for nothing more than her dowry. It had been a frightening and yet enlightening lesson. Her father had taught her all the tricks that a desperate man might employ to snag himself an heiress. Seduction being the first. As a consequence of those lessons, Blossom strived to never be alone with a man—no matter who he was or how innocent the setting. But she was safe here at the lake. The ladies were upstairs, napping and preparing for the dinner and dance that evening. The gentlemen were sipping port and playing billiards, or lounging in the library, reading the papers. No, she would not encounter anyone out here, except perhaps a few swans.

Pausing, Blossom closed her eyes and lifted her face to the sky, enjoying the warm sunlight that crept across her face. The sun was hot, but she pulled the strings loose on her bonnet, anyway. Pulling the bonnet off her head, she was aware that a lock of her hair had come loose and was dangling down her back. With a mischievous smile, she tossed the bonnet aside and, letter in hand, she made her way to the bridge.

Strolling leisurely, she took in the magnificent grounds, and stopped in the middle of the bridge to gaze down upon the dark water. Two swans, one white and one black, swam lazily beneath and she turned to the other side in time to watch them swim from out beneath the arched stone. Swans were everpresent here, a symbol of devotion and love. One always black, the other white. She had often asked her parents about the custom, but they just smiled and sent each other private glances. It was then that Blossom knew the swans somehow symbolized her parents' union.

It was romantic. Passionate. And one day she wanted something similar to share with her husband.

Strolling along, Blossom followed the winding paths that were edged with trees and bushes and flowering perennials while breaking the red wax seal of the Earl of Wallingford, and opened the missive from her brother.

Dearest Blossom,

I received your letter, and hope you are well. Your heart mended. I fear you have made too light of things. How angry you must be with the bastard. You should have allowed me to come home and box Samuel Markham into bloody pulp. You always were too kind, sister.

Smiling, Blossom continued her walk and thought of her brother, his black hair and dark eyes—how they flashed when he was riled. She could just imagine the scene that would have ensued if she had encouraged her brother's anger at Samuel.

It was no less than he deserved, Blos. My God, a dancer, when he could have had you, my beautiful sister. Why, the man must be soft in the head to desire any woman above you. How could he have done it, left you for a ballet dancer!

Because he was in love, she thought. One day, even Edward would succumb to the emotion. One day, her brother would curb his reckless ways and discover what it was to heed the urges of one's heart. A heart could lead anywhere, and Samuel had simply followed his. She did not resent him, but admired him for it. What courage it took to be true to oneself.

Mama and Papa have written to me that they are hosting a country house party. You know what it is, Blos. It's a ruse to have you meet new gentlemen. Don't fall for it. They'll have you married and whisked away before you know it. And for heaven's sake, don't consider a bloke until you've written me and informed me of his name. I know most all of the degenerates and will inform you if you've had the unlucky happenstance to engage said degenerate's interest.

I'd never want that for you, sister. You deserve something better. As your brother, I demand better!

Home soon, and remember, do not entertain a thought of a gentlemen before first writing to me.

My address follows, and so, too, does a kiss and a
buss, and a stiff upper lip, little soldier!
Your favorite, and most affectionate, brother—
Edward

Ah, Edward. As far as siblings went, Edward was ex-
ceptional. They were six years apart, she the younger. He
had always included her, dragging her off to the lake for
fishing or catching tadpoles. How she had enjoyed those
times, when anything was possible.

Folding her letter, she pressed her lips to the seal, recalling those bygone days when the real world had never
intruded upon them, and the rules of society were all
abandoned.

But she had grown up, and was now faced with the
knowledge that the world for her was not as it was for
her brother. Men were afforded far more privilege, while
women labored under centuries-old stigmas and occupations. Daughters of dukes did not don britches and boots
and scamper into the lake, fishing. They sat on the bank,
their skirts protected from the grass, their complexions
shielded from the sun, and pretended to watch the men at
their sport, while secretly envying them their freedom.

She knew all too well that would be her fate tomorrow morning when she met Lord Halston for fishing.
He would fuss over her, demanding the right to bait her
own hook, and no doubt cast her line, as well. He would
smother and coddle her so much that she would become
exasperated and would seek the bank to be rid of him.
She would then sit there, miserable, and he smug with
himself, feeling as though he could manage her.

Such was a woman's lot in life.

Lamenting that fact, Blossom paused and looked
around her surroundings, amazed to discover that she
had unconsciously strolled to the very same spot that

she had so fondly been ruminating about. Before her, in all its boyhood glory, stood the wooden fort. She hadn't come by it in years, but Papa had it kept clean and in good repair for when Aunt Sarah visited with her husband, Simon, and their three children—as well as for any future grandchildren that might come along.

Reaching for the handle, she pulled the door open and stepped inside. It was dark, a bit dingy, but it smelled the way she always remembered, woodsy, a bit musky and… spicy?

No, it couldn't be. Whirling around, she found the source of that spicy scent. It was cologne, and it belonged to a man she hadn't seen in almost a year.

"Hello, Blossom."

"Jase!"

The sound was a strangled noise from her throat. Good Lord, what was he doing here?

"It hasn't changed much, has it?" he asked as he looked up at the ceiling and the loft where they all had once sat, the remnants of a picnic lunch strewn around them. His gaze met hers, and a smile suddenly broke free. "I do believe the last time I was here, we were playing highwayman, and you were the rich heiress that was dragged from her carriage, and I was the dastardly highwayman—although, I do like to think I played him rather dashingly."

She smiled at the memory while studying him. "You bound my hands too tight and the rope left burns on my wrists."

"Indeed I did. Did I ever apologize?"

"Not properly. You were rather indignant by the fact that your father had dragged you back to the house by the scruff of your neck in order to apologize."

"Ah, yes, now I remember, a litany about how a man is to treat a lady, and it is not by leaving marks on her person. All clear now. In fact, I even recall what he was wearing as he gave me that lesson. And I do call to mind that it was not a very gentlemanly apology. Allow me to make amends, then."

He stepped close, out of the shadows. She could see him clearly now, his ruffled hair, the dark green of his eyes and the black shading on his cheeks and chin. Reaching for her hand, he lifted it up to his gaze, his green eyes lingering over her paint-stained fingers before turning her hand over and running his fingertips along the blue veins of her wrist. "No scars?"

"No."

He glanced up at her then, devilry in his eyes. "I would hate to think I marked you."

Her hand suddenly felt a bit damp in his, the heat of the day and her stroll no doubt catching up with her.

"Blossom. Please accept my humblest apologies for tying you up too tight." His smile turned from boyish to wicked, and Blossom saw instantly how successful he must be in making the opposite sex swoon with delight. "I vow, the next time I find myself tying you up, I won't leave marks. And you definitely won't go crying to your papa."

CHAPTER FOUR

"THE NEXT TIME!"

He laughed despite himself. She was so riled and enraged. Her cheeks were flushed pink, making her dark blue eyes glisten. He could hardly breathe she was so beautiful—and so close to him. It was utterly unimaginable how Samuel could not find himself hopelessly smitten with Blossom. He was besotted, that was for certain. One look at her and he was thinking all manner of improper, base thoughts. Lust and Blossom had a way of becoming symbiotic in his brain.

"Jase, you beast, you're teasing me. You always teased me."

"Perhaps." Although, the image of Blossom bound in scarlet ribbons teased him far more.

"What brings you to the fort, of all places?"

He shrugged, trying to find his footing. "I suppose I felt a bit reminiscent."

"I understand. As I was strolling the paths, reading Edward's letter, it brought back many childhood memories of us playing in this fort, and fishing in the lake."

His eyes dropped to the white folded paper she held in her hand. "How is Edward? I haven't seen him in a month. We last were together at the Black Swan, in York."

"He's gone to the Lake District." She smiled as her thumb passed over Wallingford's seal. "He claims to return home."

"And when is that?"

"Soon, he says. But I don't fully believe him. He's restless and unsettled, searching for something, but I don't believe he knows just exactly what he's looking for."

Jase wondered what he himself was truly looking for. He had always thought himself contented with life, but these past few days, traveling back from Yorkshire, he had found himself thinking on his future more and more. He had thought of his future, and not for the first time, a fleeting image of a home and a woman who loved him flickered to mind. That woman looked remarkably similar to Blossom. But he forced it to the back of his mind. Desire was one thing. He had never confused it before. But this was Blossom, and for some strange damn reason, the desire felt different. Deeper. Why, he could not fathom. They had never even shared a kiss, let alone their bodies. So how his desire for her felt so much more powerful, he could not fathom. He could only acknowledge that it was the truth—and that it frightened him.

A moment of awkward silence passed between them, a minute of him staring down at her, taking in every inch of her being, and wondering what he was about, coming there to see her; and her, avoiding that gaze.

"So, you're home at last. What was the inducement?" she asked.

You. "I thought it time."

The last time he'd been home was when Samuel had announced his engagement to her, and he had been forced to endure a celebratory dinner in their honor. The next morning, he had packed his bags for his northern estate and focused his attentions on his horses and stables. He had, or so he thought, convinced himself that he didn't really care about Blossom. He'd wanted only to bed her. He'd believed it, too, until that night spent with Trevere and the Carringtons, when their inebriated talk had turned to marriage, and the image of Blossom had reared up.

He thought if he saw her again, he might get the crazed thoughts out of his head, once and for all. But they were still there, and the thoughts were getting more and more absurd the longer he gazed down at her.

"I understand your parents are hosting a party?"

He saw her expression change, heard the almost imperceptible groan from her lips. "Indeed they are."

"And are you not enjoying yourself?"

"As much as I ever did at these sorts of functions. Parties and balls interfere with my work, I'm afraid, and I'm most selfish with my time. I don't like it interrupted."

Smiling, he reached for her hand and unfurled her fingers so that her fingertips lay in the center of his palm. Her thumb and index finger were tinged with smudges of black and blue and a small smearing of white. *Charming.*

One of his most guilty pleasures was to secretly watch Blossom paint. She was transfixed by the canvas before her, lost in a world that only she could see. Her hair, which was red as a young child, had turned onyx. It was now black and shining, usually dragging loose from its pins. The aprons she wore to protect her clothes were always covered in paint, and he'd fantasized about coming up behind her and pulling the strings loose, kissing her neck, dragging his tongue up her throat to catch her lips in a searing, passionate, openmouthed kiss. With his ministrations and caresses, Blossom would not be perturbed to find herself interrupted from her work. Indeed, his seductions might be the very muse she required.

"Lord Halston couldn't keep his eyes from my hands at tea this afternoon," she said with a smile as she looked at her hand lying in his. "I think I might have given him paroxysms."

"Halston is an ass if he can't see you for what you are." Oh, God, he could see her, and he wanted her. He wouldn't change a damn thing about her—well, perhaps her opinion of him, which seemed to be decidedly friendly, not amorous.

She pulled her hand away but not before she glanced at her fingers. "It is terribly rude to come to tea with paint on your fingers—not to mention a stained apron."

Ah, so she had intentionally set out to shock the poor bastard. Halston could have no knowledge of what lay in store for him if he were to seriously pursue Blossom. "I suppose you thought you should give him a good showing of what he might find after marriage?"

She smiled up at him. "Indeed I did. Samuel never minded my paint-stained fingers or aprons, or the odd smudge on my cheek, and to be honest, I never thought twice about such things. Since…our parting, I've come to the realization that I am not inclined to change my ways for a man. He must accept me as is. Warts and stained aprons and a decidedly distracted mind when I am in the midst of creating."

The mention of his brother soured his mood. They had been getting on rather well, renewing their acquaintance with surprising ease. But now the air was heavy, charged with uncomfortable silence.

"So you meant to warn him, did you? Let him know what will come first in any marriage arrangement he might propose?"

"Indeed. I suppose it's best to begin how I mean to go on."

He took a step closer to her, narrowing the space between them. "And how do you mean to go on?"

Her breath caught, and she took a step back. "I mean to have the sort of marriage I want, and nothing will dissuade me from it."

"And what sort of marriage do you wish for?"

Her mouth trembled and she took another step back. Immediately, she seemed recovered. "I should think that a private matter, my lord. Something to be discussed between me and my future husband."

He smiled—one of a hungry predator spotting lame prey. So easily cornered. So easily taken in his hold and consumed…

"Perhaps I am inquiring for my own edification so that I might court you and come out the winner of your lovely paint-stained hand."

The comment was out before he could stop it. He was as surprised as Blossom looked. She paled, her eyes wary, and then suddenly she brightened, her lips breaking open in a wise smile. "You're teasing me!" Her body seemed to sag in relief. "Honestly, sir, you are such a rake!" She laughed up at him. "How the silly London girls must swoon at your antics."

He frowned. How could she laugh and so easily discard what he had said? He had never said anything of the like to a woman before now.

"Oh, I could almost believe that you are truly wounded. How you have perfected that pout and narrow-eyed look!" She laughed again. "My lord, you are vastly amusing. You always made me laugh and it is good to have a laugh again."

This was most certainly *not* what he had expected. He was wounded, damn it. Grievously so.

"I should be going. I've been away from the house for some time and I have dinner to prepare for. You'll be coming tonight, with your parents, I assume? I'll tell Mama to expect one more—or two? Did you bring a guest with you on your return home?"

"No, no guest. And I will most definitely be at dinner tonight."

"How wonderful. It will be nice to have a friend there."

A friend. Well, it was a start. What had he expected,

her to throw herself into his arms and kiss him wildly? They had been friends as children; that friendship had deteriorated into a passing acquaintance during her first Season, for reasons he could not fathom. In the ensuing years, they had lost contact, mostly because she was distant, and he was tired of feeling jealous watching her with his brother.

This meeting was truly more than he should have ever hoped for, but the cordiality of it made his mood a bit sour. She had laughed at him, and he had been attempting to bare his heart. A heart he had never allowed himself to look too deeply into.

"Till tonight, then, my lord."

"Yes. Till tonight."

She left the fort without a backward glance, and he moved to the window and watched her progress down the path. Never once did she look back at the fort—at him. A sudden, most distasteful thought occurred to him. She was utterly indifferent to him.

TOSSING THE REINS TO the stable boy, Jase jumped off his stallion and all but ran up the steps that led to his home— Eden Park. It had not changed much since his boyhood days, and the ease brought him comfort. He wasn't the sort of creature who enjoyed change, and seeing the familiar white lace curtains billowing through the open window of his mother's salon made him smile.

"Welcome home, my lord," Beetle, their butler, murmured as the front door swung wide open. "If I might say so, milord, you've been greatly missed."

Pulling his hat from his head, Jase raked a hand through his unruly curls. "Thank you, Beetle. It's good to be home."

"You'll find your parents in the green salon, my lord."

Jase thrust his hat to the butler and walked the few steps to the salon, not waiting for the footman to open the door. Inside, the sun shone through the lace curtains, and a rose-scented breeze blew in. His mother was seated on a cream-colored settee, embroidering; his father, head bent, was busy at his desk, scratching away at a missive. On the floor, dark hair in pigtails, sat his sister, reading a book.

"Jase!"

"Look at you!" he cried as Julia jumped up and launched herself into his embrace. "You've grown, moppet." He chuckled as he swung her up. Her face lit up and he wondered how it was that his baby sister had grown up so quickly in just a few months.

"Well, I'm twelve now, you know. I'm not a little girl."

He smiled and let her feet rest on the ground. "I see you're wearing the necklace I sent you for your birthday."

"I am." Reaching up she tried to place a kiss on his cheek, but she was still too short, so he bent down, reaching for the little peck.

"Thank you, brother."

"You're most welcome."

"Jase." It was his mother's turn to kiss him. Quietly she came to him, her eyes glistening with tears. "We have seen you but for a week this past year. I thought we might have to send out the militia to find you."

Hugging her tight he held her close to him, then allowed his father to come to him, who hugged him tight, patting his back with strong hands. His father had always been an affectionate man. He was not one to hide his thoughts and feelings. He wore his heart on his sleeve, and Jase feared he was very much like him in that regard, although he tried fiercely to hide the fact.

"About time you got back," his father teased. "I need some advice about the new stables. And I received a letter from Crompton just the other day. He says the mare you bought to mate with your stallion has taken to him. Crompton believes she is with foal. Also there is a market in Derby next week. I was thinking of going, but now that you're here, perhaps we might go together."

"Lindsay." His mother laughed as she snuggled up to her husband. "Allow him to rest and catch his breath. He's dusty from his journey and needs a drink and a meal. Then you may talk of horses and Derby and whatever else you desire."

Grudgingly his father admitted defeat. Besides, Jase hadn't come home to talk about their breeding program, or stables. He came to see Blossom, and somehow both his parents knew it. He could see into the workings of his father's mind, and saw that he knew of his son's affliction—and the purpose behind his return home after so long an absence.

"Pet," his father said to Julia. "I believe Cook is making luncheon. Will you go and tell her that your brother has arrived, and is famished. She'll need to make more sandwiches and lemonade."

"Of course, Papa." Julia turned to him and smiled. "I missed you, Jase. I hope that this time you'll stay longer."

"Yes, moppet, I will. For a long time, I hope."

"Good, because my dance instructor has taught me the waltz, and I'd like to practice it with you."

Bowing, he reached for his sister's hand and placed a kiss on her knuckles. "It would be my honor."

Wrinkling her nose, she gazed up at him. "I do hope you're better at it than Papa. He trods on my toes."

As she skipped out of the room, Jase watched her leave. The door closed, and he whirled around to confront his parents, who had removed themselves to the settee. His father was seated beside his mother, with an arm casually draped over her shoulder. His mother was resting her head against his father's chest, her hand clutched in his free one.

The image was one of love and support. A comfort and ease with each other. He wanted that sort of relationship, he suddenly realized. After nearly thirty years of marriage, he wanted to sit on the settee with Blossom and hold her like that. He wanted to feel the weight of her head against his chest. Wanted her to hear his heart beating beneath her ear—the heart that beat only for her. He wanted to glance down to his lap and find their hands entwined, resting on his thighs, their plain gold wedding bands glinting in the afternoon sunlight.

He felt it so acutely, this desire to possess Blossom. It had been growing swiftly and steadily since the moment he read his brother's telegraph. Before, he had not allowed himself to think in such terms. She had been his brother's betrothed and therefore forbidden. But now—everything had changed. Every thought, every feeling. And while he was just beginning to accept such feelings, he was realistic enough to know that she had never felt this way about him. What he wanted was singular—for now.

"I've seen her."

There was no reason to elaborate. His mother would have most certainly told his father about Jase's unrequited lust for their neighbor. There were no secrets in their marriage, and while Jase wished his mother had not told his father, he respected the fact that they held nothing back from each other. One reason their marriage had been so prosperous.

"Sit," his father murmured. He waved to the empty chair that sat across from them. Too keyed up to sit and stay immobile, he paced the perimeter of the room.

"You must know what has brought me home."

"I would like to think it was to see your family, but I can tell from the way you are pacing the floor, that it was to see someone else entirely."

"What the devil was my brother thinking?" he suddenly exploded. "By God, her reputation! Did he not have a proper thought or care in that direction?" Bloody hell, how could Samuel not want her, when every fiber of his being cried out for her.

"Your brother followed his heart," his father began, and was interrupted with Jase's outburst of "Hang his heart!"

"Dearest, you must sit and take some tea. It will revive your spirits."

"Forgive me, Mama, but my spirits are rather invigorated. In fact, they might even be oversensitized." Good Lord, he was coming unglued—utterly unhinged. His mind was in a muddle, and his heart...well, he did not possess the courage to glimpse inside.

His mother's gaze followed him as his boots, dusty and battered, left dirt on the Oriental carpet. "Tell me," he murmured, "everything. I...I need to know."

Squeezing his wife's hand, his father took over. "Your brother took a commission this winter in the south. He was gone some weeks, and evidently, while there, he met and fell in love with Cherise, a ballet dancer."

"You'll adore her," his mother cooed. "Such a lovely French accent."

"Cherise!" he exploded. "God, she isn't even a proper English girl!"

His parents shared a glance, and his father's expression turned to a scowl. "She is a very nice young lady, and you'll like her, and accept her just as we all have."

"Bloody hell, am I the only one present who realizes how reprehensible his actions were?"

"He didn't love her."

Whirling around, he confronted his parents. "How the hell couldn't he? My God, I would—" Jase stopped and let out an aggrieved breath. His parents looked at him expectantly, their expressions knowing, his father's daring, challenging him to confess his deepest, darkest secret—that maybe, somehow, in some strange twist of fate, he might actually be in love with his brother's former fiancée. Had been in love with her for years. No. Impossible. He had lusted after her, for certain. But love…

"Well, it's just not done," he said instead. "Her reputation, the gossip, not to mention the legalities involved in a breech of contract."

"There has not been, nor will there be, any legal ramifications," his father announced. "And her reputation has not been withered by this—in fact, it has been renewed."

Jase narrowed his gaze. "What do you mean by that?"

"Blossom is even now entertaining possible suitors," his mother said. "The duke and duchess are hosting a country house party as we speak. They're having a dinner tonight. You'll have to come along—I'm certain Jane and His Grace will be desirous to see you again."

His brain shut down after hearing the word *suitors*. He heard nothing else, only saw Blossom in a ballroom surrounded by slathering piranhas in gentlemen's clothing.

"Ah, here is the tea," his mother said. "Won't you have a cup?"

Without a word, Jase left the room. In the hall, he stalked, heading to the front door. Beetle reached for his hat, and held it out to him, but Jase ignored him and wrenched the door open.

He had no idea where he was going, he only knew he couldn't stay here. Couldn't sit and take tea and make polite conversation with his parents. His mood was not polite. It was volatile. What he needed was a bruising ride through the woods, and a plan.

CHAPTER FIVE

"DO YOU LIKE THE SOUTH country, Lady Blossom?" Lord Halston inquired as he sprinkled a generous amount of salt on the fillet of trout that graced his plate. Thankfully, their somewhat tenuous meeting at tea that afternoon seemed far behind them. Halston had been eagerly talkative this evening, appearing as though he had quite forgotten the matter of her paint-stained fingers and apron. She might have been far more relieved by that if Halston would begin talking of something other than his own merits.

"Indeed, I do, my lord. Lovely scenery in the south."

"I have a grand estate on the ocean. Oh, and one in Ireland, near Cork, and another in the Peak District, and am looking to purchase some land on the coast, near Blackpool. Land, you know, particularly property which can be developed, is the best investment. Wouldn't you agree?"

They were on the third course and already Blossom had a blistering headache. How was it she had not realized how talkative his lordship was? Since they had been seated side by side at dinner, his gums had not stopping yammering on. He talked a great deal—about himself. His houses, his estates, his stocks, his mounts and the pack of hounds he was breeding. She was rather sick of him. Was this but a taste of what it would be like being married to him? She found herself wondering exactly how long it took to completely know another. She was quite taken aback by this change in him. After their few meetings and dances she thought him to be a polite, refined gentleman, not a pompous braggart. She truly loathed men who boasted about themselves and appeared self-important. That failing she could not, and would not, ignore. She had liked Halston—before this evening. With a sigh, she realized that it was time to rethink things.

"Have you been to the Peaks?" he asked, not waiting for her answer. "Lovely country, just lovely. My estate there, you know, is nearly a thousand acres—well wooded, and stocked with pheasant and deer. Rivals Scotland's grounds for hunting. Coveted, my hunting invitations are. Always have more guests than rooms and I hate to dash anyone's hopes, but I'm afraid disappointment is inevitable when it comes to one of my hunting parties, for there are always so many eager for a chance to hunt in my park. What do you think of the hunt?"

"I do not—"

"You'll have to come this fall. Spectacular scenery. And I have just the right mare for you to ride to the hounds. Smashing time we'll have of it."

"I think you'll find that Lady Blossom does not care for blood sports."

The deep voice from across the table broke through Halston's pomposity.

"Eh?" Halston glanced at her, and then at the man seated across from him. "How would you know, Raeburn?"

Jase's smile was part cynicism and part disgust. Above them, the chandeliers cast a golden glow on the table, and bathed in such light Jase's black curls shone. The light also made his moss-green eyes glow, lending him a rather mysterious aura. There was no denying that Jase Markham was extraordinarily beautiful for a man. He had the face of a romantic poet, but the body of a sportsman.

Tall, broad, well muscled. There was nothing soft about that body. Nor the look he was giving Lord Halston.

"Well?" Halston challenged.

Jase tossed his napkin aside and sprawled back in his chair. Blossom was positive she heard the Sommerton twins sigh in simpering awe at the picture he presented— all handsome, indolent rogue.

"I know, Halston, because I have known her all my life. The lady does not care for bloodshed. She is a gentle soul, and would far rather embrace the woodland creatures than shoot them dead."

"Oh."

Jase shared an amused smile. "Is that not right, Lady Blossom?"

The fish suddenly seemed tasteless in her mouth. He was making a scene. Numerous people, including her father, had ceased their own conversations and were now watching intently.

Intent on putting a halt to Jase's mischief, she graced Halston, who sat to her right, with a polite smile. "Indeed it is, I'm afraid. Although I will say that I greatly admire the woods in the autumn. Such marvelous colors, and wonderful inspiration for painting."

Halston grunted, clearly not as appreciative as her to the changing seasons. Halston would not notice anything but a flock of pheasant, and deer. Good Lord, she wondered if he was the sort of sporting man that would bring home his kill, parading it about for everyone to admire, only then to have it served that night at dinner.

Her stomach soured, and she reached for her wine. She had never thought of Halston like that, but she knew that many peers and rich merchants found great pleasure in hunting and killing.

"Well, then, perhaps the south would be better," Halston mumbled. "Nothing there to offend your sensitive feminine sensibilities."

"Yes, the ocean," Jase murmured as he lifted his wineglass to his lips, "perfect inspiration for Lady Blossom to paint."

Halston's face flushed the tiniest bit, and Blossom sent Jase a warning glare. He was teasing her by goading Halston. The bored rake, amusing himself. He arched his brow, challenging her, and they sat in silence, each staring at each other until, thankfully, her father interrupted the quiet.

"Never been one for the hunt. I consider myself a lover, not a hunter."

Amusement rang out loud and a few men lifted their goblets in toast to her father, who, with that one well-placed line, was able to set the table at ease again, and the discourse flowing freely.

Halston, fortunately, turned to his plate and ate, leaving her in silence. Jase, however, continued to stare at her from his place across the table. Just what the devil was his purpose here tonight? To humiliate her? When he had accepted her invitation to dine with them, she had thought it a marvelous idea. He was a friend—albeit, it had been a long time since they had been on intimate speaking terms—but that hadn't mattered. All she could see when she looked at him was a sanctuary of sorts. He would save her from all her zealous suitors, free her for a dance or two so she could think of nothing but the dance, not outmaneuvering her suitors. Perhaps he could escort her out into the gardens for a moment of fresh air and quiet. She had thought all those things, but now she wondered if it was wise to have invited him. He seemed more a nuisance than a savior.

"How is your painting?" Jase inquired. "I seem to recall hearing you had accepted a commission."

"Yes," she replied, conscious of the fact that Halston was watching her with curiosity. "It is a series of vignettes to be included in a retelling of *The Lady of Shallot*."

"Ah," he murmured, his eyes glistening wickedly. "I adore Tennyson. What of you, Halston?"

The earl mumbled a reply, one Blossom did not hear clearly. She had no idea if Halston's interests ran to the arts.

"I assume you still enjoy reading?" Jase asked. "Are the Brontë sisters still your favourite? I recall a spirited debate we had once, about whether Heathcliff was a villain, or an antihero."

Smiling, she bit her lip, remembering that hotly debated thought. She, of course, had believed the brooding, insolent Heathcliff a misunderstood man. Jase had accused her of romanticizing the villain.

"Ah, I see you do, too." He smiled. "You presented your side with such enthusiasm."

She had been a harridan. And he had laughed at her, making her punch him in the arm in frustration.

"I remember it fondly," he murmured, his voice dropping into a seductive purr. "In fact, I can still see you, your cheeks glowing pink with indignation."

Halston's gaze volleyed between them, making Blossom aware of the intimacy that seemed to crackle between her and Jase. She wondered if Halston noticed, or if anyone else did.

"That was a long time ago, my lord," she answered quietly. Their gazes met across the table, and Blossom looked away, lest anyone notice how they had conversed without any thought to the others at the table.

"It was not that long ago, Lady Blossom, I still vividly recall it—and you."

His voice was like a caress, and she shivered in response to the way his voice seemed to glide along her.

"I understand you've been in the north this past year," an aging viscount asked Jase, breaking the tension. "Breeding Arabians, I've heard. A spunky breed. Must be a handful."

"Indeed. But I believe that anything in life with spirit is worth the effort. Wouldn't you agree?"

The viscount laughed and tipped his fork at Jase. "And taming that spirit, eh? I've heard you're a master at it."

Jase's gaze once more found hers. "Not fully tamed. I would never change a creature's temperament or bend them to my will for my own amusement or personal gains."

Her father, Blossom noted, had suddenly taken an extreme interest in her end of the table, particularly Jase. "Spirit is a marvelous thing," her father stated. "It is up to a man to harness it, to keep it free from danger, but never to snuff it out completely. Men feel the need to tame because they are not confident enough to allow such spirited freedoms. It is a rare man who is strong enough to, say...allow a woman such spirit."

"Agreed, Your Grace."

"Oh, ho!" The viscount laughed. "Now we have left the topic of horses and have turned the conversation to something bordering on shocking!" The table laughed, even the women. But Halston, she noticed, glared at Jase.

"Trust my husband to introduce such a unusual topic of conversation," her mother said graciously. "But it would not be a Torrington country house party without a little something shocking."

"To Your Graces, then," the elderly gentleman toasted. "For your gracious hosting, your unpretentiousness and refreshing outlook. I always enjoy myself here."

They drank a few more toasts, and three more courses were served before dessert arrived. A chocolate-and-cream concoction that happened to be her favorite. Once the dessert was over, her mother rose and suggested the ladies retire and allow the gentlemen their cigars and port. Blossom had never been more eager to escape in her life. Her response to Jase unnerved her. In fact, she was so keen to put distance between her and Jase that she left half of her dessert!

THERE WAS NO FIRE LAID in the hearth, but Jase stared down into the empty grate, anyway. Closing his eyes, he thought of Blossom wearing that lovely soft pink gown. What a startlingly contrast to all that ebony hair that was wound up high on her head. And that fresh-as-cream skin that made him want to lap at her. What a dichotomy she was—an innocent little frock, covering a body made for sin. He hadn't been able to take his eyes from her. He'd thought her lovely before; tonight he thought her utterly breathtaking.

"Not so subtle in there, were you?"

His father came to stand beside him, and they kept their backs to the other men as they conversed in low tones. "Subtlety is for sneaks and weaklings," he replied. "I'm neither. I want her. And I will have her."

"So you decided to give notice to every unattached male present."

"What would you have done if you knew the woman you desired was being surrounded by venomous snakes? I at least give fair warning before I strike."

"I admire your doggedness, but you're going about it a bit strong, aren't you? You've only just arrived back home."

Jase stared incredulously. "What? You'd have me wait, and allow Halston more time with her? You're mad. No, I'm staking my claim—tonight."

His father smiled. "I can see myself in you. I guess

you could say that I went about wooing your mother in the same fashion, with single-minded tenacity."

"I wasn't trying to be rude," he mumbled, "well, perhaps bordering it. But damn it, Halston doesn't know a bloody thing about her. She was pale and fidgeting when he was droning on about the hunt. I couldn't allow it to continue."

"Nevertheless, you cannot come barging in and make such a blatant claim. People will talk no matter how veiled you might have thought that comment was."

Sighing, Jase pressed his eyes shut. Christ, he hadn't the patience for social politics. It made no damn sense to him.

His father looked at him assessingly. "It is wooing you are about, isn't it?"

The mere hint that Jase was being less than sincere riled him. Yes, he desired her, but there was so much there, more than he had ever thought possible. Just seeing her seated beside Halston had made him as dangerous as a taunted lion. He had known by his reaction that much more than desire had made him return to her.

"Here."

A new voice was beside him, so was a hand, holding out a crystal glass of whiskey.

"My thanks, Your Grace."

Blossom's father nodded, then proceeded to look him over, from the top of his hair, which he wore a bit too long for fashion, to the tip of his boots, which he'd made certain his valet had shone to a high gloss.

"Nice to see you back," the duke said. "It's been a while."

"It has."

"What is the enticement?"

There it was. The thing he most admired about the Duke of Torrington. He cut to the heart of the matter. He played the politics of politeness only so far. In this matter, Jase was absolutely relieved.

Taking a sip of the whiskey, he let it slide down his throat, savoring the heat of it. "I believe you already know, Your Grace."

"I suspect. Let's put it that way."

"Perhaps I'll take my leave." His father patted his shoulder and departed for the others, which were thankfully a safe distance away.

"You've made the right first impression," the duke began. "I believed you, back there at the table, when you spoke of spirit. I also know you weren't speaking of your damned Arabians, but my daughter."

Their gazes met, and Jase held the duke's cool blue eyes. He would not back down. He fleetingly wondered if Halston could hold his own against Blossom's father.

"It's not her dowry, or a connection to a powerful duke, I'll tell you that."

"So you'll take her without the dowry, then?"

Jase held his gaze steady on the duke's. "Absolutely."

Torrington broke out into a smile. "Prat," he muttered.

"With all seriousness, Your Grace, I have for some time…admired Blossom. But with her engagement to my brother…" Oh, God, he was starting to sweat.

"Mmm, yes, it wouldn't do to pursue her. Kindness among brothers and all that."

Relief made him exhale long and hard. Torrington was making this easy—too easy.

"Indeed. As I was saying. I've long admired her and wish to get to know her better."

Torrington's eyes narrowed. "What are you suggesting?"

"I'm asking permission to court your daughter."

"Are you indeed? How interesting. Not sure how this

sort of thing is done. You see, I already granted Halston the privilege of courting my daughter."

Jase couldn't hide the anger that suddenly burned in his eyes. The duke shrugged.

"My daughter seems to like him—well, as much as any of them. Perhaps if he can be made to come around to her way of thinking, it could be an agreeable match. Unfortunately it is that spirit issue again. So, tell me, Raeburn, what is the proper etiquette in these situations?"

"I believe, Your Grace, that in this the best man should win."

"I like your obstinacy, although I'm not quite enjoying the thought of my daughter as some prize to be won. Smacks of male pride and vanity, don't you think?" Torrington's eyes darkened, and he stepped forward. "If this were your daughter, what would you do?"

"I would allow her to get to know both men, and then consent to let her choose for herself."

"Hmm." Tossing back the contents of his glass, the duke placed the tumbler on the mantle. "I like you, Raeburn. Always have. But that doesn't mean I want you in my family."

"And Halston would suit you better?"

Torrington's smile raised the hair on Jase's neck. "I like to be in control, Raeburn—always. Halston would be far easier, I think, to keep under my thumb than you. You understand, don't you? And if you don't, you at some point will, once your daughter is being preyed upon by leagues of gentlemen who are nothing more than wolves in sheep's clothing."

Strangely, he began to see the workings of Torrington's mind, understood the profound love, and need to protect her. It would be nothing less with his own father when Julia came of age.

"Very well, Raeburn, permission granted. Although I will be watching you like a hawk circling a mouse."

"I would expect nothing less."

"By the by, I thought you might like to know that Halston will be taking Blossom fishing tomorrow morning by the lake. Perhaps you might like to join them. My gamekeeper will show you where to find rods and tackle."

With a slight nod, Torrington left him, and Jase smiled to himself. The first hurdle had successfully been jumped. Now he only had Blossom to convince that he was the right man for her.

CHAPTER SIX

LAUGHING, BLOSSOM SKIPPED down the long line of the country dance, her cheeks flaming red with her efforts. She hadn't sat out one dance, and her partner, a Mr. Thornton, was most agreeable. When it was done, he clasped her hand in his and squeezed hard.

"That was quite possibly the most enjoyable dance I've ever had." He laughed.

"I wholeheartedly concur, Mr. Thornton. But I must beg you to quit the floor. I'm parched, and in need of some fresh air."

"Shall I join you?"

He posed no real threat, she decided, and she had enjoyed his company. He was a lively man, thoughtful, intelligent, and he obviously knew how to have a spot of fun.

"I would be delighted, sir."

They would not be totally private, and that suited her just fine. If she stayed close to the door, everyone would see them, and see that they were only taking the air and having polite conversation. It was safe.

"Ah, what a glorious breeze," Thornton gasped as he led them outside. Blossom lifted her face to the sky and inhaled the humid air.

"What a relief. I thought I was going to melt."

Thornton's gaze drifted over her. "You don't look the worse for wear, Lady Blossom. In fact, you are more beautiful than when you first entered the salon. Then you were lovely. Now, with your flushed cheeks, you're breathtaking."

If possible, she flushed even more. Such flattery. She wasn't used to such bold compliments.

"I've embarrassed you. My apologies. I...forgot myself."

"No, indeed. Please, do not worry. Although I am embarrassed. There are many lovely ladies present tonight."

He smiled, then stared at her with what could only be described as a thoughtful expression. "You're really rather magnificent. There is no artifice about you at all."

Glancing away, Blossom studied the other guests who were promenading on the terrace. "I despise artifice, almost as much as I loathe the art of flirtation and coquetry. It seems silly to hide behind such things."

"I do agree."

Inhaling the cool breeze that rippled the hem of her gown, Blossom gazed up at the stars. "Do I detect a Yorkshire accent, Mr. Thornton? It's faint, but I can hear it."

"Aye, lass," he said, intentionally allowing his accent to be heard.

"I've never been to Yorkshire. I wonder," she whispered while gazing up at the black velvet sky, "if the stars are just as brilliant and beautiful there as they are here?"

"I do not know for I have never taken the time to stargaze. I doubt they are in Leeds, where I am from. The soot from the factories and the coal smoke obliterates everything."

"How unfortunate, Mr. Thornton. There is such pleasure to be had to sit idle on the summer grass and watch the stars."

"I shall have to attempt it. But tell me, is it better with company?"

A faint tremor flittered through her belly, and Blossom stepped back, surprised that she felt it.

"I believe it is, Mr. Thornton."

"Then may I request that we watch the stars together? Perhaps tomorrow night?"

"I think I would like that. Perchance you might wish to ask my father's permission."

"Of course. I shall take the opportunity to do so now. I see he is alone at the buffet. You will excuse me?"

Blossom curtsied to his bow, and the faint rolling in her stomach started once again as he reached for her hand. "Thank you for the dance, Lady Blossom."

And then he was gone, and she found herself smiling like a simpleton. That little flutter…was it a taste of what passion might be like? She had never experienced such a sensation, but it was most pleasant, and she was eager to experience it once more.

"What are you grinning about?"

Jase was standing beside her, one elbow propped upon the stone balustrade as he watched the couples on the terrace proceed back into the ballroom. The orchestra was preparing for a waltz, but mercifully she was free for this dance. She wanted to stay outside where it was cool and quiet.

"Well?"

"Nothing, really, just ruminating on the stars. They're lovely and bright tonight, aren't they?"

"Indeed." He cleared his throat. "What was Thornton doing out here with you?"

She looked away from the sky, only to find Jase staring at her. "We were taking the air. Why?"

He shrugged. "I thought you might like to know that he's broke. He's been hanging out for an heiress for the Season."

"And why would I care to know such a thing? He is not the only one here hunting for an heiress."

"No, he is not. But I saw the way you smiled at him. I thought I should let you know before you got your hopes up."

"How did I smile at him?"

He pressed closer to her, and his hand, so warm and soft, cupped her chin. "With your eyes, Blossom. When you smile at the others it is only with your mouth."

"Oh."

"I've known you long and well enough to recognize your false smiles. Halston was the recipient of one tonight, at dinner."

"I really had no idea you knew me so well."

His smile was slow, seductive, and Blossom wondered if it was really that easy for Jase—to just smile like he was now smiling at her, and have women lay down at his feet.

"But I'm wondering, Blossom, do you know me?"

Oh, she knew him all right. What sort of rake he truly was. He was beautiful and sensual, and an utter heartbreaker. He was the sort of man a woman should never dare give her heart to. Friendship was one thing, but to love Jase, it would prove too painful.

"Well?"

"I believe I do. I have known your family all of my life. How could I not know you, too?"

"How indeed."

He did not release his hold on her, but stepped closer to her. They were now all alone on the terrace, and she felt a sudden fear at the knowledge.

"Would you honor me with this dance?"

The gentle breeze stirred once more and Blossom enjoyed the way the warm night air caressed her neck and shoulders. "Would you be terribly offended if I decline?

I'm afraid the night has too strong a hold on me, and I was hoping for a respite, however small, from the gentlemen who would hound me—or my mama, who seems to be forever introducing me to new marriage-minded candidates."

"No offence taken. Shall we take a walk, to the lake? It's the best place to stargaze, if I remember correctly."

"I…I don't think that would be wise."

"I have your father's permission."

"It's not my father that worries me, but other people's perception."

"Halston, you mean."

Reluctantly she nodded. "A woman's reputation can be ruined by the most innocent of things. And I'm quite certain that sitting beneath the moon in the dark with a man would be grounds for utter ruination."

He smiled, and it momentarily knocked her off-kilter. He was wickedly beautiful, and suddenly her heart seemed to be beating irregularly. "If one's reputation is to be ruined, it would be far more enjoyable to be ruined by a friend, beneath the stars."

Laughing quietly, Blossom felt at once that the strange frisson between them was gone, replaced to their normal footing. Jase was a friend. If she remembered what he truly was, she would be safe. "Well, I suppose there are less dramatic ways to be ruined. If a young woman hanging out for a husband must be ruined, it is far more romantic to be seduced by starlight than to be dragged by carriage to Gretna Green."

"Seduced by starlight. How interesting. I'll have to keep in that mind." He grinned, showing perfect white teeth. His smile lit up his face, and Blossom, for the second time in only minutes, was left feeling a touch breathless. The intimacy that had shimmered between them at supper rose once again. She could not understand it, or put a name to it. But it was there, palpable and strong, pulling her closer to him.

"Shall we?"

She linked her arm in his and followed him down the terrace, to the garden. They walked past the ornamental gardens, and down the stone path that led to the lake. In the moonlight she could see the rowboat that was tied to the dock. The wind was still, and the water moved with the barest of ripples. In the distance crickets and frogs broke the silence, and fireflies flickered around them, lighting their way.

"This seems like a very lovely spot." Shrugging out of his coat, Jase placed his jacket on the ground and reached for her hand. She tried to refuse—his jacket would be wet from the dew on the grass—but he would hear none of it, and helped her to sit. He dropped down beside her, his weight resting on his elbows as he gazed up at the black velvet sky, which was littered with brilliant twinkling stars.

"Do you remember the constellations?"

"Of course. I was eight when you taught me."

"No one shared my infatuation with the stars like you did."

That was because she had been in the first flush of puppy love then. She had hung on to every word Jase had said. She truly had loved the stars, but there was no denying her fascination had grown after she discovered his obsession with them.

"Up in the north, they're even more brilliant. Over the open moors, there is nothing but expanses of heather and sky, and when you look up and smell the salt air from the ocean, and see the vastness of black sky, it's… indescribable."

Blossom tilted her head back and stared up at the stars. "One day I would love to see that."

"One day I'll take you."

The intimacy of his voice startled her and she chanced a peek at him, only to discover that he was staring down at her.

"Do you still enjoy riding?"

She swallowed hard. "Very much."

"And I know you still fish, from our conversation earlier today."

"Yes, I enjoy it very much."

"And painting. You've become very successful at that, haven't you? But then, I knew you would. You were always very talented."

Flushing, she glanced away from him. "Thank you, my lord."

"Jase. You never 'my lorded' me before, Blossom. Nothing has changed between us. There is no need for formality between us."

Oh, but there was. Without it, she was left feeling much too at ease. It would be far too easy to fall beneath Jase's masculine spell. There was no denying he was beautiful, and his voice was as hypnotic as the winter wind. She could not lie to herself, he had intrigued her tonight, held her enthralled. And she must not allow it. Not if she wanted to keep her heart whole.

"We have much in common, Blossom. I, too, love to ride. And fish."

And do other things, she reminded herself, to many different women.

"Starlight becomes you, Blossom. Your skin is so pale, like night-blooming flowers in the moonlight."

Her corset felt too tight, and her breath caught for the barest of seconds. She was about to catch her breath again when he raised his hand and let his fingers trail across her cheek.

"I can see why so many of your parents' guests are tripping over themselves to catch your attention."

She was mesmerized by his eyes, the scruff of his night beard, the way the soft breeze ruffled his curls—the soft, lulling words he was weaving around them. "They want only my dowry and connections with my father."

"I doubt that is all they want."

She looked away, but he caught her chin on the edge of his hand and forced her to look at him. "What do you want, Blossom? When you think of your future, what do you see?"

"What any woman does, a husband and a home. Children."

"And this husband, what is he in your mind?"

"What do you mean?"

He leaned forward, crowding her, and she moved back. It wasn't until she felt the satin lining of his jacket against her shoulders that she realized she was flat on her back, and Jase was above her, his fingertips gliding down the column of her throat, where they rested on her bounding pulse.

"What would your marriage be like, Blossom? Would it be frightfully polite? Sedate and dull?"

"Of course not. I would never settle for such a thing. Just because Samuel and I...did not suit, does not mean that there isn't someone else out there that would make me a suitable husband."

"Ah, yes, Samuel. Tell me, how are you, Blossom? Really." The question was so odd, his voice so quiet, almost strained.

She was nervous. She didn't understand this line of questioning, or the strange feeling that was coming over her. Perhaps she had imbibed too much wine at dinner. "I am very well, milord, as you can see. Do I not look it?"

His gaze raked over her, his eyes hot and gleaming,

lingering on the front of her gown where no gentleman would even look, let alone allow his gaze to linger. "You are most definitely looking very fine. But what of your spirit? Is it whole?"

"Oh." They were back to talking about that. He was inquiring after her well-being after being thrown over by his brother.

"I would apologize for Samuel and his callous handling of you."

"Oh, please don't. I'm fine. Really. I'm glad he followed his heart. And now he's very happy. And so...so am I." Something inside her flared to life. She couldn't understand it, this strange feeling. Perhaps it was the wine, or the stars, or maybe it was just Jase and his rogue's sensuality.

He was still holding her chin, but now he was rubbing the pad of his thumb along her cheek. That fluttering in her belly started once more, but this time it was a thousand times more acute. She felt Jase's touch down to the tips of her toes.

But of course she would. He was a practiced seducer. A rake. A womanizer. Making women feel pleasure was his vocation.

"I am very happy, my lord," she muttered as she sat up and put distance between them. "And I'm looking forward to finding my own love, just like Samuel did."

"Are you?" His eyes lit with interest. "And what are your requirements for this love?"

She flushed, and stammered. She must clarify the matter with him. "My lord, I believe we are speaking of two different things. When I said love, I did not mean a...a sort of affair, but rather a love that would bring about marriage."

He smiled. "I know full well what you meant, Blossom.

You're not the sort to trifle with an affair. I believe that you're a woman meant to be a wife and mother—"

"And a professional painter," she finished.

"There is that. And what else? What other requirements for marriage do you have?"

"Honesty, loyalty, fidelity, the ability to converse with ease, and the capacity to sit quietly in the silence without feeling the need to fill it with frivolous topics. And passion, I must have that in my marriage."

"Passion?"

"Yes. A most ardent and abiding passion. Like my parents have."

"And mine."

The way he said that, so deep and dark and delicious, made her body hot. What was the matter with her? This was Jase, teasing her. She no longer felt that puppy love she once held for him when she was a young impressionable girl. She was a woman now, and knew that any happiness or pleasure with Jase Markham would be fleeting at best. The regret, however, would be ever present.

"What are you about?" she asked suspiciously. "You're acting very odd this evening."

"Am I? I don't see how."

She laughed, a nervous high-pitched sound. "You've hardly even talked to me in the past five years, and now you're acting as though we are very good friends."

"Are we not?"

"No, I don't believe we are. Once, that was true, but I don't think it can be said now."

"Perhaps I want more, Blossom. Much more than friendship."

The world suddenly stopped turning and she felt as though she had been doused by a bucket of cold water. It all made sense now. His return to Bewdley. The marked attention he had paid her this evening, and his questioning about marriage and husbands. Jase was a rogue, there was no doubt about that, but one thing he had was honor. And it was that sense of honor and duty that had brought him here—to her.

"Perhaps I want to court you, Blossom."

"No." Her flat refusal made gave him pause.

"I beg your pardon?"

Jumping up, she smoothed her skirts, and hid her face from him. She didn't want him to see that her cheeks had turned red with shame. "I know what you're doing. I understand why. I mean, I know you feel that you must avenge me because of what your brother did, but really, it isn't necessary. There is no reason for you do this. Samuel and I amicably agreed to end our betrothal, there is nothing to right. As your attentions have been very straightforward, and as I am not a naive young girl, I feel very confident in saying that I believe your arrival here is to court me. And I can assure you, there is no reason for you to, or for you to…offer for me."

"What if this is not about righting my brother's wrong? What if I am truly ready to marry and settle down?"

"Then I would say that you have had the impulsive idea that with our family's long-standing friendship, marriage to me would be efficient and convenient."

He rose to his feet, his gaze dropping to her mouth. "How wrong you are. I intend to show you just how wrong your thinking is, Blossom."

"I do not have it in mind to marry you, or allow you any sort of courtship." His eyes narrowed and his body grew hard, unyielding, and Blossom knew, understood fully, the reason behind Jase's return to Bewdley. Why he had brought her out here, to the lake. It was not to gaze upon the stars.

"You do not need to feel obligated—"

"This has nothing to do with Samuel."

"You are a rake, sir," she said, halting his advance upon her, "and I would never marry a rogue. I would rather be married for my money than to suffer a libertine as my husband."

"But what of passion, Blossom?"

"I don't believe you and I could ever have that."

His smile was sin incarnate, and the strange fluttering began once more. Her hands were trembling, and suddenly she felt unsteady on her feet.

"Do you care to wager on that, Lady Blossom?"

"You are a practiced seducer, sir. I have no doubt that you could employ your learned skills on me, and as a novice in the art of seduction, I would succumb. But I am not looking for fleeting pleasure—I am searching for an undying flame. A passion deep and intense. I doubt, my lord, that whatever misplaced sense of duty and rake's attentions you bestow upon me will be either undying or intense. Now, good night to you, my lord."

She whirled around to leave him, but he captured her wrist and started to pull her toward him—that was, until they both caught sight of her father at the top of slope, watching them.

"You will run away tonight, Blossom. But I will be there in the morning, and then again in the evening. And every day after that. You cannot outrun me forever."

"I have told you, you needn't feel obligated to make amends."

"And I told you that I don't."

"Then what is your true purpose for...this?" she asked as she waved her hand at their surroundings.

"I shall leave you to ponder that, when you are alone in your bed, thinking of me."

She gasped at his arrogance. "You're very presumptuous, my lord, to think that I would even give this conversation a second thought."

"You'll give it more than a thought, Blossom. You'll dream of me."

And then he walked past her, and she was left glaring at the breadth of his back.

Ha! She thought mutinously. What did he know? He did not affect her. Not in the least. Dream of him…that would be the day!

CHAPTER SEVEN

TIRED AND IRRITABLE, Jase took the rod and tackle from Torrington's gamekeeper and headed for the lake. Already he could see the outlines of Blossom and Halston at the edge of the water. The image of Halston there with her set his teeth grating.

He hadn't slept a wink last night. He saw each hour pass, until blackness turned to daylight. Each interminable hour was spent thinking of Blossom, and how damn lovely she had looked beneath the moonlight. When she had lain back on his coat, he had wanted to cover her with his body and take her lips between his. He almost had, but then the conversation had somehow turned on him.

First she thought him obligated to marry her and mend the hurt his brother had caused. And then she had given him her true thoughts—she believed him a rake. The worst sort of rogue, if her words were to be believed. But somewhere during the night, after reliving her words over and over again, he discovered the true reason behind Blossom's distance—her disinterest in him and their friendship. She had fallen under the belief that he lived a libertine's life. She didn't approve. But that realization was swiftly followed by Blossom's words. She desired passion in a marriage. And he was just the man to give it to her. His plan was simple. Make her understand that he was really not the man his reputation purported him to be. And show her passion. It seemed a simple, straightforward idea. Much like Blossom herself, who did not partake of the coy games that women so frequently enjoyed. She had been very honest and up front with him last night. Which led him to believe that she would be very honest in her passion. Passion he knew he could bring forth.

He had no idea when the idea of actually courting and marrying Blossom had come into being. He knew only that it was what he wanted. As he lay in bed, pondering his plan, he waited for the shock and aversion to settle in. It didn't. He wanted to marry her. And now he just had to find a way to show Blossom that he was a far better candidate than Halston.

Upon hearing his footsteps, and the clanking of his tackle as he neared, Blossom glanced over her shoulder. Halston was bent over, fiddling with her hook, baiting it. She was exasperated. He could tell. She was also beautiful standing there in her fetching bonnet and gown—a gown that conformed to her figure like a tight-fitting glove. He knew that figure wasn't all the work of a corset, and the wait to see her, unlace her, was growing intolerable. Too many years of fantasizing about her had made his patience nonexistent.

She wore a straw bonnet tied with long yellow ribbons that snapped in the breeze. The contraption must be driving her mad. Blossom preferred a bare head—especially while fishing. And trousers and hip waders. He smiled, thinking how much a nuisance her yellow morning gown with layers of petticoats was going to be for her.

"Oh, hello, Raeburn," Halston called. "Come to fish, have you? They're biting. Why, look at the pile Lady Blossom has already caught."

Jase glanced at the pile of trout that lay in a bucket full of ice. "Always did have the devil's own luck," he replied as he set his tackle down and opened the box.

"Luck?" she snapped, and he saw her eyes narrow beneath the brim of her bonnet. "It is skill, sir."

Arching a brow, he silently challenged her. She responded by turning around and bending down for a worm. Giving Jase a splendid view of her backside. Oh, how he wanted to touch that lovely derriere.

"Oh, no, you mustn't get your fingers dirty," Halston was chortling. "It would be my honor to bait your hook. Raeburn," Halston muttered, "hold this rod, while I search for the perfect bait, will you?"

"Why?" he muttered as he straightened and headed to the edge of the water and cast his line far out into the lake. "She's been managing her own hooks and bait for years."

He thought he saw Blossom smile, just as Halston glared at him. "A lady of breeding should not be left to soil her delicate fingers, sir. Why, her frock would get dirty and her half boots ruined."

"I suppose that's why she normally wears trousers and hip waders, then."

The earl's eyes nearly bulged out of his head and Blossom sent him a mutinous glare. Jase hid his smile. He took no offence to Blossom in trousers. In fact, he rather enjoyed the view. But what he liked the most was fishing beside her. There were no coy games. No feminine shrieks and theatrics made to keep his attention upon her. They cast their lines, and stood side by side and chatted about all and sundry, quite comfortable in their conversation and fishing skills. At least they had, until his somewhat fabricated reputation had come between their friendship. Until now, he hadn't realized just how much he missed those moments of friendship with her.

"Why did you not wear your waders today, Lady Blossom, hmm? You could move about much more freely. I've never known you to sacrifice practicalities for fashion."

In a surprising fit of pique, Blossom stuck her tongue out at him. *Churl,* she mouthed. He laughed, causing

Halston to glance up and frown. The earl's expression recovered when he realized Blossom was observing him, and his somewhat inadequate skill at baiting her rod. For some childish reason, Jase took perverse delight in that knowledge.

"There you are," Halston said as if he were speaking to a child. "Now, then, might I suggest you cast your line over there. Or shall I do it for you?"

"I am quite capable, sir," she muttered, and Jase held his laugh. Someone else was obviously tired this morning, too.

In silence, the three of them stood, and Jase pretended that he was engrossed in his line, and the beautiful scenery surrounding him.

"What brings you out this early in the morning?" Blossom asked. There was suspicion in her tone.

"I am up at this time every morning."

"Hmph," she huffed.

"Besides, it's been an age since I had someone to fish with."

"I doubt that," he heard her mutter. She ignored him after that, and fixed a smile on Halston. "I do believe I shall move my line, my lord. I'm not even getting the smallest of nibbles at it."

"Mind the rocks," he cautioned. "Your line will catch on them."

"My thanks, my lord. I did not see the somewhat large boulders there."

Her expression was sheer mutiny, and Jase couldn't hold back his chuckle. It only got louder when Blossom reeled in her line in order to recast, only to discover that the bait Halston had placed for her had fallen off. They shared a glance, and she rolled her eyes and sent Halston a defiant glare. Poor Halston. He'd have a time of it with

Blossom as a wife. She needed a particular kind of man, and the stuffy, proper earl was not it.

"Oh, I've got a bite," Halston suddenly cried. He made a great show of struggling with the fish, and Blossom stopped what she was doing to watch. With a snort, Jase continued with his line, all the while watching out of the corner of his eye.

"My lord, he must be a great size," Blossom cried, her excitement clearly showing. "Oh, do have a care, sir. You wouldn't want to lose him."

"Indeed, he must be a rather large fellow for he is giving one devil of a fight."

"Oh, do not let him go," she said, and rushed to Halston's side to watch.

"I shall endeavor not to, Lady Blossom. And by the feel of him, we shall be able to have a picnic lunch with him today."

Jase stopped to watch. This ought to prove amusing. Halston was trying to impress Blossom with his somewhat haphazard angling skills. Jase could only hope it would backfire.

Pulling on the line, Halston struggled, once, then once more, and then with a triumphant "Gotcha," he reeled in his line, pulling his hook out of the water to reveal a fish about four or five inches long.

Blossom's expression fell, and Halston turned crimson. Jase said nothing, only smiled to himself at the absurdity of his lordship going to such theatrics to impress Blossom.

"I'll just throw him back," Halston muttered.

"Indeed, he needs a few more years to grow, I would say," Blossom replied as she baited her hook. Jase caught Halston watching her with a mixture of admiration and horror. It was clear the earl desired her. Found her enchanting, while at the same time he didn't quite know what to make of her. He certainly didn't know what to do with her.

Blossom cast her line and swung it in a graceful arch, and Halston's eyes bugged out once more. Blossom really was a natural when it came to fishing. She was better than Edward and, in truth, better than himself.

"My word, you can cast a line," Halston murmured in awe. "You must have quite an arm."

Blossom smiled, heedless of the way the earl was suddenly studying her body. Beneath that fine dress, Jase knew she would be perfectly formed—utterly feminine. What Halston imagined, he had no idea. He only knew he didn't like the earl's eyes on her.

"Oh, my!" Blossom's breath caught, jerking Jase's gaze away from the profile of her breasts to her face, which was suddenly lit up with excitement. "I've got a bite."

The line jerked, and she moved forward, just a bit, struggling the smallest fraction with the rod. The line went out more, pulling her forward, and she dug her heels into the damp ground. Her cheeks were pink, and she was smiling. When she turned in excitement, it was not to look at Halston, but him.

"Hold on to him," Jase said, then dropped his rod, and came up behind her. "I'll spot you."

He stood behind her, prepared to reach for her if need be, but he didn't touch her. Blossom could do this on her own. He'd seen her do it a hundred times. But whatever was on the other end of that line was giving her a run for her money.

She worked the reel, but the fish was strong, and it pulled at the line, pulling her forward.

"Raeburn, help her," Halston called over his shoulder as he reeled in his own fish.

"No. She can do it. She doesn't need either of us. That's

it," he murmured, "just like that. Let him tire himself out."

"He's big," she whispered breathlessly. "Strong."

"But I think you're stronger."

"I know I am."

He smiled at her arrogance, and when the fish pulled harder, struggling with the hook, Blossom inched forward. Instinctively he stood closer behind her, his hands coming up to span her waist, anchoring her close to him. He didn't dare take the rod from her. But instead allowed her to feel him behind her. He was there if she needed him.

"Your footing, is it okay?" he asked.

"It's a bit soft here and my boot is sinking. You'll stay close?"

"Absolutely." He could see her face lit up, her cheeks pink and her bosom rising and falling with her labored breathing. She glanced up at him over her shoulder, and her blue eyes were sparkling with wonder. "He's tiring."

"Reel him in," he whispered against her ear. "That's it. You're doing fine, and I've got you. Yes, just like that. Bloody hell, you're doing a fine job of it."

The line bobbed and tugged as she reeled, the rod bending forward against the fish's weight and struggle. "That's it, Blos, slow and steady. He's done. I can see it in the way the rod is loosening."

She worked hard, reeling the fish in, giving it no leverage to free itself. It pulled her once, twice, and Jase wrapped his arm around her waist, holding her tight. And then the fish was gliding on the surface of the water, and Blossom and he both gasped at the sight of it.

It landed on the rocks, flopping, gasping for breath, and with a triumphant cry and squeal, Blossom turned in his arms and hugged him tight. "I did it. Look at the size of him, Jase. He's gorgeous."

She was warm in his arms, her breasts pressed up against his chest. He was happy for her; there was no better setting for this, with Halston standing there gaping like a dying fish watching Blossom's remarkable performance.

Lifting her high in the air, he twirled her around and she laughed. When he brought her down, till her toes touched the ground, their gazes caught, stared, and as if in slow motion, he lowered his mouth to hers and kissed her.

CHAPTER EIGHT

"Jase!"

Aware that Lord Halston was behind them, packing up his gear, Blossom pushed herself out of Jase's embrace. What had she been thinking to fling herself into Jase's arms? True, she had been jubilant over her victory of the fish, but to be so brazen, and in front of Lord Halston, too!

The kiss had been nothing but a quick buss against her lips. It meant nothing and hopefully Halston would realize that. Oh, she was mortified that she had lost all semblance of control.

"Congratulations, Lady Blossom. That fellow must be a record breaker. I vow he's at least fifteen pounds."

"Thank you, my lord. Shall we see if we can catch another?"

He looked up at her and smiled as he gathered his rod, and closed the tackle box. "I'm afraid I have a matter of business to attend to this morning. Perhaps we might see each other for tea this afternoon?"

"Of course, my lord."

Blossom watched him stroll past, but the scowl he sent Jase did not go unnoticed. Halston was indignant, and she couldn't blame him.

"Of all the—"

She was stopped, midtirade, when Jase wrapped his fingers around her arm and all but dragged her to the large weeping willow that stood a few feet away. Carefully he brought her up against the trunk, and pressed his body—all lean and hot—against her.

"My God, I can't wait another second to do this." Swiftly, he lowered his mouth to hers, and Blossom felt the instantaneous jolt of excitement rush through her veins. His lips were soft, pliant, beneath hers. He pressed another kiss to her, then another, but this time he opened his mouth, allowing his heat to envelope her, and she stiffened, backing away, not knowing what he wanted. Not liking the heat and confusion he was creating inside her.

He tried again, pressing up against her, encouraging her with his lips to open her mouth for him, but she wouldn't allow him the intimacy. She couldn't.

"Blossom," he groaned. He cupped her face, holding her still as he lowered his lips to her ear. "Let me."

"No."

"Yes."

"No!"

"Just one kiss," he murmured against her ear. "I have to know what it is like—the feel of you. Your taste."

In growing frustration, he cupped her chin with both hands, kissed her hard, hungrily, until she gasped in shock at the intimacy. He took advantage then, slipping his tongue effortlessly between her lips. His hand slid up along her neck and untied the ribbon of her bonnet, flinging it from her head. Then his fingers dove in her curls, squeezing and tugging, angling her head so that he could feel every recess of her mouth as he hungrily deepened the kiss.

Blossom reeled backward, the intrusion of Jase's tongue astonishing her. It was an awkward, odd feeling, yet, she was chagrined to admit it, not totally unpleasant. He smelled of soap and sandalwood and the unmistakable scent of man, and his tongue felt as soft as velvet as he searched her mouth in slow, lazy sweeps that made her feel light-headed.

She should stop this at once, but before she could tear her lips from his he brought her against him, deepening the kiss as her traitorous legs buckled despite her considerable attempts to control them. He was doing devilish things to her with those lips. She'd known the minute she'd looked at him that his finely sculpted mouth had done many wicked things and now his lips were settled on hers, his tongue deep within her mouth, his strong fingers raking through her hair, squeezing and clasping and raking all over again.

She could barely think beyond the pleasure. Only two thoughts traveled through her mind. Samuel's kisses had never felt like this, followed swiftly by the realization she didn't want him to stop.

Damn, if she would only kiss him back, Jase cursed, deepening the kiss further, pressing his arousal against her thighs, ignoring her gasp of alarm when his cock thickened against her leg. He just needed a sign, some flicker of hope, that warmth resided in her. Would she burn for him as much as he burned for her?

Her body tensed as if she were preparing to push him away and flay him alive for his actions. He didn't give her a chance. Instead, he stabbed his tongue deep within her mouth, forcing her to kiss him back—or slap him.

She kissed him back.

Her touch was tentative, driving him recklessly on. He didn't want to overwhelm her, but damn it all, he was far too worked up. He usually needed much more than a kiss to lose all reason. He'd never actually lost his way during lovemaking, and yet Blossom was threatening him with insanity this very minute.

He opened his eyes, consumed with the need to see

her. Her eyes were closed, long lashes fluttering against pale, porcelain cheeks that appeared slack and relaxed.

Without warning, Blossom straightened, shoving herself out of his arms, and slapped him hard across his face.

"You rogue. You rakish—"

"That good, eh?" He grinned, rubbing his cheek. "I rather thought you were enjoying it. I know I certainly was."

Her breath caught and the bodice of her gown brushed his waistcoat, sending warmth snaking through his veins once again when he felt the fullness of her breasts press against his chest. He'd like nothing better than to bury his mouth in her inviting décolletage, to hear her whimper of need as he lowered her bodice and skimmed his lips across her nipples, which he knew would be firm buds waiting for the stroke of his tongue.

"You womanizing mongrel," she hissed, drawing him from the mental picture of Blossom reclined in the grass, him atop her and his hands covering and kneading her breasts. "Oh," she stamped, trying to push past him. "Have you no shame, sir?"

He reached for her arm, his grin gone. "Not when it comes to you, Blossom. I fear I'll stop at nothing to win you."

"Is this a game to you, sir? Are you toying with me, having a laugh at my expense? Or is it your purpose to seduce me in broad daylight only to have us discovered and forced to marry?"

"Do not tell me you didn't want that."

It was the wrong thing to say. He knew it the second the words left his mouth. If he didn't then, he knew now, by the incredulous, disgusted expression on her face.

"Blossom, I'm sorry. That was wrong of me to say."

"More than that is wrong with this picture, my lord."

She tried to move away, but he pinned her against him. "What is wrong with both of us finding passion in each other?"

"I already told you, I'm not looking for the sort of passion you're offering."

"What you think you know of me is a lie. It isn't who I am."

"Please. Do not try to fob me off with that tale. A misunderstood reputation? How clichéd. The romantic hiding beneath the rake's veneer? How trite."

"Damn you, it's the truth."

"You don't want me," she suddenly snapped, struggling in his arms. "And I don't want you. You're only doing this to placate your honor. You believe as the eldest sibling you must right the wrongs of your brother. But you're misguided, my lord. An alliance between us would be the worst possible thing. I won't have you, Raeburn. Do you hear me? I won't."

"Where does it leave us, then, Blossom? For I won't stop until I have you as my wife."

That made her freeze in his arms. When she looked up at him, her expression was one of confusion. "I don't understand this. After all these years you've suddenly decided that you want me for your wife."

"Believe me, it's not sudden," he growled.

Finally, after all this time, he permitted himself the truth. He had always wanted her, and now... He swallowed, allowed his words to whisper through his mind for the first time. He had always thought of her as his wife.

"I can't believe your sincerity. I won't believe it. You seek an easy alliance. Along with that, you believe you can gallantly ride in and save me from your brother's actions, but you're wrong. I'm not looking for a self-sacrificing knight. I'm looking for a man who will love me. Who truly desires me."

In desperation he pressed up against her, allowing her to feel his aroused body. "And I do not desire you?"

"It's a...momentary madness," she whispered, her breath catching as she felt his heavily aroused body pressing into hers. "A dangerous spark."

"Oh, how little you know me, Blossom. This spark, as you call it, has been threatening to ignite for years."

"You don't truly want me, Jase. It's honor and duty, and nothing more. Besides, why would you want soiled goods—and goods soiled by your brother."

Through his haze of desire, he realized what Blossom was trying to do. She was attempting to dissuade him, to disgust him, by allowing him to believe that she had lain with his brother. "Do not lie to me, Blossom. I know nothing more than chaste kisses have passed between you and my brother."

"And how would you know that?"

"You've the look of a woman who has not yet bloomed beneath a man. But I promise you, I will be that man. And you will flower," he murmured against her ear. "Beneath my hands, my body, my mouth."

"No," she whispered, but he could see the battle being waged in her eyes, the force it was taking to deny it. He could reach out and kiss her again. Skim his hands along her curves and feel her. He could make her bloom now, but he had no wish to take her like this, to force her hand. He would wait a bit longer, until the desire, the attraction, was undeniable, and then he would show her passion beyond her wildest dream. And then she would believe that she could find the sort of husband she dreamed of in him.

"This afternoon, I'll meet you for tea."

"I won't be there."

"Then I'll find you. And I won't rest until I discover

wherever it is you're hiding. And when I find you, I'll kiss you, and I won't stop. Not even if you beg."

OH, HOW THAT KISS HAUNTED her. It had been two days since that moment by the lake, and still Blossom could feel the pressure of his lips against her mouth, the sweep of his tongue against hers. Her tummy flipped, as though a legion of butterflies were circling, every time she thought of it. Try as she might, she was consumed by thoughts of him. Dreams of that kiss and what more she might have been able to experience.

She tried to console herself with the reminder that Jase was a practiced seducer. It was not difficult to make women feel the way he desired them to. But what did that say of her? That she was that weak-willed, that brainless, to fall helpless victim to him? No, she knew better than that. Somewhere, in some deep, ignored recess of her being, was her desire for Jase. She had banked and hidden that desire for so long. But one afternoon alone with him had changed all that. She tried to ignore it, to bury it deep once more, but Jase made it impossible.

He wanted her, she reminded herself. He did not love her. Passion was all well and good, but what was it, what did it mean when it did not accompany love? He had not given her his heart, and, Blossom knew, she would be a fool to give him hers. And because of that, she knew she must find a way to stop thinking of him, and that kiss they had shared.

True to his word, he found her—morning, afternoon and each night. For two days he had hunted her like a panther hunts a helpless gazelle. There were no more kisses. No, that would be too easy. Instead, Jase prowled around her, letting her desire build even as she tried not to let it. He touched her, a brief caress on her arm, a fingertip gliding along her hand. His knee would brush hers at tea, and he would cast his green eyes her way and smile knowingly above the rim of his china cup. And that was just during the day.

At night, he would sit beside her at dinner, and allow his hand to caress her thigh. He danced with her too close—and said nothing during those dances—just made her feel his body brushing against hers. When he wasn't dancing with her he was watching, prowling about the ballroom like a caged lion. His gaze would linger upon her and she would feel the heat of his stare, and when she would glance over her shoulder, she would find him watching her, and her body would heat and tremble twenty feet away from him. That was that power that Jase Markham held over her.

She had almost broke this afternoon at tea. She had almost begged him for another kiss, and damn it, she was positive he knew it, too, for he smiled, that well-satisfied masculine grin, and leaned down to whisper, "Tonight," in her ear.

She was gelatin in his hands, despite her resolve against him. He wasn't husband material—at least, not the sort of husband she desired. But he was passionate. And sinfully handsome. More handsome than any other man she had ever met. And the things he made her feel… What a curse that it would be Jase who did this to her. A reprehensible reprobate who would play fast and furious with her heart and body and then leave her to mind both on her own.

"Blossom?"

The knock and the sound of her mother's voice on the other side of the door pulled her out of her reverie. "Are you well?"

"Yes, Mama."

"Are you coming down to dance? You've been up here for over an hour."

Really? Had it been that long? It felt like only minutes

ago she had fled the dining room for the sanctity of her bedroom. She had pleaded a headache, all in an attempt to put distance between herself and Jase. She could not bear it, being so close to him, and feel herself struggle not to touch him. She was disgusted by her wantonness, demoralized that it had taken so very little to make her desire him.

"Might I come in?"

"Of course."

Blossom straightened on the window box where she had been sitting, staring sightlessly out into the night. Lanterns lit the drive, and moonlight danced upon the still waters of the lake. The window was open; the rose-scented air was humid and warm, making her itch to walk in the night.

"Oh, you are pale," her mother said as she sat across from her. She touched the back of her hand to her forehead. "You don't have a fever." The concern she saw in her mother's eyes was her undoing.

"I'm feeling much better, Mama."

"It isn't Halston, is it, Blossom? Your father and I have noticed that he's been suspiciously absent by your side. We didn't think that you cared for him in that way."

Oh, dear. She had no wish to think of Lord Halston. He most likely thought her the biggest flirt—and that was being gracious. No doubt he had told everyone that she had flung herself into Jase's arms like a doxy tart. How could he not stay away from her?

"Or is it someone else entirely?"

The tone of her mother's voice made Blossom look up sharply. One thing her mother was not was naive. She knew about Jase. How could she not?

"Blossom?"

Blowing out her held breath, Blossom leaned her head

back against the wall. "If you must know, then yes. It is Jase."

"I thought so." Her mother's smile made the hair on her arms rise to attention. "He has talked to your papa, you know."

"I can't accept anything he offers. I...I think he's only wishing to marry me as he feels obligated to because of Samuel."

"I don't think so, my love."

"What else can it be, then?"

Her mother's head dipped low to capture her gaze. "A legitimate desire to be your husband?"

She snorted. "Rakes don't want wives, Mama. They desire conquests."

"Rakes don't go about the manner of securing a conquest while said conquest's parents look on, dear."

Oh, damn him. His attentions were blatant. Marked. He had scared off all her other admirers and now he was ensuring her parents knew of his intentions.

"And what makes you think Jase's intentions aren't honorable? We've known him for years, and have never believed him to be anything but a gentleman."

"Mama," she snapped, feeling irritable. "That is just the point. I've known him for decades and never once did I get the impression that he desired anything more than friendship between us. And now, four months after my engagement ends, he's mad to marry me. It's convenience or obligation. I just haven't figured out which yet."

"Oh, darling," she whispered. "Nothing I say will make it right, will it? I guess you will have to discover the truth for yourself."

And she would, too. If it was the last thing she did, she would discover Jase's true motive in this preposterous game he was playing.

"Well, you do look pale. You've had many late nights

and I know you're used to country hours. Why don't you stay up here? I'll make your excuses."

"Thank you, Mama."

Hiding from Jase was exactly what she needed. She couldn't face him tonight. She was too weak-willed to resist him.

The door closed behind her mother, and Sally, her maid, came in to undress her. The blue satin gown was discarded for her night rail and wrapper, and a freshly laundered apron. "I shall be in my studio, Sally, if you need me."

"Very good, miss."

Opening the connecting door to her chamber, Blossom entered her studio and lit the glass lamps. She had started a new painting this morning. A landscape of the garden at night. Silently she sat on her stool and positioned the easel toward the light. Then picking up her brush and dabbing it into the yellow paint, she began to paint the fireflies that dotted the backdrop. With a few strokes of her brush, she was relaxed and calm, and all thoughts of Jase Markham were replaced by her painting.

CHAPTER NINE

HE WAS WAGING A CAMPAIGN, and Jase was not one to be easily thwarted. When the Duchess of Torrington came to him not more than hour ago with the news that Blossom was unwell and would not be joining them, he knew his battle plans would change that night.

Coward. He grinned to himself as he climbed the servants' staircase that lead to the family's private quarters. That was the advantage of years of friendship; he knew precisely how to get to Blossom's room without anyone discovering him. He had to admit, he hadn't thought Blossom the type to turn tail and hide. She was so certain of herself in everything she did, he couldn't help but wonder at why she would not face him tonight.

He hoped she was not truly adverse to him. He paused on the threshold of Blossom's chamber door. His hand was on the brass latch, and he stopped, taking stock of the thought. He thought back to the kiss by the lake, the kiss he hadn't been able to stop thinking about. The kiss that haunted his dreams and made his body ache. He also recalled the little touches, the graze of his hand on hers, the brush of his knee, the glide of their bodies during a waltz. No. She was not adverse to him; she was afraid of her own passionate response. She was a virgin—not a missish one—but an innocent nonetheless. It stood to reason that her passionate response frightened her. She obviously hadn't felt those things for his brother. Not for the first time he found himself wondering what the devil the two of them had gotten up to during their long courtship? How had Samuel resisted such temptation? He ought to be nominated for sainthood as far as Jase was concerned.

Lifting the latch, he quietly stepped into Blossom's room. It was empty. But the connecting door was opened, and he silently crept across the carpet and leaned against the doorjamb, studying the sight before him. Blossom, dressed for bed, her hair long and unbound spilling down her back, painting.

She was humming to herself while her brush moved in slow, sweeping glides against the canvas. He was transfixed by the sight, by the sounds she was making. He imagined her in his house, painting, and him lying on the settee with a whiskey in his hand watching her. Soon, he promised himself. *Very soon.*

Uncrossing his arms, he made his way to her. She didn't pause or stop her humming, but carried on painting. He now stood behind her and allowed his hand to lift her hair and watch the long black strands slide through his fingers.

"'She walks in beauty, like the night,'" he said, murmuring the opening line to Byron's poem. "Yet she hides from me and forces me to come in search for her."

Her hand was frozen, the brush tip poised just an inch above the canvas. Whirling around, she confronted him. "What are you doing here? Are you mad?"

"Desperately so," he said as he took the brush from her hand and placed it in the jar of turpentine. "I've been waiting hours to speak to you, and here you are, hiding in your sanctuary."

"I'm not hiding," she snapped.

He smiled and reached for the ties of her apron. The bow came free, and the bib of the apron fell, revealing the white lace wrapper beneath. "Then what are you doing up here—avoiding me?"

"Yes, if you must know. I'm tired of your constant stares, and you're brazen touches. They aren't welcome."

"Aren't they?" He could see her pulse wildly beating at the base of her throat, saw the way her pupils had dilated with desire.

"I'm not interested in anything you have to offer. Most especially a sordid liaison."

"I'm not offering a liaison. What I'm offering is honesty."

"Oh?"

"Yes. I want you, Blossom. You're not naive, you know what that means. But how I want you is as my wife and lover. I want to marry you. Have a life with you. I want to have a home and children. And I want it all to be with you."

She snorted disbelievingly. "After, what, three days? Your heart must be easily engaged, my lord."

That angered him, and he caught her about the shoulders, stilling her, forcing her to glance up at him in shock and perhaps alarm.

"Try years, Blossom. I've wanted you for years, but it's damned impossible to admit that when your brother is engaged to you."

Her mouth opened and closed. He saw the disbelief. Followed by shock. He had blurted that out, and hadn't meant to. It was too soon. He was too uncertain of her to make himself so vulnerable. But there it was. It was out in the open now.

"What is your hesitation, Blossom? Is it me? Do I disgust you? Tell me so I can right it. So that I can fix whatever it is and we can be together."

"Your reputation. You're hardly the type of man who could make a good husband."

"Give me a chance. I promise I can be faithful and true. Give me your dreams and I'll share them with you. I'll make them happen. You know me, Blossom, better than anyone ever has. You know I won't make you stop painting, you know you can do as you damn well please with me. Wear trousers, go fishing, ride astride. I don't give a damn, just as long as I can be there beside you when you're doing it, that's all."

The silence stretched on, and Blossom felt her blood rushing to her ears. For years he had desired her? Could it be true, or was this another ruse?

Her heart was beating so fast she didn't know what to do. She only knew that Jase appeared utterly sincere, and breathtakingly beautiful. But that was now. What would it be like twenty years from now?

"Desire if fleeting. Once passion is spent, it is gone."

"Not what we'll have Blossom. That isn't fleeting."

"What do we have?"

"Let us make a bargain," he murmured. "Give me one week to show you that I am sincere. Let me show you what sort of husband I could make you."

"I don't know…" Biting her lip she looked away, her cheeks crimson.

"Seven nights, Blossom, to prove that my offer has nothing to do with familial obligations or the desire for an easy, advantageous match, but a burning passion that I can no longer keep hidden. I offer you not a liaison, but a prelude of what our married life could be."

Oh, it all sounded too decadent and tempting. But was a week long enough to know a man well enough to marry him? Anyone could be on their best behavior for a week— even her.

Reaching for her hands, he brought them to his mouth

and closed his eyes as he kissed her knuckles. "You know me," he said in a tortured whisper. "You know the man I am. I've always been that man with you. You can trust me, Blossom. I swear it."

The scrape of his night beard against her fingers made her body ache in a strange way. He released her hands, but Blossom let her fingers uncurl, and skim across his lips. "My heart and mind tell me that this is a terribly great risk. To trust you with myself, my dreams. You have all my hopes for the future in your hands. But my body... it desires what you're offering. It wants me to ignore the warnings and rush headlong into this offer."

"Trust me," he whispered as he pulled her close. "I'll take care of you, Blossom. I won't force you. I'll let you lead in this bargain. Take what you want of me."

What she wanted was everything. Not just his body. He would readily give that, she knew. But she wanted something more. Devotion. And, God help her, love. Passion was all well and good, but without love to support it, it wouldn't last.

"I can see the wheels of your mind turning, Blossom. You're thinking too much. There is a future here for us. You just have to believe it."

She nodded, for faith was all she had. "All right, Jase. I'll trust you. Seven nights, then."

"You won't regret it. I swear, you'll never want it to end."

His mouth came down slow, deliberate, and he kissed her with controlled passion. Opening to him, Blossom pressed her tongue against his and he moaned, clutched her firmer against him as he hungrily took her mouth in his, kissing her as though he were starved for her.

Oh, God, he was beautiful like this—his mouth, his hands caressing her back. They were sliding lower, grasping her bottom, and she held on to him tight, clutching at his shoulders, as his palms moved lower to pull up the hem of her nightclothes.

The heat of his hands on her backside made her moan, mewl against him, and he broke off the kiss on a gasp and moved his lips to her throat, then his tongue flicked out, trailing a scorching line along her skin. She was wet between her thighs, aching there. She didn't know what to do with it, how to alleviate it, so she clutched him harder, shuddered as she said his name.

In a swoop he came up and captured her mouth in a hard kiss, just as one of his hands came free and shoved the wrapper and night rail over her shoulder. The warm air caressed her breast, and she looked down to find Jase staring at her.

"More beautiful than I have ever dreamed, and this nipple. Dark, like cherries." His thumb circled her, and the nipple budded even more. She watched in fascinated wonder as Jase's tongue came out and circled the tip of her breast. Her fingers flew from his shoulders to his hair, which she clutched in great handfuls. When he slipped her nipple into his mouth and sucked, Blossom was frozen, watching as he made love to her. She had no idea if it was wicked of her, but never had she imagined such a thing. Never had she thought it would feel this wonderful to have her breasts touched.

"So responsive," he murmured as he pulled her other shoulder free. Her upper body was now bared to him, and he spent long minutes studying her, touching her with his fingertips in a teasing fashion and cupping the heavy weight of her breasts in his palms.

"Jase, the bed," she whispered, and he smiled, then allowed his lips to skim over her straining nipples.

"We have seven nights, Blossom. There is no need to rush. I could spent an entire night loving your breasts and still not be satisfied."

She moaned, pulled at his hair, her body restless. "You tease me."

"No," he groaned. "Do you think that I don't want to carry you to your room and lift your nightgown and sink deep inside you? I would give my soul for that, but it isn't what you need. Not yet. Trust me to know that, Blossom."

She didn't know what she needed, but her body felt restless and taut. She actually ached deep in her belly and between her thighs.

A door slammed down the hall; it was followed by heavy footsteps. No other person had footsteps like that.

"My father," she whispered, straightening from him and tugging her gown back into place. "Hurry, he might come in to check on me."

Kissing her quick, Jase brought her up against him. "Remember, I'll share you during the day, but the nights, they belong to me, Blossom. To us."

Blossom watched him leave, and as she did so, she brushed her fingers against her lips. She was strangely aware of the keen sense of loss. She liked being in Jase's arms. The feel of him. The strength. She realized then that tomorrow night could not come soon enough.

FOR SOMEONE WHO WAS NOT skilled in the art of seduction, Blossom was doing a damn good job of it. He was wound tighter than a spring-loaded clock, and this, just two nights into their bargain. Good Lord, how would he endure the next five? He was going insane, and Blossom was the reason.

For the past two nights he had lain awake reliving every moment in her arms. She was beautiful, and her body... He was right. It was made for carnal sin. That first night, in her studio, he had seen her breasts, had liked and been aroused by her dark nipples. Last night, he had felt her, the sweet, damp place between her thighs. Her folds had been thick with desire; she'd been wet, and panting, and then they had been interrupted as the guests came out to enjoy the evening air. There had been no other opportunities for them, for the duke was a constant presence by his daughter's side.

As he prowled about the ballroom, watching Blossom dance a waltz with Thornton, Jase realized that there would be no interruptions tonight. He would give Blossom her first real taste of passion tonight, when he pleasured her to her first climax. And if he was lucky, he would get her to touch him, too.

The waltz ended and he was at her side in a flash. A light supper was set up in the next room, and he strolled with Blossom, allowing them to get lost in the guests. When he was certain no one was noticing him, he reached for her hand and dragged her away to the hall, where he tugged her inside the library, which was empty, and took her into his arms.

"My God, you torment me."

She smiled and allowed herself to be caught up in his arms. "You're being silly."

He glared at her. "No, I'm not. I'm actually crazed for you. Come here, Blos. Kiss me," he commanded, his tongue finding its way into her mouth. He gripped her tighter as one hand left her belly and cupped her chin, holding and positioning her the way he wanted.

"Put your hands on me." Taking her fingers in his, he slid them up his chest. Her fingers swept over a muscled chest until they reached the starched cravat and folded collar that shielded his throat. A rivulet of perspiration trickled down his neck, and she followed its path with her fingertip until it disappeared beneath his collar.

His breathing was harsh. She could hear it in the quiet,

could hear his beating heart over the hum of the crickets. She could smell the maleness of him despite the earthy, humid breeze.

Blossom couldn't suppress the shiver that snaked along her skin as he twirled his fingers along her curls. He brought her closer to him and she felt his lips nuzzling her hair.

"Such beautiful skin. I want to touch every inch of you. I have to touch you." The tip of his finger trailed down her throat, slowly, inexorably, to rest at the junction of her breasts. His lips met her skin, gently brushing the swells of her breasts. "I have lain awake at nights dreaming of you."

"And I you."

He grasped her waist and brought her tightly up against him. "I want to touch you and kiss you and feel your body beneath mine. You're wet for me, aren't you? I can feel it, your passion, your passion for *me*."

Oh, yes, she was wet. And she wanted to feel him touch her.

His hand reached for her skirts and she felt him slide his fingers up along her stocking-clad thigh, teasing her. "Tonight I am going to part these sweet thighs and discover the treasure you've been keeping from me."

Blossom moaned and wrapped her arms around his neck, bringing him against the full mounds of her breasts. His body tightened and he brought her closer as he deepened the kiss. She allowed him that, and she even whimpered when he skimmed his fingers along her bodice to brush his thumb against her hardening nipple. Lowering one sleeve, he exposed a full breast to his hand. He cupped her, skimming his thumb along her hard nipple. She moaned into his mouth and he broke off the kiss only to slide the remaining sleeve down her shoulder, revealing her fully to his gaze.

She was perfect. Filling his hands with both breasts, he watched the expression of pleasure cross her face. Their eyes met and he very purposely skimmed both thumbs across the taut, dark nipples. Holding her gaze, he went to his knees, all the time watching her, seeing how she followed him with her tempestuous eyes. Unable to resist the temptation she offered when she filled his palms with soft flesh, he pressed forward, nuzzling the valley of scented skin with his lips. She whimpered and clasped his head to her chest, and for a second he was content to press the side of his face between her breasts and listen to the rapid rhythm of her heart. But then he realized that her nipple, erect and searching, was scant inches from his mouth and he flicked it with the tip of his tongue, first in short flicks, then in slow, languorous circles, relishing the taste, liking the way they puckered for him.

Her knees gave out and she slid to the floor in a puddle of blue watered silk. He held her tightly, stroking her nipple, feeling it firm and quiver beneath his fingers.

"Touch me, Blossom. Oh, God, yes," He reached for her hand and brought it to the flap of his trousers. Ignoring her hushed breath, he flattened her palm against the fabric and smoothed her hand down his swollen cock. Closing his eyes he allowed himself the pleasure of imagining her small hand surrounding him, pumping him slowly until he could stand the torture no longer.

He wanted to take his time, to explore her leisurely, but pent-up desire and the fear that something would happen to interrupt them made him eager and rash.

"Will you let me?" he asked as he kissed her cheeks, then her chin. His fingers were touching her breasts, and she was slipping backward, her shoulders lying across his thighs.

"Let you what?" she whispered.

"Touch you. Between your legs."

Her eyes closed, and her back arched as his palm made the slow descent down her belly and thighs. He thought about just tunneling his hand beneath her skirt, but instead decided to raise her gown, to reveal her fully.

When he was done, she was lying on his thighs, her white stockings tied with blue silk garters; the triangle of black hair was stark against her pale flesh and his hand. The pink silk of her flesh so wet and glistening as she parted her legs and tossed her head in his lap.

He was torn where to look. Her face as she experienced this first rush of illicit pleasure, or his hand, where he was gently parting her folds.

"Oh, God, Jase!"

His gaze tore away from his hand, to watch her. She was beautiful. Wanton. So unashamed and missish in her passion. She embraced it, and bucked up against his hand as the pad of his thumb circled her. One finger slipped inside her—hot, wet and tight—and he closed his eyes, savoring the feel, imagining the time when it would be him slipping slow and deep inside her.

"Yes," she moaned as he slowly built her up. Another finger, which she accepted with a deep moan. Her fingers were clutching at his jacket, twisting and pulling as he slowly increased his rhythm. He watched as she bucked against him, saw her tongue creep out to wet her lips, and then she was shuddering, her mouth open on a soundless cry.

"Yes," he encouraged, "just like that, Blossom. Let it come over you."

He watched as her climax washed over her in waves.

Oh, she had never felt anything like this before. The pleasure, the euphoria. She curled into a ball and pressed her face to his stomach, and felt Jase rub her shoulders and spine.

She was crying. Why? She had no idea. But Jase did.

He lifted her up and had her kneel between his thighs. Her breasts were bare and he was cupping them as he kissed her tears away.

"Your first orgasm and you cry for me. My love, you undo me."

"I'm shaking. I can't stop."

"Because you need more," he whispered as he kissed her neck. "You need me to be inside you all night long."

"Yes."

He caught her lips and kissed her—slow and thoughtful. The most romantic, passionate kiss he'd ever given her. And then, suddenly, without warning, it turned hotter, carnal. It was a kiss that was consuming, all lips and tongues and hands, and the harsh rasp of impassioned breaths.

"I want to sink so deep inside you," he rasped against her ear. "I want to pulse and empty inside you and hold you for hours after."

"I want that, too. Tonight, Jase. Say you will find a way."

Suddenly the handle rattled; it was followed by the sound of the door opening. Blossom was still too dazed to react, and Jase had no time to fix Blossom's gown and get her off his lap. His first instinct was to shield her, so he wrapped his arms around her, burying her front and face in his chest.

"Just this way, Thompson," he heard the duke's voice. It was followed by the indigent sound of air being drawn in. "Just a moment, my lord. I've just recalled that I've left the book in the salon."

Jase looked up as the door was closing. He met the duke's furious gaze. "I shall return in precisely two minutes. You had better be here, Raeburn."

The door slammed shut, and Blossom gazed up at him.

"That was my father, wasn't it? He always did have impeccable timing."

"Shh," he soothed her. "Let me help you."

"What are we going to do?" she shrieked.

"The only thing that can be done. We'll be married as soon as possible."

CHAPTER TEN

CLOSING THE LIBRARY DOOR, Jase stepped into the masculine domain of the Duke of Torrington. It looked much the same as it had five nights ago, when he had petitioned the duke to court his daughter. Then, there had been smiles, and slaps on the back. Tonight there was to be none of that. The duke was brooding, his shoulders stiff and set as he stood at the long window that overlooked the immaculate grounds of his estate.

Jase knew the duke heard his entrance, but Torrington ignored him, allowing him to stew in his own juices until His Grace was damn good and ready to acknowledge him. Well, he was no longer the young lad that His Grace had known. He was a man now, and he could be just as stubborn and brooding as the man standing before him.

The duke might have cowed a lesser man, but Jase would not give in. Not when the stakes were so high. Blossom was worth any amount of suffering her father might make him endure.

"What the bloody hell were you about in there?"

Closing his eyes, Jase struggled to find an answer. *Begging to get beneath your daughter's skirts, Your Grace,* hardly seemed appropriate given the circumstances and the present company.

"Goddamn you!" the duke thundered. "I can't believe this. My daughter. My house..."

He wouldn't apologize for it. It would smack of a lie. He wasn't sorry that they had shared those charged kisses, and the illicit embraces. How could he, when it was what he'd wanted for years? He'd been fantasizing of touching her, of revealing those lovely, perfect breasts and touching her quim, since the second she opened the door of the fort and saw him standing there.

"To think I actually believed, Raeburn, that you were sincere that night I agreed to allow you to court Blossom."

He had been. He *was,* he corrected himself. But the duke was in a rage, and nothing he said would change that.

"Well, what have you to say for yourself?"

What could he say? There were no words for this sort of thing, and apologizing for wanting Blossom went against everything he felt.

"When I agreed to allow you to court my daughter, Raeburn," the duke growled, clearly not composed, "I did not think you the sort of man who debauches young ladies during parlor games. I certainly did not expect to find you...mauling her in such a fashion. Good God, man, there were guests outside the door. What were you thinking?"

"I did not intend for you to witness that."

The duke swung around, his gaze narrowed, his expression murderous as he confronted him. "I'm not so sure you didn't."

Now it was Jase's turn to be affronted. "I'm not sure what Your Grace is implying."

"That you forced my daughter into a scandalous, illicit embrace hoping that I would find you and force you to wed." Torrington straightened, his big hands curled into fists at his sides. "My daughter has made it very clear to her mother and me that she believes your desire to wed her is out of some misplaced belief that you ought to right your brother's wrong."

"Not to mention the ease of convenience to myself, I'll wager."

"She mentioned that, as well."

"So you think I intentionally coerced her into my arms so that you could find us and force us to marry?"

"Precisely."

"Well, you're dead bloody wrong! I didn't need for you to find us. I was convincing Blossom rather well to accept my hand. I didn't need this. And in fact, by you discovering us, it has set my suit back considerably."

"You little prat," the duke spat. "What do you think you're about?"

"Marrying your daughter."

"Like hell." The duke paced to his desk, sunk into a large leather chair and lit a cheroot. He puffed away on it, eyes narrowed as he sized Jase up. "If you think I'll allow you to have her now, you're stark bloody mad."

"As you said, there were guests in the hall, well aware of what was happening. I cannot allow her reputation to be tarnished."

"You should have thought of that before you allowed things to progress as they did."

Jase winced. Matters had gotten a bit far, but damn him, he hadn't been able to stop. She had felt so warm and soft beneath his hands. Had found her first orgasm with him. He could still hear her whispered pleas, the way she moaned his name.

He cleared his throat and forced away the memories. "I do regret that you stumbled upon us. It cannot be easy for a father to, er…"

"Discover his daughter in a state of undress being ravished by the neighbor? No. It is rather unsavory, and it is only by the grace of God, and my wife, that you are still breathing now."

"So it is your intent to extract a pound of flesh, is it?"

Torrington sat back in the chair and kicked his feet onto the desk, studying him through the cloud of smoke. "I'd strip you of your hide if I could, but my wife, and your father, mean too much to me to tear you to pieces. They are civilized. I am not. I'd love to have my pound of flesh, as you call it. That and a good deal more." He gave a meaningful glance in the direction of Jase's trousers.

Jase nodded. He understood. If that had been his daughter, he would have acted first, then asked questions. His daughter...with Blossom. The thought ran rampant in his mind.

"Sit," Torrington commanded, motioning to the chair opposite the desk.

For the first time since entering the room, Jase felt as though there might still be hope. Blossom might yet be his. Numerous scenarios had run through his mind as he and the duke squared off, the most prominent being what he was going to do if the duke denied him Blossom's hand. He knew what he'd do—take her away with him and marry her. They'd go to Gretna if they had to. But he would not be denied her. He had come too far to be deprived of her once again.

Taking the offered chair, he sat before the duke, suffering beneath his glacial stare. Silence descended, heavy, encompassing and more than a damn bit discomforting.

"You have a reputation, Raeburn," Torrington said as he studied the glowing tip of his cheroot. "I hope that ravishing ladies in salons is not *de rigueur* for you."

Shifting uncomfortably in his chair, he forced himself to meet the duke's probing gaze. "My reputation is overblown, Your Grace."

He smiled, raising the hairs on Jase's neck. "Oh, I doubt that. I know from what sort of stock you come from. You forget that your father and I were in swaddling clothes together. We cut our teeth together and ran a swath through society ourselves."

"I have not forgotten, Your Grace." No, his father was going to have his hide when he got him alone.

"Where there is smoke, there is fire, Raeburn. Do not expect me to believe that your reputation is the result of some misunderstanding. There were a few people in my time that believed that my reputation had been maliciously maligned, that I couldn't possibly be as bad as what I was rumored to be. I assure you, they were wrong. I was everything my reputation was reputed to be—and then some."

"My reputation is a careful cultivation, Your Grace. It is the truth that I'm not nearly as experienced as what is reported in the tabloids. But it suited me well to hide behind the facade."

Frowning, the duke raised his cheroot to his mouth and took a long inhalation. Tipping his head back he blew out the smoke. "Let us get to the heart of matter? I believed I knew what sort of man you were when you requested the *honor* of courting my daughter, but it seems I was wrong. So, let's have it out, shall we? Tell me, what kind of man are you really?"

"Hardworking," Jase supplied. "Honorable. Trustworthy. Dependable."

"All wonderful merits I could find in a hound, but I don't give a damn about that right now. What I want to know is, what sort of man will my daughter be getting if I allow you to marry her?"

"Very well. What is it you wish to know?"

"Do you sleep with many women?"

Jase bristled at the duke's impertinence. "No."

"Are you careful when you do? I would feel compelled to murder the man who gave my daughter a disease."

"I have no diseases and I use protection."

"Any children tucked away in charming cottages that my daughter may find out about?"

This was going too damn far, but he answered, anyway. "Absolutely not."

"Do you seduce other men's wives?"

"No."

"Defile virgins—other than my daughter, that is?"

"Of course not."

"Keep a mistress?"

"*Emphatically* not."

"And do you plan to, after you take my daughter to wed?"

"No!"

Torrington sat forward, his gaze narrowing danger-ously. "See that you don't because if you disgrace her with another woman, if you hurt her by betraying her heart, I will gut you."

"You have my word. Now, is that all?"

"No. Habits. What of those? Do you drink?"

"Socially."

"When is the last time you've been in your cups?"

"Two weeks ago, with my friends and a night of cards."

"And what friends are those?"

"The Duke of Trevere, the Marquis of Winterborne, his twin, Maxime, and your son."

The duke grunted. "You will not be saved by throwing your friendship with my son in my face. If Edward were here, we wouldn't be having this conversation. He would have hung you by your bollocks the minute he discovered you with his sister."

"I am well aware of that, Your Grace."

Admiration lit in the duke's eyes. Finally he realized

that Jase was not afraid of him. He would stand up and match him, an honest answer for every prying question.

"You were drunk two weeks ago—were there women there?"

"No."

"No? Then when was the last time you seduced one—and I hope you're not going to answer that you've had one of my maids, or my guests."

Jase flushed. The duke was a bully, and he ought to tell him to sod off, but his future with Blossom was at stake. It was submit to the examination or find himself shoved aside forever. "Months," he finally admitted. "I've been in the north, busy with the stables, and visiting friends. I haven't the time or the inclination for seduction."

"Apparently that has all changed since you found adequate time this evening."

Jase did not rise to the bait, and the duke arched a mocking brow.

"No mistresses, no excessive drinking, no women for months—you're a model paragon for gentlemanly behavior."

"Would you care to know the amount of my investments and bank accounts? I realize you already know the extent of my properties and what I will inherit."

The bastard smiled, utterly unrepentant. "No, I've already had my man of affairs look into it, and you're as stable as a rock. You have a fortune, but you're a bit of a tightwad, I understand."

"Not with Blossom," he answered. "I'll give her anything she wants."

"Hmm," he mused. "She's not one to be persuaded by trinkets and tokens. I would have thought that you knew that."

"I know the kind of husband and marriage she wants,

and I am pleased—and more than eager—to give it to her."

The duke flushed. Obviously Blossom had informed her parents that above all she desired a blistering passion in her marriage. Served the pompous duke well, he thought. After prying into his personal life, Jase could not help but discomfort the duke, as he had done to him.

"Well, then, have you asked everything, Your Grace?"

"For now."

"Then may I have my turn?"

The duke looked surprised but then he spread his arms wide. "Be my guest, Raeburn. But I'll not tell you how to win my daughter's affections if that is what you're going to ask, nor am I going to decide anything about marriage tonight."

"You've asked many questions tonight, but the most important one, you haven't."

Gaze hooded, the duke glanced out the window, into the blackness beyond. "I don't know what question you mean."

"The reason why I asked to court Blossom in the first place."

"I hope the answer is not because you are in need of a wife and you find our family's long-standing friendship easy and convenient."

"I love her."

He hadn't intended to state it so boldly, but the words slipped out—clipped, hard and full of passion. And damn, it felt good to finally admit it to himself.

"I have loved her for so long and I was forced to stand by while my brother wooed her. Even when I tried not to, when I told myself I didn't, I have loved your daughter. Despite everything, that love has never wavered, and in fact has only grown. It was my personal hell knowing she was marrying another. It was my salvation when my brother had the deplorable manners to run off to Gretna Green with another."

Torrington's mouth hung open in shock. Jase knew he was being far too bold and familiar, but damn it, this was important. He needed Blossom's father to understand that what he had witnessed was not staged to entrap.

"Your Grace, I have waited ten years to kiss your daughter. I regret you walked in on us, but I do not regret kissing her. I will marry her, and I will spend the rest of my life convincing not only Blossom but you that I am worthy of her."

"Oh, good, there's no blood."

Jase glanced back to see his father step into the library. There was relief in his father's expression, but disappointment as well when his stare lingered upon him.

"Come to defend your offspring, Weatherby? I confess, he's rather a chip off the old block."

"Torrington," his father growled. "Let us be reasonable."

"I think I am. I put a cheroot between my hands, not your heir's neck."

"You have every right to, of course."

"Of course. But I'm quite certain that in our youth we might have ravished a lady or two in a salon. It wasn't quite as sordid as it is now, is it?"

"Then we weren't fathers."

"Hmm," the duke murmured.

"I wonder what Raeburn will do when he walks into his salon only to find his beloved daughter being manhandled."

He did flush then. So did his father. He couldn't imagine it—his child with Blossom.

"Enough of this," Jase exploded, unable to stand it any longer. "I have submitted to your questions, I've been honest about my feelings—now I want to know what is to be done."

"The only thing that can be done, my boy," Torrington drawled. "You're going to marry my daughter."

Sagging, Jase sprawled out in the chair and breathed a sigh of relief.

"If…" the duke murmured, "my daughter agrees."

She will. After what had happened in the salon, there could be no doubt in Blossom's mind the passion between them. She may not love him yet, but she would. He wouldn't stop trying to make her, until she did.

"I'll speak with her now. I'm quite certain the estate chapel can be readied within a day."

"No," Jase said, standing. "That's not the wedding of her dreams."

"I doubt that matters now, Jase," he father muttered. "There's no time for fairy-tale weddings and such. People are already murmuring about what the devil was going on in that study."

"She'll be married the way she wants, on the bridge, overlooking the lake, with only immediate family and a posy of lilies. Something simple and intimate. That's what she wants. And I'm going to give it to her."

Torrington nodded. "Fine. You'll spend the wedding night here."

It was not a question but a command.

"No. Once we're done here, I'll make arrangements for a honeymoon. A cottage, in the Lakes."

The duke's eyes narrowed. "You seem to have everything in hand, Raeburn, but you forget, my daughter has not yet agreed, and until she does, there will be no wedding."

"I will speak with her now."

"Not on your life. Weatherby, take him home. I don't want him near my daughter."

His father reached for him, but something inside him snapped. "You'll not keep her from me, Your Grace. I mean to have her as my wife, and I will."

"Do you really believe that I am impressed by this little speech of yours? Do you think it changes my mind about you, because you know what sort of wedding she dreams of and what type of damn flower she wants for a bouquet?" the duke thundered. "It means nothing to me. You have seduced my daughter, and have forced my hand. In case you haven't heard, Raeburn, I deplore manipulations, and while it might be the right thing to do, I won't have my daughter wed if she doesn't wish it. I don't care about reputations and other such nonsense. I won't have her living a miserable life because she lacked the where-withal to ignore the advances of a practiced seducer. So," the duke snarled, "you will take yourself off and appear before me at one in the afternoon, and then you may have your answer."

Dismissed. That was what he was. But what the duke did not realize was that Jase was every bit as stubborn as he was. He would not leave tonight with his tail between his legs, ashamed of what had happened. By God, he would see Blossom once more, and explain to her that she was the only woman in the world he wanted to marry. He had to tell her of his love, to make her understand that this was not a marriage of convenience.

"WHAT COULD BE TAKING so long?" Blossom muttered as she wore a path on the carpet of her mother's sitting room.

"Sweetheart," her mother murmured as she gently took her arm. "Come and sit by the fire and have a drink. It will do you a world of good."

"How can you be so calm!" she exploded.

"Well, I've had a few minutes to gather my wits—and

you would, too, if you had a sip of sherry. Another, Anaïs?" her mother inquired of Lady Weatherby as she held up the crystal decanter.

"Please, Jane."

How could they be sitting on the settee sipping away on sherry like nothing was happening? Dear heavens, there were guests in the house, and here was her mother and Jase's mother hiding out in a private salon, drinking sherry!

"Dearest, your pacing is not going to make things go any faster. Your father, as you well know, will be finished with Lord Raeburn when he is good and ready and not a moment before."

"What must he think of me?" she gasped as she collapsed into a chair.

"I should think that was obvious," her mother murmured.

"Not Jase," she snapped, "Papa."

Her mother arched her brow and sipped her drink. "Two peas in a pod you are. I've heard that tone a time or two from your father."

"Forgive me, Mama."

Shaking her head her mother put her drink aside and captured Blossom's gaze. "It is not as though your father is a stranger to scandal, my dear. Far from it."

"I don't want to lose his good opinion." Or have him murder Jase, she silently added.

Reaching for her hand, her mother clutched her fingers. "I don't believe that there is anything you could do that would turn your father away from you. Besides, your papa is the least of your worries. What of Lord Raeburn?"

Blossom cast her gaze toward the settee where the marchioness was busy looking every place but at them. She was making a grand show of appearing not to listen, but Blossom knew she had her ears wide open.

"Mama," Blossom muttered, which turned to a warning when her mother smiled.

"Blossom, you worry too much. It is only us in the room, three women, nothing more than that. There is nothing you cannot tell us. Believe me, we might have entertained a scandalous kiss or two in our time."

Swallowing hard, she glanced away, unable to speak her true feelings.

"I believe I'll look for my husband," the marchioness murmured. "Excuse me."

Blossom watched Jase's mother stroll from the salon. When she reached the door, she hesitated and turned back toward them. "I must speak on behalf of my son. I realize he isn't like his brother, but he's worthy, Blossom. He'd make you an excellent husband. I...I cannot condone his actions tonight, but...I can understand them. You'll at least think on his offer, won't you, and not dismiss it out of hand?" Nodding, Blossom grasped her mother's hand. "Things have a way of looking much clearer after a good night's rest," Lady Weatherby reminded her.

And with that she closed the door, and Blossom promptly fell against her mother, hugging her.

What in the world was she to do now? She'd been caught in a most compromising position, by her father no less. Damn Jase and his seductions. She was no match for him. Could not defend against such machinations...

No. She could not play the wounded virgin now. She'd been willing. More than willing. She had encouraged him, had all but dared him. Deep inside she had known what he would do when she challenged him about passion, and whether or not they would have it.

She had thrown the gauntlet and he had picked it up.

It was not entirely Jase's fault. But that said, she didn't want to be married because of a scandal. What woman did?

"Shh," her mother soothed, hugging her tightly, "all will be well. You'll see."

"I don't want Papa to force him to marry me," she gasped. "I...I don't want that, Mama."

"I know, darling. We'll figure something out."

The tears that she had allowed to fall fell faster, until she was sobbing. Her body wanted Jase. Her heart wanted him, too. That young, tender love she had once felt for him had needed little encouragement to grow and flourish. While her heart and body desired him, her mind warred with her. Could she trust him? Would he only break her heart with his rakish tendencies? Was his pursuit of her out of desire, or a misplaced sense of honor and obligation?

Was she merely convenient?

"There is nothing so dangerous as passions, Blossom," her mother whispered as she smoothed her hair back. "They make us feel alive, fulfill us, and make us soar. But they confuse us. Make us frightened because it changes who we are."

Pulling away, Blossom blinked back the tears and tried to listen.

"You're just discovering that, I'm afraid. Nothing is easy when the heart and soul are engaged. Tonight, you followed where your heart led—and it led you to Jase."

"But what if I'm just a convenient wife? What if he wishes to marry me because he desires to right a wrong he perceives his brother has done to me?"

"Do you truly believe that?"

"I don't know. At first, yes. But then...I don't know. What if, Mama, he took me to the salon and intended for us to be found?"

"I don't believe that for a second. That is not the action of a gentleman, but a desperate man. If you think matters through, Blossom, you'll soon realize that there is no real reason that Jase needs to marry you. None but one."

One reason. Desire? Or love? Desire was all well and good, but what happened when it waned? What would be left to sustain a marriage?

"Excuse me, Your Grace," a footman said from behind the closed door. "But His Grace is wishing to speak with Lady Blossom in his study."

"Mama," she whispered. Her lip was trembling and her hands were shaking. "Come with me."

Her mother's smile was full of love and acceptance. "Tell him what is in your heart, and everything will be well."

She did not want to face her father. Or Jase. She wasn't ready to bear witness to her father's disappointment, and Jase's satisfied smile. He had wanted to marry her. Claimed he would stop at nothing to have her, and here she was, ruined in the eyes of society—the only remedy to marry him.

"PAPA?" SHE MURMURED as she stepped around the study door. It was dark and gloomy; the only light was from the hearth. The embers were dying, but a spark flickered and illuminated the chair where her father sat, watching the flames.

"Come," he ordered her.

She had never disappointed him. Had never given him cause to be ashamed of her. She had been his darling little girl and she felt sickened at the thought that she might lose not only his love, but his regard, as well.

Padding softly across the carpet, she stood before him, head bowed, hands folded demurely before her. He was looking at her. She could feel his cool, assessing gaze upon her. And then he reached for her hand, smoothed his thumb along her knuckles, forcing her gaze up from her slippers and into his face.

"You've been crying?"

She didn't trust herself to speak. Her eyes were welling up once again and a small hiccup escaped her. So she nodded and bit her lip to quit it from quivering.

"Blossom—"

"Papa, I'm sorry," she cried as she clutched his hand. "I don't know what came over me. I mean…I don't—"

"Shh," he whispered. "There is no need. I understand completely. I am not so old that I cannot remember what it was like to desire someone so completely."

"Mama."

"Yes. Mama." His smile was wistful, his eyes darkening like they always did when he spoke of her mother, or looked at her. "I want your happiness, Blossom. It's all I've ever wanted. You were minutes old when I held you and gazed upon you and swore that very thing to you. Tell me," he asked as he squeezed her hand, "what will make you happy?"

"The sort of marriage that you and Mama have."

"It has not been without pain, Blossom."

"I know." And she did. When she was old enough, she had been told their story. Theirs was a love against all odds. After witnessing such love, after experiencing it firsthand, how could she not wish for the very same thing?

"Is he what you want, Blossom?"

Was he? She hardly knew anymore. From the moment she saw him again, her heart had opened to him. Her body warmed for him. Every waking thought was of him, and every dream was about them—and the way she felt when she was with him.

She thought of what it would be like to never see him again. To turn from him and walk away. She thought of him married to another. Him kissing and touching another woman the same way he had done to her tonight. Oh, God, the pain those thoughts evoked robbed her of breath.

"Well?" her father prodded. "Is he the sort of man you've always dreamed of marrying?"

"Yes, Papa," she said through a fresh flush of tears. "It has always been Jase. I just made myself believe that I wanted something different—*someone* different."

Her father held out his arms, and Blossom flew into his embrace. "He will be a good husband to you, and that is the only reason I will allow this. I don't give a damn about gossip or tittle-tattle among the *ton* and the servants. What I care about is you. Your happiness. Your future."

He hugged her tight, and kissed her cheek. "I wouldn't part with you for anyone who I felt was unworthy, Blossom. You're too special to just give away to any man."

"Thank you, Papa."

"How I love you," he murmured softly. "And how I will make him suffer if he hurts you."

"Papa."

"One day, sweetheart, Raeburn will be the father of your children, and he will sit in his study and hold his beloved daughter in his arms and say the very same thing to her. It is one of the reasons that I'm allowing this union. He's the sort of man I have always wanted for you—a man who will take care of his own. A man who risked your father's wrath and a host of insolent questions just to have you."

"Did he really? Papa, you were hard on him."

"Hard? My darling, I was rather easy on the fellow. Besides, it was a test, to see just how much he wanted you for a wife. After all, in taking you, he gets me. A most daunting thought for any perspective bridegroom."

Laughing, she hugged him tight. "You are the best father a girl could ever have."

"I have tried my best. Now, if I could only bring Edward to heel."

"That, Papa, will take a miracle."

Smiling, her father tweaked her nose. "Now run along and send your mother in here, if you please."

As if on cue, her mother was waiting outside the library. With a smile she breezed by her.

"Ah, Jane." Blossom heard the deep rumble of her father's voice. "Come and sit on my lap and hold me. I've just given our baby girl away."

"Matthew," her mother whispered, "is the pain so very bad?"

"Quite lethal, Jane. Make it go away."

And then Blossom shut the door, allowing them their privacy. After all these years of marriage her parents were still so ardently, and passionately, in love.

CHAPTER ELEVEN

IN THE END, BLOSSOM HAD seen very little of the man who was to be her husband. And when she did see him, their visit was supervised by her father or mother. Blossom was literally bursting to speak with him, and she could tell that Jase was just as eager. But her father demanded that they would not have a second alone until they departed for their honeymoon.

It took only two days for Jase to obtain a special license, and only one for her parents' houseguests to depart. They fled back to London amid a brewing scandal. Her mother had worried the tiniest bit; her father had laughed and reminded her that it was not a proper Torrington house party if there was not a hint of scandal.

It was her wedding day, and despite Jase's attempts to make it the wedding of her dreams, it did not happen that way. First was the rain. Second was the complete deluge that would not stop.

"I think it's a sign from God," she whispered as the carriage jolted forward. She waved at her mother and father, who were huddled beneath an umbrella, and then again at Lord and Lady Weatherby.

"Nonsense," Jase muttered, "it's good luck if it rains on your wedding day."

"Not for the bride it's not," she said as she lifted her leg and showed him her muddied boots and soaked stockings.

"Then let me make you comfortable. We have a bit of a journey to the train station."

"Where are we going, exactly?"

"To the Lakes. My friend the Duke of Trevere has a cottage there."

"Oh."

Jase reached for her foot and began unlacing her boots. "Will you like that, do you think?"

Nodding, Blossom continued to look out the window. She hadn't expected to feel so awkward in his presence. It was as though they were strangers. He seemed to know it, because when he was done removing her boots, he slid himself to her bench and began to untie her bonnet. With a careless air he tossed it onto the now-empty bench and clutched her face in his palms.

"At last," he whispered, "I can give my wife the proper kiss she deserves."

Jase's mouth was warm and soft, his tongue sheer pleasure. They kissed for a long while, until Blossom could hardly breathe, and when they broke it off, Jase did not leave her, but rested his forehead against hers.

"I've missed you. Your smiles. Your cheeky little taunts. But mostly I missed this, just being beside you."

"Really?"

"Really."

She smiled, the awkwardness slowly retreating. "A week ago I could never have dreamed I would be married to you."

"I could say the same. Although, I've been fantasizing about our wedding night for what seems like years now."

"You're fibbing."

"Blossom." He reached for her hand and placed it over his heart. "I can tell you with utmost sincerity that I've wanted you in my bed for years. I would stand back and watch my brother with you and wish to strangle him. It's the whole reason why I was gone so much. It shattered my soul to see you so happy with him, because, you see, I wanted you to be happy with me. Blossom?" He pressed her hand hard against his chest, and held steady on to her gaze. "I love you. I have loved you silently and secretly from afar for so many years. And this—the fact you're now mine—is almost too surreal. When I look at you I'm afraid you're going fade into the mist and I will wake up to the realization that this is only another dream."

"Oh, Jase."

He held a finger to her lips. "This isn't the way I wished for it to happen. But it's what transpired and I'm not sorry for it. But I promise you, Blossom, I will worship you with my body for the rest of my life, and one day you'll realize that I'm not the man behind the reputation. One day, you'll feel safe enough with me to give me your love. And I will wait patiently for it, I promise you."

He kissed her again, and when he ended it, she felt how hard and fast his heart was beating beneath her thumb. "Sleep, my love. Because tonight when we get into our little cottage, I will be keeping you very much awake."

BLOSSOM GLANCED UP FROM her book to see a pair of birds dip low in the sky, squawking and singing as they landed on a thick branch of a pine tree. Heedless of her position below them, they cocked their heads to one side and addressed each other with a high-pitched warble.

"That must be the female," a deep voice resonated behind her. "A right saucy wench, isn't she?"

Jase. Her body tingled at the sound of his voice. She was a wife now, in every respect. Their first time had been magical, intimate. He had been very careful with her, and she had felt nothing more than a pinch and a burn. It had been a bit awkward and Blossom had been self-conscious.

But that had been three nights ago. Now she was eager. Gaining confidence and experience. Now she wanted what her husband had purposely kept hidden inside him. She wanted his passion—all that dark, beautiful rakish passion she knew he was hiding.

Shading her eyes, she looked up to see him standing before her, the sunlight acting as a halo, making his hair shine in the bright rays. His face was in shadow, but she could make out his lips, which were grinning wickedly. How she was coming to adore those lips. She could still feel them, soft and full as they covered her body, searching for her sensitive spots. She wanted that again. To feel him moving inside her. The deep connection of being together. She wanted his love—to hear him say it again. And God help her, she wanted to tell him of the love for him that was growing inside her.

"Come." He motioned for her to follow him. "Let us get out of this heat. The cook at the pub has packed a bowl full of cream for the strawberries and she'll be horrified if I let it spoil. Join me for lunch and allow me to enjoy your company."

"And that is all?" she asked in a teasing voice as they stood on the threshold of the cottage that they were using for their honeymoon.

"That, and you must allow me to feed you at least one strawberry."

"Only one?" she said, ducking her head as he picked her up and carried her into the sunlit cottage. "Very well, then, but we are only to discuss books and fashion and weather as any newly courting couple would."

"Agreed." He put her down so that the tip of her half boots touched the floor, but the rest of her body was tightly held in his arms. "Of course, I'm flexible. I shall not hold you to the agreed-upon agenda if, shall we say, the course of the afternoon takes a decidedly different turn."

"It won't," she said in a husky voice. After all, it had been Jase's idea to embark on a real courtship. Not hers.

"Well, then, here we are." He stepped over the threshold and placed the basket atop a round table that sat before a blue brocade lounge, decorated in the airy Chinese style.

He released her wrist, only to capture her hand in his as he maneuvered her behind the lounge to where brocade curtains were drawn. He parted them, revealing brilliant sunlight filtering through the panes of a long bank of French doors, which he opened. A gust of rose-scented air washed over them, heavy and humid, tranquil and sensual. Below the cottage was a ha-ha, a valley that had been dammed and filled to resemble a lake. Beyond the dam lay sloping hills that reminded her of emerald velvet. The vista was a patchwork of squares, all symmetrical and outlined with stone walls or hedgerows winding down to the lake, and the mountain behind. Dotted on the green tapestry were sheep, cattle and horses all moving languidly in the midday heat, resembling tiny insects flickering on a felt cloth.

She hadn't any idea that something so basic in nature could be so breathtaking. When Jase wasn't making love to her, she was painting. In truth, they hadn't even begun to explore the beautiful landscape. They'd only gone as far as the inn and the pub when their stomachs protested in hunger.

His hands came up to rest on her shoulders and tiny tremors snaked down her spine when she felt his fingers play with her curls. He'd discarded his jacket and waistcoat and his cravat lay draped over the back of a nearby chair. He wore only his shirt, which was unbuttoned. She refused to look him in the eye, but he wouldn't let her avoid him. Instead, he tilted her chin in order to make her meet his steady gaze. How very wicked it was of him to hold her entranced like this.

"Shall we not recline on the lounge?" he asked, strolling to the lounge and stretching his body on the brocade. "The breeze is lovely from here." He pulled his shirttails over his shoulders and discarded his shirt onto the floor. "Come." He patted the cushion beside him. "Recline with me."

"I really don't think—"

She squeaked when he reached for her and pulled her down alongside him. "The trouble is, sweeting, you think far too much. Now, then," he said after he had propped her with numerous pillows and ensured her comfort. "Shall we begin with a drink?"

Blossom nodded, unsure of her own voice. It would be weak and breathless she was certain, and if it wasn't, then it surely would be now that he was leaning over her. His chest was brushing hers, and she swore her bodice became five times too tight in the time it took him to remove the cork from the champagne and pour it.

He handed her a glass, then slid back beside her, his elbow propped along the rolled arm of the lounge, his green eyes glistening with amusement as he peered down his long lashes at her.

"To a beautiful afternoon." He held out his glass so that it chinked with hers. "Strawberry?" he asked, holding out a plump, red specimen for her perusal.

"No, thank you," she croaked, taking far too big a sip of her champagne. Not a sip, really, more like a gulp. It was cool and bubbly, refreshing in the humid heat, and just what she needed to put her addled wits in order.

He shrugged, then leaned across her once more, dipping the berry into a bowl of clotted cream. Without preamble he popped it into his mouth, licking a dollop of cream from his lip. "I adore clotted cream. I vow I could eat it with anything." He looked her over and grinned lazily. "Strawberries, blueberries, you."

Blossom took that opportunity to take another gulp from her champagne, this time finishing it.

"Let me get you another."

"No really, I hardly ever imbibe," she protested, feeling her head already starting to become fuzzy. She fanned herself, suddenly feeling overheated.

"Unseasonably warm weather we're having, is it not?" he asked, reaching for another strawberry and offering it to her. "One would wonder what changes will occur in fashion if this is a glimpse of what our summers are to be like."

He dipped the strawberry into the cream and she watched in fascination as he softly squeezed it, the juice trickling out in red drops that landed on the cleft of her bosom. His tongue followed, licking every red bead in little strokes.

"Wh-what are you doing?" she gasped, wishing her breasts would stop inching above her bodice.

"Eating."

It was uttered in the darkest of tones and Blossom did suck in her breath then. He reached for another strawberry and bit a portion of the soft flesh, letting the juice drip— drop by red, glistening drop—onto her lips. Her heart skipped when she felt his tongue, soft and light, licking away the sweet juice from her lips. "You really should think of joining me," he whispered against her mouth.

She tried to focus on the conversation, tried to ignore the heat infusing her veins, attempted not to notice how Jase's eyes kept roaming over the expanse of her breasts. Breasts that were pushed up into high mounds in her current semirecumbent position. It was she who was supposed to be teasing him. Not the other way around.

"Shall we continue our discussion of fashion?" he drawled, tracing the curve of her breasts over her bodice. "What do you think the ladies will be wearing next year?"

"I…I…" Lord, she was rendered mute. Her brain was fuzzy and her heart was pounding much faster than what was good for her.

"Perhaps they will be wearing nothing but a chemise and bare feet, hmm?" He grinned while his finger dipped beneath the lace edging her gown.

"I doubt that."

"No? Perhaps they'll wear nothing at all."

"My lord, we are to be talking about the weather and books."

"And fashion."

A strangled sound escaped her pursed lips when his fingers raked through her hair, dispelling the blue ribbon she'd used to manage her riotous curls. His lips grazed her cheek, then throat, as he reached over, setting his glass atop the table. "Speaking of weather, you look a trifle warm, Blossom. Might I entreat you to refresh yourself by removing some of these heavy layers? I could assist you, you know."

"Lord Raeburn," she warned as her breasts firmed beneath the stroke of his finger. "You're not supposed to be doing this."

"Doing what?" he asked innocently while fiddling with the tapes of her gown with anything less than innocence. "You are my wife. Is it not right that I see to your every comfort?"

"Jase," she said, trying to muster up the appropriate amount of reproof to make him cease his attentions, but the set-down came out as a breathless entreaty.

"I'm the most attentive of hosts, Blossom, and I assure you I shall not rest until I see you in a state of comfort."

Her gown came off and he tossed it aside in a rustling, crinkling lump of blue satin.

"Now, then, your stockings."

The fight, or whatever fight she pretended to have, left her. She could only smile and nestle her head deeper into the cushions as his wicked fingers set about stroking her calves, working their magic up past her knees to the inner facings of her thighs.

"Such a garment is unnecessary in this heat, don't you think? Let us start a new craze—bare legs. Yes, this will most definitely be all the rage," he said appreciatively as his hands and eyes roamed over her. "Lovely alabaster legs. What man could resist stealing a glimpse?"

"Jase," she moaned, feeling restless and languid at the same time. It was like she was floating, as if the heaviness of her heart and mind suddenly sprung wings and lifted away from her soul, leaving only a weightless body waiting, hungering for the feel of his touch. When he touched her like this she forgot everything, even the fact she was supposed to be resisting his charm and rakish skills.

"Yes, Blossom?" he asked, his eyes, which had only seconds ago been shining brightly, now dimmed. "Are you going to tell me I can't? That I shouldn't? That we shouldn't?" He placed a soft kiss on her navel through her chemise. "We are supposed to be courting, isn't that right? A bit too forward for courting, I think."

"N-no." She shivered despite the heat in the room and the warmth flowing through her veins.

"Then what?" he asked, his wicked mouth covering every inch of her belly through the thin linen. Blossom sunk farther into the silk cushions, her legs spreading, trying to cradle his hard thighs between hers as he slowly raised the hem of her chemise and bared her to his gaze.

"I know what it is you want," he said, stroking her with his finger. "It is the same thing I want, sweeting. You want my hands all over you." He slid his warm palm up her thigh to her belly where he circled her navel with one long, roughened finger. "You want my mouth covering you."

She squirmed when he sunk his hand between her thighs. She waited to feel his fingers inside, but he did not indulge her. Instead, he cupped her, waiting for her to look into his green eyes. "Here is where you want my mouth most of all, I think."

She twisted beneath him, but he stilled her with his heavy thigh. "You want to feel me inside you. You only have to admit you want it, Blossom, and I shall give it to you. Anything you want."

"Yes." The word whispered past her lips before she could think to stop it.

He slid up the length of her, his chest slick with perspiration, the evidence of his arousal rubbing against her belly from beneath his trousers. Flinging her arms around his neck, she kissed him, and Jase allowed himself to sink onto her, let her kiss him thoroughly while she commanded the pace and the performance.

She deepened the kiss, and reached for his trousers, fumbling with the buttons until she at last tore them free from their openings.

"That's it, sweeting, take me in your hand." When she freed him into her palm he moaned a deep, guttural, "Yes," and began to pump himself into her hand, all the while nipping and tugging at her hardened nipple through her chemise. "Firmer, Blossom, take it tightly and stroke it."

"Like this?"

"God, yes. Like that." He groaned when she swirled her fingertip atop the swollen tip of him. "My, what a quick learner you have become."

"I have had a most excellent tutor. Now, what else would you like?" she asked, trailing her fingertips down the silken length of him.

"You're mouth on me."

"Like this?" She kissed his shoulder and sucked at it, tasting the saltiness of his skin.

"Lower," he commanded, spurring her into abandoning every moral edict she'd ever been taught. She teased him with her tongue on his nipples, flicking and laving as he had done to her.

He straightened, then reached for her, bringing her next to him so that they were eye to eye. "I would sell every acre of my estate to feel these beautiful lips around me." He traced her mouth with his forefinger before his eyes slowly met hers. "I'd sell my soul to watch as you do it."

Sliding along the silk, she lowered her body and set her mouth to his straining flesh. She kissed him before flicking her tongue along the tip of him. "I will pleasure you as you wish. I only ask that you will not find me wanton or immoral after."

"Never," he growled as she kissed him again. "There is nothing immoral among lovers." His hands raked through her hair and she heard his breath coming in short pants. Leaning back, he spread his legs, allowing Blossom to kneel between them. She tormented him with sultry looks, peeking up at him as she flicked her tongue from the base to the glistening tip.

Close to finding his release, he reached for her and positioned her so that she sat astride him. Her sex was wet as she lowered her bottom onto his lap. She was as much aroused by what she had done as he was, and the thought pleased him. She was most definitely passionate, and she would bring no end of pleasure to his bed.

"Take this off," he commanded, hooking his finger beneath her chemise strap. "Slowly. I want you to unveil yourself to me inch by inch."

Her face was flushed, as were the tops of her breasts as they strained against the chemise, but she gathered the hem tightly between her hands and raised it up along milky-white thighs till the lace edge skimmed her bottom and rested below the dark V between her legs. "Look at me, Blossom." He tilted her face up to meet his. She looked him in the eye; a womanly challenge sparkled in them, encouraging him to be as bad as he wanted to be. And he so desperately wanted to be bad.

"Show me your breasts."

With a tilt to her lips, she dropped the hem of her chemise and reached for the straps, then stopped before she slid them down her shoulders. She didn't lower them; instead, she fixed him with her blue gaze and pushed the bodice of the chemise down so that her breasts bobbed out, teasing him with their bouncing. Her smile when she heard his growl of appreciation made him feel reckless. She would not lay cool and unfeeling beneath him, enduring the obligations of the marriage bed.

He took his time studying her in the light, watching as the afternoon sun highlighted her hair and cast her skin in a peach glow. His gaze flickered up to the gentle slope of her shoulder, to the curve of her neck, and beyond, to where a mirror rested against the wall opposite the lounge.

Reaching out, he trailed his fingers along the indentation of her waist and up and over her hip, all the while watching in the mirror as his hand roamed along her alabaster flesh. Gooseflesh sprung to life beneath his fingers, and he felt as well as saw Blossom sway into him.

His hand at last found her bottom and he squeezed it. He rather enjoyed this position, he realized, tipping his head to the side so he could see his finger skimming down her derriere and disappearing into the dark curls that were already damp for him.

"Cup your breasts, Blossom. I want to watch you. I want you to see me watching you."

He fitted her hands around her breasts, making certain her pink nipples peeked out between her fingers. At first she didn't understand what he wanted of her, but she soon learned as he showed her how to pinch and tweak her nipples.

Lifting her, he positioned her so that she slid her sex along his throbbing cock. He was aching to take her, but he wanted to take things slower, to savor the moment.

Blossom watched as Jase's dark hands roamed her body, heating her with each touch of his fingers on her belly and his lips at her back. When she sat frozen atop him, mesmerized by the beauty of his hands on her, he nipped her shoulder and said in a dark and thrilling tone, "Make them hard for me, Blossom. Make them so that I can flick my tongue along them."

He was so very wicked, she decided, even as she indulged him. Yes, he was so very wicked and she knew that she wouldn't want him any other way.

Her eyes went wide when he raised her up from his lap and took his erection in his hand, thrusting slowly into her, telling her to sink down onto him.

"Ride me," he encouraged. He supported her with his knees as he lifted her onto his arousal.

She arched then, the action thrusting her breasts toward him, the movement making them bounce in a way that begged for his hands to cup them.

Good God, he'd never experienced this before; never had lovemaking felt this right, this complete. As he

watched her body move atop him, he realized he was at
last satisfied, his hunger appeased, his soul fed. He loved
her and it was only a matter of time before she realized
that it was safe to love him back.

She moaned again, raising herself up and down without
the least bit of encouragement while her nails bit into his
thighs. She was molten in his arms.

Resting her back against his knees while she ground
her hips onto him, Jase watched her match his rhythm. A
thin sheen of perspiration trickled between her breasts and
he captured it with his fingertip, circling her nipple with
it until it glistened like a shining cherry. The sight made
him grow uncomfortably thicker, but Blossom's loving
body stretched around him, welcoming him deeper.

"Come for me," he commanded, quickening his pace
until they were deep stabs that made her suck in her
breath. His finger found her clitoris and he flicked it in
time to his strokes. She was beyond wanton now. She was
wild and writhing, and not until he was certain she was
satiated did he let himself indulge in his own pleasure.

God, how I love you. He hugged her slick body to his
and nuzzled his face between her breasts, feeling more
contented than he ever had in his life.

This was love. This was the future. He had never been
happier in all his days than he was right now, vulnerable
and weak, with only Blossom's arms to keep him safe
from the tempest raging in his heart.

BLOSSOM STOOD AT THE French doors, staring at the
patchwork of farms, trying to think of anything other than
the man sprawled gloriously naked, soundlessly sleeping,
on the lounge behind her.

Chancing a glance over her shoulder, she saw that Jase
still slept, his black hair a tousled mass that was brushed
back from his forehead. Shivering despite the heat,

Blossom brought her arms tight around her waist. She'd donned Jase's shirt when she'd risen from the lounge. His scent still lingered and she swore she could feel remnants of his body heat clinging to the material.

With a heavy sigh she closed her eyes and rested her head against the wall. She loved him. Desperately. Forever. How it had happened was so strange. But then maybe that was the mystery of love, it came upon you swiftly, without warning, ensnaring you. It had happened that way for Samuel. Why shouldn't it have happened for her in the same way?

Suddenly Jase's heat engulfed her. He caged her with raised arms, his fingers curving around the molding on the door frame while he proceeded to nuzzle her hair.

"Sorry to fall asleep on you, love. You should have woken me instead of standing here all alone. Although," he whispered wickedly, "I rather enjoyed waking up to the view. You look rather fetching in my shirt. It's very alluring, you know, what you look like in white linen." He traced the outline of her bottom that peeked out from beneath his shirt while he nuzzled her neck. "Come back to bed, sweeting. Let me love you till the sun goes down. Then I will seduce you by starlight."

She smiled and caressed his face. "You already did that, that very first night."

"Did I?"

"You did."

"Tell me what you were thinking just now, when your eyes were closed."

"How beautiful it is here, and how much it reminds me of your estate. The countryside is very similar. I'd like to paint it."

"I can't wait to bring you home, Blossom. I can't wait to stand at our bedroom window, just like this, and look out upon the fields.

His grip tightened and he turned her to face him. "I want to share this with you—all of it. I want the estate to bear the fruits of our labor. When I look out our window I want it to be with you."

His fingers cupped her thigh, and he hooked her leg over his. "Can I take you like this?" he asked, his fingers sinking deep inside her.

Immediate desire flared to life within her and she writhed against his hand. "Take me any way you want, Jase." She sighed as he slipped inside her and stroked her deeply. He moaned and thrust deeper into her, his fingers biting into her waist with the force of his desire.

"I want you hard, Blossom, so that you never forget that it's me inside you."

"Jase," she cried as he reached for her breasts and bared them from beneath his shirt. He fondled them, cupping them in his hands and squeezing.

"I have to feel all of you. I have to see you." And then he pulled out of her body and turned her around so that her back was against the wall. He opened the fastenings of his shirt and roughly shoved the material aside, baring her. Greedily he nuzzled her breasts before he slipped her nipple into his mouth. When she was moaning and tugging at his hair, he grasped her legs and wrapped them around his waist. His arms were above her head, resting against the wall, as he thrust hard into her waiting body. Their eyes were locked and their breaths mingled together with each pant, each sigh, each erotic whisper.

She clutched him close to her bosom as her climax loomed closer. "I've fallen, Blossom," he rasped as he filled her once more and allowed his seed to empty into her. "I've fallen so damn hard for you."

"Jase." His name was a shaky whisper on her lips, and she clutched him closer. "I've fallen, too. How have you done it?"

He raised his head from her breasts and smiled slowly. "You feel it, too?"

The unspoken words hung between them, and Blossom shivered. "Jase, my love."

His breath caught and he looked at her. "Am I? Am I your love?"

"Forever and always. Through health and sickness, and my inattentive moods when I'm painting. For good and happiness and those times when I'm miserable and grouchy. I love you, Jase."

"My God, you've made me the happiest man in the kingdom! And you should know, my love, your love is not in vain. You have my heart and soul, and my love. You always did."

He stared down at her and smiled as his fingers brushed against her lips. "Now you finally have the look of a woman who has flowered beneath a man."

"You're still a rake."

"A rake who wants to seduce you beneath the stars night after night until our own lives fade into starlight."

* * * * *

#1 New York Times *and* USA TODAY
bestselling author

NORA ROBERTS

evokes love's most beautiful melodies
with two timeless tales.

UNFINISHED BUSINESS

Vanessa Sexton thought she knew what she wanted…glamour,
fame and applause. But at twenty-eight nothing is easy. She
wants peace and space to figure out the future, but that's
impossible when Brady Tucker is around. How can Vanessa give
herself away when she's not even sure who she is anymore?

LOCAL HERO

Hester Wallace is proud of her independence. She needs only
one man in her life—her nine-year-old son, Radley. When Rad
starts idolizing neighbor Mitch Dempsey, Hester wonders if
she's cheated her son out of a male role model. But inviting
Mitch into their lives is dangerous. Because she might start to
rely on Mitch—or worse, she might fall in love with him.

EXPERIENCE THESE TIMELESS LOVE STORIES,
APPEARING TOGETHER FOR THE FIRST TIME
IN

Perfect Harmony

Available now.

REQUEST YOUR FREE BOOKS!

2 FREE NOVELS
FROM THE ROMANCE COLLECTION
PLUS 2 FREE GIFTS!

YES! Please send me 2 FREE novels from the Romance Collection and my 2 FREE gifts (gifts are worth about $10). After receiving them, if I don't wish to receive any more books, I can return the shipping statement marked "cancel." If I don't cancel, I will receive 4 brand-new novels every month and be billed just $5.74 per book in the U.S. or $6.24 per book in Canada. That's a saving of at least 28% off the cover price. It's quite a bargain! Shipping and handling is just 50¢ per book in the U.S. and 75¢ per book in Canada.* I understand that accepting the 2 free books and gifts places me under no obligation to buy anything. I can always return a shipment and cancel at any time. Even if I never buy another book, the two free books and gifts are mine to keep forever.

194/394 MDN FDC5

Name _____ (PLEASE PRINT) _____

Address _____ Apt. # _____

City _____ State/Prov. _____ Zip/Postal Code _____

Signature (if under 18, a parent or guardian must sign) _____

Mail to the **Reader Service:**
IN U.S.A.: P.O. Box 1867, Buffalo, NY 14240-1867
IN CANADA: P.O. Box 609, Fort Erie, Ontario L2A 5X3

Not valid for current subscribers to the Romance Collection
or the Romance/Suspense Collection.

Want to try two free books from another line?
Call 1-800-873-8635 or visit www.ReaderService.com.

* Terms and prices subject to change without notice. Prices do not include applicable taxes. Sales tax applicable in N.Y. Canadian residents will be charged applicable taxes. Offer not valid in Quebec. This offer is limited to one order per household. All orders subject to credit approval. Credit or debit balances in a customer's account(s) may be offset by any other outstanding balance owed by or to the customer. Please allow 4 to 6 weeks for delivery. Offer available while quantities last.

Your Privacy—The Reader Service is committed to protecting your privacy. Our Privacy Policy is available online at www.ReaderService.com or upon request from the Reader Service.

We make a portion of our mailing list available to reputable third parties that offer products we believe may interest you. If you prefer that we not exchange your name with third parties, or if you wish to clarify or modify your communication preferences, please visit us at www.ReaderService.com/consumerchoice or write to us at Reader Service Preference Service, P.O. Box 9062, Buffalo, NY 14269. Include your complete name and address.

MROM11